"Come closer." The intensity of his gaze drew her in, enticing her to lean toward him.

"Closer," he said.

When she didn't move, he took hold of her arm and pulled her forward until their lips were only inches apart. Suddenly in his space, she felt every bit of the magnetism he held for the women of the world and realized she wasn't immune to it. She'd never be immune to it. No matter how maddening his arrogance could be, no matter how much she protested to the contrary, she'd be drawn to this man until her dying breath.

"Listen up, Bernie," he said softly. "Are you listening?"

He was so close now that she could feel his breath as he spoke. In the darkness of the car, each second seemed to drag on endlessly.

"I'm listening," she said.

"I told you the truth. I was jealous. Don't ask me why, because I'm still not completely sure myself. All I know is that I'd already decided that if any man was going to touch you tonight…" His voice dropped to a near whisper. "It was going to be me."

Believe in Happily Ever After in
TALL TALES AND WEDDING VEILS

"A romantic comedy romp, this book has fun, endearing characters... Graves writes fun, sassy, and sharp characters that may be opposites, but definitely attract!"
—*Parkersburg News and Sentinel*

Buckle Up for Sexy Fun with
HOT WHEELS AND HIGH HEELS

"A delightful, funny read with a unique twist as a former trophy wife discovers herself, and true love, in the most unexpected place. A total winner!"
—SUSAN MALLERY,
***New York Times* bestselling author**

"Jane Graves is a pro at blending romance and comedy... *Hot Wheels and High Heels* is a delightful story packed with heated romantic tension, colorful characters, and a fast-paced story line that keeps the reader hooked."
—RoundtableReviews.com

"Sassy and smart!"
—SUSAN ANDERSEN,
***New York Times* bestselling author**

"Absolutely hilarious! Jane Graves has done an outstanding job with this book."
—RomanceReaderatHeart.com

"An interesting and fun novel with plenty of fascinating characters, this story starts fast and doesn't lose momentum."
—*RT Book Reviews*

Black Ties
and
Lullabies

ALSO BY JANE GRAVES

Hot Wheels and High Heels
Tall Tales and Wedding Veils

Black Ties
~ and ~
Lullabies

Jane Graves

FOREVER

NEW YORK   BOSTON

Copyright © 2011 by Jane Graves
Excerpt from *Heartstrings and Diamond Rings* copyright © 2011 by Jane Graves
All rights reserved. Except as permitted under the U.S. Copyright Act of 1976, no part of this publication may be reproduced, distributed, or transmitted in any form or by any means, or stored in a database or retrieval system, without the prior written permission of the publisher.

Book design by Giorgetta Bell McRee

Forever
Hachette Book Group
237 Park Avenue
New York, NY 10017
Visit our website at www.HachetteBookGroup.com.

Forever is an imprint of Grand Central Publishing. The Forever name and logo is a trademark of Hachette Book Group, Inc.

The publisher is not responsible for websites (or their content) that are not owned by the publisher.

Printed in the United States of America

First Printing: July 2011

10 9 8 7 6 5 4 3 2 1

To Michele Bidelspach, for being the patient, supportive, insightful editor every writer should have.

Black Ties
and
Lullabies

Chapter

1

Bernadette Hogan wished that when this night was over, she could tell Jeremy Bridges to go to hell. She was about ten times more emotionally stable than the average person, but if she had to spend one more evening watching him pick up vacuous blond women for fun and recreation, she was going to go insane. Yeah, he attended all these charity events as the philanthropic CEO of Sybersense Systems, but in the end it wasn't about generosity. It was about putting one more notch in his hand-carved Louis XIV bedpost.

But it wasn't Bernie's job to plan a principal's itinerary. Her job was to protect him wherever he decided to go. And, of course, there was the small matter of the outrageous amount of money he paid her to put up with this nonsense, money she was going to need desperately in the coming years. So she kept that resignation letter only in her head, staring at it longingly with her mind's eye every time he aggravated her to the breaking point.

Tonight would be one of those times.

Carlos pulled the limo into the driveway of the San Moritz Hotel behind a string of unusually small and sedate vehicles. Tonight, it seemed, the filthy rich of Dallas society had left their Mercedeses and Beemers and gas-guzzling Hummers in their five-car garages, opting instead for their hybrids and electric cars.

Bernie sighed. "So which environmental cause are we championing this evening?"

Jeremy's brows drew together thoughtfully. "Hmm. Good question." He reached into his breast pocket and pulled out an invitation. "Ah. Global warming. Emphasis on diminishing polar bear habitats."

"And here you are in your limo. Last I checked, it gets about nine miles to the gallon. People are staring."

"People are hypocrites."

"True, but it's all about appearances."

"It's all about comfort," Jeremy said. "I didn't make all this money to cram myself into a car the size of a shoebox."

"You don't seem to mind cramming yourself inside your Ferrari."

"The Ferrari doesn't count. It's the only vehicle on earth that makes it worth giving up my wet bar and HDTV."

With that, he drained his Glenlivet and set the empty glass down with a contented sigh. There wasn't much that Jeremy denied himself in the way of creature comforts. He drank the best Scotch, lived in a gazillion-dollar house, traveled the world, and dated women who were knockout gorgeous with brains the size of golf balls. *Nice to look at,* Jeremy had told Bernie more than once, *without all that pesky intelligence to get in the way of a good time.*

Bernie sighed. With that one statement, he singlehandedly set feminism back fifty years.

There had been a time when total professionalism had dictated the way she dealt with Bridges. *Yes, sir. No, sir. Very good, sir.* But the longer she worked for him, the more she spoke her mind. Her attitude didn't mean she didn't take her job seriously. It just meant she had an outlet for the irritation she felt around him just about every minute of every day. Fortunately, because Jeremy was a bored rich guy who refused to play by the rules, a smart-ass bodyguard seemed to suit him just fine. Good thing, because if she had to hold her tongue around him, she'd probably end up killing him herself.

"Are you planning on tying that tie?" she asked him.

Jeremy looked down at the tie dangling around his neck. "The invitation said I had to wear a black tie. It didn't say how I had to wear it."

"Did it also say you had to wear athletic shoes?"

"No," he said with a smile. "That's my fashion statement."

Truth be told, Jeremy could show up in what he usually wore in his spare time—crappy cargo shorts, a Rangers' T-shirt, and flip-flops—and they'd still let him in. If he wrote a big enough check, he could show up stark naked. But it wasn't like him to be in their faces about it. He always dressed well enough that they would admit him without question, but just shabby enough that they wished they didn't have to. Now that he was thirty-seven years old, Bernie thought maybe he ought to knock off the eccentricities and play it straight, but hell would probably freeze over first.

Over the years, the press had tried to dig up any dirt that might explain his quirkiness, but except for the basics, his background remained something of a mystery. He had grown up in Houston with his father. Mother unknown. Graduated from Texas Southwestern University. Short stint as a software engineer before starting his own company, which eventually became Sybersense. Except for more current professional and civic activities, that was about it.

Bernie looked at the rich folks strolling into the hotel and sighed. "Must we do this?"

"Now, Bernie. This is a very special occasion. After all, how many times in this city does somebody have a benefit for such an outstanding cause and invite all the rich, pretty people?"

"About once a week."

"Exactly! Not nearly often enough. It's time for us to party."

"Us?"

"Okay. So it's time for me to party and you to watch for bad guys. Everyone should stick with what they do best."

Bernie glared at him. "It's a credible threat this time, you know."

"That also happens about once a week."

He was right. When a man had Jeremy's money and influence, somebody was always out to get him. She was reasonably certain the recent death threat had something to do with Sybersense's new medical management software that was due to launch early next year. Word on the street was that it was so revolutionary that it would forever change the way the medical industry conducted its business and bring untold riches right to Bridges's doorstep. But in order to accomplish that, he'd executed hostile takeovers of two of his hottest rivals, which allowed him, among other things, to cherry-pick the best and brightest programmers and other employees who could help him develop and market his new product. Then he kicked the rest to the curb. Unfortunately, that had removed a lot of formerly wealthy, high-powered executives from the gravy train at their respective companies and given them a reason to want to see Sybersense fail or Jeremy dead. Or both.

But in Bernie's experience, the threat could also be coming from somebody who drove a taxi or washed windows who decided he didn't like rich guys, which was why she had to stay vigilant.

Bernie felt pretty certain this event would be the harmless experience it seemed to be on the surface, but there was no way for her *or* Jeremy to know that for sure. All Bernie knew was that every time she tried to figure out why he behaved the way he did, she realized how pointless that was and merely concentrated on keeping his body and soul together.

"Don't you ever get bored doing this?" she asked him.

"What? Going to charity events?"

"No. Going to charity events, picking up Paris Hilton wannabes, and having your way with them."

"Oh. Well, when you put it like that..." His mouth turned up in a cocky smile. "Nope. Doesn't bore me at all."

"Good *God*, I hope you practice safe sex."

"Of course. You never know when some dread disease will rear its ugly head. Your concern is heartwarming."

"Concern, my ass. I just want you to do the world a favor and keep your genetic material to yourself."

"Not to worry," he said, patting his pants pocket. "I'm nothing if not prepared."

She shook her head. The man singlehandedly kept the latex industry afloat.

"Why go to all the trouble of attending these events?" she asked. "Why not just stay home and order out?"

"Order out?"

"Haul out your little black book and take your pick. Send Carlos to pick her up."

"But if I did that, I wouldn't have the opportunity to... what is it we're doing again?"

"Saving the polar bears."

"Oh, yeah. We have to think of the wildlife."

"Come on, Bridges. The only species you're interested in preserving is the Perpetual Bachelor. Unfortunately, the world's never going to run out of those."

"Now that's where you're wrong, Bernie. Polar bears are at the forefront of my consciousness nearly every minute of every day."

"And I'll believe that the moment polar bears grow blond hair and big breasts."

"If you object so much to this event, stay in the limo. I restocked the DVD collection. *Terminator, Alien, Die Hard*—all your old favorites."

"I'm paid to stick close to you."

"Not too close. You have a tendency to cramp my style."

"I have a tendency to keep you alive."

"Do you have to be so dramatic?"

Bernie narrowed her eyes. "Are you forgetting the London incident?"

"That was an accident."

"That was an out-of-control car that may not really have been out of control."

"We'll never know for sure, will we?"

"Fine. Die. See if I care."

"Of course you care. Would you be able to abuse another client the way you abuse me?"

"*Abuse* you?"

Jeremy leaned forward and tapped the Plexiglas window. "Carlos?"

The window came down. "Yes, sir?"

"Would you categorize Bernie's attitude toward me as abusive?"

"Oh, yes, sir. Absolutely."

"Thank you, Carlos."

As the window went back up, Jeremy turned to Bernie. "Now, there's a man who knows who signs his paychecks."

Bernie glared at Carlos. "Ass kisser."

"Tell me something, Bernie," Jeremy said.

"Yeah?"

"Exactly where do you hide your weapon when you're wearing a skirt?"

She met his gaze evenly. "That's none of your business."

Jeremy's gaze slid away from her eyes, slithered down to her breasts, fell to her thighs, then lazily made its way back up again. "So you're leaving it to my imagination?"

For a moment she felt the oddest twinge of awareness, as if she was one of those glowy, showy, magazine-perfect women he was so fond of. Just the sound of his voice made her heart beat a little faster. And those gorgeous green eyes. Good God, it was no wonder women fell in his wake.

It wasn't as if she didn't know he was pushing her

buttons. Jeremy thrived on knocking people off guard, and he wasn't above using every weapon in his arsenal to do it, including sex. But that didn't mean she was immune to him as a man, and when he looked at her with that unrelenting stare, she couldn't help the hot, sexy thoughts that entered her mind.

In a few minutes, though, he'd be zeroing in on some dazzling daddy's girl or elegant divorcee, at which time he'd suddenly go Bernie-blind. In the end, she was just one more employee at his beck and call, like his housekeeper or his pool boy. And that was fine by her.

"Knock it off, Bridges. All you need to know is that I'm armed, I'm dangerous, and whether it's good for the world or not, I'll get you home in one piece."

"Actually, I doubt you'd even need a weapon," Bridges said. "Didn't I hear that you once killed a man with a Popsicle stick?"

"A Popsicle stick?" She made a scoffing noise. "That's ridiculous."

"So the rumor isn't true?"

"Of course not." She paused. "It was a Q-Tip."

Jeremy just smiled, then turned his attention to a glittering Barbie doll standing near the front door of the hotel beside a planter full of periwinkles. Her mile-long legs protruded from beneath the hem of a sheath of silvery fabric that clung to her body like Glad Wrap, and her headful of stunning blond hair glinted in the evening light.

The car ahead of them drove away, and Carlos pulled to the curb directly in front of the hotel. A uniformed man opened the door of the limo and gave Jeremy a deferential smile. "Good evening, sir." Then he turned to Bernie, and his smile faltered. She could read it in his eyes as clearly as if he'd shouted it: *What's a woman like you doing with a man like him?*

He cleared his throat. "Uh . . . good evening, miss."

Miss? Bernie cringed. Nobody had referred to her as "Miss" since . . . well, *ever*. And it was none of his damned business what she was doing with Jeremy, anyway.

The man dutifully held out his hand to her, as if she needed help getting out of a car. She ignored him and climbed out, quickly scanning the area for anything out of place. She and Jeremy headed for the front door of the hotel, and she got a good look at the blond for the first time.

Even though the woman wore enough mascara to sink a freighter, Bernie thought she recognized her. Two days ago, outside the gates of Jeremy's house, a woman had been standing at the curb, watching as they pulled through the gates. Bernie also remembered a woman loitering outside a restaurant yesterday where Bridges had met his chief financial officer for lunch. Bernie couldn't say with absolute certainty that it was the same woman, but her instincts rarely failed her. Two sightings was a coincidence. Three was a pattern. And even though the woman was dressed to the nines, she didn't mesh with the sophisticated crowd here tonight. Bar hopping in the West Village seemed more appropriate. Her makeup was too extreme, her dress too flashy, her heels too high. When somebody didn't fit the profile of the occasion, it was always a reason for a heads-up.

As they passed her on their way into the hotel, the woman turned slowly and gave Bridges a suggestive smile. Not surprisingly, he matched her smile with one of his own. But Bernie sensed something about the woman's demeanor that went beyond the usual high-society mating ritual she'd witnessed a hundred times before.

Then the woman shifted her gaze to Bernie.

Her smile vanished, replaced with an oddly irritated expression that made a chill snake between Bernie's shoulders. In spite of the fact that Bernie had arrived with Jeremy, there was no way on earth this woman considered her a romantic rival. Something else was going on, which meant Bernie needed to keep a close eye on her for the remainder of the evening.

As Jeremy stepped into the ballroom, the same feeling of déjà vu passed over him that he always felt on nights like this. Interchangeable hotels. Interchangeable causes. Interchangeable, ingratiating people who wanted his money.

Mile-long buffet—*check*. Silent auction—*check*. Bar in every corner stocked to the hilt—*check*. Young, sexy society women looking for husbands—*check*. Just once he'd like to see something different at one of these events. Maybe a margarita machine or a beer bong. A rock band instead of the symphony strings. Karaoke. A wet T-shirt contest.

Anything to keep him from being bored out of his mind.

But if he showed up at these things, Sybersense held on to its reputation as a philanthropic leader in the community, and he held on to his reputation as a wealthy, eccentric bachelor. Then, at the end of the evening, he invariably had several incredibly gorgeous women to pick from to entertain himself with later. As for the events themselves, he got his laughs by watching the looks on the faces of the old biddies as they tried to ignore whatever fashion faux pas he'd decided to perpetrate for the evening. They were all about propriety—almost all about it, anyway. In this crowd, money trumped taste, but just barely.

"Mr. Bridges! Good evening!"

He turned to see one of those old biddies waddling toward him. Genevieve Caldwell was a chunky senior citizen with silver hair, a brassy voice, and a gold-plated portfolio of oil fields all over the world.

"I'm just so delighted you could make it here this—"

He knew the exact moment she caught sight of his slack tie and scuffed Nikes. Her voice faltered, and for a split second, he saw it. That look of disapproval. That expression that said, *You're not one of us.* That vibe of superiority that the socially blessed radiated to those less fortunate. But, as always, he consoled himself with the fact that for all her riches, he could buy and sell her ten times over.

In spite of her momentary gaffe, she recovered like a pro, pasting on a smile and holding out her hand.

"—this evening," she finished.

Jeremy took her hand and kissed it, then flashed her a dazzling smile. "Mrs. Caldwell. What a joy it is to see you again."

The old lady practically quaked with delight, her disapproval momentarily vanishing in a wave of pure ecstasy.

Jeremy nodded toward Bernie. "Mrs. Caldwell, I'd like you to meet Bernadette. She's a family friend visiting from Arkansas. *Rural* Arkansas. It was a slow time at the chicken farm, so she put on her best dress, hopped a Greyhound, and here she is."

At the same time he got a furtive eye roll from Bernie,

Mrs. Caldwell's nose crinkled as if she'd smelled something rotten. Hearing *rural, chicken farm,* and *Greyhound* all in one sentence made her disgust meter shoot through the roof.

"It's a pleasure to meet you," Mrs. Caldwell said, even though it clearly wasn't a pleasure for her in the least. Then she tilted her head questioningly. "But I'm certain I've met you before." Her eyes narrowed. "Do you know you look remarkably like Mr. Bridges's astrologer?"

"My astrologer?" Jeremy said.

"Yes. Three months ago at the Sunshine Gala for Solar Energy, you had your astrologer with you. You said she told you that your moon in Pisces simply demanded you give an extra thousand dollars." She looked back at Bernie. "There *is* a resemblance."

"Ah, that's because she *is* my astrologer," Jeremy said. "Did I not mention the connection before?"

"Why, no, I don't believe you did." Mrs. Caldwell turned to Bernie. "Do you do readings for others?" She smiled. "I can only hope for more moons in Pisces tonight."

"It's more of a hobby of hers," Jeremy said. "She wouldn't want the responsibility of suggesting another person's path in life."

"But you'll be happy to know, Bernie said, "that Jeremy's moon is in Gemini today. The Twins. Which means he's going to give twice as much money as he did at the Sunshine Gala."

"That's wonderful!" Mrs. Caldwell said, beaming. "You're such a generous man, Mr. Bridges. With patronage such as yours, the polar bears will live on for generations to come." She glanced over Jeremy's shoulder.

"Please excuse me. I have other guests to greet. I hope you and your friend have a lovely time tonight!"

Mrs. Caldwell moved toward her next victim, and Jeremy turned to Bernie. "You just set me up for twelve grand," he muttered. "Thanks a bunch."

"Consider it penance. Now maybe you won't go to hell for lying."

"That might cover *this* lie. But what about all the others?"

"You have no respect at all for these people, do you?"

"Their games aren't my games."

"So you make up games of your own."

"Exactly."

"Just don't make me your financial planner again. I don't know a damned thing about the stock market."

With that, she turned and fanned her gaze over the crowd with the same intensity she always did, never relaxing for a moment, never cracking a smile. Bernie was nothing if not predictable. She wore the same plain black dress she always did whenever she shadowed him at events like these, one that hit her legs midcalf. It was so shapeless that it was impossible to get a mental picture of what her body beneath it looked like. Dark hair that grazed her shoulders in no particular style. Not a speck of makeup. Flat, sensible shoes. No stockings, of course. He couldn't imagine Bernie wiggling into a pair of pantyhose. Jewelry? Perish the thought. In this room full of peacocks, she looked like a plain brown starling, so bland she faded right into the wall and so unmemorable that he was surprised Mrs. Caldwell had recognized her at all.

Sometimes he cocked his head and narrowed his eyes and looked at Bernie when she wasn't aware he was doing it, just to see if there was an actual woman in there some-where. Occasionally he got a glimpse of one, but it was like seeing something fleeting on the periphery of his vision that was there one second and gone the next.

He wondered what she did with all the money she made working for him, because it sure didn't go toward nice clothes or a decent apartment. She wore discount-store clothes and lived in a mediocre complex in east Plano full of questionable people. Not that it wasn't safe for Bernie. Somebody would have to have a death wish to mess with her. Aside from paying somebody to hack into her bank account or personal email, Jeremy didn't have any way of finding out much more, and hell would freeze over before she offered any personal information of her own accord.

Her professional history, though, was a different story. He might show the world a cavalier attitude, but he never hired anyone without vetting that person from top to bot-tom. As bodyguards went, Bernie was the best of the best. Ex-military, she was a top-notch marksman and a martial arts expert. She had observational skills out the wazoo. And Jeremy had no doubt she could be lethal if the situa-tion ever warranted it.

Still, she *was* a woman, and every once in a while he imagined what would happen if he sent her for a day at one of those stupidly expensive spas, then took her to Nei-man's and sprang for the works. Just for fun. Just to see the result. Of course, if he ever actually suggested such a thing, he'd probably end up as one more notch on her Q-Tip.

"I'm heading for the bar," Jeremy said. "Can I interest you in a glass of outrageously expensive champagne? I have to recoup my twelve thousand somehow."

"You know I don't drink on the job."

"Do you drink *ever*? Or smoke, or park illegally, or spit gum on the sidewalk? What do you do for fun, anyway?"

"I am having fun," she deadpanned. "Can't you tell?"

"Lighten up, Bernie. This is friendly territory. Not much chance of a kidnapping attempt around here."

Bernie's laserlike eyes zeroed in on something across the room. "I'm not so sure about that."

"What are you talking about?"

"Do you know that woman?" Bernie asked. "The one by the buffet table in the silver sequined skirt up to her ass?"

Jeremy turned to look at the woman in question, who turned out to be the same women he'd seen as he was coming into the hotel. She was indeed showing a few more inches of thigh than the average woman here tonight. Bernie didn't seem to approve, but—funny thing—he didn't object in the least.

Did he know her? No. Was he going to get to know her? Absolutely. Before this evening was out, he intended to get to know her very, *very* well.

"Never seen her before tonight," he said.

"I have. A couple of times in the past few days. She may be following you. She was outside the gates to your house two days ago, and on the street in front of Rodolpho's yesterday when you were having lunch with Phil Brandenburg. And she's barely taken her eyes off you tonight."

Jeremy smiled. "Ah, women...they just can't seem to control themselves around me, can they?"

"There *is* a chance she's just a groupie. She probably saw the article they did on you in *Dallas After Dark* and she's hoping to snag a handsome millionaire."

"So you think I'm handsome, do you?"

"I'm just quoting the article."

"Well, if it's in print, it must be true."

"Right. *Dallas After Dark*. Journalism at its finest."
Bernie continued to eye the girl, then shook her head
grimly. "There's something fishy about her. She doesn't
belong here. She's dressed too slutty. And she's standing
alone."

"Maybe you're right," Jeremy said. "Maybe I should
check her out. Get closer to her. Infiltrate her evil plot."

"You're not taking this seriously."

"Now, that's where you're wrong. I'm very, *very* serious about taking her home with me." He glanced back at
the woman. "And look at that. I don't even have to go on
the hunt. The prey is coming to me."

Chapter
2

If Bernie had to endure one more word of this woman's incessant babbling, she was going to reach down her throat and permanently remove whatever organs afforded her the ability to speak.

Even after moving to her post along the wall, Bernie could still hear Miss Ashley Preston telling Jeremy that she'd seen him in *Dallas After Dark,* and she just hadn't been able to get his photograph out of her mind. When Jeremy asked her about her family, she said she was the daughter of Mr. T. J. Preston, a man who, according to Ashley, "dabbled in oil, real estate, that kind of thing." She went on to say that she was between careers because she hadn't found her calling yet, though she did have her volunteer work with her sorority sisters from Southern Methodist University. To Bernie, all of that said she was either supported by daddy or had a never-ending trust fund from another rich relative.

Mrs. Caldwell swung back by and Ashley greeted her by name, reminding her that they'd met briefly at the Faces of Hunger benefit at the Adolphus Hotel three months before. Bernie waited for Mrs. Caldwell's reaction, which included a short but definite lapse of memory. Within a second or two, though, she greeted Ashley as if they were old friends. Unfortunately, Bernie couldn't tell if Mrs. Caldwell had finally remembered Ashley, or whether it was merely a social cover-up because she thought she was supposed to.

If it was the former, all was well. If it was the latter, Bernie could be dealing with somebody who'd done her homework for the event to ensure she wasn't found out for the impostor she was. Unfortunately, a possible memory lapse on Mrs. Caldwell's part wasn't enough to start any whistle blowing.

As Ashley started on her second glass of wine, the hair twirling began, and before long she was practically shoving her breasts right into Jeremy's chest. Bernie sighed, wishing to God he would just go ahead and make his move and get all this over with.

Fortunately, she didn't have to wait much longer.

Jeremy leaned in to talk quietly to Ashley, who leaned away with a raised eyebrow and a seductive smile. "Now, Jeremy. Just what kind of girl do you think I am?"

"One who loves fine wine," Jeremy said, nodding down at her glass, "and rich men."

Ashley laughed in that way that only beautiful blond women could, with a toss of her head and music in her voice. "You already know me so well," she said slyly. "I do believe we're a match made in heaven."

A few minutes later, Jeremy made nice with Mrs. Caldwell, thanking her for the evening and assuring her that his check would be forthcoming. Then he and the

blond deposited their wine glasses on the nearest bar and
headed for the hotel lobby. Bernie called Carlos, and by
the time they reached the circular drive in front of the
hotel, the limo was pulling to the curb.

Ashley glanced back at Bernie, her sunny disposition
growing a little cloudy. She leaned in and whispered to
Jeremy, but Bernie heard her loud and clear. "Your bodyguard isn't hanging around all night, is she? To tell you
the truth, she kinda scares me."

Jeremy whispered back, "To tell you the truth, she
kinda scares me, too."

"Then you'll send her away?"

"As soon as we get to my fortress."

Carlos got out and opened the door, escorting Ashley
inside. Bernie started to get into the passenger side of the
front seat, when all at once something dawned on her.

"Bridges," she said quietly.

One foot in the limo, Jeremy stopped and turned back.
"What?"

"Can I talk to you for a minute?"

Bernie stepped away from the car. Jeremy reluctantly
followed.

"Did you tell that blond I was your bodyguard?" she
asked.

"No. Why?"

"She knew. She asked you if your bodyguard was going
to hang around all night. How did she know who I was if
you never told her?"

"Come on, Bernie. It isn't that hard to deduce."

"I'm a woman. Most people don't."

"Maybe she's smarter than she looks."

"Maybe she's more of a threat than she looks. Do you

remember how she greeted Mrs. Caldwell by name, but Mrs. Caldwell didn't seem to remember her?"

"Mrs. Caldwell is pushing eighty. Do you have more than that?"

Bernie pursed her lips, wishing she did have more. But she had to tell the truth. "No. Nothing specific. I've just had a bad feeling about her from the beginning."

"And I've had a good feeling. We're going with mine."

He turned around and got into the limo. Bernie wished she could take him by the lapels of his thousand-dollar tux and shake some sense into him. Nothing was more intolerable to her than his putting his sexual conquests above her recommendations about his personal safety. *Nothing.* She hadn't gotten to be the best at her profession by ignoring her gut instincts, and the people she worked for hadn't stayed alive by ignoring them, either.

Bernie got into the car, and as Carlos pulled away from the curb, Ashley was giggling in the backseat. Bernie could only imagine where Jeremy's hands already were, but she had no intention of turning around to find out for sure. Carlos let out a soft whistle and whispered, "Wow. She's a hot one."

"Knock it off. You're old enough to be her father."

"Which does *not* make her any less hot."

Bernie just rolled her eyes and stared out the passenger window. *Someday soon,* she told herself, *I'm outta here.*

Twenty minutes later, they arrived at Jeremy's estate. Carlos punched a code into the box by the front gates, and they swung open to allow them entry. He drove down the long, winding driveway. On either side, petunias and coleus overflowed their brick-lined beds, shaded by precisely spaced live oak trees that were tall and broad enough that, in a few years, they'd form a canopy over the driveway. With luck, Bernie would be long gone before that ever happened.

Carlos pulled the limo beneath the portico on the west side of the house. He got out to open the door for Jeremy and Ashley. Ashley emerged, still giggling in that grating way that made Bernie wish she were stone cold deaf. Jeremy told Carlos that he was in for the night, which was his signal to garage the limo and head home. Then Jeremy and Ashley disappeared into the house, shutting the door behind them without so much as a backward glance.

To hell with you, Bernie thought. *I hope she blows your head off.*

Carlos pulled the limo into the garage. He and Bernie got out, and they went to their respective cars that were parked nearby.

"Later, Bernie," Carlos said.

Bernie nodded. Carlos got into his car and headed back down the driveway. Bernie started her car, intending to follow him, only to have another thought occur to her.

She grabbed her iPhone and Googled T. J. Preston, which was supposedly the blond's father's name. Seconds later, she came up with a dean of a college in California and a veterinarian in Cleveland as the leading results. She scrolled through that screen and two more, revealing the MySpace page of a freshman at Ohio State. A chemist in Maine. A children's book author. Other assorted T. J. Prestons, but nobody in oil or real estate. If he was any kind of mover or shaker in the city of Dallas, his name would have popped up before now.

The bad feeling she'd had all night suddenly grew worse.

She thought about calling Jeremy. But would he listen?

Probably not. Still, what was the downside? That she delayed his recreation for the evening?

She hit Jeremy's speed dial number. Six rings, no answer. But that wasn't unusual. If Jeremy was in the company of a woman, he probably wouldn't even look to see who was calling.

Just then, the kitchen door opened and Jeremy's housekeeper, Mrs. Spencer, came outside. Small, compact, and grandmotherly, she was dressed as she always was in a starched white shirt, a plaid skirt, and a pair of highly sensible shoes. She walked across the courtyard to the stairs leading to her apartment above the garage, waving to Bernie as she passed by. Bernie waved back. If Jeremy had dismissed his housekeeper, he must really be gearing up to make a night of it.

Just go home. It's his own damned fault if something happens.

Bernie put her car in gear. Started to hit the gas. But for some reason, she sat there a few minutes longer, unable to put the pedal to the metal. If wasn't as if she cared what happened to Jeremy Bridges. But she cared very much for her professional record. If something went down tonight, who would be blamed?

Huffing with irritation, she killed the engine and got out of the car. Using her key, she went inside the house. She listened for a moment. Hearing nothing, she walked through the kitchen and into the den. When she saw what was going on, every nerve went on red alert.

The security panel that was usually hidden in the wall beside the bar had been opened. Jeremy stood next to it. And the blond stood six feet away from Jeremy, holding a handgun pointed directly at him.

Chapter
3

"Don't move," the blond said, "or he's history."

"I hear you," Bernie said.

"I was hoping you'd just drive away."

"Sorry to disappoint you."

"Give me your gun."

"I'm not armed."

"Bullshit. Let's have it."

Bernie paused just long enough to look at what was on the security screens. One camera was pointed to the courtyard, where Bernie's car sat. Another screen showed a large truck making its way up the winding road toward the house. In only a few seconds, it would be there. She had to do something *now*.

Slowly she reached beneath the hem of her dress to pull her Beretta out of the holster strapped on the inside of her thigh above her knee. Just as she kneeled down to slide it across the floor, she heard the truck's engine outside. Seconds later, the muffled thud of doors slamming and boots on the ground told her that men were heading into the house, and when they got there, all hell was going to break loose.

The kitchen door opened. The blond turned toward the noise, angling her gun away from Jeremy. Already in a crouching position, Bernie dove at the woman, grasping her around the hips. She fell backward, her hand smacking the floor and dislodging the gun from her grasp. It slid across the hardwood floor to crash into the wall. Bernie was on her feet in an instant, still holding her gun, but the men were almost there.

"Safe room!" Bernie shouted to Jeremy. *"Now!"*

Bernie shoved Jeremy in front of her as they raced to the hallway at the back of the house and into his office. She slammed the door behind them, locked it, then ran to the bookcase on the far wall. She reached beneath one of the shelves, grabbed the handle, and swung the bookcase open to reveal a silver keypad on the wall behind it. Heavy footsteps clattered down the hall.

She spun around, double-fisting her Beretta, pointing it at the door. "Punch in the code!" she shouted at Jeremy, just as the office doorknob rattled. An instant later, somebody started kicking the door.

Jeremy hit the last number, and the safe room door clicked. He yanked it open. Bernie turned and shoved him inside at the same time a gun went off. Glancing behind her, she saw pieces of the lock on the office door go flying, and with one more smack on the door, it swung open hard, bouncing against its hinges. As the men entered the room, Bernie pulled the door closed behind them.

Then . . . silence.

Not only were the walls concrete, reinforced with Kevlar, they were also soundproofed. Absolutely nothing got into or out of this room unless Bernie decided it would. She paused for a moment to catch her breath, then went straight to a communications panel connected to a secure phone line and called 911.

"Robbery at 4536 Emerald Creek," she said. "The home of Jeremy Bridges. Perpetrators are still on the premises."

"Where are you and Mr. Bridges?"

"Safe room."

"Anyone else in the house?"

"No."

The operator told Bernie that the cops were on their way. Bernie told her to call them back for an all-clear when the incident was over. Then she called Mrs. Spencer and told her to lock her door and move away from the windows until the police arrived, assuring her that the burglars were most likely on the run by now. Bernie heard the apprehension in the woman's voice, but she was a calm, levelheaded soul. Of course she was. How else could she have continued to work for Jeremy all these years?

After she hung up, Bernie pressed her palms against the wall, closed her eyes, and took a deep, cleansing breath. That had been close. Too close. Then she turned around, and any relief she felt was overwhelmed by a surge of irritation.

In the few minutes it had taken to her to make sure the room was secure and the authorities notified, Jeremy had poured himself a drink. Now he was lounging in an over-stuffed leather chair, basking in the ambience of a space that looked more like a gentlemen's club than a safe room. It came complete with walls paneled in cherry wood, a wet bar, an entertainment center that included a state-of-the-art music system, and a forty-two-inch HDTV. As he relaxed in that chair, instead of showing fear, relief, thanks, *something,* he looked smug. Slightly bored. Not the least bit distressed at the possibility that he might have ended up dead, and she might have, too.

"Well," he said, with a big sigh of satisfaction. "That was fun, wasn't it?"

For a moment, Bernie was speechless. Then her anger shot through the roof. "Fun?" she shouted. *"Fun?"*

"Yeah," Jeremy said, taking another casual sip of his drink. "Really gets the old blood rushing. But I am a little disappointed. You had your gun. I think you could have taken them."

Bernie looked at him incredulously. "Taken them? There were three of them!"

"Let's see ... three against one ... when the one is you ... *hmm.* Now, there's a fair fight."

"My job isn't to take out the bad guys," she said hotly. "It's to get you out of the situation alive."

"And I appreciate that. But I've always been a fan of old westerns, you know. I was hoping for a showdown."

She looked at him incredulously. "Does anything bother you? Anything at all?"

"It wasn't a kidnapping attempt. They were robbing the place. Low-end criminals. Don't make it out to be more than it was."

"So the blond was the inside man. She got you to disable the security around the house."

"Exactly."

"She must have had that gun from the time we left the hotel. Didn't I tell you she was up to something? Didn't I *tell* you?"

Jeremy shrugged. "All's well that ends well."

Anger and frustration roiled inside Bernie. This was it. The last straw. She'd had Jeremy Bridges up to her eyeballs, and she had no intention of dealing with him one more day.

She stalked over to his bar, grabbed a bottle of Crown Royal. She didn't drink often, but suddenly it seemed like a really good idea. She poured a shot and tossed it down. And if one was good, two was better.

"I thought you didn't drink on the job," Jeremy said.

"I'm not on the job," she said, pouring another shot. "As of this moment, I no longer work for you."

He sighed dramatically. "Okay. How much is it going to cost me to get you to reconsider?"

She tossed down the second shot, loving the way it burned her esophagus and instigated even more anger, making her feel as if she could strangle him with her bare hands and walk away without so much as a backward glance.

"Nobody has that kind of money," she said. "Not even you."

"Five hundred more a month."

She slammed the shot glass down on the bar. "I told you to get yourself another bodyguard."

"A thousand."

"I warned you not to bring that woman home," Bernie said, her voice quivering with anger. "I told you I smelled trouble. And you did it anyway. I don't give a damn if you have a death wish. But you're not dragging me into it anymore."

"Now, Bernie. Don't go away mad."

"That's a done deal. I am mad, and I am going away.

I'm done with following you around, watching you pick up women. I'm done with your cavalier attitude. I'm done with *you*."

"Everybody has their price. Even you. We just haven't found it yet."

"Why do you care if I quit? We don't even like each other. But for some unknown reason, you still want me around. Why is that?"

"I'm a masochist?"

"Nope. I'm the masochist for working for you longer than I ever should have. You want to play Russian roulette with your life? Fine. But you're not playing it with mine any longer. The moment we get the all-clear, I'm out of here."

"You didn't have to come back. Why did you?"

"I don't lose principals. Not even you."

"Once they got what they wanted, they'd have been gone."

"And within the hour, you'd have been pointing out their faces in a mug book. Maybe they were only burglars, but that doesn't mean they weren't *ruthless* burglars. Why do you think they came after us instead of clearing out? Because they didn't want us turning them in, and they'd have done anything to stop us."

Jeremy just shrugged. His nonchalance infuriated her. "I saved your ass," she growled. "Don't you *ever* forget that."

"I know Mrs. Caldwell won't. After all, I haven't sent the check yet."

"You just love jerking people around, don't you? Then you fix everything by doling out just enough cash that they put up with you being a snarky pain in the ass."

"I get my laughs where I can."

"Laughs?" She shook her head. "If you think that's funny, you have one screwed-up sense of humor."

"And you have no sense of humor at all. I bet you've never laughed a day in your life."

"You don't know a damned thing about me."

"You're right. I don't. As far as I know, what I see is what I get. You're all business. Not a shred of emotion. Tough girl all the way to the bone."

"It beats having nothing under my skin but silicone and Botox."

"Actually, I think you should try those things sometime. You might like them." He looked her up and down with a deliberate sweep of his eyes. "Why, I might even be persuaded to pick up the tab."

Bernie felt that twinge of sexual awareness that always flickered whenever Jeremy looked at her like that, and she hated herself for letting it happen. *It's nothing but a power play. Don't give him an inch.*

"Keep your money, Bridges. The older you get, the more those twenty-year-old bimbos are going to cost you."

"I believe I can still spare twenty thousand or so," he said, tilting his head and focusing directly on her breasts. "I know a surgeon in Houston who does some damned fine work. He can take a woman from B to D and never break a sweat."

Bernie resisted the urge to fold her arms across her chest. "Have you ever considered dating a real woman? Just once in your life?"

"Define 'real.'"

"Smart. Sensible. A woman who thinks plastic surgery

is for accident victims, and that's about it. Instead, you sleep with every living, breathing, blond-haired D-cup you can find. It doesn't get much more juvenile than that."

He swirled his glass, ice cubes clinking. "An attraction to beautiful women is juvenile?"

"When those beautiful women are nothing but boobs and asses to you, yes."

"Not every encounter has to be a cerebral experience."

"How about *one*, Bridges? Just one? My God. I don't think I've ever heard you have a conversation with a woman under age thirty that wasn't designed to get her into bed."

Bernie knew she was losing it. Saying things she might regret. But for one of the very few times in her life, she couldn't stop. Didn't want to stop. She was full to the brim with anger fueled by a really nice alcohol buzz, and she wanted to take out every bit of frustration she'd felt with this man over the past two years and face the consequences later.

"But it's not the conversation that gets them into bed," she went on. "It's your money. Without it, you're nothing. You might be able to get by for a few more years on your good looks alone, but pretty soon you won't even have that." She made a scoffing noise. "And when that day comes, a real woman wouldn't have anything to do with you."

Jeremy's demeanor shifted, and for the first time, anger flickered across his face. Very deliberately, he set his glass down on the coffee table and stood up. "A real woman, you say?" He took a few steps toward her, closing the gap between them. "Such as yourself?"

"You're *such* an asshole."

She turned to walk away, but he grabbed her by the arm and spun her back around. She looked down at his hand, then slowly turned her gaze back to meet his, giving him a look so frigid it could have turned Death Valley into a polar ice cap. "I wouldn't do that if I were you."

"Oh, yeah? Why not?"

"Because I know a dozen ways to kill a man. I'm thinking number five."

"You could do that," Jeremy murmured, his gaze wandering over her face. "But you won't."

"I wouldn't bank on that."

"You want to do a lot of things to me right now," he murmured, "but killing me isn't one of them."

As she imagined what kinds of things he was talking about, her face heated up as if she were standing in front of an open furnace. She closed her hands into fists and realized her palms were sweating. She wanted to object. Tell him she didn't care if he lived or died. But as he continued to challenge her with an unyielding stare, she was forced to admit the truth.

God help her, he was right.

There had been times when she watched Jeremy lust after beautiful women that she wondered what it would be like to be the object of his singleminded attention. *Look at me like that,* she'd thought sometimes, as her mind wandered to forbidden places. As furious as she was with him right now, just the feel of his hand against her arm triggered the kind of sexual thoughts she hated herself for having, the kind of fantasies about this man no *real* woman would even begin to entertain.

All at once everything seemed mixed up together—the alcohol, the flaming-hot anger shooting between them, his green eyes boring into her. Her heart had settled into a heavy, sluggish rhythm, refusing to drive enough blood to her brain to ward off the fuzzy, incoherent feeling that came from one too many whiskey shots. Light seemed to fade around the edges of her vision, blurring the room around her until the only thing she could see clearly was his handsome face and his mocking eyes.

"If you're one of those real women," he said, easing closer still, "why don't you show me what I've been missing?"

"Why don't you go screw yourself?"

"Good. At least you're thinking about sex. I wasn't sure that was possible."

"Which is just more proof that you don't know a damned thing about me."

"Then maybe it's time I found out a thing or two."

With that, he wrapped his arm around her waist, yanked her up next to him, and slammed his mouth down on hers.

For several seconds, Bernie couldn't fathom what was happening. She was stunned into submission, her head swimming with disbelief.

He was *kissing* her?

She'd expected verbal sparring, but not this. Never this. Her brain, still disoriented, refused to react, which gave him the opportunity to slide his other hand up her back and clamp it around the nape of her neck. He kissed her long and hard, consuming her mouth with his until she couldn't catch a breath. She cursed herself for downing those shots of Crown. Her brain felt so hazy that it was several seconds before she finally wrenched her lips away from his.

"What the *hell* do you think you're doing?" she said.

"Nothing you haven't been asking me to do."

"Asking you to do? Are you out of your freakin' *mind*?"

"If I am," he said breathlessly, "then stop me."

He smothered her lips with another kiss. He moved forward, one step, then another, until he'd backed her against the wall. She made a halfhearted move to shudder away, but he held on, kissing her until the room spun around her.

Stop him, stop him, stop him…

The words swirled around in her mind but never took hold. She'd always imagined Jeremy to be cool and calculating with women, but something had bubbled to the surface she'd never anticipated, something wild and scorching and out of control.

And it was making her hotter by the second.

He was right. She could have smacked her knee right to the place that would shut him down in an instant. But now that the dark, hidden fantasy she'd denied for so long was finally coming to life, all she wanted to do was melt into his kiss, to feel like the woman he had never believed she was.

But he wasn't on the same page. Not even close. She knew he felt nothing for her. His kiss was intimidation. Proof he could control her whether she liked it or not. A power play designed to ultimately humiliate her. If she didn't put a stop to it right now, she'd regret it forever.

She jerked her head to one side, dislodging her lips from his, only to feel his hot breath skate along her cheek. "I'll have you *arrested* for this, you son of a bitch."

"It's only a crime when a woman isn't willing."

"Willing? What the hell makes you think I'm *willing*?"

He pressed his forearm against her shoulder, trapping her against the wall as he cradled her chin between his thumb and forefinger. With his other hand, he clutched the hem of her dress, pulling it upward until his palm rested against her bare thigh. She jumped as if he'd touched her with a lit match. He inched his palm upward, staring at her with an expression of lust so primitive and powerful it paralyzed her. She had the sudden irrational thought that a surge of superhuman strength might be waiting beneath that lust, and if she so much as blinked, it would come roaring out. But worse than that, she discovered something truly insidious about that irrational fear.

It made her even hotter than she already was.

She fought to hold on to her anger, but it seemed to melt into the wall behind her, leaving her more vulnerable to him than she'd ever felt before. He moved his knee between hers, pressing them apart at the same time his hand burned a path upward along her leg. He reached the apex of her thighs and cupped the crotch of her panties, teasing one finger lightly back and forth. Just one small touch, and she shuddered with pleasure. Knowing her expression was giving her away, she tried to turn her head, but he grasped her chin more tightly and turned it back, tormenting her with those unrelenting green eyes. She held her breath, desperate for his touch even as she cursed herself for it. Then he curled his finger around the edge of her panties and slid it beneath them, discovering the truth she couldn't hide.

She was hot and slick with desire.

When a smile of satisfaction crossed his lips, it was as

if he'd shaken her awake from a rapturous dream to the harsh reality of day. Humiliation surged through her.

"You bastard," she said. "Let *go* of me!"

"Come on, Bernie," he said, his voice low and raspy. "We both know that if you really wanted me to stop, you wouldn't be talking at all. I'd be on my back on the floor before I knew what hit me."

In that moment, something shifted inside her. Yes, she wanted him. She wanted him like a woman crawling through the desert wanted a drink of water, and denying it any longer would only make her look like a fool. But suddenly she didn't feel the least bit vulnerable to the games he played. Jeremy lived to control everyone and everything in his midst, but he sure as hell didn't control her.

Thanks for the suggestion, Bridges.

She took him by the shoulders, spun him around ninety degrees, drove her hip into his, and flipped him onto his ten-thousand-dollar Persian rug. Before he could recover, she was on her knees beside him, her hand wrapped around his throat. She saw the shock on his face, but to his credit, it took him only a few seconds to erase that expression and replace it with one that was considerably more unconcerned.

"What a disappointment," he said, his voice a little breathless. "Does this mean sex is off the table?"

"Oh, no. It's very much on the table. But from here on out, *I'm* running this show."

Chapter
4

Jeremy had never felt so flabbergasted in his life. Not
that he objected. In the last five minutes, he'd been
reevaluating every assumption he'd ever had about Bernie. He'd taken it for granted that if he hit her with a little
sexual intimidation, it would just piss her off. She'd snap
back at him, and that would be that. In reality, the woman
he'd believed to be stone cold was hot as a river of lava,
and he'd been standing on the rim of the volcano when it
exploded.

Her gaze traveled leisurely from his chest to his abdomen, and then to the area below his belt, where it lin-
gered for several seconds on the monumental hard-on he
couldn't have hidden if he'd wanted to. She met his eyes
again, giving him a wicked smile.

"Take off your pants," she said.

Jeremy blinked with surprise. *Take off your pants?*
Had those words actually come out of Bernie's mouth?

She removed her hand from his throat and slowly stood
up, towering over him. Under normal circumstances, his

first inclination would have been to give her a smug smile. Turn on the sarcasm. Find a way to get back on top, figuratively speaking. But since any of those things might short-circuit what was getting ready to happen here, he kept his mouth shut. He'd never had even a passing thought of having sex with this woman, but right now he wanted it as much as he wanted his next breath.

He came to his feet, kicking off his shoes. He unbuckled and unzipped, dropping everything from the waist down, only to catch one foot in the leg of his pants as he tried to pull them off. He lost his balance and hopped on the other foot to his oversized leather sofa, letting out a string of curse words all the way there. He fell onto the sofa and finally jerked off his pants, pausing only to retrieve the condom from his pocket and put it in place. Breathing hard, he turned to see Bernie glaring down at him like an Amazon woman hell-bent on revenge. She still wore her dress, but she'd kicked off her shoes.

And her panties dangled from one fingertip.

With a flick of her wrist, she tossed them aside. She took three hip-swiveling steps forward, smacked her palm against his chest and shoved him to his back on the sofa. In the next breath, she was straddling him, gripping his shoulders as she slid herself along the length of him. Once. Twice.

Then again.

And again.

He sucked in a breath, astonished at the sheer carnality of it, at the unbelievable sensations she was creating. On the next stroke, she shifted her hips and took him inside.

Holy shit.

He closed his eyes with a heavy groan. She rose, almost

sliding away from him, only to slam her hips down again.
She began a steady rise and fall, slowly picking up the
pace until her strokes were hard, fast, and punishing. At
the same time her dark-eyed gaze bored into him so completely that she could have pinned him to the sofa with that
alone. His entire adult life, the instant he had felt another
human being reaching for control over him, he had cut
that person off at the knees and done everything in his
power to ensure that he or she never tried to run over him
again. But right now, with his head swimming in a sea
of alcohol and lust, all he wanted was her next ferocious
stroke. He remembered earlier in the evening when he'd
wondered if there was a woman inside her somewhere.

He wasn't wondering now.

Then her gaze seemed to lose focus. A crimson flush
spread across her chest, then rose to suffuse her cheeks.
Still riding him relentlessly, she squeezed her eyes closed
and ducked her head, as if she'd forgotten all about him
and was lost in sensation. The raw sexuality of her expression, the pressure she was creating, the heat, the friction, the astonishment that it was Bernie on top of him
right now, bringing both of them to a place he'd never
counted on—all of it was pushing him to the edge so fast
it shocked him.

Seconds later, a wave of indescribable pleasure hit him
with the force of a battering ram. He gripped her thighs
and thrust his hips up off the sofa, driving up into her as
she drove down onto him, jerking convulsively as sear-
ing pulsations tore through him. Seconds later, Bernie
threw her head back, clasping his shoulders with savage
force. He knew he'd have bruises in the morning, but he
didn't feel the pain. All he knew was that the woman who

usually controlled every move she made was suddenly shuddering like a leaf in a violent wind, a groan of satisfaction ripping from her throat.

Then little by little, the shuddering stopped. She dropped her chin to her chest, her hair clinging to her sweaty temples, her breath coming in short, shallow gasps. Then she raised her head and opened her eyes to look down at him.

For a moment, she seemed lost. Disoriented. Those eyes that spent all day every day narrowed sarcastically slowly widened with bewilderment. Her mouth dropped open slightly, as if she wanted to say something but the words wouldn't come. It was as if a window had opened just enough for him to catch a fleeting glimpse of the woman inside, and she was as stunned as he was at what had just happened.

And then the telephone rang.

She jerked around to look at the phone, then turned back to him. In the blink of an eye, her expression became hard and impenetrable again. She moved away from him and rose from the sofa, giving her skirt a couple of quick tugs to put it back in place as she walked over to pick up the phone.

He sat up slowly, making out just enough of what she said to know that the danger was over. After she hung up, she turned and walked back across the room, grabbed her shoes, and put them on. She scooped up her panties, stuffed them into her purse, and headed for the door.

"Wait a minute," he said. "Where do you think you're going?"

"Anywhere but here."

"But you'll need to talk to the police."

"I no longer work for you."

"The hell you don't."

"I'd have to be willing to take a bullet for you. As of right now, I'd step aside and let the bullets fly."

"But—"

"I told you I'm done with you. Once and for all."

Jeremy felt the strangest trickle of desperation. But why did he care if she walked out? He wasn't completely sure. He only knew that women didn't walk away from him. He walked away from *them*.

"So you're done, are you?" he said.

She unlocked the door. "Completely."

"I notice you didn't mind screwing me on your way out the door."

Bernie froze, then slowly turned back, her expression cold as ice. "You started it, Bridges. I just finished it."

God, how she'd finished it. He felt as if he'd been hit by a freight train.

"And by the way," Bernie said, "if you ever get the urge to tell *anyone* what happened here, I'll deny it to my dying breath."

With that, she turned and left the room, closing the door behind her.

Jeremy just sat there, furious that she'd had the nerve to leave. Most of the women he'd been with barely climbed out of bed before they were on the phone to tell their friends they'd screwed a multimillionaire, so Bernie's reaction stunned him. Then again, in the past half hour, pretty much everything about Bernie had stunned him.

He went to the bathroom. Cleaned up. Yanked on his pants. He knew the cops were out there waiting to talk to him, but he couldn't seem to focus on that. Instead he went to the bar, anger and irritation still eating away at him. He picked up the bottle of Crown, but instead of pouring a drink, he slammed down the bottle, grabbed the glass, and hurled it across the room. It hit the wall and shattered into a thousand pieces, which did not one blessed thing to make him feel better.

Damn it. Why should he even care what she thought of him? There were dozens of bodyguards in this town who could do everything she could, and without the endless barrage of insults she fired at him. But for some reason, when he imagined a big, nameless guy shadowing him saying, "Yes, sir," and, "No, sir," he felt sick inside.

He shouldn't have pushed her, but he hadn't been able to stop. From one second to the next, he'd gone from lobbing his usual sarcastic remarks at her to wanting her so badly he'd do anything to have her. What the *hell* had gotten into him? Whatever it was, it had made him feel helpless and exposed and out of control, which meant he needed to bury it thoroughly and completely so it never saw the light of day again.

When she came back—and she *would* come back, because money talked—he'd be calling the shots again, and everything would be back to normal.

Chapter

5

Bernie pulled her SUV into a parking space at her apartment complex, glad the day was over. Since early that morning, she'd been on a security detail for a high-profile chef on his whirlwind book-signing tour of the Dallas metroplex. Why his publisher thought he needed security, Bernie didn't know. Forty-something housewives hoping to get an autograph of the star of their favorite Food Network show didn't exactly pose a security risk. Boredom set in about the time she picked him and his publicist up at the airport that morning, and it didn't end until she driving out the north exit of Dallas–Fort Worth airport eight hours later. But Bernie was paid to stay vigilant, and that was exactly how she'd behaved.

The biggest drawback to her assignment today, though, was all the food talk she'd had to endure. Since late morning, even the thought of eating had turned her stomach, the nausea fading in and out, never quite taking hold, but never really going away, either. She felt somewhat better now, but maybe that was only because she was no longer hearing a certain chef repeating his story about going to Osaka and eating whale testicles.

She got out of her car and started up the stairs to her apartment. She put her hand on the iron railing. It shuddered beneath her hand, practically falling out of the wall.

With a muttered curse, she climbed the rest of the stairs, pulling her phone out and hitting speed dial eight. How bad was it to have the manager of her apartment complex on speed dial so she could complain about the latest code violation?

Five rings, no answer. Of course not. The last person Charmin wanted to talk to was Bernie.

Without a doubt, Charmin Brubaker was the most unpleasant, unmotivated, unlikable person Bernie had ever met. She spent a good portion of her day on the Internet playing Mafia Wars on Facebook. She had permanent orange Cheetos stains on her fingers. And whenever a tenant requested something, she went out of her way to "lose" the order three or four times before finally doing something about it. And since the owner, Harvey Farnsworth, was a tightwad who didn't mind letting costly repairs slide, Charmin's incompetence didn't bother him in the least. As long as she kept the occupancy rate up and the delinquency rate down, she could run a prostitution ring for all he cared.

Charmin had successfully browbeaten most of the tenants until nobody wanted to go head to head with her. Bernie had no such fear. If there was one thing she hated, it was seeing somebody like Charmin screw people who couldn't help themselves. Evidently that was the kind of person you turned into when your mother named you after toilet paper.

Bernie reached the landing in front of her apartment just as she heard the beep to leave a message. "Charmin. This is Bernie Hogan. I want these railings fixed. The one by my apartment, and the ones in buildings five and nine, too. If you don't fix them, I'm reporting you to the city. Again. Old people live here, Charmin. They need those railings! Do you hear me? Now, *fix them!*"

With an angry huff, she disconnected the call, shoved her phone in her pocket, and stuck her key into her door.

"Hey! Who you calling old?"

Bernie spun around to see Ruby Wilson standing in her doorway, a Marlboro hanging out of her mouth and her gnarled fingers wrapped around a bottle of Bud. A Hawaiian shirt was stuffed inside the stretchy waistband of her denim pants, which were pulled up under her breasts. She had a face that looked like a relief map of Appalachia, and every time a puff of cigarette smoke wafted past it, a dozen more skin cells gave up the ghost.

"Ruby. You're eighty-two. Most people think that's old."

"Yeah? Well, you're almost forty. Some people think *that's* old."

"Okay, then," Bernie said. "We're both old. And we both need that railing fixed."

Ruby took a long drag off her cigarette. "That Charmin's a real bitch. Wish I knew how to do one of them evil eyes, or stick a voodoo doll, or something. That'd teach her."

No, if Ruby fell and broke a hip and sued, *that'd* teach her.

"I'll follow up with her tomorrow," Bernie said. "In the meantime, don't touch that railing."

Ruby sighed. "Guess I'll have to build in an extra ten minutes just to get down the stairs."

"Just be careful, okay?"

Ruby nodded. "Goin' to the Choctaw on the bus tomorrow with my girls. If you're not workin', why don't you come along?"

Oh, yeah. Sounded like a blast. Going to a casino and plugging nickel slots with three chain-smoking senior citizens. Ruby had won a five-hundred-dollar jackpot on her sixty-seventh birthday, and she'd had the once-a-month habit ever since.

"No, thanks," Bernie said, her stomach still upset enough that an hour-long bus ride on the Casino Express sounded like torture. "I'm sticking close to home tomorrow."

"Okay. Holler if you change your mind."

Bernie went inside her apartment, found a bottle of Pepto-Bismol, and downed a dose. She took a deep breath. Let it out slowly. The queasiness was starting to subside, so it probably wasn't the flu, which was a very good thing. She had a week-long assignment starting on Monday. She hadn't missed a day of work in years, and she wanted to keep that record clean, because she'd never taken kindly to being thought of as the weaker sex. Men accepted any kind of sickness from other men—flu, cold, migraine, hangover, bronchitis, poison ivy, blue balls, *anything*— but the moment a woman was sidelined, it was because of female problems. She could have a flesh-eating bacteria that had consumed one leg and was starting on the other one, and they'd still say she hadn't shown up that morning because Aunt Flo had paid her a visit.

She went to her fridge and grabbed a bottle of Gatorade to drink as she flipped through her mail. Electric bill. Postcard with a coupon for an oil change and lube.

Solicitation from a local real estate agent. Weekly grocery ads.

Wait. A copy of *Home & Hearth*? Where had that come from?

She checked the mailing label, figuring the mailman had gotten it wrong. Nope. There it was. Her name and address, as if she'd subscribed. She thumbed through the magazine, saw the headlines, and realized she didn't need to read the articles to know the answers.

"Secrets to an Always-Clean House." Ajax, a sponge, and elbow grease.

"Real-Life Exercise Strategies That Work." Weightlifting, kickboxing class, and five-mile runs.

"Dinner in Under Ten Minutes." Lean Cuisine in the microwave.

She was sure this magazine had good advice for most women. She'd just never been like most women.

Suddenly her phone rang. She looked at the caller ID, and when she saw her cousin Billy's name, her stomach felt even sicker than before. She waited until he left a message, then picked it up.

"Hey, Bernie, it's Billy. I need your help."

Bernie sighed. Of course he did.

"I applied for a job, and I need a reference. They'll be calling you tomorrow. Can you tell them I'm a good guy? Hard worker, and all that?"

Translation: *Will you lie for me?*

"Now, I swear it won't be like my last job at the video game store. That wasn't my fault. My boss was a real bastard who had it in for me. No matter what he said, I did *not* steal that copy of *Assassin's Creed*. Somebody must have put it in my backpack. So this time it'll be different.

I swear. It's a job at an auto parts store. You know I love cars. This is my dream job, Bernie. You have to help me."

Dream job? Not likely. Her cousin Billy's dream job didn't exist, unless there was an opening somewhere for a TV-watching, pot-smoking, freeloading deadbeat.

So what was she supposed to do this time? If she told them he'd be a good employee, she'd be lying through her teeth. If she didn't, he might not get the job, and within a few weeks, he'd be on her doorstep asking for money.

She was damned if she did, damned if she didn't.

She just wanted him to take care of himself. That was all. Just get a decent job and hold on to it. Was that really too much to ask?

She heard a knock at her door. With a heavy sigh, she went to answer it. Looking out the peephole, she saw her mother. She was wearing her mint green dress and carrying a small white box, which meant she'd come from some church function and Bernie was going to have to hear all about it. She loved her mother, but sometimes it got to be too much.

Bernie opened the door, and Eleanor Hogan strode inside. "When I was getting out of my car," she said, "I saw a man lurking by the stairs with a bunch of little silver rings in his eyebrow. Just one eyebrow. Would you tell me the purpose of that? Five rings in one eyebrow and none in the other?"

"So you'd rather see him put five in each eyebrow?"

"Heavens, no. But at least that would make sense. And that odd little woman across the way was looking at me through the window as I was coming up the stairs."

"Ruby is harmless."

"I'm sure she's very nice," Eleanor said. "But she was

smoking and drinking, of all things. At her age. That can't possibly be good for her."

"Wait a minute," Bernie said, suddenly remembering. "The stairs. You have to be careful going back down, Mom. That railing is broken."

"Everything's broken around here. This isn't a decent place for a woman to live. If I were you—" All at once Eleanor stopped short and stared at Bernie, her brow furrowed with worry. "Bernadette? What's wrong? You're white as a ghost. Are you sick?"

"No. Of course not. I'm fine."

"There's Pepto-Bismol on your kitchen counter. Do you have stomach problems? Nausea? Gas?"

Bernie sighed. "I really don't want to discuss my gastrointestinal system with you, Mom."

Eleanor put her hand against Bernie's forehead. "Hmm. No fever. You didn't eat at that new restaurant on Branson Street, did you? Sushi is unnatural. Only grizzly bears should eat raw fish."

"No, I didn't eat sushi. I'm fine now. The Pepto Bismol did the trick."

"You're still pale."

"That's because the Pepto-Bismol pink hasn't made its way to my face yet."

Eleanor looked unconvinced. "Okay. Just be careful. Get plenty of rest. So many terrible things are going around this season." Then she spied the copy of *Home & Hearth* on the counter between Bernie's kitchen and dining room. She set down her purse and the white box and picked it up. "Oh, how nice! You've started getting the magazine. It was only an extra eight dollars to give a gift subscription when I renewed mine. I couldn't turn down a bargain like that."

Bernie heaved a silent sigh. She should have known.

In recent years, her mother had begun to recognize the futility of overtly begging her daughter to marry and procreate, so her game plan had shifted to subtle hints. Bernie couldn't imagine that her mother actually believed she'd sit down with a *Home & Hearth*, read an article or two, slap her forehead, and say *How could I have been so blind? This is the life I want!* But that was her mother. She stuck to hope like gum to a tennis shoe.

"Did I tell you Katherine's daughter Susan was getting married at the church this afternoon?" Eleanor said. "I wouldn't have chosen yellow Gerbera daisies for a bridal bouquet, but it was lovely just the same."

Eleanor Hogan had definitely found her calling as head of the altar guild at the Sunnyside Baptist Church. It was all weddings, all the time. According to her mother, everything about them was *lovely*, from the cakes to the dresses to the flowers to the nut cups to the blissful expressions on the brides' faces as they pledged undying love to their grooms. Statistically speaking, within a few years, half those brides would be hurling china at their grooms' heads on their way out the door to hire a divorce lawyer, but Bernie refrained from pointing that out.

To stem the tide of wedding talk that was sure to begin, she grabbed the book she'd brought home. "Mom, look. You know that guy you watch on the Food Network? The chef who does all that international cuisine stuff? This is his cookbook. I had him sign it for you."

Her mother took it reverently, her eyes wide with awe. "You got Chef Allen's autograph? *The* Chef Allen?"

"Yeah. He was in Dallas doing some book signings. I was on his security detail."

Eleanor frowned, her brows pulling together again. "Security detail? For Chef Allen? Was there any... trouble?"

"Yeah. Those ladies who showed up for his signings were really pushy. I think one of them stepped on his toe."

"Don't joke," Eleanor snapped. "Your job worries me to death."

"No need to worry. About 99 percent of the time, it's a real bore."

"It's the other one percent that concerns me."

Bernie was tired of rehashing this. Yes, she knew her mother worried, but in the end, her biggest objection had to do not with what her daughter was, but with what she wasn't: a secretary, schoolteacher, librarian, or stay-at-home mom with six kids and a minivan. On her mother's side of the family, women were shuttled onto a bullet train that sped straight into a blackened tunnel of Kool-Aid spills, diaper changes, and perfunctory sex with the lights out. And when they emerged on the other side, what was waiting for them? Social Security, TV remotes, and ungrateful children who never came to visit.

Bernie remembered when she was fourteen and her mother made an appointment so they could have a spa day together. A spa day. God, was there anything worse than that? Evidently Eleanor thought if she shoved that pendulum really hard in the other direction, her daughter would end up somewhere in the middle. Bernie would have licked the spout of every drinking fountain in town if it meant she'd pick up the flu and be forced to stay home. Unfortunately, the hundred different strains floating around that season had bypassed her, so she'd been stuck enduring an afternoon of people's hands on her from her hair to her toenails, buffing, polishing, massaging, and scrubbing until Bernie had lost an entire layer of skin and any semblance of privacy. And through it all, her mother had said, *Now, isn't that nice? That's a lovely shade of pink nail polish, isn't it? And I don't think your complexion has ever looked prettier.* And Bernie had come home reeking of jasmine and vanilla and hating every minute of it.

"Billy said he was going to call you," her mother asked tentatively. "Did you hear from him?"

Bernie closed her eyes. "Yeah, Mom. He left me a message."

"I hope you'll help him out. The job sounds very promising."

"A reference from a blood relative doesn't count for much."

"But you present yourself so well. Anything you say will help."

"He stole from his last employer."

"He says that was just a misunderstanding."

"Yeah. He misunderstood that he wasn't supposed to steal things."

"But it's been so hard for him," Eleanor said sadly. "Growing up without a mother."

Oh, God. Here it comes. "Mom, your sister died when Billy was eight years old. He's twenty-nine now. Don't you think it's time he stood on his own two feet?"

"Bernadette. If I were the one who had died, I would have wanted Rose to help you."

Ignoring, of course, the fact that Bernie hadn't needed any help from anyone in approximately thirty years. But that was logical, and her mother had never run on logic.

"Okay, Mom," Bernie said on a heavy sigh. "I'll give him a reference."

"I'm sure you can think of something nice to say."

Yeah. She could say he had good manual dexterity and superior powers of persuasion. As long as they didn't realize she was talking about him punching a TV remote and begging for a loan, maybe she wouldn't be struck dead for lying.

"Sorry to be abrupt," Bernie said, "but I have plans this evening. I need to take a shower."

"Dinner with friends?"

"No."

She blinked hopefully. "A . . . date?"

As if she could speak it into existence. "No."

Her mother frowned. "You're playing poker again, aren't you?"

"Yeah, Mom. I'm playing poker. I like poker."

"It's gambling."

"Given the guys I play with, there's really not much gambling involved."

Eleanor let out a weary sigh. "You do take after your father."

Yes. She did. And if only her mother would accept that someday, Bernie would be the happiest woman alive.

Her father had been a cop, shot in the line of duty when she was only sixteen. She didn't know if she'd been a tomboy from birth, or she'd just loved her father so much that she wanted to be just like him. He took her fishing. To baseball games. Taught her how to play basketball. The first time he took her to the shooting range, she'd hit a bull's-eye. He told everybody within range of his voice that his baby girl was a hell of a shot. It had been a losing battle for her poor mother to get her to wear perfume when her favorite scent was gunpowder. To this day, every time Bernie smelled it, it was as if her father was smiling down at her from heaven.

"Can't I make you dinner before I go?" Eleanor said. "Maybe some chicken soup to help you feel better?"

"No, thanks."

"You still don't look well. Promise me you'll get home early and get some rest."

"I will."

Eleanor grabbed her purse and walked to the door.

"Wait," Bernie said, picking up the white box her mother had left there earlier. "You forgot this."

Eleanor turned back. She froze, looking at the box, then tilted her head. "Is that mine?"

Bernie felt a tremor of apprehension slither between her shoulders. "Yeah, Mom. It's yours. You brought it here."

Her mother swallowed hard, her hand slinking to her throat, her eyes blinking anxiously.

"Did it come from the church?" Bernie asked. "The wedding?"

"Oh!" Eleanor said, exhaling, her eyes falling closed, then opening again. "Cake. It's cake. From Katherine's daughter's wedding. I just forgot for a moment. Such a busy day." Her mouth turned up in a shaky smile. "It's why I dropped by. To bring you the cake. It's delicious. White buttercream frosting on the outside, but the cake itself is chocolate. Not exactly traditional, but what woman ever complained about chocolate? And such pretty yellow roses on top. With a vase of yellow roses beside it, it made such a beautiful cake table."

Bernie winced at the information overload. *See, I*

remember all the details. Every one. So there's no problem. No problem at all.

"Well, I'd better be going," Eleanor said breezily. "You have things to do. Enjoy the cake. And thank you for the book. If you'll come for dinner sometime soon, I'll try one of the recipes."

"I will." Bernie followed her to the door. "Mom?"

Eleanor turned back. "Yes?"

"Have you been feeling okay?"

"Me? Of course I have."

"Are you sure?"

"Bernadette," she said, her voice laced with nervous laughter. "It's nothing. I'm sixty-eight years old. Sometimes it's just...just normal forgetting. You know."

Don't panic. It was just a momentary lapse. Things are still okay for now. "Yeah. I know."

"I'll call you tomorrow. See how you're feeling."

Bernie started to say that it wasn't necessary, but she stopped herself. She could see now that she couldn't let a day go by without talking to her mother, without judging each day's experience in light of the one before. Sometime soon there would be a tipping point, and Bernie needed to recognize it when it happened. She had the terrible feeling that day was coming sooner than she expected.

"Yeah, that'd be good," Bernie said. "Give me a call in the morning."

Her mother nodded and slipped out the door, and Bernie closed it behind her. She turned and leaned against it for a moment, taking a deep breath and letting it out slowly. Damn it. *Damn it.* She hated that life had thrown her this curveball. And she hated that she hated it. A good daughter would remain calm and sympathetic instead of feeling the undertow of responsibility dragging down until she could barely breathe.

Why on earth had her mother let her health insurance lapse?

If Bernie could count on help from the rest of the family, it might be different. But all she had was a grandmother who was too old and too eccentric to take care of anyone. Billy, who was allergic to work and sponged off anybody he could. There were others who were less of a pain but loony in their own right, or they weren't local, so how much help could they be? If only her father were still alive to run interference and take care of her mother, Bernie would be free to live her own life. But now it fell on her to be the sane one, the voice of reason, the one strong thread that kept the ragged fabric of her family from falling apart at the seams. To make sure her mother was protected, now until the end.

She thought about what had happened with Jeremy. About the money she wasn't making now. For all her complaints about him, she never would have quit that job unless she'd done something so stupid that quitting had been her *only* option. It wasn't until now, almost two months later, that the sting of that experience had even begun to fade. She'd just been so damned angry, and then she'd tossed down those shots, and then Jeremy had taunted her, then kissed her...

No. There was no excuse for what she'd done. None at all. She'd never been one to blame anyone else for her own actions. It was the only time in her adult life she'd behaved in a way that made her ashamed to think back on it, and now she had to live with the memory of it forever. And in the coming months and years, she'd just have to

find a way to keep things afloat that didn't involve a great
big paycheck from a womanizing millionaire.

She drained the Gatorade bottle and headed to her
bathroom to take a shower, then head to Bill's house for
poker. Just for tonight, she was going to lose herself in
Texas Hold 'Em and a few longnecks and pretend everything was A-OK.

Chapter

6

A couple of hours later, Bernie sat at Bill Ramsey's dining room table, playing poker with some of the other security specialists from Delgado & Associates. Only a few faces were missing—those who had an evening assignment or were on a job out of state. Bernie had already won a couple of hands, which was a good thing. These days, every penny counted.

She took a break and went into the kitchen. Gabe followed. She grabbed two beers from the fridge and handed one to him.

"Got a call from Bridges today," he said, taking the bottle. "That's the third time in the past few weeks. He wants you back."

Bernie froze for a second, then opened her bottle. "You know I'm not interested."

"You don't even want to know what he's offering now?"

"Nope."

"Seriously, Bernie. You might want to consider—"

"He only wants me because he can't have me. He'll throw all kinds of money around just to get his way."

"That's the key. He wants *you.*"

"Fine. But I don't want him."

"You never did tell me why you requested reassignment."

"You never asked. And I appreciate that."

"I assumed you had your reasons."

"I do."

"But I'm asking now. Does this have anything to do with the robbery attempt at Bridges's house the night before you quit?"

Bernie turned away. "That was nothing."

"I know the robbery wasn't. The police made an arrest later that night. But did something else happen?"

Bernie took a sip of her beer, wishing this topic had never come up. "Could my answer jeopardize my job?"

"Hell, no."

"Then my answer is that I'd rather not answer."

Gabe stared at her a moment longer. Finally he nodded. "Okay. I'll tell Bridges he'll have to keep putting up with Max."

And Bernie would bet her last dollar that Max drove Jeremy crazy. Max was six-five, big as a house, and could be scary as King Kong if he set his mind to it. But Jeremy wouldn't have a problem with those things. What he would hate was that Max never spoke unless it was absolutely necessary. Jeremy wasn't one to tolerate silence for long without filling it with some random comment or smart-ass remark, but with Max, it would become obvious very quickly to Jeremy that he was talking to himself.

"I know it's more money for both of us," Bernie told Gabe. "But I just can't consider it right now."

"Forget the money," Gabe said. "You're one of my best. I'm not putting you anywhere you don't want to go."

Bernie nodded, truly appreciating that about her boss. Gabe Delgado was an ex-cop in his midforties who was too rugged to be handsome and too rigid and unsmiling to be approachable by the average woman. Whether by choice or by fate, marriage didn't seem to be in the cards for him, but some woman's loss was his employees' gain. Fiercely dedicated to his business, Gabe was a fair man who ran a tight ship, which meant Bernie had a boss she could respect.

They went back to the table and sat down again. Lucky dealt the next hand. Bill picked up his hand, looked at the flop, and his mouth twisted with irritation. After three beers, his poker face had deserted him, if he'd ever had one in the first place. He was a family man through and through, with two kids and a great big mortgage. He kept mostly to local short-term assignments, which usually meant odd hours, but at least he was home most evenings. His wife, Teresa, was one of those perfect moms who made motherhood look easy. Their house always looked beautiful, the children were well-behaved, and Teresa looked as if she hadn't broken a sweat.

"So how's the gig with Bridges going?" Bill asked Max.

"It's a job," Max said.

An image of Jeremy flashed through Bernie's mind—his hands, his mouth, the sound of his voice—and a heavy flush of heat went to her cheeks. *Fever,* she thought. *It's just fever. Fever that goes along with whatever this thing is you have.*

Bill turned to Bernie. "Still don't know why you

backed out of that assignment. Bridges was paying you through the nose."

"That's my business," Bernie said.

"Was it some woman thing?" Lucky said. "Did he offend your feminist sensibilities?"

"No, Lucky," Bernie said, "*you* offend my feminist sensibilities."

Lucky grinned. "Every chance I get."

"Like that time you told her she had a nice ass," Max said. "You're lucky she didn't split your ribs and rip your heart out."

Lucky shook his head sadly. "A guy just can't give a woman a compliment anymore."

Lucky's taunting rarely bothered Bernie, but right now, she didn't feel up to dealing with it. He was good at his job, with a resume that was nearly as sterling as her own, so Bernie couldn't fault him there. But when it came to chasing women, he was second in line only to Bridges. But while Bridges rationed his glowing smiles, using them only when they suited his purposes, Lucky was as quick to laugh as he was to move in on any woman within range of his voice. He'd probably banged two girls on the way there tonight and had one waiting for him when he got home.

Bernie tossed in her bet for the round, only to have it hit her again. The nausea. She took a deep breath, which did nothing to ease the pain.

"Wow, Bernie," Bill said. "You don't look so good. What's up?"

"He's right," Gabe said. "You do look a little green."

She felt green. A nice shade of bile, to be exact.

"You got the flu or something?" Bill asked.

"Bernie can't have the flu," Lucky said. "She's too mean for the germs to survive."

"I'm fine," Bernie said, even though she was beginning to believe she wasn't.

And then she felt it again. An even bigger wave of nausea, undulating like a riptide dragging her out to sea. She did her best to keep her face impassive, but it was a hard-won battle.

Bill stared at her, his eyes narrowing. "You know, Teresa looked like that once for three solid months."

"Teresa had the flu for three months?" Gabe said.

"No. She had morning sickness for three months."

In unison, the other three heads swiveled around and looked at Bernie expectantly. Until that very moment, the possibility hadn't even crossed her mind. But now . . .

No. No way. She'd seen Bridges put on a condom. She was sure of it. Pregnant? That was ridiculous.

But just as she was blowing off the possibility, another wave of nausea hit. She gritted her teeth against it, sliding her hand against her stomach.

"There!" Bill said, pointing. "That's it! The look! White as a ghost, weaving back and forth, hand on stomach—"

She jerked her hand away and sat up straight. "I told you already. It's nothing."

"So you're telling me you couldn't possibly be pregnant?"

"For God's sake, Bill!" Teresa called from the kitchen.

Bill leaned in. "When's the last time you got laid?"

"Bill!" Teresa shouted. "Will you *stop*?"

"Well," Lucky said, "if she was with a guy, he's a goner now. Don't black widows eat their mates?"

When Bernie didn't honor that nasty remark with an

equally malicious comeback, Bill sat back in his chair and eyed her carefully.

"Hmm. The suspect is being evasive. Gentlemen, it looks as if we have a possible crime scene here."

Bernie sighed. Okay. Fine. She knew the drill. Not one of these guys thought she could actually be pregnant, but they sure loved getting under her skin. They were all that way. Like a pack of wolves. The second they sensed vulnerability, they circled around and went in for the kill. She remembered the time a pair of Bill's tightie whities ended up in the wash with the colored stuff and they turned pink. Once word got out about that, they took up a collection and made a donation in his name to the National Center for Gay and Lesbian Awareness. He was still getting fundraising phone calls.

Right now, Bernie was simply the target du jour.

"Will you guys just shut up and play?" Bernie said, taking a swig of beer. Big mistake. The instant the liquid hit her stomach, her insides felt like puzzle pieces rattling around in the box.

Bill gave her a smug smile. "Looking a little woozy there, Bernie."

If she'd been operating at a hundred percent, she would have countered the smart remarks by reminding Bill of the time he'd gotten drunk on a fishing trip, cast his line, and hooked himself in the ass. But feeling the way she did right then, most of her attention was focused on keeping that swig of beer from sneaking back up her throat.

It was time to get out of there before it succeeded.

But just as she'd decided to fold her hand and clear out, Bill picked up a twenty and tossed it in the middle of the table. "I've got twenty bucks that says I'm right."

"Are you nuts?" Lucky said. "We're not even sure Bernie is an anatomically correct woman, and you're betting good money that she's *pregnant*?"

"Jesus," Teresa muttered from the kitchen. "This is why I can't take him to Vegas." She came out to the dining room and grabbed Bill's half-empty beer bottle. "I'm cutting you off."

Bernie slumped back down in her chair. Now why did Bill have to do that? She'd been born way too competitive for her own good, and dealing with these guys over the years had only sharpened that inclination.

Bill grinned. "We can find out if it's true right here and now." He turned toward the kitchen. "Teresa! Where's that home pregnancy test?"

She stared at her husband dumbly for a moment, then thunked her head against the door frame with a heavy sigh.

"You have a home pregnancy test lying around?" Lucky asked.

"Yeah," Bill said. "Teresa's excessive fertility demands it." He turned to Bernie. "So how about it? Shall we see if you should be drinking for two?"

Unfortunately, this had just turned into one of those "damned if you do, damned if you don't" situations. If she backed down now, these guys would harass her endlessly, giving up only when nine months passed and nothing popped out. But if she went ahead and did it, they were going to laugh their asses off because Bill got her to pee on a stick for twenty bucks. At least with the latter, the harassment would die down faster and she'd be twenty dollars richer.

She pulled out a twenty and slapped it on top of Bill's. "You're on."

To a round of applause and a few catcalls, she rose from the table and followed Teresa. As she entered the bathroom, she started to worry. Just a little.

What if she really was pregnant?

No. No way. She wasn't even going to entertain the possibility. After all, what were the odds?

Still, it wasn't as if there was no chance at all...

Teresa grabbed a blue and pink box from a cabinet, muttering that she was cutting Bill off forever from more than just alcohol, so she sure wouldn't be needing a pregnancy test again anytime soon. Then she gave Bernie a crash course in how to use the test, apologized again for her husband, and slipped out the door.

Okay. She was supposed to pee on the indicator thingy and then wait five minutes. One line meant she wasn't pregnant. Two lines meant she was.

She pulled out a few tissues and put them on the counter, then peed in the appropriate place. She shook it off and rested it on the tissues, then closed the toilet lid and sat back down again, leaning her head on the wall behind her to wait the requisite five minutes. No doubt Bill would be watching the clock, so she had to, too.

She closed her eyes, wishing the light wasn't so damned *bright* in there. Not only was her stomach throwing her a curveball, but her head was getting into the game. Her brain felt as if it was booming against her skull. She'd had the flu before, but she didn't remember it feeling like this.

It seemed as if eons passed before the second hand swept past twelve for the fifth time. She stood up, grabbed the stick, and started to leave the bathroom.

Then she saw the two lines.

For a few seconds, the sight didn't register. She just

stood there staring at it, thinking whatever dire disease she had was making her see double. Something. *Anything*.

Then her hands actually started to shake. She could squeeze off a shot at a target two hundred yards away with a high-powered rifle and never so much as twitch, yet suddenly her hands were trembling as if she was standing naked on the tundra. Like a DVD gone haywire, her mind leaped back to that evening with Jeremy. She saw him putting on a condom.

He *had* put on a condom, hadn't he?

Yes. Yes, of course he had. No doubt about it.

But condoms weren't a hundred percent, and suddenly she couldn't remember the last time she'd had a period. She squeezed her eyes closed, thinking about how she kept track of the rest of her life so carefully. Why the hell didn't she keep track of that?

Because she didn't have much of a need to before.

Suddenly her brain wouldn't function. Her lungs wouldn't breathe. Nerve synapses ceased firing. She slumped against the counter like a puppet without strings, overcome by the most horrendous feeling that she'd taken one step too many and fallen right off a cliff. The one man on earth she despised above all others . . . the man she'd vowed she'd never speak to again for the rest of her life . . .

She was carrying his baby.

Chapter
7

Bernie just stood there in that bathroom, staring at that stick and watching her life come to an end.

"Come on, Bernie!" Bill shouted. "Give us the verdict!"

She wondered how long she could survive in there on tap water and toothpaste. Nine months, maybe?

She opened the door. Slumped against the door frame. They all turned around to look at her. Bernie knew her expression said it all, but she couldn't seem to wipe it away. She waited for the taunts, the laughter, the ridicule, but strangely, none of it came. They just sat there staring at her, and suddenly Bernie knew why. They were no longer looking at a colleague. A security specialist like themselves. Just one of the guys. They were looking at a *pregnant woman*, and the very idea of it short-circuited their brains. Even Teresa couldn't hide her expression of disbelief. *You? Bernadette Hogan? Pregnant? How in the hell did that happen?*

Okay, so the *how* was pretty obvious. It was the *who*

they were all wondering about, but they'd get that information out of her only over her dead body.

"Bernie?" Teresa said.

She opened her mouth to say something, but the words got lost between her brain and her lips.

Teresa turned to the men. "Okay, you guys. Out."

They looked at her dumbly.

"I said out! *Now!*"

"But I live here!" Bill said.

"All of you!"

Bill and Lucky took flight like a pair of startled birds, scraping their chairs against the tile floor, stumbling over each other in their haste to get as far away from the pregnant woman as they could. Gabe was more measured in his exit, but Bernie could tell he'd still rather be anywhere else. Max, who never got in a hurry to do anything, stared at her a long, analytical moment before picking up his winnings and following the other guys to the door.

"Wait!" Bernie shouted.

They froze. Turned back.

"If one of you so much as breathes a word of this to anyone," Bernie said, her voice low and malevolent, "I'll rip your eyeballs out and squash them with my bare hands. Are we clear on that?"

Bernie didn't make threats often, and these guys knew it. If they opened their mouths, they were blind men.

Bernie turned away and collapsed on the sofa, and the guys took that as permission to clear out, closing the door behind them with a solid *thunk*. The sudden screaming silence and Teresa's sympathetic expression as she sat down beside Bernie made her want to duck her head under a cushion and leave it there until she asphyxiated herself.

"How accurate are those tests?" she managed to croak out.

"It depends. When was your last period?"

"I . . . I don't know. I don't really keep track all that well."

But it had been a while. Maybe more than a month. Maybe more than two months. Maybe she didn't know.

"Who's the . . . I mean, do you have a boyfriend?" Teresa said.

As sick as Bernie had felt all day, the very idea that there was only one candidate for fatherhood made her stomach curdle with dread.

"I really can't talk about it," she said.

"So if it's true, would it be a . . ." Teresa paused, wincing as she spoke. "*Bad* thing?"

Bernie turned slowly to look at her, feeling her own face falling into a you-gotta-be-kidding-me expression.

"Okay, then," Teresa said. "You don't have to panic just yet. Really. It was just a dumb over-the-counter test. Sometimes they're wrong. Get another test. Do it again. It'll probably be negative."

"Have you ever had a false positive before?"

"Well . . . no."

"Ever known anyone who did?"

"No, but I've heard that it does happen."

I don't want anecdotes! Bernie wanted to shout. *I want somebody to tell me that these tests are worthless pieces of crap!*

"I'm thirty-six years old," she said. "Don't the odds of getting pregnant diminish with age?"

"Yeah, if you're forty-five or fifty," Teresa said. "But thirty-six-year-olds get pregnant all the—" She stopped short. "But I'm sure not *this* time. It's probably just—"

"I need to go."

"Uh . . . yeah. Okay." They rose from the sofa, and Teresa opened the door. "Let me know what happens. And tell me if I can . . . you know. Do anything for you."

Bernie nodded. "Thanks. But I think it's a mistake, you know? I'll probably be laughing about this in the morning."

"Probably," Teresa said, just about as unconvincingly as Bernie had ever heard anyone utter a single word.

She left the house and headed for her car parked at the curb. There was no sign of Lucky or Gabe—apparently they'd *really* cleared out. Bill came back up the sidewalk, passing by her without a word, and returned to the house. Only Max remained, leaning against the driver's door of Bernie's SUV, his arms folded, staring at her.

No. *No.* She didn't want to talk to anyone right now. Not even him. She stopped in front of him. "Go home, Max."

"Not just yet."

"Get out of my way," she snapped, "or I'll *move* you out of my way."

"Under normal circumstances, I'd take that threat seriously. But right now you don't look strong enough to beat up a kitten."

"You're right. So I don't feel like arguing. Will you just let me go home?"

"Nope. We've been watching each other's backs for years. I don't intend to stop now."

He was right about that. The military had brought them

together. Delgado & Associates had kept them together. They were friends, nothing more, but she'd always been able to count on Max, like the big brother she'd never had. The way she felt right now, though, she'd rather count on him *tomorrow.*

"There's no reason to get all worried about this," Bernie said.

"I'm not the one who's uptight."

"I'm not pregnant, you know."

"The test was positive."

"The test was wrong. I can't be pregnant. No way."

Max nodded thoughtfully. "Uh-huh."

She threw up her hands. "I told you I'm not pregnant!" Then she closed her eyes in frustration. "Damn it, would you at least try to be as oblivious as other men? Just once?"

"I'd ask who the father is, but I'm guessing you'd rather keep that to yourself."

She started to say that there wasn't a father because she *wasn't pregnant,* but it would have fallen on deaf ears. And first she had to believe it herself.

"Do another test," Max said.

"I intend to."

"Tonight. If it's negative, maybe you can actually sleep."

A nice thought, but Bernie could hear what Max wasn't saying. *And if it's positive, you're screwed.*

"You okay to drive home?" he asked her.

"Of course I am."

Bernie clicked open her car door. Max stepped aside and opened it. As she settled into the driver's seat, her stomach did a slow, sickening heave. Good Lord. If this was what pregnancy felt like, how did the average woman stand it?

"Can I count on you to keep this quiet? Not a word to anyone? You know—until I find out for sure what's up."

"Hell, yes, I'll keep it quiet," he said with a tiny smile. "You think I want my eyeballs squashed?"

"Come on, Max. You know I wouldn't *really* squash your eyeballs. Lucky's maybe. Never yours."

Squashed eyeballs notwithstanding, she didn't know why she worried about Max. If the population dwindled away and there was only one discreet person left on this planet, it would be Max Delinsky.

"Don't sweat this until you're sure there's something to sweat, okay?" Max said. "Get another test, rule it out, and then you can forget about it."

Bernie nodded. She got into her car, and at the first red light she came to, she grabbed her iPhone and found a twenty-four-hour drugstore. It was twelve miles away, but she didn't care. She tossed her phone to the passenger seat and drove there, where she picked up another pregnancy test. She was careful to get a different brand from the one she'd already taken just in case that particular manufacturer wasn't quite up to par. As she made her way to the checkout counter, she felt as if everyone in the store was looking at her, so she also grabbed a Snickers bar, a bottle of shampoo, and a pack of razor blades, as if those would distract from her real intent: *I'm hungry, my hair's dirty, I have hairy legs, and…oh, yeah. I need to see if I'm pregnant.* The teenage girl behind the counter didn't blink as she rang the stuff up, but Bernie still felt as if a gigantic spotlight had appeared from nowhere to shine directly on her.

All the way home, her heart beat like mad at the same time her stomach flip-flopped like a fish on the deck of a bass boat. She came through her apartment door and headed straight for her bathroom, where she yanked the directions out of the box and read them from beginning to end, including a statement about the effectiveness of the test. "Supersensitive in detecting hCG levels" and "99 percent accurate after seven to nine days" didn't exactly fill her with hope.

A few minutes later, there it was. Corroborating evidence. She was going to have a baby.

In dazed disbelief, she tossed the test into the trash. She made her way to the living room, where she plunked herself down on the sofa. She stared straight ahead, her hand on her stomach, trying to reconcile the test she'd just taken with the reality of an actual baby growing inside her. She'd always been proud of the fact that she had a job that one in ten thousand women couldn't have qualified for, yet here she was in a situation any brainless teenager in the backseat of a car could have gotten herself into.

Then she thought about Jeremy. Oh, *God.* What was he going to say when he found out?

She couldn't think about that now. Not when the majority of her energy was consumed with trying to keep from throwing up. Morning sickness? Wrong damned time of day. And it sounded so benign. There had to be another name for it, something more like *bubonic plague.*

She lay down on the sofa and tucked a pillow beneath her head, stifling a groan as she curled up in a semifetal position. She closed her eyes, willing the nausea to subside, only to hear a knock at her door.

No! Whoever you are, go away! I want to die in peace!

She closed her eyes again, only to hear more knocking. Finally she got up and staggered to her door, intending to open it only if somebody was carrying a five-foot-long Publishers Clearing House check for a million bucks. She looked out the peephole.

Oh, God. Her mother?

More knocking. "Bernadette? Open the door. I saw your car. I know you're home!"

Bernie felt a twinge of panic. If her mother saw her looking like this, she'd call 911.

The flu. She'd just say she had the flu, because she sure couldn't tell the truth. Not until she had a chance to think about it when she felt better. Whenever that might be.

She opened the door. "Mom? What are you doing here this late? You know you shouldn't be driving after dark."

"I tried to call you, but you didn't answer. I got worried."

"You called? I didn't hear—" She stopped short. "Oh. I must have left my phone in the car." And what a dumb, dumb move *that* had turned out to be.

Eleanor came into the apartment, her brows drawing together. "Oh, my. You really are sick. I can tell. You're feeling worse, aren't you?" She pressed her palms against Bernie's cheeks. "Hmm. Still no fever. Do you have a headache? Muscle aches?"

"Yeah. I think it's the flu."

"Are you nauseated?"

Just hearing those words was all it took for Bernie's stomach to turn upside down one more time. She yanked herself away from her mother and hurried to the bathroom. When she reached the toilet, she dropped to her knees, flung up the lid, and started to heave. A few moments later her mother was beside her, sitting on the edge of the tub, holding her hair and patting her back. When Bernie finally stopped throwing up, she took the wet towel her mother offered her and wondered what she'd done in a former life that was so bad that she'd get stuck with karma like this.

"Poor baby," her mother said.

"It's just the flu," Bernie croaked. "I'll be over it in a few days."

"Don't you usually get a flu shot?"

I do. But flu shots don't prevent pregnancy. "Yeah. Usually. It just got past me this year."

"You need water. Fluids will help you feel better. I'll get you a glass of—" When she stopped short, Bernie looked up to see her staring down at something. The trash can. When her mother reached inside, Bernie froze with dread, but there was no stopping her now.

She pulled out the box the pregnancy test had come in.

She looked at it. She looked at Bernie. At the box. At Bernie. It was as if she was finding it impossible to reconcile the two, but feminine barfing in the presence of a used pregnancy test would eventually lead anyone to the truth.

"Bernadette," Eleanor said finally, her voice quivering. "It isn't the flu, is it?"

Bernie scoured her brain for a really good lie, but absolutely nothing came to her. "No, Mom," she said on a sigh. "It's not the flu."

When Eleanor slid her hand to her throat, her eyes wide, her jaw slack with disbelief, Bernie actually began to tremble with dread. After all, how had her mother reacted when Sharon Binkley, the biggest slut at Bernie's high school, had gotten pregnant? *What's wrong with these girls?* she'd said in a hushed, horrified whisper. *Having relations outside of marriage? Do they have no shame? No shame at all?* Then came the lecture she subjected Bernie to, the one about boys and their motives and the dreadful things that happened to any girl dumb enough to fall prey to their manipulation. Eleanor had done her best to pray for poor Sharon, but Bernie knew the truth as her mother saw it: The shameless, spineless pregnant girl was going straight to hell.

Now, twenty years later, it was Eleanor's own daughter on the hot seat, and nothing had changed. Bernie had no doubt her churchgoing mother was going to bring down the wrath of God right onto her head. And in the event that God chose to spare her an instantaneous death, Eleanor would simply drag her to church every day for the rest of her life to save her from eternal damnation.

"Bernadette?" she said slowly, carefully. "Are you ... p-pr ... ?"

Oh, God. She couldn't even say the word. This was going to be bad. Very, *very* bad. But there wasn't much that Bernie could do now to stop it from happening.

"Yeah, Mom," she said. "I'm pregnant."

Bernie braced herself. As much as Eleanor loved her daughter, a sin was a sin, after all, and any moment she was going to throw her arm skyward and beseech God to send down that thunderbolt. But to Bernie's total amazement, the whole Old Testament thing never happened.

Instead her mother started to smile. A look of delighted relief swept over her face. She dropped the box and threw her arms around Bernie, hugging her so tightly Bernie swore she was going to throw up all over again.

What the hell…?

Eleanor pulled away and took Bernie by the shoulders. "So it's really true? You're pregnant? You're going to have a baby?"

"So…you're not mad?"

"Mad? *Mad?* Why would I be mad? I'm going to be a *grandmother*!"

And then she was hugging Bernie all over again. For several stunned seconds, Bernie just let it happen, wondering what portal she'd fallen through to land in this alternate universe. Then Eleanor slowly backed away, putting her hand on her chest, and closed her eyes, taking a deep, relaxing breath. When she opened them again, they glistened with tears.

Bernie blinked. "Mom? What's wrong?"

"Nothing, dear. Nothing." She wiped beneath her eyes with her fingertips. "It's just that…" She exhaled. "I'd given up hope. You're so independent, and since you've never said you have any interest in getting married, I assumed that having a baby was out of the question. I've always wanted to be a grandmother. So much. At church, they show me photos of their grandkids. Katherine has eleven. Did you know that? Eleven grandchildren, and I don't have even one. And I always smile and tell them how beautiful they are—and I'm not lying, they are—but I can't help it. I'm always so envious. That's one of the seven deadly sins. Envy. I know that. But surely God understands, doesn't he? How I feel? How much I want just *one*?" Then her eyes grew wide with understanding. "That's it! He must know! He must, because look at what he's done!" She took Bernie's hands. "This is a blessing, Bernadette. A blessing from heaven."

Bernie didn't have a clue what to say. A blessing? *This?*

"How far along are you?" her mother asked.

"About two months, I think."

"You have so much to do. But don't worry. I'll help you. Have you called Dr. Underwood?"

"No, not yet. But—"

"You need to get an appointment right away. Prenatal care is a must. Have you been eating properly?"

"I've been eating just fine," Bernie said.

"Well, you have to make sure to from now on. You're eating for two, you know."

Her mother kept prattling on, wearing an expression of pure ecstasy. Given her diagnosis, Bernie thought she'd never see that look on her mother's face again. But everything about this wasn't wonderful, and Bernie couldn't let her go on thinking that it was.

"Hold on, Mom. Wait a minute."

Her mother stopped short. "Yes?"

Bernie swallowed hard. "I haven't really decided..."

"What?"

"What...you know. To do about it."

For several seconds, her mother looked bewildered. "Wh-what do you mean?"

When Bernie just stared at her, her mother's face slowly fell. Bernie could actually feel the joy slip away from her, leaving her body as if she'd drawn her last breath.

"Oh," Eleanor said, leaning away. "I see." She drew herself up in the way she always did when emotion was getting the better of her and she was trying not to fall apart. "I just thought that maybe, for just a little while, I'd have a grandchild, you know? Even if the time comes when I don't remember, at least I'd have had one for a little while."

Please don't say that! "Mom—"

Eleanor held up her palm. "No. It's okay. It's your decision, Bernadette. Not mine. I know that." She took a deep, shaky breath, trying to get a grip, but her eyes still filled with tears. "And contrary to what you might think, I'll love you no matter what you choose to do. No matter what. I mean that. I just hope you're thinking of adoption. Not . . . not the other."

Bernie felt her own eyes filling with tears. The thought of having a baby was so overwhelming that she almost couldn't imagine it. "The other" was out no matter what. But adoption . . . could she have this baby, only to give it away?

No. She couldn't. And not just because it would break her mother's heart. Now that she was facing the reality of the situation, she realized it would break her heart, too.

At first she'd been in total disbelief that her life had taken such a drastic turn, but now she was starting to think that maybe this was a shot of good luck, not bad. She'd never had a relationship with a man that had leaned toward marriage, and the older she got, the less she expected that would happen. And if it didn't, she'd always assumed she'd never have a child.

Now she was going to.

The longer she sat there, the more her conviction grew. Maybe her mother was right. Maybe this really was a blessing. This was probably going to be her only chance to be a mother, and if that were true, she didn't want to let it go.

She took her mother's hands. "Oh, no, Mom. You misunderstood."

Eleanor blinked, and another tear went south. "I did?"

"I didn't mean that I don't know what I was going to do about the baby. I just meant that I don't know what I'm going to do about my job. It's going to be kind of hard to be a bodyguard and pregnant, too, you know? But I'll figure out something."

"So . . . so you're going to have the baby?"

"Well, of course."

And then her mother was smiling and hugging her all over again. And for the first time since she'd seen those two lines, Bernie was smiling, too.

So what now? Gabe already knew she was pregnant, so that was the last she was going to see of any personal protection jobs. But even with this incredible nausea, maybe she could still fill some kind of contract position for Delgado & Associates that didn't involve carrying a weapon and protecting somebody's life, a job that wouldn't put her or her baby in danger or under stress. One way or another, she was going to work it out.

Her mother eased away, tears still shining in her eyes. "Bernadette?"

"Yes?"

"Have you . . ."

"Have I what?"

"Told the father?"

Not a question Bernie wanted to hear right now. But it was one she'd eventually have to answer. She could beat around the bush, or she could get the issue out of the way right now, once and for all.

"The father won't want to be part of this," she told her mother. "And believe me, Mom—it's for the best."

Her mother's brow furrowed with consternation. "A man who doesn't want to know his own child?" Eleanor said. "Are you sure that's the case?"

"Yeah, Mom. I'm sure."

"Maybe things will change as time goes on."

"Please don't count on that."

"Can you tell me who the father is?"

Bernie bowed her head with a heavy sigh. Then she looked up again. "I'd rather just pretend he was never in the picture at all. Do you think you can do that, too?"

Her mother's expression fell. "Oh. Yes, of course. I won't say another word about it." She paused. "But that isn't going to stop me from praying that he somehow sees the light and you all eventually become a family."

Bernie gave her a shaky smile. "Nobody's ever been able to stop you from praying, Mom."

And speaking of the father, there was something Bernie had to do before her pregnancy progressed one day further. Bridges might be the biological father, but the last thing she wanted was for that heartless, soulless, controlling man to have anything to do with her baby.

She'd watched him in business. He wasn't above getting what he wanted by any means necessary, as long as it was legal. She'd watched him with women. Even as he smiled and seduced, she'd never seen a shred of a connection on an emotional level. It was one thing for her to enjoy the mental challenge of bantering with a man whose IQ dwarfed the average person's, but it was quite another to imagine him as the father of her child. When she thought of her own father, of the warmth and acceptance she'd felt from him, it nearly brought her to tears. To subject her own child to the complete opposite of that was something she refused to do.

It could take her a week or two to get the legalities in place, but by the time she was finished, she was going to make sure Jeremy had no hold over her, or her baby, for the rest of their lives.

Chapter
8

Jeremy crossed the motor court behind his house and approached his black Lincoln sedan, his briefcase in one hand and his laptop case slung over his opposite shoulder. Max Delinsky stood beside the back door of the car, waiting to drive him to work just as he had every weekday morning for the past few months. For the short drive to the office, Jeremy opted for the sedan over the limo, which meant Max acted as both his bodyguard and his driver. But even though it was only a fifteen-minute drive to the office and back, Max still drove Jeremy nuts from the moment he got into the car to the moment they arrived.

It had nothing to do with the protection he offered. He was six-five, two-forty, with a body like a slab of granite, wearing the rugged, deadpan expression of a lifer in Huntsville. Nobody would think twice about messing with Jeremy when Max was around. Not groupies, not kidnappers, not assassins. Hell, Max Delinsky could take down a pit bull. A mountain lion. A charging rhino. He'd annihilate a zombie or a mutant creature from outer space before it knew what hit it. But just once Jeremy would like to have a decent conversation during his downtime in this car, and Max seemed to do everything he could to keep communication to a bare minimum. And unless it was practically dark outside, he insisted on wearing a pair of mirrored sunglasses. With his eyes obscured and his face immobile and not a word coming out of his mouth, Jeremy was at a total loss when it came to getting inside the man's head.

When he reached the car, Max opened the door for him.

"Good morning, Max," Jeremy said.

"Sir."

"Nice morning, isn't it?"

"Yes, sir."

In the World According to Max, they'd just had an extensive conversation and now had absolutely nothing left to say.

After Jeremy slid inside, Max circled around, got into the driver's seat, and started the car.

"Watch the Rangers game last night?" Jeremy asked.

Max flicked his gaze to the rearview mirror. At least Jeremy thought he did. Hard to tell with him wearing those damned mirrored sunglasses. "Yes, sir."

"Good game, huh?"

"Yes, sir."

"What do you think of their pitching game these days?"

"It could be better."

Well, that was a real conversation starter. Unless every Rangers pitcher threw a perfect game every time, it could *always* be better.

As Max steered the car along the tree-lined drive leading to the main road, Jeremy started to bring up another subject, maybe global warming, or possibly the state of Britney Spears's career. Something had to get Max's attention. Then he thought, *oh, screw it,* and pulled out his iPod and earphones. It was like trying to talk to Koko the gorilla. Maybe if he learned sign language, they could actually communicate. Unfortunately, just having Max around reminded him of who *wasn't* around.

Damn it, when was it ever going to stop?

When several calls to Gabe Delgado failed to bring Bernie back no matter how much money he offered, he decided he'd been humiliated enough and quit picking up the phone. But that didn't stop him from thinking about her, which irritated him no end. No matter where he was or what he was doing, even the most insignificant trigger could shift his thoughts to her. In this limo, Max and his silence made him wish she was around to argue with. At his house, all he had to do was glance down the hallway leading to his safe room, and she popped into his mind. And every time he so much as looked at a member of the opposite sex, he heard Bernie's voice in the back of his mind, asking him if he had any clue what it was like to be with a *real* woman.

And then the memory would come roaring back—the wildness of that night, the breathtaking heat, the indescribable sensation of sex with a woman he'd barely realized was a woman at all until that night, only to have her become a woman he couldn't drive from his thoughts if he'd wanted to. Several times he'd come close to asking Max about her, but fortunately he'd stopped himself. How pitiful would that have been?

But no matter how much his thoughts were consumed with Bernie, he was starting to get some perspective on what had happened between them. He knew now that the reason he couldn't get her out of his mind had nothing to do with sex. It had nothing to do with wanting her back. It had to do with the fact that she'd walked away from him before he'd had the chance to tell *her* to go to hell, and he hated unfinished business.

A few minutes later, Max checked in at the guardhouse in front of the Sybersense office complex, then pulled through the gates. He circled the western edge of the man-made lake, which was enhanced with fountains and stone retaining walls. Green hills undulated around the various buildings, dotted with perfectly placed crape myrtles alive with dark pink blooms.

Jeremy felt the same swell of pride he always did when he looked at this place. He'd built every bit of it from the ground up with money he'd sweated to earn even when the whole damned world said he couldn't, creating a thriving business empire in a place where he controlled every inch of the environment. The moment he saw anything that wasn't quite right—a brown patch on the lawn, a cracked sidewalk, a sprinkler head shooting a few degrees in the wrong direction—all he had to do was pick up his phone. Within a few hours, perfection was restored.

Max pulled up to the entrance. Jeremy tucked his iPod away, grabbed his briefcase, and got out, the August sun already beating down relentlessly even though it was only seven-forty-five in the morning. As he walked into the building, Max pulled away from the curb, leaving Jeremy covered by the security force at the Sybersense complex. Max would be on call for the remainder of the day, but

Jeremy allowed him to use the car any way he wanted to as long as he stayed fewer than fifteen minutes away. A bodyguard on call didn't come cheap, but that was one of the reasons Jeremy had amassed the fortune he had—so he could create a world where his convenience was the only issue.

He could have used the private elevator leading to his fourth-floor corner office, but he rarely did. Instead, he enjoyed walking through the front doors and hearing the low buzz of his employees' voices echoing through the four-story atrium. He loved how the morning sunlight streamed through the windows, making a crisscross pattern on the polished mahogany floor. His running shoes squeaked as he walked across it, and he loved that, too. It was a sound that said he'd risen to the point where he made his own rules and nobody could tell him what to do, and that included wearing dress shoes to work.

Phil Brandenburg came through the door from the parking garage and fell into step alongside him, carrying his usual Starbucks Venti Cappuccino and wiping the sweat from his brow with the shoulder of his shirt.

"Christ, it's hot out there," Phil said. "Thought I was gonna melt on the way here. Dallas in August—*God*. Swear I'm moving to Siberia."

"Might want to turn on the air conditioner in your car," Jeremy said.

"Had it going full blast."

"Or skip the hot coffee."

"You know I can't think without coffee."

Not only could Phil not think without coffee, he couldn't eat, watch TV, drive, play golf, or probably have sex without it, either. He subsisted on caffeine, fried food, and beer, which meant that in ten years, when he reached age fifty or so, he'd be in danger of dropping dead. But Phil had always said he'd rather live it up and die young than eat crap he hated and wear himself out exercising. When they were in college, he was the kind of guy who smiled a lot, partied hard, and found a reason to like just about anybody he came into contact with. They'd both taken potluck on roommates their freshman year and ended up with each other. Jeremy had sworn Phil's exuberance would drive him nuts before the first semester was out, but as it turned out, Phil was the perfect foil for his own relentless intensity. Jeremy learned to lighten up around Phil. Learned that women were actually interested in him now that he wasn't the poor scholarship kid at a rich private high school. Learned to ditch his bad attitude and charm the world with a smile instead. He could leave his past behind and re-create himself any way he wanted to. And the result, twenty years later, was that he was living a life not one man in ten thousand had any chance of experiencing.

Three years ago, he'd reconnected with Phil and brought him on as his chief financial officer, and it was as if twenty years had never passed. Not only was it a plus to have a trusted friend in such an important position, Phil also had a knack for identifying acquisitions that turned out to be pure gold for Sybersense's bottom line, which also made Jeremy very, very happy.

"Fair warning," Phil said, as he pushed the button for the elevator. "Alexis has you in her sights for a benefit on the sixteenth."

"Which does she want this time? My money, or me? Can I get out of it by writing a check?"

"Not this time. A donation is always nice, but what she really wants is to introduce you to 'the future Mrs. Jeremy Bridges.'"

"Ah, God."

"Sorry. She's matchmaking again. You know Alexis."

He did. From the time he brought Phil on board at Sybersense, his wife had made it her personal mission to fix Jeremy up. *You have everything else on earth,* she told him just about every time she saw him. *Now it's time for a wife.*

Jeremy couldn't even fathom it. For nearly twenty years he'd had blinders on, running at warp speed toward his target, almost fanatically staying on course, building his company into the juggernaut it was today. Women were a pleasant diversion, but the moment one got in the way of his business, she was history. And that was never much of a loss, because there was always another one waiting just around the next corner.

"You haven't poked your head above water for several weeks now," Phil said. "What's up?"

"With everything going on at Sybersense, you have to ask?"

"Alexis tells me this woman she wants to introduce you to is knockout gorgeous. You might want to put it on your calendar."

"I'll think about it."

The elevator doors opened, and they got off on the fourth floor. "It isn't like you to hole up at home," Phil said. "Is everything all right?"

The truth was that it *had* been weeks since he'd been out of the house in the evening. With Sybersense's new software package only a few months away from hitting the market, he'd been so busy that he'd barely bothered to go out at all. Lately he'd just worked late at the office and then headed home, where he ate whatever Mrs. Spencer left him for dinner, flipped around on ESPN for a while, then went to bed. Maybe if he took Alexis up on her offer to introduce him to a beautiful woman, he could get back in the swing of things. For the first time in a long time, maybe he wouldn't be going to bed alone.

"Everything's fine. I just have a lot to think about right now."

"Meant to ask. How are you and Max getting along these days?"

"Okay."

"Frankly, he scares the crap out of me. Almost as much as Bernie did."

Jeremy flinched a little at the mention of her name, but he kept on walking.

"You never told me why you dumped her," Phil said.

"I didn't. She had to quit."

"Why?"

"Personal reasons."

"What personal reasons?"

Jeremy stopped short. "Phil? Will you stop being so damned nosy? A bodyguard's a bodyguard. Who gives a damn?"

Phil held up his palms. "Hey. Sorry. Forget I said anything."

Jeremy hadn't meant to snap at Phil, but really. Why was the man even asking?

"Are we all set for this morning?" Jeremy asked.

"Right on target," Phil said. "The team's ready. We'll see you at eight to wrap up the last-minute details, but we're on track to be at the Simcon building by ten-thirty to start due diligence. If everything looks good, we can get this acquisition wrapped up in a hurry."

After they passed through the glass doors leading to the executive suite, Phil veered to the left to head to his office, while Jeremy strode ahead toward another set of doors leading to his.

He entered his outer office, where Ms. Keyes sat behind her computer, staring at the screen through her bifocals. He swept by her desk just as she was pulling a hard copy of his schedule off the printer.

"Good morning, Mr. Bridges," she said.

"Good morning, Ms. Keyes. Nice day, isn't it?"

"Yes, sir."

"I don't believe I've ever told you how attractive you look in that shade of beige."

"Thank you, Mr. Bridges," she said, never looking up, her expression never changing. "How kind of you to say so."

She might as well have said *I put a new box of paper clips in your desk drawer* for all the emotion in her voice. It had become a game he played just for the hell of it. Could he get a reaction out of her? Coax a faint blush to her cheeks? A demure smile to her lips?

So far, no luck.

For years he'd hired secretaries who were young and stunningly beautiful, only to have them get married and then pregnant in short order, or have them show up every morning with happy-hour hangovers. Finally he decided that sooner or later he needed some work done, so he'd hired Ms. Keyes.

She took no personal calls at work. She took no time off with sick kids because she didn't have any. In fact, she'd never even been married, so she had no husband issues to deal with. She leaked nothing to the press. She didn't question or comment on anything concerning his personal life. He could moonlight as a serial killer, and she'd ignore the bloody scratches on his neck the next morning when she brought him his cup of Colombian dark roast with a splash of cream. In short, he'd hired a highly dependable, highly efficient secretarial robot, and if he could find a way to mass produce her and send the resultant product into the marketplace, his net worth would shoot straight into the stratosphere.

He grabbed the hard copy of his schedule, knowing she'd also sent it to his iPhone and synched it with the calendar program on his PC.

"Your coffee is brewing," she said. "I'll have it for you in five minutes."

"Thank you," Jeremy said, as he swept his office door open. He headed for his desk, only to realize that somebody was sitting on the sofa. Slowly she turned around, and his heart missed a couple of beats.

Bernie?

Chapter
9

Jeremy's shock disappeared immediately, replaced by the strangest feeling of relief. *She's come back. She's going to work for me again. She's—*

Then he saw the look on her face—an intense, narrow-eyed expression he'd seen more often than he cared to count, and every single time it had been on the face of an adversary.

"Bernie," he said, striding nonchalantly past her to his desk. "What a surprise. Ms. Keyes didn't tell me I had a visitor."

"That's because I didn't pass by your gatekeeper."

"Then how—"

"I still have a key to the back elevator, which means you need to have a word with your security people."

He put his briefcase on his desk. "I'm afraid this is a bad time. I have a meeting in five minutes."

"They'll wait. After all, you're Jeremy Bridges."

She said the words matter-of-factly, but Jeremy heard the hint of derision in her voice.

"Clearly you have something you'd like to discuss with me," he said.

"That's right."

"Sounds like business."

"Not entirely."

"Then meet me later at my house."

"This is a private matter. There's nothing private about the inside of your house unless you intend it to be. I'm still not completely certain where all the audio and video recording equipment is in that palace of yours."

"And you think it's any safer here?"

"Now it is. You really do need to have a word with your security people."

Jeremy eyed her carefully, taking note of the way she was dressed—jeans, boots, black T-shirt, even in this heat. He had a feeling she owned about a dozen of each, which probably constituted her entire off-duty wardrobe, even in August. As always, no makeup. Zero jewelry. She looked no more sexy or alluring than she had any other time in the two years he'd known her. So why did just the sight of her make his temperature shoot up ten degrees?

Because he'd experienced the fire beneath the ice.

He sat down in his chair, elbows on the armrests, steepling his fingers in front of him. "All right, Bernie," he said evenly. "Why don't you tell me what this is all about?"

"It's about a certain evening we spent together in your safe room."

Jeremy held his gaze steady at the same time his nerves felt anything *but* steady. His thoughts shot back to those hot, intense moments when he'd backed her up against that wall, kissing her and touching her in ways he never

could have imagined before that night. He only hoped
those thoughts didn't show on his face, because if they
did, this woman would have him at a disadvantage before
he knew what hit him.

Then he noticed she was tapping her fingertips against
the sofa cushion. Just the slightest bit of movement, but for
Bernie, who controlled every move she made, she might
as well have been chain smoking. What did it mean? She
was nervous, yes, which meant that maybe *she* was the
one at a disadvantage. But why was she nervous? He had
no idea. What could she possibly—

And then the truth came to him. He froze for several moments, turning the thought over in his mind. He
couldn't imagine that a woman like Bernie would ever do
such a thing, but what other explanation was there?

Then he got angry.

He stood, grabbed a few papers he needed for his meeting, and shoved them into his briefcase. "I don't have time
for this right now," he said, zipping the briefcase shut.

"Wait a minute!" Bernie said. "Where are you
going?"

"I told you I have a meeting."

"Five minutes," she said, standing up. "For God's sake,
at least you can give me that."

"It's not necessary. Just give me the name of your attorney; we'll let the professionals handle it."

"Professionals?"

"Though you must know that I hire only the best.
Think twice about what you're doing, Bernie. My people
will eviscerate yours in court."

"Court? What the *hell* are you talking about?"

"You know what I'm talking about."

"I'm afraid I don't. Maybe you'd better fill me in."

He took several slow, menacing steps forward and stared down at her. "Don't insult me. I can hear a sexual harassment suit coming from a mile away."

Her mouth fell open. "A *what*?"

"Save it. I know where this is going."

She barked out a tiny laugh. "No, I don't think you do."

"You'll say I coerced you. But you and I both know it was mutual. You'll tell me I was in a position of authority over you so there was no such thing as mutual consent. Then I'll tell you that most of the time we were having sex, you were over *me*, so the very idea that—"

"I'm pregnant."

For the count of five, Jeremy stopped talking. Stopped moving. Stopped *breathing*. When his power of speech finally returned, his voice was choked with disbelief. "*What* did you say?"

"You heard me."

Pregnant. The word bounced around in his head, refusing to stay put long enough for him to absorb it. His gaze traveled south, looking for some kind of indication—

"Will you cut that out?" Bernie snapped. "There's nothing down there to see. Not yet, anyway."

He jerked his gaze back up and assumed an air of nonchalance. "So you're pregnant. Congratulations."

"Congratulations to you, too. You're the father."

Jeremy's heart jolted hard. "No, I'm not."

"Believe me. You are."

A tremor of apprehension crept up his spine. There was no way. He *knew* there was no way, but still...

Just then his office door opened, and Ms. Keyes came

in holding a cup of coffee. She looked at Bernie with surprise, then turned to Jeremy. "Mr. Brandenburg and the others—"

"Not now," Jeremy said.

"Your eight o'clock meeting—"

"Tell them to wait."

"I have your coffee—"

"Go!" Jeremy snapped.

Ms. Keyes backed quickly out of his office, her heels clicking like machine-gun fire, and closed the door behind her. With a deep, silent breath, Jeremy sat on the edge of his desk and folded his arms, slowly turning his attention back to Bernie.

"Do you even know for sure you're pregnant?" he asked her.

"You're insulting me. Do you think I'd be here if I weren't sure?"

He remembered with total clarity the expression on her face as she left his safe room that night. It was the look of a woman who'd had more than enough, who'd stepped over a line she'd never meant to cross, who couldn't wait to put every moment of it behind her. He'd thrown all kinds of money at her, but nothing had brought her back.

Until now. Until *this*.

"So," he said carefully, "you're pregnant, and you think I'm the father?"

"I don't *think* you're the father. Unless I'm experiencing the second case of immaculate conception in recorded history, I *know* you're the father."

"If there have been other men—"

"There haven't. You can insist you're not the father, but you and I both know it's a waste of time."

"Since you're telling me about this," he said, "I assume you intend to go through with it?"

"Yes. I do."

"Are you sure? You must have just found out. Have you really had a chance to think about it?"

"Don't patronize me," Bernie said. "I know what I'm doing."

"Why would a woman like you burden herself with a child?"

"I have my reasons."

"Which are?"

"None of your business and never will be."

Jeremy felt this situation slipping out of his control, his mind spinning in a dozen different directions. He had stay on top of it. *Get a grip, and get it now.*

"Fine," he said. "You're pregnant. But I'm telling you—the baby's not mine."

"I know you're thinking that because you used a condom, it couldn't have happened," Bernie said. "But they're not a hundred percent effective, and you know it."

"They certainly make pregnancy much more unlikely."

"So you think I'm lying?"

"Are you?"

Bernie narrowed her eyes, her lips tightening with anger. "Once the baby's born, DNA testing will prove you're the father, so why would I bother lying now?"

He made a scoffing noise. "That's pretty clear, isn't it?"

"No, I'm afraid it's not."

"Let's cut to the chase. How much money do you want?"

Bernie's mouth fell open. "You think that's why I'm here? To extort money from you?"

"You wouldn't be the first woman to try it."

"But if you think I'm lying and you could eventually prove it, what would be the point of my asking for money now?"

She was right. And with her staring back at him the way she was right now, her eyes unblinking, her expression resolute, he was reminded once again that she wasn't like some women he'd known, who would sell their own souls to have access to his bank account.

"If not money," he said, "then what do you want?"

When she turned to the sofa, reached into a manila folder she'd brought with her, and pulled out a stack of legal-sized papers, Jeremy's mouth went dry. Papers like those meant she'd retained an attorney, and that was *always* a red flag, telling him he'd damned well better stay on his toes.

She rose from the sofa and tossed the papers on his desk. "I want full custody."

Jeremy blinked with surprise. "What?"

"You heard me. Sign these papers, and you never have to see me or this child ever again."

Jeremy was stunned. "I never took you for a fool."

"What are you talking about?"

"If you really are pregnant and you believe I'm the father, why aren't you demanding child support?"

"Because it's better for a kid to have no father than a lousy one, no matter how much money that lousy father is forced to give him."

Jeremy was surprised at how much that stung. "What makes you think I'd be a lousy father?"

"Are you telling me you'd be a good one?"

The question caught him off guard, and it was a moment before he answered. "Quite frankly, I've never even thought about it, since I never planned to be one."

"In other words, if you ever got a woman pregnant, you figured you'd just pay her off and that would be that?"

"Do you really think so little of me?"

She paused, looking away. "Sometimes I don't know what to think of you."

"Most of my enemies don't."

She whipped back around. "Damn it, I'm not your enemy!"

"Then stop acting like one. Do we really have to drag lawyers into this?"

"I'm just trying to handle this situation in a way that's best for both of us."

"By shutting me out completely?"

"Come on, Bridges. I'm doing you a favor. You've said time and time again that you'll never marry, much less have a family, and you like it that way. Do you really *want* to be a father?"

No. He didn't. Or at least he hadn't up to now. But he'd also never been faced with a situation like this.

"If you're so sure I want nothing to do with this child you say I've fathered," Jeremy said, "then why all the legalities?"

"You're a businessman. If there's something you want, do you rely on a handshake, or do you get it in writing?"

"If I sign these papers, what do you plan to tell this child about his father?"

"That I don't know who he is. And not only will my child not know, nobody else will, either. I'll leave it blank on the birth certificate, and I won't tell a solitary soul. The truth will go with me to the grave."

The baby will never even know who you are.

For a moment, Jeremy felt a stab of anguish. A child growing up in this world without a father was a very specific kind of hell no kid should ever have to experience.

But was this child really his?

If she thought he was the father, she should at least be demanding some kind of shared custody. But she wasn't asking him to sign papers to ensure he did something. She was asking him to sign papers to ensure he did nothing.

Which meant she was telling the truth.

He picked up the papers. Looked at them but didn't *see* them. Page after page of legalese that could have been written in Chinese for all he comprehended it right now. He flipped to the last page. Saw the signature line. His name typed beneath it. Even those words seemed to blur until he was having a hard time reading them clearly.

He needed time. Time to think about this. Time to come to terms with the situation.

"I'll give you my decision tomorrow."

Bernie blinked. "What? Why not now?"

"That's none of your concern."

"I don't get it. What is there to decide? I'm not asking for money. I'm not asking you to take any physical responsibility for a child. I'm not asking you for anything. So why not just sign the papers and be done with it?"

"I may very well do that. Tomorrow."

"Why the delay? So you can run it past your attorney?"

"Again, that's no concern of yours." He stood up and held out the papers to her. "I'll be in touch."

She stared at him dumbly. "You're *such* a control freak."

"What?"

"I could hand you the keys to heaven, and you'd tell me you need time to consider whether you should take them or not."

"You're probably right about that. But it changes nothing. I'll be in touch tomorrow."

She yanked the papers out of his hand. Without another word, she left his office, shutting the door behind her so hard that the glasses on his bar clinked together.

Jeremy circled around his desk and sat down, feeling weirdly dizzy and disoriented. Fatherhood. Just the possibility of it rattled him like nothing else. But Bernie wanted him to go away. To have nothing to do with this baby. To be out of the picture for good. He had millions, and she wanted nothing. Instead, she was telling him what a dismal failure he'd be as a father and doing everything she could to make sure he never even laid eyes on his own child.

He knew what Bernie wanted. The question was, what did *he* want?

His office door opened. He spun his chair around to see Phil walk in with two members of the acquisition team in his wake.

"Ms. Keyes said you were free now," Phil said, then tilted his head quizzically. "Is this a bad time?"

"Can I see you alone for a minute?" Jeremy asked.

Phil turned to the other men and told them he'd give them a call when they were ready to meet. They left, closing the door behind them.

"What's up?" Phil said, plopping down in a chair

in front of Jeremy's desk. "Did we hit a snag with the acquisition?"

"No," he said, tapping a pen against his desktop. "It has nothing to do with business."

"Then it has to do with Bernie."

Jeremy jerked his head up. "What?"

"She was leaving as I was coming in. And she didn't look too happy. You have the same look on your face. What's the matter?"

Jeremy took a deep breath and let it out slowly. "You're not going to believe it."

"Believe what?"

The very thought of it was so mind-boggling he could barely get the words out. "Bernie just told me..." He paused, then finally just spat it out. "It looks as if I'm going to be a father."

For at least the count of five, Phil's expression remained blank. "What?"

"She's pregnant."

Phil blinked. "Come again?"

"Good God, Phil. Do I have to explain the birds and bees to you?"

Phil slumped back in his chair. "You're kidding me. You? With *Bernie*?"

Okay. So that reaction wasn't unexpected. Jeremy knew Bernie wasn't exactly the kind of woman the world was used to seeing him with. But how could Phil ever understand what those few scorching minutes with her had been like? How they'd blasted away the memory of the dozens of women who'd come before her? How was he supposed to explain that when he didn't even understand it himself?

"So..." Phil said. "You two are having a baby." He said

the words haltingly, as if just the act of passing them over his tongue was a chore.

"Not exactly," Jeremy said. "Bernie has other thoughts on the matter."

"What do you mean?"

"She wants me to sign my rights away. Walk away as if this had never happened."

Once again, Phil looked stunned. "Wait a minute. That makes no sense. She wants nothing?"

"That's right."

Phil blinked. "But you have millions. Why wouldn't she—"

"Because she doesn't want my money. She just wants to make sure I have no contact with the baby."

"Why?"

"Because she thinks I'd make a lousy father."

"That's crap."

Phil's quick response took Jeremy by surprise. "Come on, Phil. Do you really believe I'd have any chance at all of being a decent father?"

"Of course."

Jeremy tossed the pen to the desktop. "You're bullshitting me. I hate that."

"No, I'm not. Being a father would be no different than anything else you've ever done. Any time you ever decided you wanted to do something, pretty soon you were better at it than anyone else."

"This isn't writing software code. What the hell do I know about parenthood?"

"Look, Jeremy. I know where you come from. I know why you shy away from anything that looks like a family. God knows you have good reason for that. But sometimes things happen for a reason, you know? Maybe this is the universe's way of giving you what you really need rather than what you think you want."

Jeremy twisted his mouth with irritation. "Do you have to be so damned philosophical?"

Phil shrugged. "I minored in philosophy. Remember?"

"Accounting and philosophy. *God*. What made you do that?"

Phil gave him a sly smile. "Interior design classes were full?"

Jeremy shook his head. "You were so weird back then." He made a scoffing noise. "Hell, what am I saying? You're weird now."

"And yet you put the financial future of your company in my hands."

"Only proves what an idiot I am." He paused. "I sure as hell was that night with Bernie."

"There's something you're not talking about here."

"What's that?"

"How do you feel about her?"

Jeremy's heart skipped. "I don't feel any way at all. There's nothing between us."

"Are you sure about that?"

"Of course I'm sure."

But he wasn't. Not completely. If he was so sure she meant nothing to him, why the hell couldn't he get her out of his mind?

"Okay," Phil said. "It's clear what Bernie wants. The question is, what do you want?"

"I don't know. It's hard for me even to imagine what it would be like. I wouldn't know the first thing to do with a kid."

"Take him to ballgames. Give him a mitt to catch foul balls. Let him eat hot dogs until he throws up."

"What if it's a girl?" Jeremy said.

"Take her to ballgames. Give her a mitt to catch foul balls. Let her eat hot dogs until she throws up."

"No ballet recitals? Barbie dolls? Tea parties?"

"Maybe. But this is the twenty-first century. Sexism isn't allowed."

Jeremy rested his head in his hands for a moment, feeling overwhelmed at the very thought of it. A child had always been number one on his list of things he had no clue how to deal with.

"It's simple, really," Phil said. "Just do all the stuff with a kid you wish your father had done with you."

His father. The moment an image of that man entered Jeremy's mind, all he wanted to do was drive it away again.

"I know what you're thinking," Phil said. "You're thinking about how your own father sucked as a father, so you can't imagine going there yourself."

Jeremy rubbed his temples. "It's not that."

"Then what is it?"

Jeremy sighed heavily, wishing he could protest, but he had the most sickening feeling Phil was right. Part of him was still that scared, angry kid who'd had only one example of fatherhood to follow. A bad one.

He remembered a time thirty years ago when he'd spent one lonely night after another huddled in bed, fantasizing that his father wasn't a shiftless alcoholic who sometimes didn't even bother to come home at night. Instead he was a rich guy with a big house and shiny new cars who took him to ballgames and for rides in his jet and to Disney

World, who smiled all the time and said yes to everything. Then Jeremy would wake the next morning to the squalor of his real life and his father at the breakfast table. The old man's face would be gray and unshaven, his eyes hangover-bleary, his voice harsh and gravelly as he snapped at his son for whatever small transgressions he chose to focus on that day to keep from facing the despair of his own life.

The older Jeremy got, the more the childish fantasies gave way to nothing more than the desire for his father to dry out, get a job, and recognize that he had a son. But that never happened. Instead, day in and day out, Jeremy lived with the anguish of having a runaway mother and a father who couldn't have cared less about him.

"Yeah, maybe that's part of it," Jeremy said.

"Well, get it out of your head. You're not your old man. Not by a long shot."

Intellectually, Jeremy knew that. Emotionally, though, Bernie's opinion of him hit way too close to home. He just didn't know if he had it in him to be a decent father to a child of his own.

"You want me to tell you a secret about raising kids?" Phil said.

He had two kids of his own, so Jeremy was inclined to listen.

"Just be there."

Just be there? "It can't be as simple as that."

"Okay. I lied. There's also the diaper-changing when they're babies and the door-slamming when they're teenagers. But I think you get my point."

He did. If he had ever looked up at a school event and simply seen his father's face, it would have meant everything to him.

Maybe Bernie was wrong. Maybe there was something worse than a bad father, and that was a father who didn't bother to show up at all.

He felt a shiver of awareness, a sense that maybe Phil was right. Maybe the universe knew what the hell it was doing no matter how crazy it looked. And the more he thought about it, the more his determination grew.

The baby Bernie was carrying was his, which meant he had a stake in this, too. And if she thought he was going to sign away rights to his own child, she needed to think again. He might not have a clue how to be a father, but facing that uncertainty wasn't nearly as intolerable as knowing that someday a child of his would be wandering through this world thinking his father just didn't give a damn. In that moment, he made a decision, as resolutely as anything he'd ever felt in his life.

Whether Bernie liked it or not, they were having a baby together.

Chapter
10

When Bernie heard the knock on her apartment door, she looked out the peephole, her heart thudding with anticipation. Sure enough, Jeremy was standing at her door. She had no idea why he hadn't signed the papers on the spot yesterday, but with luck, in the next few minutes they'd be putting this matter to rest once and for all.

She opened the door to find him wearing his usual scruffy jeans and faded Polo shirt. Any other man wearing those things might look unkempt. Not Jeremy. He'd once entertained some business associates in a sky box at a football game wearing a pair of cargo shorts, a Cowboys T-shirt, and flip-flops. She'd watched silently from the corner, thinking the only way he could have looked more handsome was if he took off his clothes altogether.

"Bridges. What a surprise."

"Surprise? Didn't I say we'd talk today?"

"I assumed you'd summon me to your office."

"I was in the neighborhood." He glanced back over his shoulder with an expression of disgust. "Okay, so that's a lie."

Don't bite back. Just keep things friendly until you can get his name on the dotted line.

"Is Max with you?" she said, stepping back to allow Jeremy to enter.

"I took this trip on my own."

"That's not wise."

"Concerned about me?"

"Old habits are hard to break."

"This is private business, so I came alone. Where are the papers?"

Thank God. This was going to be easier than she had thought.

She walked over to pick them up. "I'm glad you've decided to sign," she said, turning back and handing them to him. "It really is better for both of us. I know the last thing you want is to be saddled with a..." She paused, watching as he turned the papers sideways.

"What are you doing?"

He ripped them in half. Bernie's mouth fell open. "What the hell are you *doing*?"

Then he tore those pieces in half.

"Bridges!"

He handed her the decimated contract. She stared down at the jagged pieces in total disbelief. "Are you out of your *mind*?"

"Not last time I checked."

"Well, you haven't accomplished anything," she said. "I have another copy."

"Great. Hand it to me. I'll tear it up, too."

She tossed the pieces of paper down on her dining room table. "Why are you doing this?"

"I told you I'd make up my mind in twenty-four hours." He nodded toward the torn-up contract. "There's my decision."

She glared at him. "A simple *no* would have sufficed."

"I doubt that. If I hadn't torn it up, you'd still be trying to shove it in front of me."

"That's right. I would. Because the best thing for both of us is for you to go away and pretend all this never happened."

"But it did happen, and both of us are going to have to live with it."

A swirl of nausea kicked up in Bernie's stomach, and not just because of the morning sickness that had plagued her like a bad case of the flu that wouldn't go away. This couldn't be happening. She knew Jeremy. She knew his biggest fear had to be that he'd get a woman pregnant and have to deal with the consequences. So why was he being so obstinate?

"You just can't stand for anyone to tell you you can't have something," she said hotly. "Even something you don't want."

"Who says I don't want it? I never really thought about having a baby, but you know, I'm not getting any younger. So why not?"

"Damn it, Bridges! You could find a dozen women in the next hour who would have your baby! *Don't take mine.*"

"Ours."

That single word said she was tied to him forever, and she hated the sound of it.

"Why are you doing this?" she asked. "You know you don't want to be a father."

Jeremy's expression darkened. "Stop making assumptions about what I want. You'll be wrong every time."

Bernie searched his face for any sign of insincerity, but she didn't see it. Still, it was so incomprehensible to her that he'd want anything to do with fatherhood, so completely at odds with the life he'd so deliberately built for himself, that she found it impossible to believe him.

Maybe it was time to find out just how serious he was about being involved with this baby.

"You know what?" she told him. "You're right. You're the father. You should have input."

"I'm glad you see it my way."

"But any involvement you have comes with conditions."

"Conditions?"

"You're not just going to sit in that big house of yours and play dictator. And you're not going to be one of those men who just throws money at his kid as if that's all a kid needs. You have to give to get. If your name is on the birth certificate, you're going to be a father in every sense of the word."

His smug expression vanished. "What do you mean?"

"Well, for starters, I have an ultrasound scheduled for tomorrow afternoon. I expect you to be there."

He blinked with disbelief. "You want me to come to your *doctor's* exam?"

"All good fathers do."

"I should think you'd want your privacy."

"Where you're concerned, my privacy disappeared weeks ago."

"Tomorrow's out of the question. I'm right in the middle of an acquisition. Things are happening very quickly, so now's not really a good time."

"Fine. I'll reschedule for next week."

"I have a full schedule next week."

"Then the week after that."

"I'm late for a meeting. I'll have to check my schedule and get back to you." He headed for the door.

"Just as I figured," Bernie said.

Jeremy spun around. "What?"

"A father in name only. My child could do so much better. Unfortunately, he's stuck with you."

His jaw tightened with irritation. "I have responsibilities."

"I understand completely." She nodded toward the pieces of paper on the table. "Shall I get the other copy?"

For a few unguarded moments, Jeremy's Adam's apple bobbed with a heavy swallow. When he eyed the pen on her dining room table, it looked as if she'd been right. Jeremy didn't care about this baby. He just cared about winning. The moment she forced his hand by putting the image of real fatherhood squarely in front of him—

"I'll be there," he said.

Bernie blinked. "What?"

"I said I'll be there tomorrow for your ultrasound appointment."

"But I thought you said—"

"It's what you want, isn't it?"

Bernie's knees suddenly felt weak. Could Jeremy be more serious about this than she'd thought?

No. He thought she was bluffing. That was all. And he

was calling her on it. What could she do now but go along with it?

"Yes, of course," she said. "My appointment is at Dr. Marge Underwood's office on K Street in East Plano. One o'clock."

He nodded. "One o'clock it is."

With that, he left her apartment, closing the door behind him.

Bernie stood there for a moment, dumbfounded at what she'd just done. She'd intended to end this day with Jeremy out of her life and her baby's forever, and now he was coming to her doctor's appointment with her?

She walked to the door in a daze and locked it behind him. She moved to the sofa and sat down, thinking back to her first obstetrical appointment a few days ago. Across from her in the waiting room sat a young pregnant woman and her husband. She remembered how the two of them had been chatting quietly, and then the woman's eyes lit up. She grabbed her husband's hand and rested it on her belly. Both of them froze for a few seconds, waiting. The woman let out a soft gasp, and they turned to each other with a smile. When he leaned in to give her a kiss, Bernie felt a stab of envy that went straight to her heart, a feeling so powerful she'd been forced to turn away.

And now, when she thought about Jeremy sitting next to her in that waiting room tomorrow, the crack in her heart widened and bled just a little bit more. She'd made the right decision to have this baby. She'd never regret that as long as she lived. But was it wrong to want a husband, too? Someone she could turn to when she felt so tired and overwhelmed she just couldn't take another step?

Someone who would love her just as much as he loved their baby?

She sighed. No. It wasn't wrong to want that. It just wasn't going to happen anytime soon.

And it certainly wasn't going to happen with Jeremy.

Chapter
II

The next day Bernie sat in Dr. Underwood's waiting room, flicking her gaze to the clock every ten seconds. Was Jeremy actually going to show up? Or did he go home last night, think about the prospect of a trip to the obstetrician's office, and realize fatherhood involved way more than he wanted to deal with?

If he was going to bow out, she hoped he'd do it now. Now, before she started to count on him. Now, before he became one of those whenever-he-felt-like-it fathers who disappointed his child over and over. If he wasn't serious about being there for the long haul, she truly hoped he'd just stay home. As the clock hands crept past one o'clock, she became convinced that he really wasn't going to show up.

Then all at once the door opened, and Jeremy walked in.

He stopped for a moment to slowly remove his sunglasses. Then he fanned his gaze around the room, until every woman in the place noticed he was there. And they were all staring at him, not overtly, but with little sideways glances that had to be wearing out their eyeball muscles. Did they recognize him from photos in the media? Or was he just so damned good-looking that they couldn't keep their eyes off him?

That really irritated Bernie. They were all married, for heaven's sake. Well, maybe not married, but committed. Okay, maybe not committed, but they were going to be mothers, right? It was time to keep their eyes off handsome men and concentrate on the task at hand. Having a baby.

So why was she having trouble taking her own advice?

Then Jeremy zeroed in on her. With a smile of supreme confidence, he made his way across the room to take the seat beside her.

"Did Max bring you here?" she whispered.

"Yep."

"What reason did you give him for coming to a medical building?"

"I'm the boss. I don't have to account for my actions."

"Where is he now?"

"I convinced him to watch for bad guys from the comfort of my car."

Thank God. Even though Max knew she was pregnant, Bernie was happy to keep the identity of the father under wraps for now. She could only imagine what Max was going to think when he found out.

"Bernadette Hogan?"

Bernie looked up to see a nurse she didn't recognize standing at the door leading to the exam rooms. She looked nothing like Dr. Underwood's usual nurse, a fifty-something woman with iron-gray hair and a depilatory issue on her upper lip. This one was slim, gorgeous, and not even thirty, with auburn hair and big blue eyes. Somehow the shapeless Snoopy scrubs she wore only made her look that much more feminine, as if she were a supermodel who'd slipped on a man's flannel shirt over her baby pink undies. Bernie sighed inwardly. If she put on a set of Snoopy scrubs, she'd look like...Snoopy.

Out of the corner of her eye, she swore she could practically see Jeremy's antennae rise from the top of his head and tune in to Nurse Goodbody, and that irritated her more than it should have. After all, that he was the father of her baby didn't mean there was anything between the two of them, nor would there ever be. And she was likewise certain that there was nothing about fatherhood that would ever shut down his legendary libido. But at least he could have the good grace not to look at other women as if he'd popped into his favorite club on ladies' night.

Bernie grabbed her purse and rose from her chair, and when Jeremy rose right along with her, suddenly she was the one who was hit with the reality of the situation.

"Where are you going?" she whispered.

"With you."

"No. You can't go back there."

"Sure I can. I'm the father."

"And I'm the mother. It's my body. I get to choose who sees it."

"But there's something in that body that's half mine."

She leaned in closer. "And in a few minutes, this body will be half *naked*."

He shrugged. "That's okay. I've seen you half naked." He paused. "Will it be the same half?"

She didn't want to stand here and argue with him. She just didn't. And since the other people in the room were starting to stare, Bernie decided it was time to just get it over with.

"Oh, for God's sake," she muttered. "Come on."

"How y'all doing today?" Nurse Goodbody said, her smile revealing pristine orthodontia.

"Just dandy," Bernie said.

"Right this way," the nurse said, leading them down the hall. Bernie glanced at Jeremy, whose gaze was trained dead center on the nurse's ass, which was proof positive that to him, even a doctor's office might as well be a singles bar.

"Just think, Bridges," she whispered. "In just a moment you're going to experience the miracle of pregnancy."

"Can't wait."

"I can practically feel the estrogen in the air, can't you?"

"Oh, yeah. It's my favorite hormone."

Bernie sighed. There was only one place on earth more estrogen-filled than an obstetrician's office, and that was Jeremy's bedroom. The last place he'd ever be uncomfortable was around a bunch of women. And the fact that most of them were pregnant didn't seem to change his perspective one bit.

They followed the nurse into an exam room, where she motioned for them to sit. She spread Bernie's chart out on the desk. "So you're here for your first ultrasound?"

"That's right," Bernie said.

"How exciting. The two of you seeing your baby for the first time. You'll even get a photograph to take home with you!"

"Did you hear that, Bernie?" Jeremy said. "A picture of our baby. Imagine that."

"The baby's the size of my little finger," Bernie snapped. "A black-and-white blob on a blurry screen. You'll barely be able to tell what's baby and what isn't."

"Oh," Jeremy said, looking distressed. "So I guess this means we won't be putting the photos on our Christmas cards?"

Bernie closed her eyes. Maybe this had been a mistake. A big one. She'd given him carte blanche to get in the big, fat middle of this situation when what she really wanted was for him to go away and never come back. But she knew if she continued to act irritated that he'd shown up, he'd only irritate her by pretending to enjoy it even more.

The nurse took Bernie's blood pressure and her temperature, then asked her to step on the scales. "One hundred and forty-five pounds," she chirped, and Bernie cringed.

"I'm sure that's just water weight," Jeremy said.

"Bite me," Bernie said.

Jeremy turned to the nurse. "This is what I get for trying to be supportive."

"And I'm sure deep down she appreciates it," the nurse said, patting Jeremy on the knee. "It's just those pesky pregnancy hormones," she whispered. "They make some women a little testy."

Jeremy gave her a million-dollar smile, and just like that, he was elevated to generous, supportive partner and Bernie became the bad guy.

The nurse rose and led them to an exam room. "Undress from the waist down," she told Bernie. "Put on the gown, open in the back. The doctor will be with you in a moment."

As the nurse shut the door behind her, Bernie headed for the small curtained changing room. She took off her clothes and put on the paper gown. It rustled as she wrapped it around herself as best she could, refusing to think about Jeremy sitting in the other room. She was *not* going to be self-conscious about this.

She came out of the changing room, clutching the gown closed behind her. Jeremy was sitting in a chair beside the exam table. With an amused smile, he watched her shimmy up onto the table at the same time she made sure the two sides of the gown were adequately pulled together before she grabbed the paper drape and placed it over her lap.

"Damned paper gowns," Bernie said.

"I know," Jeremy said, tilting his head. "You can see right through them."

Bernie's heart skipped a beat or two. "It's nothing you haven't seen before."

"On other women, maybe. Unfortunately, we were far too goal-oriented during a certain encounter for me to remember much of anything I happened to see."

She turned and gave him a deadpan stare of disbelief. "Do you *ever* think about anything but sex?"

"Sure. Sometimes I think about...uh...well, let's see. Oh, yeah. Football."

"Imagine that. A man who thinks about sex and football."

"Which makes me think about the Cowboys. Which makes me think about the Dallas Cowboy Cheerleaders. Which makes me think about—"

"Sex with Dallas Cowboy Cheerleaders." She shook her head. "So when you're not having sex, you're fantasizing about it."

"When it comes to the Cowboy Cheerleaders, it's not a fantasy." He smiled. "It's a memory."

Just then the exam door opened and Dr. Underwood came in. She was pushing fifty, with prematurely gray hair cut short. She wore gray slacks, sensible shoes, and a white coat over her navy-blue blouse. No frills, just competence. Bernie liked that in a person.

"Hey, Bernie," she said. "How are you feeling? Morning sickness letting up?"

Just the mention of it made Bernie's stomach turn over for the hundredth time that day. "The barfing's better. But I'm still a little queasy."

"If it keeps up, let me know. I'll write you something for the nausea." She turned to Jeremy and stopped short. "And you are ... ?"

"I'm the father," Jeremy said, holding out his hand. "Jeremy Bridges."

Dr. Underwood looked a little confounded as she shook his hand. Bernie didn't think it was because she recognized the name. It was because she recognized that somebody who looked like Bernie and somebody who looked like Jeremy rarely ended up combining genetic material.

A few moments later, she was on her back on the table. The doctor lifted her gown to expose her abdomen. Bernie distracted herself from Jeremy's gaze by telling herself that he wasn't seeing anything more than the average woman showed on the average beach.

The doctor squirted some cold, goopy stuff on her

abdomen, then grabbed a thing that looked like a microphone that was attached to the scanning machine by a
cord.

"What's that?" Jeremy asked.

"A transducer. It sends out high-frequency sound waves
and then listens for the returning echoes from whatever's
inside the body. That forms an image on the screen."

She spread the goop around with the transducer, and
then stopped and pressed it gently into Bernie's abdomen.
Sure enough, a blurry image popped up, but nothing in
it looked remotely like a baby. Dr. Underwood moved
the transducer around a little more. Finally she pointed.
"There's your baby. See?"

Bernie looked closely, finally reaching the conclusion
that she'd have to take the doctor's word for that.

"Is it a boy or a girl?" Bernie asked. *Boy, boy, boy,* she
said to herself. A boy she could deal with. She'd take him
hunting and fishing and teach him to play basketball. But
what if she had a girl who wanted to play with Barbies
and dance in a tutu?

"It's a little too early to be able to tell," the doctor said.
"In a month or two—"

She stopped short, staring closer at the screen, then
rubbed the transducer around a little more. "Well, lookie
there."

"What?" Jeremy said.

"Just a minute... let me make sure... yep. Okay, if
you'll look closely..."

Bernie and Jeremy both leaned in.

"...there's your baby."

"Uh... okay," Bernie said, taking her word for it all
over again.

"And right there," she said, pointing to another blob on the screen, "is your other baby."

Bernie's heart seized up. "Wh-what do you mean?"

The doctor just stared at her, slowly raising an eyebrow.

"Oh, no," Bernie said, her voice suddenly edged with panic. "No. Don't tell me that. Please don't tell me—"

"Congratulations, Bernie. You're having twins."

Chapter

12

Jeremy just sat there, stunned. Had he heard that right? Bernie was having not one baby, but *two*?

The doctor looked back and forth between him and Bernie, clearly sensing she hadn't presented the best news possible. She hurried through the rest of the exam, gave Bernie some perfunctory instructions, and left the room.

Bernie shimmied to the edge of the table and stood up, awkwardly holding the paper gown closed. "Go away," she told Jeremy. "I have to dress."

"I was here when you undressed."

"I can't deal with you right now."

"Deal with *me*?"

"In fact, why don't you just go back to your office? There's really no need for you to hang around."

"Come on, Bernie. Your doctor just dropped a bomb. We need to deal with the fallout."

"We? There is no 'we' here."

"First you want me here, and now you don't? Which is it?"

"Get out of here, Bridges," she said, her voice growing shakier by the second. "I mean it."

"I'm not going anywhere."

"When I told you I know a dozen ways to kill a man, I wasn't joking. And make no mistake this time. That's *exactly* what I intend to do if you don't get out of here."

"Bernie—"

"Get out of here now!"

Jeremy drew back. When the hell had this happened? When had Bernie stopped being calm and rational and coolly sarcastic and turned into a raging crazy woman?

Okay, so maybe it was the moment she discovered she was getting two babies for the price of one. Toss that together with overactive hormones, and she clearly wasn't thinking straight, which meant he needed to take control of this situation.

As soon as she stopped *shrieking* at him.

"I'll be in the waiting room," he told her. "Get dressed. *Then* we'll talk."

He strode out of the room with as much authority as he could muster, which didn't feel like much right about then, and went back to Pregnancy Central. As impossible as it seemed, there were even more pregnant women in the waiting room than there had been twenty minutes ago. He sat down in the only empty chair and grabbed a magazine. A moment later he realized it was a copy of *American Baby* and threw it back down as if it was on fire. He felt a sudden nervous energy that made him want to get up. Walk around. Maybe punch something.

No. That reaction was for hormonal crazy women.

Twins. Good Lord. Jeremy knew that very, very soon he'd have his own private mental breakdown over that, but as of right now, he was more concerned with Bernie's state of mind. It wasn't like her to fall apart over anything, and it rattled him more than he could have imagined.

Being a father was one thing. Being a father of twins? He couldn't even fathom that. Then he thought back to something Bernie said yesterday that sounded like a challenge he had to rise to.

My child could do so much better. Unfortunately, he's stuck with you.

When she said that, Jeremy felt as if she'd slapped him. Where fatherhood was concerned, he knew he stood an excellent chance of screwing it up. But when he realized Bernie thought so, too, something inside him had snapped, and he felt as if he had as much to prove to her as he did to himself.

He took a deep breath. Let it out. Spent the next few minutes trying to think of a controlled, workable way he could deal with her and the babies she was carrying. He would have thought that magnifying the problem times two might make it easier to sort out, but it only made things even more complicated. *Two babies, two babies, two babies…*

The words reverberated inside his head until he thought his skull was going to explode.

A few minutes later, his phone rang. He looked at the caller ID, then answered. "Max? What's up?"

"Bernie's gone."

Jeremy snapped to attention. How did he even know she was here in the first place? "What do you mean, she's gone?"

"She left the building through the back door and drove away. Five minutes later, you're still in there, so I thought maybe you weren't aware that she'd left the premises."

Jeremy couldn't believe this. Bernie had given him the slip? He'd been sitting in here waiting for her, and she was already out the door?

Well, that was just great. And wasn't it great, too, that Max saw Bernie and assumed she was the reason Jeremy was here? Why else would Max alert him to the fact that she was gone?

"Bring the car around," Jeremy said.

"Yes, sir."

Jeremy stuffed the phone back into his pocket and headed for the door. As he walked outside, Max swung the car to the curb and he got in the backseat.

"Where to, sir?" Max asked, putting the car in gear.

Jeremy slipped out his iPhone. Opened his address book. "Creekwood Apartments. Fifteenth and Sycamore. Apartment two-fourteen."

Max glanced in the rearview mirror. "I wouldn't recommend that, sir."

"Excuse me?"

"That's Bernie's apartment, and it seems she doesn't want to talk to you."

Jeremy raised an eyebrow. "Watch yourself, Delinsky. This is none of your business."

Max shifted the car back into park, then turned around to face Jeremy in the backseat. "I know she's pregnant."

That statement didn't come as a huge surprise to Jeremy. Chances were that everybody at Delgado & Associates knew it.

"And from what I've seen today," Max went on, "it appears you're the father."

Jeremy froze. He hadn't expected such an in-your-face accusation from a man with barely functioning vocal cords. He considered denying it, but it was pretty clear what was happening here, and this was all going to come out in the open soon enough, anyway.

"That's right," Jeremy said. "I'm the father."

"There's an obstetrician's office inside that building."

"Yes."

"Why did she leave without you knowing it?"

"That's none of your business."

Slowly Max slipped off his sunglasses, revealing those dark, piercing eyes and a wicked slash of a scar on his left orbital bone. "Bridges?"

Jeremy was instantly aware of the absence of the "Mr." that Max always inserted before his last name.

"I don't know what's going on between you and Bernie," Max said, "and I don't need to know. But I will tell you this. She's a good person. If you hurt her in any way, you'll answer to me. Are we clear on that?"

Jeremy was flabbergasted. Was this man actually *threatening* him? He leaned toward Max with an unblinking stare. "One phone call to Gabe Delgado about your insubordination, and you no longer work for me. Are we clear on *that*?"

Max's gaze never faltered. "Make the call."

Jeremy slumped back against the seat. "Good God, do you *want* to lose this job?"

"Nope. I just want to make sure we understand each other. Do we?"

For a second or two, Jeremy was on the verge of making good on his threat, only to think again. If Max was this protective of Bernie, they were better friends than he'd realized, so firing Max wouldn't exactly put him in Bernie's good graces. And right now, that was where he needed to be until he could get this whole mess sorted out.

Jeremy swallowed his anger and spoke evenly. "I have no intention of hurting her."

With a slight nod, Max put his sunglasses back on and turned back around in his seat. *Great.* From now on, Jeremy was going to be forced to spend time in this car with a grizzly bear of a man who was just looking for a reason to rip through his jugular.

"She's upset because she just found out she's having twins," Jeremy said.

True to his nature, Max didn't overreact. He merely glanced at Jeremy in the rearview mirror. "Then you can take my warning times two."

Bastard.

Jeremy had to practically sit on his hands to keep from calling Delgado, but what would it accomplish? It would only make Bernie even more irritated with him than she already was. Still, somebody needed to take control of this situation, and judging from Bernie's state of mind, Jeremy had already decided that somebody was going to be him.

Chapter

13

Bernie sat on the sofa in her living room, staring like a zombie at the wall, her hands resting on her abdomen. She'd managed to absorb the fact that she was having one baby, but to find out she was having two made her brain waves flatline.

This isn't real. It's a nightmare. Be patient—you'll wake up in a moment and this will all be over.

Then she heard a knock at her door, jolting her out of her trance. Was that part of her nightmare, too?

She rose and looked through the peephole. Yep, nightmare. Jeremy had actually followed her home.

She didn't want to talk to him. She felt stupid for flipping out the way she had at the doctor's office, but if she hadn't shut him down, he would only have started in with his usual way of handling things, which included commanding and controlling at all costs. And if she let him in and he went off like that, she might just rip his head off, and the last thing she needed was a murder accusation.

Being pregnant with twins was one thing. Being pregnant with twins in prison was quite another.

Jeremy knocked, louder this time. "Bernie! Answer the door!"

Bernie continued to look out the peephole, willing him to go away.

"I'm not going away!" he said.

So much for her willpower.

Bernie grabbed her cell phone and dialed Max's number. The line clicked. "Hey, Bernie. What's up?"

"I assume you're in Jeremy's car downstairs?"

"Yep."

"Uh . . . you probably know the whole story by now, don't you?"

"What? That Bridges is the father, and you're having twins?"

Leave it to Max to get right to the point. "Yes. And right now, he's banging on my door, and I just don't want to deal with him now. Can you make him go away?"

"Sorry, Bernie. No can do."

"Come on, Max. Help me out here!"

"For now, Bridges is calling the shots on my end. Here's some advice."

"What?"

"If you don't deal with him now, you'll deal with him later, so just go ahead and deal with him now."

"Bernie!" Jeremy shouted. "Open the *door*!"

She slumped with resignation. Max was right, of course. Avoidance only bought her another day or two of worry until he showed up again.

"Bernie?" Max said.

"Yeah?"

"Gotta admit it was a hell of a surprise. How did you and Bridges...you know—get to where you are now?"

Bernie sighed. "I'd have to be extremely intoxicated to tell that story."

"I'll be looking forward to it."

Yeah, buy me a six-pack in about eighteen years.

With a sigh of extreme frustration, Bernie laid down her phone, took a deep breath, and opened the door.

"It's about time," Jeremy said as he swept into her apartment. "I was beginning to think you hadn't come home, except your car is out front. Which suggests—crazy as it seems—that you may have been ignoring me."

"*May* have been ignoring you?"

"You shouldn't have left alone. You're not thinking straight."

"Will you stop being so condescending? Of course I'm thinking straight!"

"Yeah? Then why do you have your shirt on backward?"

Bernie flicked her gaze down to look at herself. *Damn.*

The longer he stared at her, the dumber she felt. She brushed past him and went to her kitchen. For what, she wasn't sure, but she was absolutely sure she wanted to escape his prying eyes. "You can go home now, Bridges. I'm perfectly capable of dealing with this by myself."

"Yeah? Well, you went a little nuts in the doctor's office."

She grabbed a bottle of water from the fridge. "I was just surprised at the news. That's all."

"Freaked out is more like it. But you know, I've been thinking. This might actually work out pretty well."

"Oh, yeah? How's that?"

"You're having twins," he said. "One for me, one for you."

Bernie wheeled on him. "For God's sake! They're not a pair of Twinkies!"

"Will you laugh a little? It won't kill you."

"Is everything just a big joke to you?"

"Sometimes you gotta laugh, or you'll cry."

Suddenly, out of nowhere, Bernie felt her eyes fog up. Then they burned a little. *Oh, God.*

Tears?

For one of the few times in her tightly controlled life, the power of suggestion had power over her. She tried to blink them away, but she wasn't having much luck. If it were up to her, she'd damn all female hormones to hell.

"Oh, crap," Jeremy said, his joking expression vanishing. "I didn't mean you actually had to *choose*."

"I'm not choosing," she snapped, turning her back to him as she unscrewed the cap of the water bottle. "And I'm not crying. *I don't cry.*"

"Oh. My mistake."

Damn it, now her nose was running. She set down the water bottle, grabbed a napkin, and wiped her nose surreptitiously. "Two babies is just kind of overwhelming, and crying is a reflex. That's all."

"Right. A reflex."

And just like that, the reflexive action kicked in again, and she grabbed another napkin to wipe her eyes. *Don't do this. Don't start crying, or you may never stop.* She started toward her bedroom, just in case the eternal weeping was about to begin.

"Where are you going?" Jeremy asked.

"To turn my shirt around."

"The shirt doesn't matter. Sit down for a minute."

"I don't want to sit."

But as she brushed past him, he grabbed her arm and pulled her to the sofa. "Forget the shirt."

"Bridges—"

"*Sit.*"

With a heavy sigh, she sank to the sofa. He went to the kitchen, grabbed a stack of napkins, and plopped them onto the coffee table in front of her. But she didn't need them, because by God, she was *not* going to cry. At least, not much.

But *two* babies? How was she ever going to deal with that?

"Look, I have enough problems already," she said. "The last thing I need is you adding to them."

"Problems? What problems?"

"None of your business."

"Have you been able to work?"

"That's none of your business, either."

"Let's get something straight, Bernie. You're carrying my children—"

"*Our* children."

"—which means 'none of your business' is no longer an acceptable answer. Are you going to be able to work?"

She paused. "Not as a bodyguard."

"Yeah. Pregnancy would tend to make that a non-starter. So what are your job plans?"

Bernie hated this. Saying it out loud made it sound even more mundane, boring, and dead-end. "If you must know, I talked to Gabe Delgado. He has a contract job for me at the Lone Star Museum of Art monitoring their security cameras."

Jeremy shook his head. "You're not cut out to sit at a desk all day. You'll be miserable."

"For the next week or two at least, I probably won't feel like doing much else." She dropped her head to her hands, then rubbed her temples.

"What's wrong?" Jeremy asked.

"Head's swimming a little. That's all."

"Uh-huh. Probably aggravated by all that crying you're not doing."

"It's just morning sickness."

"I thought that was a stomach thing."

"Nope," she said, lifting her head again. "It's more like an 'every organ in your body' kind of thing."

"How can you have morning sickness when it's not morning?"

"I don't know why they call it that. It lasts all day and halfway into the night. But it's way better than it was, which tells you how bad it used to be."

She took a deep, cleansing breath that did no good at all. Another breath. Same story. Maybe she should stop breathing altogether. That would definitely solve her problem.

The distant sound of music wafted through the air. Jeremy glanced out the window, where her neighbor across the way sat on his balcony playing his guitar. The guy had spiky red-tipped hair and was tattooed just about everywhere that showed. Bernie had met him. He was nice enough. He just looked a little . . . alternative. Judging by the way Jeremy twisted his mouth with disgust, he thought the guy was a little *too* alternative.

"I can't believe you live in a place like this," Jeremy said.

"What's wrong with it?"

"Weird people. Potholes all over the place. Peeling paint. The stair railing outside is falling out of the wall."

Damn. With everything going on, she'd forgotten to call Charmin again about that damned railing.

"I paid you really well for two years," Jeremy went on. "You could have spent an extra three or four hundred a month and found a decent place to live. Why didn't you?"

"Because I like saving money."

"Yeah? What good will those savings do you when you're attacked by some lunatic?"

"Do you have to be so dramatic? You know I can take care of myself."

"Under normal circumstances, of course you can. But pregnant women make excellent targets."

"Will you stop? You're just comparing this place to that castle you live in. This is where normal people live."

"Yeah? I saw a few out front who were decidedly abnormal."

"Yeah, well, I've met a lot of men in business suits who were rotten to the core. Most of the people who live here are just regular people who are trying to get by."

"I'm the father of the babies you're carrying," Jeremy said, "so I should have some say-so when it comes to your health and well-being. And you won't be healthy and well very much longer living in a place like this. Move somewhere else."

Bernie wanted to pull her hair out. Here he was, acting as he always did, as if the entire population of the world should fall in line the moment he snapped his fingers. He saw absolutely nothing wrong with that, but in Bernie's eyes, there wasn't anything that *wasn't* wrong with it. The moment she let him dictate something as basic as where she lived, she'd be under his thumb from now on.

"You're not telling me where to live," she said. "And it's a moot point anyway. Even if I wanted a nicer apartment, I couldn't afford it."

"Uh... have we met before?" He held out his hand. "Hello, I'm Jeremy Bridges. I'm a multimillionaire."

She took his hand. "Hello, Mr. Bridges. I'm Bernie Hogan, the mother of these babies, and you're keeping your money to yourself."

He pulled his hand away. "So you're telling me you'd deprive your children of a decent place to live when their father can easily foot the bill for it?"

"When that money comes with so many strings attached that it chokes their mother to death, you bet your life I would."

"I'm just offering to help. What's wrong with that?"

What was *wrong* with that? Was he *serious*?

"It might interest you to know," Bernie said, "that your paternity can't be legally established until after these babies are born. Until then, I have sole custody and all the rights that go along with that." She stood up, suggesting it was time for him to go. "In other words, I don't have to listen to a damned thing you say."

Jeremy stared at her a moment through narrowed eyes, then stood up beside her, shaking his head. "My God. Tell me you're not that naive."

"What do you mean?"

"Do you actually think a recitation of your legal rights is going to make me go away?"

He spoke with such conviction that she couldn't help feeling intimidated, especially with him staring down at her as if he held all the cards. She inched closer, folding her arms and staring up at him.

"You have no idea what you're getting yourself into," she said. "Having a baby is no walk in the park. Neither is taking care of one. Or two, as the case may be."

"People have been doing it since the dawn of time."

"How did you like going to the doctor with me today? Feel right at home? Can't wait to go back?"

"It was an interesting experience."

"Interesting. Uh-huh. Trust me when I tell you—it's only going to get harder from here."

"I built a multimillion-dollar business from the ground up in an economic climate that should have chewed me up and spit me out. Do you really think I can't deal with a baby?"

"Business. Right. Try telling a screaming baby what a big-shot businessman you are. *That'll* put him to sleep." She paused, raising an eyebrow. "Then again, maybe it will. I know it makes me yawn."

Jeremy gave her a small, knowing smile. "Trust me, Bernie. I have skills I haven't even begun to show you yet." He moved closer. "Want me to give you a preview?"

With a slow, deliberate sweep of his eyes, he lowered his gaze to her lips. Memories came flooding back of that moment in his safe room when he'd swooped in and kissed her with an unrestrained carnality that made her knees buckle. And when her legs wobbled a little all over again, she wondered: What the hell was it about this man that made her want to kiss him and slap him all at the same time?

"This is just amazing," she said.

His gaze came up slowly to meet hers again. "What's amazing?"

"The more you try to intimidate me, the more I get the urge to open that door and throw you down the stairs."

He shook his head sadly. "Bernie? Have you ever thought about trying sex *without* anger?"

"From now on, where you're concerned, I think I'll stick to anger without sex."

"Never say never. It makes it so much harder later when you're dying to change your mind." He glanced at his watch. "I have to go now. But don't worry. You'll be seeing me again soon."

On his way out the door, Jeremy gave her one of his smiles that looked charming on the surface but was calculating underneath, making her wonder what he was up to. Because he was always up to something.

Always.

She watched as he trotted down the stairs. He grabbed the handrail at the same time, clearly forgetting how he'd complained about it on the way up. When it wobbled beneath his hand, he stopped, cursed beneath his breath, and gave it a hard shake. One end came free, falling to the stairs beneath it with a clatter, and a couple of rusty screws went flying. He stepped back suddenly, then glared down at it.

"Gee, thanks," Bernie said. "That made things *much* better."

"This place is a dump," he muttered.

"I'm still not moving."

"You've made that clear."

"So you can stop trying to talk me into it."

"Oh, I'm through talking. That's not getting me anywhere."

"Well, thank God."

"It's time for action. Later, Bernie."

As he trotted the rest of the way down the stairs and into the parking lot, Bernie felt a rush of apprehension. *It's time for action?* What the hell did he mean by that?

Max swung the car around. Jeremy got in, and the car sped away. Just then, the door across the breezeway opened and Ruby peered out, a half-smoked Marlboro between her fingers. She wore pink terrycloth slippers and a leopard-print housecoat. Ruby was fond of leopard. Said it was way better than zebra or cheetah for hiding cigarette burns.

"Is he gone?" she asked.

"Ruby. You're spying again."

"What else have I got to do? Is he a friend of yours?"

"Not exactly. With luck, he won't be back."

"I don't know," Ruby said. "Maybe you're being too picky. Men don't wander up here very often." She hobbled out to the landing and glanced down at the half-collapsed railing. "Then again, he does kinda tear things up." She looked back at Bernie. "So when *are* you gonna get yourself a man?"

"Same time you do."

"Nah. I'm old enough to know what a pain in the ass they are. You're young enough to still get taken in. So who was he, anyway?"

Bernie sighed. "He's the father of my baby."

"Huh?"

"I'm pregnant."

Ruby's eyes widened. "Yeah?"

"Yeah," Bernie said. "Imagine that. Me, thirty-six years old and pregnant."

"Hmm. I take it you're not loving the idea."

"Let's just say I have mixed emotions."

"Yeah, I hear you. If men are the biggest pains in the ass, kids are a close second."

"Particularly when you're having two of them."

"Two of them?" Ruby raised an eyebrow. "Twins?"

"Uh-huh."

She shook her head. "Holy crap. You really are screwed."

So there it was. Confirmation of exactly how Bernie felt right then.

"Well," Ruby said. "Look at the bright side. He's good-looking, so at least the babies won't be ugly."

Bernie couldn't argue with that. She had no doubt that Jeremy's genetic material was as domineering as the rest of him and would shove her right out of the way. Unfortunately, attractive children would be a small consolation for having to put up with a man like him.

"If I can help you out," Ruby said, "you let me know. You hear?"

"I hear."

Ruby headed back to her apartment, only to look back over her shoulder. "Meant to ask."

"What?" Bernie said.

"How come your shirt's on backward?"

Bernie sighed. "Long story."

"Better turn it around. People will think you're weird, or something."

Bernie's phone rang. She grabbed it from her pocket and looked at the caller ID. "Gotta take this."

"Okay," Ruby said. "But when you get a chance, can you light another fire under Charmin? Now that handrail really is screwed up."

"Sure," Bernie said. "I'll call her in a minute."

Ruby shuffled back into her apartment, and Bernie hit the TALK button. "Hey, Max."

"Hey, Bernie. You okay?"

"I'm fine. Bridges has been driving me nuts for years. Nothing new there."

"You sure about that?"

"I appreciate you looking out for me," she said, going back into her apartment. "But I can deal with him."

"You let me know if the day comes when you can't. Because trust me—I can."

Bernie couldn't help smiling at that. Max wasn't exactly all bark and no bite. He was just a very big dog who didn't have to resort to biting very often.

"He's listening to every word you say, isn't he?" Bernie said.

"Yep."

"Is he pissed off that you're talking to me?"

"Yep."

"Good. Let him stew for a while. Thanks, Max."

Bernie tossed her phone aside and collapsed on her sofa, a dozen emotions pulling her in a dozen different directions. She hated that feeling of things being up in the air. Of not knowing when she'd turn around and find Jeremy standing there again. Of not knowing why, when she'd given him a gold-plated ticket right out of this situation, he'd chosen not to take it.

She didn't know what his motives were, but she did know one thing: The fact that Jeremy hadn't walked away didn't mean he'd suddenly taken a 180-degree turn and decided he was going to leap into fatherhood with both feet. And even though he was making a lot of noise right now about running the show, when a father wasn't also a husband, there was only so much he could do even if he wanted to.

In the end, she knew the truth. Raising these babies was going to be up to her.

Max returned his phone to his pocket and kept driving without saying another word. Jeremy thought it took a lot of gall for him to carry on a conversation with Bernie right there in front of him, but what was he supposed to do? Complain about it? All that would accomplish would be to make Max hate him even more.

"So," Jeremy said offhandedly, "you were talking to Bernie."

"Yes, sir."

"Given that I'm still breathing, I take it you're not feeling the need to beat my brains out on her behalf?"

"That's right, sir."

"But the possibility still exists?"

"That's completely up to you, sir."

Sir. God, how he hated the sound of that coming out of Max's mouth. He might as well have said, *That's completely up to you, asshole.*

"She's going to need some help," Jeremy said.

"Depends on where that help comes from."

"Believe it or not," Jeremy said, "I only want what's best for her."

"That remains to be seen, sir."

"Will you stop with all the yes sir, no sir crap?" Jeremy said. "It's getting a little old."

"Just showing respect, sir."

But Jeremy didn't miss the scorn in Max's voice. "No, Max, you're not. You don't respect me in the least."

When Max didn't respond, Jeremy felt the strangest twinge of irritation. He didn't remember a day in his adult life where he'd wasted a single minute worrying what anybody else thought of him. But this . . . *this* bothered him, and it was because Max was close to Bernie. But he just couldn't understand why they both had such a big problem with him when all he was doing was trying to help.

He had to figure out a way to get Bernie to see things his way, to do what was best for her and the babies, even with Max in the mix. And he would. It was just a matter of time.

Chapter
14

The security system at the Lone Star Museum of Art consisted of thirty-two cameras placed strategically within the building, wired directly to the surveillance room on a closed-circuit system. Inside that room, a bank of six monitors allowed Bernie to swap around to see what was happening within the overlapping radii of each camera. If she saw any irregularities, she phoned the information to the security guard posted downstairs and he investigated.

That was her job in a nutshell.

A building like this, unoccupied at night, normally wouldn't even have twenty-four-hour manned security, but with the donation three years ago of approximately a gazillion dollars' worth of Egyptian artifacts, the board had decided the extra cost was worth it. But it was pure PR, designed to assure that donor, as well as other potential donors, that any private collections they chose to give up would have a safe home forever.

She'd started this job several days ago, and already the boredom factor had shot through the roof. Nobody had tried to steal anything. Vandalism had been nonexistent. Even schoolchildren on tour had behaved themselves. It was so quiet that sometimes that she imagined one day she actually would go crazy. She'd rip open the door and go screaming through the building. They'd call the EMTs, who would strap her down and send her to a psych ward, where she'd spend the rest of her life in a padded room so drugged up she didn't know her own name.

But so what if that happened? Would that life really be much different from this one? Wouldn't it be *better* than this one?

Shut up. It's a job. One you desperately need.

As long as she didn't actually go stark raving mad.

Of course, if this job didn't cause her to go completely insane, her mother would drive her the rest of the way. As much as Bernie thought she'd prepared herself for her mother's intrusiveness, her expectations didn't even approach reality. She called twice a day to see how Bernie was feeling, offering advice on everything from prenatal vitamins to the kind of crib she should buy to the preschools she should consider. Or she'd drop by to show Bernie some random pacifier or baby socks she'd bought. When Bernie told her mother she was having twins, she fell into paroxysms of swooning delight, launching the annoyance level straight into the stratosphere.

Unfortunately, it had been a few days since she'd stopped by her mother's house to check on things, so she decided she needed to do that as soon as she left work today. Her mother would make her a cup of tea and feed her a homemade muffin, then launch into another round of baby talk. Bernie hadn't yet told her that Jeremy was in the picture, and at least for now, she didn't intend to.

That he was here today didn't mean he wouldn't be gone tomorrow. If that was a disappointment she could spare her mother, that was what she was going to do.

She heard a commotion behind her. The door opened, and Lawanda came into the room. Bernie loved the sound of that door opening. She checked her watch. Yep, three o'clock. Time for Lawanda to take over and for her to go home.

Lawanda dropped a Subway sack on the desk, clunked her tote bag down beside it, and set a small cooler on the floor. She wore a lime-green baby-doll top with layers of sequin-lined ruffles, a pair of jeans, astronomical green pumps, and silver hoop earrings so huge they grazed her shoulders. False eyelashes stuck out approximately a foot in front of her face, and her cherry-red lipstick glowed by the light of the security monitors. Lawanda's sense of style entered a room before she did. And because she was a plus-size woman, it filled every molecule of space once it was there.

She flopped her considerable bulk into the chair beside Bernie. The chair groaned and squeaked, making Bernie wonder just how much more the poor thing could take.

Lawanda had gone to work for Gabe three years ago doing contract jobs like this one, and she'd worked the evening shift here at the museum for the past six months. Bernie went crazy watching those monitors when the building was occupied. She couldn't imagine the boredom when it wasn't. But the only thing Lawanda seemed to hate about the evening shift was that she missed their once-a-month poker games with the guys.

"Hey, girl," Lawanda said, the light from the monitors reflecting off her blinding white smile. "What's up?"

"What's ever up around here?" Bernie said.

"Good point."

Lawanda dug through her cooler, pulled out a Red Bull, and popped the top. "Anything happen on your shift I need to know about?"

"Nope," Bernie said. She stuck her iPhone into her backpack and stood up. "I'm out of here."

"You hate being here, don't you?"

Bernie glanced back. "Gee, how could you tell?"

"I know job disgust when I see it."

Bernie sat back down. "How do you deal with it?"

"Deal with what?" she said.

"The boredom."

"Oh, yeah. That." She reached into her tote bag. "I got my magazines. I got my music. I got my Subway and my Red Bull. I got my phone. You train yourself to look up every twenty seconds or so and to swap around the cameras on a regular basis, and you've done your job. The rest of the time you read, you text, you drink, you eat. It's still like spending eight hours a day sitting in a traffic jam, but it sure beats the hell out of being a prison guard. Try getting cussed at and spit on eight hours a day. After putting up with that, this job is heaven."

"I'll have to take your word for that," Bernie said, thinking that if she were getting cussed at and spit on, at least *something* was happening.

"And you ought to try wearing a prison guard uniform," Lawanda said with disgust. "At least on this job, I'm free to express my personal fashion sense."

"But nobody's around to see it."

"But I get to *feel* it," Lawanda said with a smile, her palm against her chest. "Contributes to my positive mental health."

"Sounds like a small consolation for being bored to death."

"I figured you'd like this job, being pregnant and all."

"I don't have much of a choice."

"So how you feeling these days?"

"Okay."

Lawanda asked a few more baby-related questions that seemed innocuous on the surface. But Bernie knew they were designed to zero in on the burning question everybody at Delgado & Associates was wondering about: Who was the father of her baby? But until Bernie knew just how far Jeremy intended to take the issue of fatherhood, it was a question she had no intention of answering, and she was certain that Max wouldn't tell anyone, either. She stood up and tossed her purse over her shoulder.

"Wait," Lawanda said. "Forgot to ask. Could you stay a couple of extra hours this Friday? I got a meeting with that lawyer, the one my friend Sylvia recommended. All I could get was an evening appointment, and she's in Mansfield."

"Mansfield? That's a long way from here."

"Chick's worth it. She handled Sylvia's divorce. Took her husband to the cleaners. If she can do the same for me, I'll fly to the freakin' moon to meet with her." A wicked smile spread across her face. "Teddy isn't gonna know what hit him."

Two months ago, Lawanda had found out her husband of three years was having an affair with their next-door neighbor. It had been a tough sell, but Bernie had finally convinced her that legal action was preferable to homicide.

"Sure," Bernie said. "I can stay. See you tomorrow."

As Bernie left the room, Lawanda was already unwrapping her Subway sandwich, settling in for the long eight hours ahead. When the heavy metal door clanged closed behind Bernie, she was already dreading having to come back there tomorrow.

After the babies were born, surely she could find another job. But for now, she was stuck. Pregnant or not, as long as she could make it to this room every day, sit upright, and stare at the monitors, she was employable. She made money. She had health insurance. And right now, those were the only things that mattered.

Half an hour later, Bernie was driving down the street toward her mother's house. She slowed down when she saw a couple of kids playing too close to the curb, then stopped completely when their ball bounced into the street and they went after it. Did they bother to check for traffic? Of course not. Kids. Good God. It was a wonder most of them made it to adulthood without getting stuck to the bottom of a Uniroyal.

A few minutes later, her mother met her at the door with a big smile. They went into the living room, which was filled with overstuffed furniture, a thousand knick-knacks, and the too-heavy aroma of Glade "Always Spring" air freshener. Bernie was convinced that her childhood memories of dainty doilies, china cabinets, and giant silk flower arrangements had been a big reason she'd decided to go into the military and shoot things.

"How are you feeling?" her mother said.

"Better every day."

"How's the job?"

"Good. It's good."

"You just sit right down, and I'll get you a cup of tea. And I made some lemon poppy seed muffins." She scurried toward the kitchen, only to turn back. "Oh! I went to that new baby store in the strip center by the mall. They have such cute things! Just a minute. I grabbed a catalog—"

Suddenly Bernie heard the toilet flush. "Mom? Who's here?"

"Uh…"

The bathroom door opened, and Billy emerged. Just the sight of her worthless cousin made Bernie's blood pressure shoot through the roof.

As always, he wore holey jeans and a crappy T-shirt, and his muddy brown hair hung down in his eyes. He had the kind of face that showed up regularly on *America's Most Wanted*. Of course, to be on that show, he'd have to be something like a serial killer, and Billy just didn't have the work ethic to pull off more than one murder before he expected somebody else to do his killing for him.

"Billy?" Bernie said. "What are you doing here?"

He flopped on the sofa and picked up the remote. "Aunt Eleanor said I could stay in her spare bedroom for a few days."

Bernie snapped to attention. "Why?"

He clicked on the TV. "My roommate freaked out."

"What do you mean he freaked out? Did you stiff him again on the rent?"

"Hell, no. I was just a little short, and he went nuts."

"In other words, you were three months behind and he finally kicked you out. Which does *not* mean that you're going to come here and—"

"Aunt Eleanor?" Billy said sweetly. "You did tell me I could stay here, didn't you?"

Eleanor gave him a smile. "Of course, dear."

Billy gave Bernie a smug look before turning back to the TV, jacking up the sound so he wouldn't miss a single critical moment of monster truck rally commentary.

"Mom?" Bernie said. "Can I see you in the other room?"

Once they were in the kitchen, Bernie turned to face her mother. "What is he doing here?"

"He just needs a place to stay for a little while. Until he finds another job."

Bernie's eyebrows flew up. "He lost that job? The one I gave him a reference for?"

Eleanor shrugged weakly. "You know Billy has problems. His panic attacks—"

"Mom. The only time Billy has a panic attack is when he thinks he might actually have to work for a living."

"He won't be staying long."

"Are you forgetting what happened last time he conned you into letting him stay here? He left cigarette burns in the guest room dresser and pawned your microwave!"

"He took my microwave only because he had too much pride to ask for a loan."

"So why doesn't his pride stand in the way of him *stealing* from you?"

Eleanor turned away, picking up a dishtowel to wipe away a few imaginary water spots on the counter.

"Where's his car?" Bernie asked. "I didn't see it out front."

"It's in the shop."

"Has he asked to use your car?"

"No."

"You mean not yet."

Her mother didn't respond.

"Why do you do it?" Bernie said. "Why do you help him when he refuses to help himself?"

"Because he's family," Eleanor said. "You always take care of family. *Always.*"

Family. Every time her mother invoked the "F" word, Bernie realized her hands were tied. For Billy, being "family" was nothing more than a fortunate accident of birth that prevented Bernie from taking him out back and giving him the ass-kicking he desperately needed. But what really pissed Bernie off was that Billy knew what her mother was facing in the next few years, and still he took advantage of her. But Eleanor Hogan had always believed the best about everyone even in the face of overwhelming evidence to the contrary, and that was never going to change.

"It'll be okay," her mother said. "He's going job hunting tomorrow, and he's only staying for a week. Then he says he's moving in with a friend."

Bernie wanted to pull her hair out. The blind spot her mother had where family was concerned was positively gargantuan.

"Promise me you won't tell him to leave," Eleanor said.

"No, Mom," Bernie said with a sigh, feeling as if she wasn't in control of anything anymore. "I won't tell him to leave."

Her mother smiled. "It'll be okay. You'll see."

No, it wouldn't. And when things fell apart, Bernie would just have to be there to pick up the pieces.

"Did you get groceries this week?" Bernie asked her mother.

"Of course, dear. And I got the ingredients to make a salmon recipe from the Chef Allen cookbook you gave me. Would you like to come for dinner one night this week?"

Bernie glanced into the living room with heavy sigh. "It's really best if I don't."

"I understand. But Billy will be gone in a week. Then you can come over, okay?"

Bernie knew better. One week would turn into three—or more—before he finally cleared out.

"I'm sending a guy over here tomorrow," Bernie said. "It's getting near fall, and I want him to service your heating unit."

"That's fine," her mother said, putting a teakettle on the stove. "What kind of tea would you like?"

"I think I'll pass on tea today, Mom. I have a hundred things I have to do. I just wanted to drop by and see how you're doing."

"Here's the catalog I talked about," her mother said. Bernie took it and thanked her for it, then said good-bye and headed for the door. As she went through the living room, she glanced at Billy, who was lounging on the sofa with his dirty feet on the coffee table.

Changing course, she strode over, jerked the remote out of his hand, and muted the sound. Standing over him, she spoke in a low, harsh voice. "Listen to me, Billy. You're going to behave yourself while you're here. That means no smoking in the house, no dragging your friends over here, and no eating every morsel of food in the refrigerator. And you're not borrowing any money this time. Do you understand?"

He gave her a smug smile. "Sure, Bernie. Whatever

you say." He reached for the remote, but she held it away from him.

"You behave yourself, or I swear to God—"

"What? What are you going to do? Beat me up? You want to make your mother cry? That'll do it." That smug look again. "After all, I grew up without a mother."

"You little—"

Billy snatched the remote back. "Man, what is it with pregnant women and all the bitchiness?"

He pointed and clicked, and the sound came up again.

Just go. Go before you really do commit murder.

Bernie spun around and walked out the door, feeling as if a two-ton stone was pressing down on her until she couldn't breathe. It was hard enough dealing with her mother's condition and a job she hated and a freeloading cousin. What about when the babies came? What then?

And then there was Jeremy. The wild card in this whole thing. The man who seemed born to irritate her, to tease her with the idea that maybe he wanted some real involvement with the babies instead of just swooping in to drive her nuts. Somewhere in her life, sometime soon, she wanted to be sure of something, but right now she was sure of absolutely nothing.

She got into her car and closed the door behind her. She put her hand against her belly and closed her eyes, imagining what her life was going to be like when she had to get up in the middle of the night to feed two babies. How tough it was going to be to find decent child care. How two babies had to be at least twice as hard to raise as one. She took a big, deep breath, telling herself everything was going to be fine. Things would level out, and sooner or later she'd have things under control.

She reached down to put the key into the ignition, only to drop her hand to her lap again. Her throat tightened, and damned if she wasn't on the verge of crying all over again.

Under control? Who was she kidding? She didn't have anything under control. Where the babies were concerned, she hadn't even made any plans yet. For a woman who'd always prided herself on her organizational skills, she couldn't seem to get any of her thoughts together. Last night she'd pulled out some of the magazines and catalogs her mother had given her and started to make a list of the things she was going to need for the babies, but before long it all felt so overwhelming that she shoved it aside, turned on *CSI Miami*, and pretended she wasn't pregnant with twins.

No more pretending. It was time to face things head-on and get something concrete done. She needed some advice from somebody other than her mother, who persisted in talking about things like how darling baby girls looked in those stretchy headbands with bows on top.

She grabbed her phone, called Teresa Ramsey, and asked if she could drop by for a little while. Teresa seemed happy at the propect of having a chat, and Bernie was happy at the prospect of hanging out for a while with a woman who made motherhood seem effortless. How Teresa pulled it off, Bernie didn't know. But right about now, when she was picturing the motherhood experience as nothing but chaos, she was dying to find out.

Ten minutes later, she pulled up in front of Bill and Teresa's house. She knocked on the front door. Waited a bit.

Nothing.

She knocked again. Still nothing. She looked over her shoulder to be sure Teresa's car really was in the driveway, then started to knock one more time. Suddenly the door swung open.

"Hey, Bernie," Teresa said, a big smile lighting her face.

No. Wait. This wasn't the Teresa she knew. This was Teresa's slovenly twin sister, who wore a pair of tattered gym shorts and a faded blue T-shirt, and had her hair pulled up into a pink scrunchy. She held a baby on her hip who was clad in nothing but a diaper with something questionable dribbling down his chin.

As quickly as Teresa answered the door, she turned and walked away. "Come on in and have a seat," she called back over her shoulder. "I'll be just a minute—crisis in the kitchen."

Bernie stepped into the entry hall and closed the door behind her. "I hope you don't mind that I dropped by. I just have a couple of questions about—"

And then she turned and saw the living room.

As Teresa disappeared into the kitchen, Bernie stopped and stared, unable to believe what she was looking at. It was as if a tornado had swept through the room, scrambling a pile of toys into a haphazard mess. Sofa pillows were in a heap on the floor. Two juice cups sat on the coffee table. Five-year-old Sarah was lying on her stomach in front of the TV, which was currently tuned to one of those very loud, very busy kids shows Bernie had always thought should be outlawed. Sarah turned to look up at her with wide blue eyes as if to say, *Who the hell are you?* Then she went back to watching the TV at a sound level in the supersonic range.

"Careful!!" Teresa called from the kitchen. "Don't trip over anything!"

Bernie appreciated the warning. She stepped over a pile of blocks and bypassed a wooden puzzle before finding her way to the sofa. This couldn't be Bill and Teresa's house. It just *couldn't*.

"Bernie?" Teresa called from the kitchen. "Can I get you anything? Coffee? Coke?"

"No, thanks," Bernie called back, still looking around in disbelief, willing her bugged-out eyeballs to relax back into her head. A few minutes later, Teresa came back into the room.

"Sarah!" she said. "Turn your show down."

Sarah grabbed the remote, which looked huge in her tiny hands, and hit the volume button, blessedly bringing the sound down into a range that didn't burst eardrums. Teresa sat down next to Bernie and plopped the baby onto her lap.

"Sorry," she said. "Soon as you knocked on the door, Matt here had a puke attack in the kitchen, so I had to do a little cleanup." She sighed wistfully. "I am such a terrible mother."

Bernie came to attention. "Terrible mother? Why?"

"Because good mothers aren't supposed to gag at spit-up. They're supposed to smile at their little angel like he didn't just barf. I gag every time. I swear this one's a spit-up machine." She turned to the baby. "Hey, kiddo. Keep it down next time, will you?"

She set the toddler on the floor. He took a few wobbly steps before falling to the carpet and crawling up next to his sister, who was still glued to the TV.

"I guess kids watch a lot of TV, huh?" Bernie said.

"Yep. Some people say it rots their brains, but I don't

sweat it too much. I limit it as much as I can, but sometimes it's a godsend. Ninety-five percent of mothers say they use it as a babysitter at least some of the time." Teresa leaned in and whispered confidentially. "If you ask me, the other five percent are liars."

Bernie was glad to hear that. Every time she imagined plunking her kids down in front of the TV now and then, she also imagined being branded an unfit mother for the rest of eternity. One worry put to rest.

She had only about a thousand more.

Teresa turned and tucked her legs up beside her on the sofa. "Bill said you missed poker at Lucky's this week. Everything going okay with your pregnancy?"

"Yeah. Fine. Actually, I had a little news this week."

"Yeah? What's that?"

Bernie was still having trouble verbalizing it. "Turns out I'm having twins."

Teresa gasped, and a big smile lit her face. "You're kidding me. *Twins?*"

"Believe me," Bernie said, "I wouldn't joke about something like that."

"That's so exciting!" Teresa said, and then her smile faded. "Isn't it?"

"Yes. Of course it is. It's just that…" Bernie closed her eyes. "God, Teresa. I'd barely gotten used to the idea of one, and now I'm having two."

"Yeah, I guess that would be a little bit of a shock."

"You have no idea." She sighed. "I guess it's like poker, huh? I just play the hand I'm dealt?"

"Just be glad you drew a pair and not three of a kind. Now, *that* would be tough. Might as well just tack on five more and have your own reality show."

Bernie shuddered at the very thought.

"Why do I feel like every other woman on earth was born for this, and I'm the odd woman out?" she asked.

Teresa laughed. "Come on, Bernie. Ninety-five percent of women feel that way with their first baby."

"And the other five percent are liars?"

Teresa smiled. "Now you're getting it."

"I don't even know what to buy for a baby. I've gone through catalogs, looked online, poked around in a few stores—"

"Wait a minute," Teresa said, holding up her palm. "Don't get caught up in all that. There are only a few things you really need."

"Like what?"

"Disposable diapers," Teresa said, counting the items out on her fingers. "Formula if you're not breastfeeding. Enough clothes that you don't have to do laundry every five minutes. Someplace for the babies to sleep. A couple of car seats." She thought for a moment. "And a diaper bag. Oh! And a stroller. One of those double ones, I guess, since you're having twins."

Bernie blinked. "That's it?"

"Pretty much. Well—except for the musical potty that plays 'It's a Small World' to reward your kid every time he pees."

Bernie drew back. "They make those?"

"Yep. Can you believe it? But you can also just stick your kids on the john and tell them to go. If they do, give them an M&M. Works like a charm. Musical potty chair, forty bucks. Sack of M&Ms, two ninety-nine."

"Aren't you setting them up to have to have an M&M every time they pee?"

"Nah. And even if you are, which would you rather have? A kid who can't pee unless he has a pocketful of M&Ms, or a kid who can't pee unless he hears 'It's a Small World'?"

Bernie smiled. "Excellent point."

"And with the M&Ms, you always have a stash of chocolate if you really need it."

The longer Teresa talked, the more Bernie felt worry being lifted from her shoulders. This was exactly what she needed. Practical advice from somebody who could assure her that the challenge of motherhood wasn't insurmountable.

"I don't know how you do it," Bernie said.

"Do what?"

"Every time we come here for poker, your house looks perfect. *You* look perfect."

Teresa laughed. "Thank God for poker nights, or I'd probably never clean house."

"Oh, boy. So you're telling me that once the babies are here, my apartment will never be clean unless I'm hosting poker?"

"No. I'm just telling you that cleaning isn't important. No kid ever became a happy, healthy, well-adjusted adult because he grew up in a house with a spotless kitchen floor."

Yet another good point.

"Motherhood isn't rocket science," Teresa went on. "Even with two kids at once. Can you hold a baby? Change a diaper? Read to them? Stick Band-Aids on their boo-boos? Tell your daughter hell *no*, she can't pierce her labia? Tell your son he'd damned well better treat women right or else? Can you do that?"

Bernie couldn't help smiling. "Yeah. I can do that." Then her smile faded. "The question is, can I do it all by myself?"

Teresa sat back, eyeing Bernie carefully. "Are you going to have to?"

Bernie sighed. "I'm not sure."

"Does the father want to be involved?"

"He acts like he wants to be, but I'm not sure I can completely trust him."

Teresa nodded. "Are you in love with him?"

Bernie was thunderstruck by the question. "In *love* with him?" She shook her head wildly. "No! Of course not. "

"Oh. Okay."

"No, really. What happened between us was a mistake. We hadn't even been seeing each other. Not like that, anyway. And what happened between us is never going to happen again."

"Okay. So there's nothing between the two of you. It doesn't mean he can't still be a good father."

"If you knew who the father was, you might not be so quick to say that."

Teresa paused. "Care to tell me?"

What was the point in keeping it quiet any longer? The whole world was going to know soon enough, anyway. She might as well just spit it out.

"Jeremy Bridges."

For several seconds, Teresa just stared at her. Then her eyelids fluttered. She tilted her head, her brows drawing together. "Jeremy Bridges? That gazillionaire you used to work for?"

"Yes."

"Well, I'll be damned." She shook her head a little, as if trying to make that sink in.

"I know it seems a little weird," Bernie said. "Believe me, I know. A man like him, a woman like me..."

"Why? Because he's filthy rich and you're not?"

"No," Bernie said, feeling just a little bit pitiful. "Because he's dated some of the most gorgeous women on the planet, and guess which one he gets pregnant?"

"Hey!"

Bernie snapped to attention. "What?"

"Don't you dare put yourself down like that. You're one of the best women I know. I look *up* to you."

"What do you mean?"

"Look at everything you've done. You have a college degree. You were in the military. You're a bodyguard. You've traveled all over the world. Have I done any of that? No. And in spite of the fact that he gives you a lot of shit, Bill's more scared of you than he is of Max." She smiled. "I like that."

Teresa was kind to say all that, but the truth was that sometimes Bernie would trade every one of those accomplishments to be the kind of woman a man couldn't take his eyes off.

"What I'm trying to say," Teresa went on, "is that Jeremy Bridges would be lucky to get you, assuming you'd have him."

Bernie couldn't believe Teresa had just said that. Jeremy, lucky to have *her*?

Then again, why not? Maybe it would do him good once in a while to look at a woman as something more than a repository for silicone, bleach, and Botox. To dig a little deeper and find out what a woman was like on the inside. To have his brain challenged by a woman who read something more than Facebook entries and cereal boxes. But he clearly didn't believe in the importance of any of that, and she doubted he ever would.

"Thanks," Bernie said. "I appreciate all that. But to tell you the truth, I'm the one who looks up to you."

"Huh?"

"Why do you think I'm here? Because you're really good at something I don't have a clue about."

"You know I'll help you any way I can," Teresa said, then gave Bernie an offhand shrug. "And you never know. Maybe Jeremy will, too."

Maybe. But she wasn't about to count on that. If she wasn't careful, she'd start to depend on him, and pretty soon he'd realize that she and the babies were too big a drain on the lifestyle he'd so carefully built, and she'd be all alone again. In fact, it had been days since he'd last been at her apartment, telling her she needed to move. Was it possible he'd already reconsidered his role in all this?

She didn't know. She only knew that the biggest mistake she could make in this situation would be to count on anyone but herself.

"Even if he did want to be a part of all this," Bernie said, "it's probably not a good idea."

"Why not?"

"Because Jeremy Bridges is the most infuriating man I've ever met. If we stay in the same room for too long, we're liable to kill each other."

"Then how did the two of you ever... well, you know. Get together?"

"That was why it happened. Because he's so infuriating."

"I don't understand."

"One night when we were together, he made me mad. *Really* mad. For the first time in two years, I told him exactly what I thought of him, and God, did it feel good. But then everything went a little crazy. I remember we were arguing, and all of a sudden he was kissing me, and before I knew it…"

"Ah," Teresa said knowingly. "Anger sex."

"Anger sex?"

"Anger and passion. Potent combination."

"*God,* I wish somebody had told me that." Bernie dropped her head to her hands. "I've never done anything like that in my life. *Ever.* And now look what's happened."

"Yeah. You're going to have two beautiful babies."

Yes. She was. And if only she'd learn to think as positively about it as Teresa, she might actually get through it.

"Mama!"

Bernie whipped around to see Matt roll to his hands and knees and start crawling back toward Teresa. When he reached the coffee table, he put both hands on it and pulled himself to his feet. Teresa held out her hands.

"Can you walk to me, sweetie? Come here. Walk to Mama."

He took one shaky step, then a couple more, before falling into Teresa's arms. She scooped him up and plunked him onto her lap.

"Yay!" she said, clapping her hands. "You did it!"

He grinned and smacked his fists on his thighs, bouncing up and down, his diaper rustling. Teresa nuzzled his neck and made growly noises until he squirmed and squealed and giggled. Bernie basked in the moment, thinking if only she could conjure up the maternal feelings that seemed to come so naturally to Teresa, she'd be okay.

And she felt that right up to the moment Matt threw up all over again.

Teresa instantly pulled back, but the damage was already done, and her nose crinkled with disgust. "Oh, God. I would have sworn he didn't have any left in him."

Bernie winced. "I guess it's like shaking up a soda."

"Uh...yeah. You might want to keep that in mind for the future."

"I will," Bernie said as she rose from the sofa. "Gotta go."

Teresa smiled. "Don't blame you a bit."

"Thanks for the advice."

"Any time. And Bernie?"

"Yeah?"

"I know everything seems a little crazy right now, but someday soon you're going to look back on all this and say it was worth it. Will you trust me on that?"

"Yeah," Bernie said. "I hear you."

She left the house and got into her car, feeling just a little bit better about everything. Calmer. More in control. With a better perspective on motherhood. On life in general. She decided she'd go home, haul out those catalogs again, and this time it wouldn't look like a sea of stuff she had no idea how to navigate. She'd pick and choose wisely, make a list, and feel as if her life was in order again.

Ahh. She felt so much better.

Then she got home and saw the fence, and everything went nuts all over again.

Chapter
15

At first, Bernie couldn't believe her eyes. She blinked. Blinked again. It was still there, an eight-foot wrought-iron fence separating the street from the scraggly lawn of Creekwood Apartments. For a moment, she thought she'd taken a wrong turn and ended up at another apartment complex. She actually turned to look at the battered sign so she could make sure she was in the right place. The workmen scurrying around still had a ways to go before the place would be completely encircled, but that seemed to be the plan.

She pulled over, rolled down her window, and called out to a fifty-something guy in a grungy baseball cap with sweat rolling down his temples.

"Hey! What's with the fence?"

"Upgrading. The gate goes up next. Controlled entry."

Bernie blinked. "Here?"

The guy shrugged. "Believe me. I double-checked the address."

She couldn't believe it. Farnsworth had finally decided

to put a little money into this place? Granted, a new coat of paint for the siding and filling a few potholes would have been a better start, but maybe this was his way of doing something visible to improve things that the residents could feel good about. And she felt pretty good about it herself. She felt even better when she pulled into a parking space in front of her apartment and started up the stairs. The handrail that had been half pulled out of the wall was gone, and in its place was a brand-new iron railing screwed so securely to the wall that it could withstand a nuclear explosion.

She stared at it in awe for a moment, then looked over her shoulder at the building across the parking lot, where she knew there were others that needed replacing. But all she saw were the original rickety, rusty ones. She walked to the next building to check it out, but all the handrails there were the original ones, too. After a little more investigation, she came to the conclusion that hers was the only one that had been replaced.

That was weird.

Okay, so maybe Charmin had designated hers to be replaced first since she'd been the one screaming about them on everybody's behalf. But the new fence was something else entirely. That was a generalized safety issue the owner really wasn't obligated to address.

Wait a minute. A *safety* issue?

She stood there a moment longer, turning that over in her mind. And the more she thought about it, the more she smelled a rat.

She pulled out her phone. Hit speed dial six. A few moments later, Jeremy picked up.

"Bernie. How nice to hear from you."

"A fence. A controlled-entry gate. A new handrail,"

she said, as she strode back toward her apartment. "Do any of those things sound familiar to you?"

"Familiar? As in, did I have anything to do with them?"

"Yes."

"Of course I did."

For a moment, Bernie was speechless. "Then it *was* you? *You* got the owner to do those things?"

"Yep. And he was actually pretty easy to persuade."

"But it's not your place to persuade him!"

"But it was a piece of cake. See, it turns out the owner sees things my way. And he's such a nice guy, too. Handsome, intelligent, successful..."

Bernie stopped at the foot of the stairs leading to her apartment. Farnsworth was neither handsome nor intelligent, and what man could be considered successful if he ran a place like this?

"Bridges?" she said, a shiver of suspicion running up her spine. "What did you do?"

"What do you mean, What did I do?"

Then she felt silly for even thinking it. "Never mind," she said with a tiny laugh. "Even you couldn't have gone that far."

"Gone how far?"

"Far enough to buy my apartment complex."

"My God, Bernie. Do you think I'd actually *do* that?"

"Oh, all right," Bernie said. "That was crazy. I was dumb to even think it."

"No, you weren't. I bought your apartment complex."

For at least the count of three, Bernie was stunned into silence. Then it all came pouring out. "Bought it? You bought it? The *whole thing*?"

"One doesn't generally buy half of an apartment complex."

"No. No way. You couldn't have bought it. Not that fast."

"It's amazing how motivated one seller can be, particularly when he's looking at a cash sale. A standard contract, an expedited title search, thirty minutes at a title company, and voilà. Done deal. I've been looking to buy a little commercial real estate, anyway. And the price was certainly right."

"You didn't buy it as an investment," she said hotly. "You bought it because you're a big, fat control freak!"

"Hey, if you wouldn't listen to me and move out of that hellhole, what else was I supposed to do?"

"Are you completely out of your *mind*?"

"I bet you liked those improvements just fine until you found out I was the one behind them."

"You mean until I found out what a manipulative jerk you are?"

"I try to protect you, and this is what I get?"

"I don't need you to protect me!"

"Get used to it, Bernie. As long as you refuse to make the right decisions concerning our babies, this is how it's going to be."

Bernie heard the line click. He'd hung *up*? She held out the phone, staring at it in disbelief. Then she hit speed dial six again.

"Yes, Bernie?"

"Small flaw in your plan," she said.

"What's that?"

"You seemed to think my neighbor across the way was a little iffy. What are you going to do about the riff-raff you think is already inside the gates?"

"Ah," he said. "That's where the armed security guard comes in."

Bernie's jaw dropped. "Armed security?"

"Ostensibly for the entire complex, but just between you and me, he'll be focusing most of his attention on building six. See what an advantage it is to have friends in high places?"

With that, he hung up again. Bernie stabbed speed dial six. *Again.*

"Bernie," Jeremy said. "So nice to hear from you. It's been ages since we've talked."

"You know what? I think you were right in the first place. I need to move."

"Nah. You're not going anywhere. See, I checked out the local rental market. Turns out you're actually getting a deal there. As undesirable as your complex is, it's at least borderline livable. If you were to pay that price anywhere else, you really would be living in a slum. Give those workmen another few days, and you'll have a nice fence around the property and a shiny new keycard for access. Now, won't that be nice?"

And then he hung up on her for the third time, and for the third time, the sudden silence infuriated her. She gritted her teeth and dialed him back to give him an even bigger piece of her mind. But this time all she got was his voice mail.

"Damn it," she muttered, stuffing her phone back into her pocket. She'd had the opportunity to toss him down the stairs a few days ago. Why the hell hadn't she taken it?

She walked up the stairs toward her apartment. Ruby stepped out onto the landing.

"Nice handrail, huh?" she said.

"Yeah," Bernie muttered. "Nice."

"And did you check out the fence we're getting with the gates and all? You must have told Farnsworth you were going to blow his brains out, or something. Did you hold a gun to his head like in the movies?"

"It wasn't Farnsworth."

"Then who?"

Bernie unlocked her apartment door, then turned back. "You remember that guy who was here to see me a few days ago? The gorgeous one with the bad attitude?"

"The father of your baby?"

Bernie winced. Would she ever get used to hearing those words? "Yeah. He bought the place. He's our new landlord."

Ruby screwed up her face. "Why would he buy a crappy place like this?"

"Because he was born to piss me off."

"Nice things around here piss you off?"

"You have no idea."

"Well, they sure don't piss me off. Not for one minute. Would you tell him that while he's at it, I got a few things in my apartment that could stand to be fixed? Like maybe my leaky shower and the ants in my pantry closet. And I'm not so crazy about the holes in the carpet, either."

"Sorry, Ruby. I don't think he's interested in—"

And that was when it struck her.

Jeremy was the new owner. As far as she knew, Charmin was still around, but Bernie had already determined what a bottleneck she was. And if she was a bottleneck, who was left for the tenants to go to with their problems?

Why, the new owner, of course.

• • •

The next afternoon, Jeremy sat in his office, listening to his cell phone ring for approximately the twentieth time. This time he didn't even bother looking at the caller ID, much less answering it. He knew it was yet another call from one of the residents of Creekwood Apartments just dying to complain about something, so he let it roll to his voice mail with all the rest. Ms. Keyes wasn't faring much better with his office phone. She hadn't fielded this many calls since he'd dated a French supermodel who made Glenn Close in *Fatal Attraction* look like a cloistered nun.

He didn't even want to know what was going on with his home phone.

As the day had worn on, he'd come to two very important conclusions. He was sick to death of his own ringtone, and Bernadette Hogan had been born to piss him off.

It was almost five o'clock. She hadn't answered her phone all day, but by God, that didn't mean he wasn't going to keep trying. Heaven forbid he inconvenience her.

He grabbed his phone and dialed her number for the umpteenth time. Finally, after five rings, she came on the line.

"It's about time you answered your phone," he snapped. "God knows I've been answering mine."

"Oh?"

"Don't play stupid. I know what you're up to. Eighteen voice mail messages on my cell phone alone. My *personal* cell phone. How did they get that number, Bernie? You want to tell me that?"

"Who are 'they'?"

"You know who 'they' are! The tenants at that godawful apartment complex!"

"So today it's godawful? Yesterday it was a good investment."

"The calls are coming to my office phone, too," he said, standing up to pace across the room. "After today, Ms. Keyes is going to be demanding a raise."

"Stop being a tightwad and give it to her. She's worth more just for putting up with you."

"How about my home phone, Bernie? What's going on there?"

"With luck, there were so many incoming calls that the lines melted."

"Then it *was* you," he barked into the phone. "*You* gave them my numbers!"

"Well, in all fairness, you are the new owner. I've always heard it's best for a landlord to have a cordial relationship with his tenants."

"Cordial relationship? All they were doing was complaining! Stopped-up drains. Nonfunctioning appliances. Holes in the wall. Bugs. Everybody had something."

"So what does that tell you?"

"That Creekwood Apartments is a disaster area!"

"Exactly. And now you're the owner, which means it's your responsibility to fix all of it."

"I'm not fixing a damned thing. In fact, if I'm smart, I'll bulldoze the place and sell the land it sits on. And then I'm going to throttle you for having the nerve to give out my confidential phone numbers."

"I'm the mother of your children. I thought your goal was to protect me."

"I'll wait until the babies are born. *Then* I'll throttle you."

She sighed. "I suppose you're going to insist on coming over here to have a word with me about this."

"You're damned right I am."

"Well, whatever you do, don't come tonight."

"Will you be home tonight?"

"Yes, but—"

"Then I'm coming tonight. I'll be there at seven o'clock."

"Bridges! No! I don't want you here. Will you just—"

"Seven o'clock, Bernie. We have some talking to do."

Jeremy punched the button to disconnect the call and tossed the phone to his desk, trying to remember the last time he'd been this livid about anything. It was going to be a monumental pain in the ass to have his phone numbers changed, but if he didn't, he'd be a sitting duck. All those people would have carte blanche to disturb him night and day, seven days a week, and the thought of that was intolerable.

At seven o'clock that night, Max drove Jeremy into the parking lot of Creekwood Apartments. Jeremy eyed the partially constructed fence on his way in, a wrought-iron creation that looked totally out of place surrounding an apartment complex like this one. But if a security fence was what it took to show Bernie just how serious he was about her safety, he didn't care if it looked like the Great Wall of China wrapped around a pup tent.

Jeremy could tell Max was curious why they were going to Bernie's house, but he didn't ask questions. He'd probably just call Bernie later to make sure Jeremy had stayed in line. But Jeremy didn't want to stay in line. He wanted to throttle her just as he'd threatened, which meant Max would throttle him. But as mad as Jeremy was right about now, he decided it might be worth it.

He got out of the car. Three parking spaces away, a

pair of teenage boys leaned against a beat-up Camaro, smoking and trying to look tough. They were eyeing his Mercedes with a hungry look, most likely scoping it out for anything stealable. Given the security features on the car, they couldn't make off with much, but they could sure break a few windows trying. Then Max got out of the car and stood next to it, and suddenly those tough guys had someplace else to be. At least with him on the job, Jeremy felt relatively certain he'd come back downstairs later to an intact vehicle.

He climbed the stairs to Bernie's apartment, admiring the new handrail he'd had installed. He hoped it had made an impression on Bernie, but knowing her, she'd refuse to touch it just to spite him.

A moment later, he rapped his knuckles against her door three times. *Sharply.*

He heard a commotion inside, and it was a little while before she finally came to the door. The moment she opened it, he breezed past her into her apartment. "Sit down, Bernie. We have some talking to—"

It wasn't until he was well into the living room that it dawned on him that they weren't alone. Not by a long shot.

At least fifteen other people were in her apartment. The guy with spiky red hair from the balcony across the way. A bleached blond with gigantic silver hoop earrings whose last makeup purchase must have sent Maybelline stock soaring. A twenty-something guy wearing a tie-dyed T-shirt and five silver rings in his right eyebrow. A couple of old ladies, one in a leopard housecoat who looked approximately 130 years old. A young Hispanic woman with a baby in her arms and a toddler beside her.

One person who was so androgynous Jeremy couldn't begin to tell what sex God had meant *it* to be. An assortment of Texas good ol' boys in jeans and boots. Tattoos all around.

Jeremy stared in rapt disbelief, feeling as if he'd entered the Land of Misfit People.

"Folks," Bernie said, "this is Jeremy Bridges, the new owner of Creekwood Apartments." She turned to Jeremy with a sweet smile. "Mr. Bridges, these are your tenants. And they're just dying to meet you."

Chapter
16

Jeremy seriously considered turning around and walking out exactly the way he'd come in, dragging Bernie along with him to give her a considerable piece of his mind. But then one of the old ladies offered him a chocolate chip cookie, and another one handed him a glass of punch, and before long everybody in the room was hitting him with their problems like machine-gun fire and escape became impossible.

For the next hour, Jeremy heard about everything that was wrong with Creekwood Apartments—its management, its landscaping, its appliances, its floor plans, its sidewalks, its lighting, its sewer system, its location, and its orientation to the sun at the summer solstice. That last complaint came from a New Age Looney Tune with frizzy blond hair and a row of silver stars and moons lining the curves of her ears, who also believed that the complex sat on a seventeenth-century Indian burial ground. And through it all, Jeremy nodded and pretended to listen, but inside his head something different was going on.

He was seeing a very large, very loud bulldozer flattening this place until it was nothing more than a pile of rubble. Once the lot had been reduced to dirt, the dead Indians could ascend to the Great Spirit and his short but eventful career as a slumlord would come to a blessed end.

Finally he was able to maneuver people out the door by thanking them for coming and assuring them that their concerns would be addressed in due time, even though it was possible he'd be addressing them with the business end of that bulldozer. Then he had to endure every one of them shaking his hand on their way out and thanking him for showing up.

As if he'd chosen to deal with any of this.

Bernie closed her door behind the last person, then slowly turned to face him, still wearing that infuriatingly smug, self-satisfied expression he was dying to wipe right off her face.

"That," he said, stabbing his finger toward her, "was the most rotten, manipulative thing I've ever seen *any-body* do."

"Coming from the master manipulator, I'll take that as a compliment."

"What was the point of dragging me over here to hear in person what they griped about on the phone?"

"I didn't drag you over here," she said, circling her living room to pick up empty Styrofoam cups. "As I remember, you insisted on coming."

"You told me *not* to come. What was with that?"

She stopped in front of him, smiling sweetly. "It got you over here, didn't it?"

As she continued into the kitchen, he felt like the biggest fool alive. With a few carefully calculated words, she'd lured him in like a matador waving a red cape in front of a charging bull.

"After what you just did," he said, "you're lucky I'm not sticking you six feet under with the dead Indians."

"There may actually be some truth to that Indian burial ground thing," she said, dumping the cups in the trash. "I think that's why the lights flicker around here. Restless spirits."

"The lights flicker because the wiring in this place *sucks*."

"That's okay. You're going to fix it."

"Wrong. I'm not fixing a damned thing."

Bernie frowned. "What do you mean, you're not fixing anything? You could gold plate these buildings and never miss the money."

"I didn't get where I am by making bad business decisions."

"So putting a fence around this place was a good decision?"

Jeremy opened his mouth to speak, only to shut it again.

"So you're not above spending a ridiculous amount of money just to make a point, but you'd hate like hell to actually do some good with it."

"I donate to all kinds of causes, Bernie. You of all people should know that."

"Right. If you give to a good cause, it's because you're schmoozing somebody on the board of directors you need to do business with. Have you ever thought of doing something good that *didn't* further your bottom line?"

"These buildings are forty years old. Renovating them would be like putting a Band-Aid on a severed artery."

"Yet you bought the place," she said, raising an eyebrow. "And you call yourself a businessman?"

God, how he wanted to kick the crap out of himself for that. Yeah, he'd gotten this place for next to nothing, but when it was worth nothing, *next* to nothing was paying a premium. It was true he'd never miss the money. The problem was that he'd led with his emotions instead of his brain, and Bernie was making sure he paid the price for it.

"What about Charmin?" Bernie asked. "Does she still have a job?"

"The manager? She's staying on, at least for now."

"Have you actually met her?"

"Not yet. But Farnsworth said she's just the person I need."

"Right. This is the woman who found a potato chip that looked like Jesus and spent an entire afternoon in her office taking pictures of it so she could list it on eBay."

"She comes cheap."

"That's because she goes out of her way to do nothing. She locks the office door for two hours every afternoon so she can watch her soap operas. And when somebody complained once that her smoke alarm wasn't working, Charmin told her if that was true, maybe she ought to think twice about smoking in bed. That's the kind of crap these tenants have to deal with."

"Nothing's stopping them from moving somewhere else."

"You said it yourself. Any other place at this price is a slum."

"That's not my problem."

"Well, let me tell you what *is* your problem. You never look at anything from somebody else's point of view.

Lupe Alvarez's, for instance. The woman with the two little kids. Do you know she works two jobs just to make ends meet? All she wants is a working stove so she can feed her kids a hot meal."

"Bernie—"

"And Frieda Jackson. The older lady in the flowered pants. She's on Social Security, and she can't even afford the heart medication she needs, much less afford to live someplace else. You know. Someplace where the owner will make sure her kitchen sink drains like it's supposed to."

"Bernie—"

"And the skinny guy in the cowboy boots. Do you know he—"

"Bernie!" Jeremy said, holding up his palm. "Will you stop? This isn't a damned telethon."

Bernie glared at him. "Doesn't matter if it is or not. You wouldn't donate a dime."

"Where's all this coming from? You've never struck me as the bleeding-heart type."

"I'm not. It's just that the only problems that ever seem to get fixed around here are the ones I complain about. People found that out, so these days I pretty much do the complaining for everyone."

"And an interesting group of people they are," he said.

"Frankly, I had the same reaction when I moved in. I was in the military for years, where everything's uptight, upright, and squeaky clean. Then I started to figure out that what you see isn't always what you get. Yeah, there are a couple of rotten people who live here, but most of them are just people who are trying to get by. Don't you have any sympathy for them at all?"

"I'm going to say it one more time. I'm a businessman. And that's about it."

"So where you're concerned, what I see is *exactly* what I get."

"That's right."

"A heartless son of a bitch who puts money above everything else."

Jeremy felt a spark of anger. "Hey, I didn't ask for all this personal interaction. You're the one who shoved that on me."

Bernie's expression went cold. "Why did you have to buy this place? You could have just left well enough alone, but no. Now these people think you're actually going to do something for them."

"And that's my fault? Aren't you the one who handed out my phone numbers, invited them over for punch and cookies, and then duped me into coming over here?" He glared at her. "You did all that just to piss me off."

"Wrong. I did it because I hoped if you met the tenants face to face you'd see how much they need your help and you might actually *do* something about their problems."

"I'm a businessman, not a social worker. Why is that so hard to understand?"

Bernie gritted her teeth, glaring at him as if he were the most despicable human being ever to draw breath. "You know what? You're right. You have absolutely no obligation to these people at all. You've made your point. Will you just go?"

"Bernie—"

"No. Seriously. I want you to leave."

Frustration ate away at Jeremy until he wanted to hit something. He'd be a complete fool to spend the amount of money it would take to renovate this place, no matter how many people wished he would. Why didn't she get that?"

"Okay, Bernie. I'm out of here. Just understand that things aren't as simple as you make them out to be."

"You're filthy rich. Everything is simple for you, and to hell with the rest of us."

With that, she disappeared into her bedroom and closed the door behind her.

Jeremy stood there for a moment, fuming mad. He was right, of course. The best thing he could do with this place was to level it. It was within a few blocks of the train station, which meant the land was actually worth something. How much, he didn't know, but even a total moron could see that the buildings that sat on this land were liabilities, not assets.

He yanked open the door and stepped out onto the landing, stopping short when he saw he wasn't alone. The old lady in the leopard housecoat was leaning against the wall, puffing away on a cigarette. He thought he remembered her name was Ruby.

"You two were really having it out in there," she said.

Jeremy shut Bernie's door, then turned back to the old lady. "Do you always eavesdrop?"

"Yep. Every chance I get." She took a long drag off her cigarette. "So I guess you're just gonna let the place rot like Farnsworth did."

How had this happened? How had he gotten himself into this situation up to his neck? A week ago, his life had been going along just fine. Then Bernie had shown up pregnant, and everything had gone to hell.

"I haven't decided what I'm going to do with it," he told her.

"She helps us out a lot, you know."

"Bernie?"

"Uh-huh. Ever since she moved in. Why she lives in this godawful place, I don't know, because I think she could do better. But we're all pretty glad she's here."

That was becoming more and more evident with every moment that passed. Jeremy had never once thought of Bernie as a do-gooder, but he did think of her as somebody who took no crap from anyone. Maybe in this instance those two things were one and the same.

"She said you'd help us, too," the old lady said. "Guess she was wrong."

"I wouldn't hold that against her."

"I'm not holding it against her. I'm holding it against you."

Jeremy looked down the stairs and across the scraggly lawn, where an old man waited for his Boston terrier to pee on a holly bush. It was getting dark, and the shadows of dusk made the stained stucco on the building behind him look even more ugly and depressing.

"It's just business," he told Ruby.

"Hmm. With you being the father of Bernie's babies and all, it seems to me it's not business. It's more like family."

So she knew. He wondered who else Bernie had told. Then again, did it really matter? His relationship to her wasn't the issue here.

So why couldn't he get that word out of his mind? *Family.* It was a concept he'd always had such a hard time grasping, and as the years passed, it seemed to move farther and farther away, until it felt like a dream he'd had once that he couldn't quite remember.

"She's good to us," the old lady repeated. "So you'd better be good to her."

With that, she waddled back into her apartment, shutting the door behind her.

Jeremy couldn't believe it. Another threat? First Max, and now Ruby? How many more people were there out there who would come after him with torches and pitchforks if he so much as raised his voice to Bernie?

Shaking his head, Jeremy trotted down the stairs. Max stood leaning against the car, his arms folded, and there wasn't a potential car thief in sight. He opened the back door for Jeremy, then circled around and got into the driver's seat. As he drove out of the complex, Jeremy couldn't stand the silence any longer.

"I bought this place, you know," he said.

Max flicked his gaze to the rearview mirror.

"Yeah, that's right. I own this godawful apartment complex. She wouldn't move, so I bought it and put up the fence so she'd be at least halfway safe."

Max moved his eyes back to the road again.

"I bet you're wondering what was going on in Bernie's apartment."

Max was silent.

"She ambushed me," Jeremy said. "Had a bunch of tenants there with every complaint in the book. She thinks I should renovate the entire complex, even though it'd cost me an arm and a leg and leave me in an even worse negative position. The smartest thing I could do would be to bulldoze the place. Then the land might actually be worth something."

More silence.

"Okay. It's true I'd never miss the money. But how can

Bernie expect me to pour money down a rat hole? I'm a businessman. That's bad business."

"Do you want to make her happy?" Max said.

Jeremy blinked, startled that Max had finally spoken. And he was even more startled by the question he asked. Now it was Jeremy's turn to say nothing, mainly because he didn't know how to respond. What was Max asking him, exactly? If he wanted to get stuck with an underperforming asset just to make Bernie happy? Commit to months of construction and repairs just to bring a smile to her face? Spend thousands upon thousands of dollars to prove to her he actually had a heart? Was *that* what Max was asking him?

"Yes," Jeremy said. "I want to make her happy."

"Then you know what to do, don't you?"

Jeremy sat back in his seat, his shoulders slumping with resignation, unable to believe it had come to this. If he did what Bernie wanted him to, it meant his spine had morphed into a wet noodle, his intelligence had been neutralized, and his well-honed business sense had deserted him completely.

Good Lord. If any of his business rivals ever discovered what a sap he was, his professional life was over.

Chapter
17

The next afternoon after she got off work, Bernie drove to the entrance of Creekwood Apartments, both surprised and annoyed to see that the workers had finished installing the new gate. It was closed and locked. Opening it required sliding a keycard, but since she didn't have a card yet, she rolled down her window and punched the call button on the console. Waited several seconds. Punched it again. Waited again. She'd just reached out to push it a third time when she heard a voice boom through the speaker.

"For God's sake, will you keep your pants on? I'm coming!"

Charmin. Sounding even crabbier than usual.

"Charmin. It's Bernie. Can you open the gate?"

"Crap. It shouldn't be locked yet. Nobody's got their cards. I don't have time for this. I'm too damned busy."

Busy? What on earth was keeping Charmin busy? Was she trying to watch *All My Children*, order a pizza, and play Spider Solitaire all at once?

"Charmin?"

"Okay, okay! There. That should do it."

Bernie heard a click, and the gate swung open in front of her. She drove through it and started toward her apartment, only to let curiosity get the better of her. It was a little early to give Charmin a rent check, but it gave Bernie a really good reason to drop in and see what was contributing to her bad humor.

Bernie parked in front of the manager's office. When she went inside, she got the shock of her life. The TV was off, and Charmin's butt was actually *out of the chair.* She was digging through a file cabinet, the phone pressed to her ear. She looked as if she was actually . . . working?

"Yes, damn it, you have to be here at eight in the morning," Charmin snarled into the phone as she pulled a file from the cabinet. "Because those are your hours, Miguel!" She paused, listening, then raised her voice. "Since you hired on here, that's since when! Get your ass in here first thing in the morning, do you hear me? If I gotta be here, you gotta be here!"

She walked back to her desk, slammed down the phone, and tossed the file folder on top of a stack of folders already there. She ran a hand through her dark, frizzy hair and blew out an angry breath.

"Bad day?" Bernie asked nonchalantly.

"How is stuff supposed to get done tomorrow if my maintenance man just wanders in here late like he always does, two hours after he finishes his Egg McMuffin?" She picked up a piece of paper from her desk and waved it. "I got a complaint list a mile long!"

"What's new about that? You always have a complaint list a mile long."

"Yeah, but I didn't used to have an owner crawling up my ass to make sure it all got done."

"Wait a minute," Bernie said, suddenly coming to attention. "The new owner? He's the one making you do all this?"

"He e-mailed me this list this morning," she said. "Some of this stuff I've never even heard about, and he wants all of it done ASAP. Today was hell. Appliance deliveries. Unstopping johns. Replacing more of those damned handrails. I had to coordinate all of it. And starting tomorrow, a painting crew is coming in."

Bernie couldn't believe it. Jeremy had decided to renovate this place?

The most amazing feeling of delight and satisfaction shivered through her, bringing a smile to her lips. She didn't know exactly why he'd changed his mind. She only knew that right at that moment, she was very, *very* glad he had. And the fact that it was driving Charmin nuts was just icing on the cake.

"What are you smiling about?" Charmin snapped.

"The fact that things are getting done around here. That's a good thing."

"Good, my ass." Charmin tossed the list back to her desktop, practically snarling with disgust. "I missed *All My Children* today because I've been running around taking care of all this crap for the tenants."

"Isn't that what a manager is supposed to do?"

"If I wanted to actually work, I'd go get a real job." She picked up the remote. "I missed one of my shows today already. If he thinks I'm missing *Bridezillas*, he can think again." She turned her back to Bernie and hit the button to turn on the television. "I'm telling you, the guy's a major dumbass who doesn't know a damned thing about business. Why else would he spend all that money on a dump like this?" She made a scoffing noise. "What's he trying to do? Turn this piece of crap complex into Buckingham Palace?"

"Excuse me?"

Bernie spun around at the sound of the man's voice. And when she saw who the voice belonged to, the satisfaction and delight she'd felt earlier took a quantum leap.

The remote still in her hand, Charmin glared at him over her shoulder. "Who are you?"

"Who am I?" Jeremy took a few steps forward, his hands shoved into his jeans pockets. "I'm the dumbass who's spending all that money to try to turn this piece of crap complex into Buckingham Palace."

Charmin spun the rest of the way around, her eyes snapping open wide.

"And you must be Charmin," he said.

For maybe the first time ever, Charmin seemed unable to find her voice. Her mouth just hung open, as if her jaw had finally snapped from overuse. Behind her on the TV, a blond Bridezilla was insisting that the doves released at her wedding had to be dyed Tiffany blue.

"Charmin?" Bernie said, nodding toward the television. "You're missing your show."

Charmin quickly pointed the remote, silenced the TV, then slowly turned back around to face Jeremy, swallowing hard.

"Can I...help you?" Charmin said.

"Nope. This is something I can handle all by myself. You're fired."

Charmin's jaw dropped. "Fired? You can't fire me!"

"I just did. And I want you out now."

"Now?" She looked around the office, then zeroed in on the TV. "But my stuff—"

"Write down a forwarding address. Your things will be delivered within twenty-four hours."

Her eyes narrowed angrily. "If you think you're screwing me out of severance pay—"

"You'll get two weeks and whatever vacation pay you have coming. But I want you out now."

"This is discrimination!"

Jeremy drew back. "Excuse me? *Discrimination?*"

"You're firing me because I'm a woman! I'm going to sue!"

He looked at her dumbly for a moment, then turned to Bernie, shaking his head with disbelief. "God, she's awful."

"I believe I told you that," Bernie said.

"From now on, when you have a point like that to make, make it a little stronger, will you?" He turned back to Charmin. "Out."

Charmin's face was quickly turning purply red with anger, her teeth clenched so tightly her molars were in danger of cracking.

"You'll be hearing from my lawyer!" Charmin said. She scribbled her address on a sticky note pad, grabbed her purse, and headed out of the office.

"God, I hope she sues," Jeremy said, as Charmin slammed the door behind her. "I'd get all kinds of satisfaction watching my attorneys take her down in court."

"If you need somebody to attest to her incompetence on the job, I'd be happy to testify."

"And I'd be happy to take you up on that." He picked up

the to-do list from Charmin's desk. "I'll send somebody over here from my facilities department to fill in as manager for a while until I can get somebody in here permanently."

"It'll be hard to find the right person to manage this place," Bernie said. "Lots of work, but not exactly a lot of prestige."

"I know of an agency that can do some looking for me. I'll have them solicit some candidates and send me their resumes."

"So," Bernie said, taking a few casual steps toward Jeremy. "You've decided to renovate the place."

"Yes."

"You said that was like putting a Band-Aid on a severed artery."

"As it turns out, I can get a big tax break for neighborhood revitalization," he said, focusing on the list he held. "Then once the renovation is finished, I can raise the rents for new tenants. My accountant put together a five-year plan that shows that this place could actually be a moneymaker."

"Look me in the eye and say all that."

Jeremy looked up. "What?"

"God, you're a terrible liar."

"What do you mean?"

"You're going to lose your shirt on this place, aren't you?"

Jeremy turned back to the list, and for a long time, he didn't say anything. "I know you've never seen my bedroom closet," he said finally, "but losing one shirt is hardly a problem for me."

"You're not the kind of man who takes kindly to losing anything. So what happened to this just being business?"

"If I don't fix this place, you'll stay on my back for the rest of my life, so what choice did I have?"

"You always have a choice."

"But what would people say if they knew I owned this place and it looked like a slum?"

"You don't give a damn what people think, remember?"

"I need a business loss," he said. "Something to offset the obscene amount of money I make every year."

"Well, this place ought to give it to you. I'm starting to think you really are the dumbass Charmin said you were."

He shrugged offhandedly. "Maybe I am."

"And maybe you're finally doing something good just for the hell of it."

"Knock it off, Bernie. I'm no saint."

She took a few more steps toward him. "True," she said, her voice softening. "But you're not quite the sinner I thought you were, either."

He glanced up and met her eyes, then looked away again.

"I'm only thirty-seven years old," he said. "Where sinning's concerned, I'm just getting started."

"Glad to hear it. If you didn't do a little sinning now and again, you wouldn't be you."

"You're starting to aggravate me. Better quit while you're ahead."

She smiled. "Okay. I'm out of here."

She dropped her rent check on the desk, gave him one last smile, and headed for the door. She couldn't remember the last time she'd felt this good. He was going to take care of these residents. Whether he knew it or not, now that she'd seen this tiny glimpse inside him, he could never completely hide from her again.

A few evenings later, Jeremy sat in the back of the limousine, sipping Scotch and staring out the window at the dusky Dallas skyline as Carlos headed for the Lone Star Museum of Art. The starkness of that particular museum—a monolith of concrete, soaring ceilings, and hollow, empty space—had always depressed Jeremy, and the prospect of viewing the new exhibit of pre-Columbian art tonight didn't do much to instill the warm fuzzies into him, either.

Carlos pulled the limo to the curb in front of the museum. Max got out first and scanned the area like the good bodyguard he was. Jeremy got out of the car and walked into the museum with Max in his wake. Max moved off to take his position against one of those cold concrete walls, which seemed to suit his personality just fine. Maybe if he stood there without moving, partygoers would mistake him for one of the chunky, lifesize terra cotta figures in the exhibit, then gasp in horror when they saw him breathe. That might liven things up.

"So you decided to come after all."

Jeremy turned to see Phil standing behind him holding a martini.

"Why, I wouldn't have missed it for the world," Jeremy said, grabbing a glass of wine off a passing waiter's tray. "You know how much I love pre-Columbian art."

"Right. You love pre-Columbian art like a dog loves fleas. You're here because Alexis promised to introduce you to a beautiful woman."

"Yes. I'm looking forward to meeting her."

"Of course, ever since the news that you're going to

be a father, Alexis thinks the woman of your dreams is already right under your nose."

Jeremy sighed. As soon as Phil told Alexis that Jeremy was going to be a father, she assumed a marriage was also going to be in the works. It took Jeremy a good thirty minutes to assure her that wasn't the case. It wasn't until he agreed to meet the astonishingly beautiful, accomplished woman Alexis had in mind for him that she finally decided he meant what he said.

"That's because Alexis believes in fairy tales," Jeremy said. "Bernie is the mother of my children. That's it."

"Are you sure about that?"

"I told you I'm not interested in her."

"Yeah? You were interested in her at least once."

"That was a mistake."

"So she was just a one-night stand like all the rest?"

Like all the rest? Hardly. Even weeks later, Jeremy could still close his eyes and conjure up every nerve-zapping moment.

"Pretty much," Jeremy said, looking away.

"I think you're lying."

Jeremy whipped back around. "What the hell makes you think I'd have any interest in Bernie?"

"Because she's the only woman I ever saw who refused to take any crap from you."

"And that's supposed to be a *good* thing?"

Phil just smiled and took another sip of his martini.

"Jeremy! It's about time you showed up!"

Jeremy turned to see Alexis approaching, impeccably dressed as always.

"Hello, Alexis," he said, as they exchanged air kisses. "You're looking beautiful this evening."

"You're such a flatterer. I never believe a word you say."

"Now you're hurting my feelings."

"Impossible. You're a cold, cold man, Jeremy. At least that's what the press is saying."

"All that acquisition stuff? Now, you know that's just business. Sybersense is simply doing what's best for its shareholders."

"You'll get no argument from me," Alexis said. "There's nothing I like seeing more than our stock going through the roof."

"And where is this woman I just have to meet?" Jeremy said.

"Right over there," Alexis said, nodding her head across the room.

When Jeremy turned to look, he had to hand it Alexis. The woman was a knockout. Even at a distance, he could tell her eyes were a brilliant blue. She wore an emerald green dress that showcased her long, lithe body, and her chin was tilted up a degree or two, highlighting her sharp, patrician features.

Alexis waved at the woman, and she turned to look at them. Those ice-blue eyes instantly locked onto Jeremy's. She smiled and walked over, her gaze playing over Jeremy with the kind of self-assurance that only the most beautiful women in the world displayed.

Alexis introduced the woman as Madeline Rayburn. One of her perfectly manicured hands was wrapped around a glass of Chardonnay, and she shook Jeremy's hand with the other.

"Madeline is new in town," Alexis said. "She's the museum's new development director."

Jeremy smiled. "Congratulations."

"I'm sure you remember me telling you about Jeremy," Alexis said, as if she hadn't already spilled everything to Madeline, from his stock holdings to his favorite restaurant to his underwear preference. "He's the CEO of Sybersense."

"Yes," she said coyly. "Of course I remember."

Alexis leaned in and spoke confidentially. "He's also a shameless womanizer. Be careful, Madeline. He'll break your heart and not think twice about it."

Madeline let out a dramatic sigh. "Well, I suppose some men are just born to play the field."

"True," Alexis said, shooting a glance at Jeremy. "And some men just haven't found the right woman yet."

"And which one of those might you be?" Madeline asked Jeremy.

He gave her a suggestive smile. "I suppose that's up to you to find out."

"Well, it looks as if my work here is done," Alexis said. "You two get to know each other." She looped her arm through Phil's. "The mayor just arrived," she told him. "Let's meet and greet."

As they walked away, Madeline moved closer, and after only a few minutes of conversation, Jeremy had to hand it to Alexis. She was right. Madeline was beautiful, cultured, well-spoken, and well-educated, not to mention oozing with the kind of sex appeal that made him wonder how she'd gotten to her late twenties without a ring on her finger. Basically, she was all a man could want in a woman in one very attractive package. So why, as he imagined kissing her, undressing her, running his hands over her body, did he feel nothing?

Okay, so he felt *something*. He'd have to be dead and buried to feel nothing. But while Madeline might be a little more intelligent than most, when he could afford to be with the most stunning women in town, pretty soon there was nothing unique about any of them and he found himself wanting more.

He found himself wanting Bernie.

She worked right here at the museum. Day shift, but that didn't stop him from imagining her looking at him right now on one of the security cameras. If she were to see him, she'd see Madeline, too. And he could only imagine what she'd be thinking.

Come on, Bridges. Tall, blond, and gorgeous? Isn't it time you climbed out of that rut?

She's after your money, you know. They all are. Gold-diggers are a dime a dozen.

How many times do I have to tell you? The bigger the boobs, the smaller the brain.

God, how he missed having her with him for hours on end, tossing out sarcastic remarks like candy at a Mardi Gras parade.

Madeline was saying something about one of the pieces in the exhibit, but all Jeremy could hear were his own thoughts. The memory of that night in the safe room flashed through his mind. To say he had a preoccupation about making love to Bernie again was a serious understatement.

He even knew exactly how it would go.

It would be different next time. He'd make sure of that, because next time he'd be running the show. Of course, she'd protest at first, but only because they were oil and water, fire and ice, with the push-pull between them practically built into their DNA. But after a single sizzling kiss, her resistance would be gone, and he'd be controlling every moment. Choreographing every heartbeat. Dialing back the animosity. Turning up the sensuality. Shifting the furious heat of their first encounter into a slow, scorching feast for the senses. He'd take her slowly, deliberately, even as she begged for more, but he had all night to make love to her, and the next night, and the next...

"Jeremy? *Jeremy*."

He snapped to attention. Madeline was looking at him as if he'd grown two heads.

"You seem a little lost in thought," she said.

"Uh...yeah. Sorry. What were you saying?"

"Never mind. I think we need to change the subject." She smiled seductively and inched closer, reminding Jeremy of his promise to Alexis to show up and play nice, which meant he needed to put Bernie out of his mind. He'd worked endlessly these past several years to have the business, the money, the cars, the houses, and the jet-set lifestyle he'd always wanted. But the number-one hallmark of his success was the undivided attention of beautiful women, and he was going to try to do everything he could tonight to enjoy it.

"Hey, girl," Lawanda said as she bustled through the door. "Thanks for staying till I could get here."

"No problem," Bernie said, already gathering up her things so she could go home. "Did you get everything taken care of?"

"Done," Lawanda said, plopping down her cooler and her McDonald's sack. Evidently this was Big Mac night.

"Did you like the lawyer?" Bernie asked.

"Yep. Chick's badass. By the time she's through with my soon-to-be ex, the son of a bitch won't know what hit him." She dug through her cooler, pulled out a Red Bull, and popped the top. "Anything happen on your shift I need to know about?"

"Nope," Bernie said, sticking her iPhone into her purse. "Boring as always. Oh, wait. Some kid tried to climb up on one of the mummy cases. I radioed Carl to take care of it. That was my excitement for the day."

"Well, things are getting ready to pick up here in a minute," Lawanda said, clicking one of the monitors. "Yep. Lookie there. Fundraiser tonight. The rich folks are showing up already."

Bernie glanced at the monitor, which showed one elegant vehicle after another dropping the cream of Dallas's social crop at the museum's front entrance. The scene was far too familiar to Bernie, which was why, for the past twenty minutes, she had done only cursory checks of that camera, as well as those in the atrium where the event was being held. Now that Lawanda had finally shown up, she could get the hell out of there.

"It's kinda like watching the stars show up to the Oscars," Lawanda said. "Stick around and we'll rate the women's gowns."

"No, thanks," Bernie said.

"Better yet," Lawanda said, switching the screen to an interior view of the atrium, "we can pick us out a couple of rich men."

"Right. Those men wouldn't give us the time of day."

"Hey! Don't you go raining on my parade. As of tonight, I'm ready to do some man shopping."

"Well, good luck," Bernie said, pulling her backpack

up to her shoulder and heading for the door. "I hope you find the guy you're looking for."

"Well, I'll be damned," Lawanda said. "That didn't take long."

Bernie turned back. "What?"

"There he is."

"Who?"

"My dream man, of course."

Bernie's eyes flicked automatically to the screen just as Lawanda zoomed in, and what she saw nearly made her faint dead away.

Jeremy?

Chapter
18

Bernie stepped closer to the monitor, her gaze following the sculpted angle of his cheekbone, then sliding down to the sensual curve of his mouth. Even at the
distance the camera was pulled back, there was no doubt
about it.

It was Jeremy.

Bernie remembered the last time she'd seen him
dressed like this. Then undressed. She closed her eyes for
a moment, trying to drive the memory back to her sub-
conscious where it belonged.

No such luck.

"Mmm, *mmm*," Lawanda said with a swooning sigh.
"I do love me a man in a tux. Makes him look all James
Bond and everything."

Bernie swallowed hard, trying to keep her cool. Given
the fact that Jeremy attended events like this one all the
time, she'd always known the possibility existed that
someday she'd see him on one of these screens, likely
with a beautiful woman or two.

She just hadn't expected it to happen so soon.

She'd even imagined how she'd react. She would just shrug and move on to the next camera view as if he meant nothing to her. He *did* mean nothing to her, at least in that way. But if that were true, why were tingles spreading across the back of her neck like tiny fireworks exploding?

Lawanda pulled the camera back a little. Bernie saw the woman Jeremy was with, because of course there had to be one. It was Madeline Rayburn, the museum's new development director, one of those tall, gorgeous, genetically blessed women Jeremy was always drawn to. Without a doubt, he'd be taking her home, because women didn't say no to Jeremy. The party would start in the back of his limo, then continue all the way to his four-poster bed.

"Shit," Lawanda said. "He's with that new chick at the museum. Little hussy." Lawanda lifted her chin. "I'm twice the woman she is."

Pound for pound, Lawanda was twice the woman most women were, but Bernie didn't bother pointing that out.

She knew this was dangerous. She knew she should just walk away, but for some reason she was mesmerized by the sight on the screen, her feet glued to the spot where she stood. She knew a woman's worth had nothing to do with her appearance. So why, when she looked at Madeline, did she feel pea-green with envy?

She watched the way Jeremy was smiling at Madeline. When Bernie had been with him, there had been no smiles. Passion, yes, but only the kind fueled by anger. Lust, absolutely, but as primitive as it got. Hearts and flowers belonged to women like Madeline. Bernie was the kind of woman men like Jeremy denied having had sex with to their dying breath.

Of course, given her pregnancy, he'd have a hard time denying it now.

"I can see by your reaction that you're thinking about fighting me for him," Lawanda said, shaking her finger at Bernie. "But let me warn you. You may have your black belt and all that, but being pregnant will slow you down. And even though I'm short, I'm scrappy."

"You'd beat up a pregnant woman?"

"Honey, for that man I'd beat up a pregnant *nun*."

Bernie nodded toward Madeline. "Forget me. She's the one you're going to have to go three rounds with."

"Ha! That skinny bitch? I can take her in a heartbeat." She turned back to the screen. "Wonder who he is?"

"Jeremy Bridges," Bernie murmured. Just the sound of his name passing her lips made another little shot of fireworks sizzle between her shoulders.

"Jeremy Bridges? Wait a minute. That's the guy you used to work for, isn't it? The really rich guy?"

Bernie tore her gaze from the screen. "I have to get home."

Lawanda rolled her eyes. "Oh, all *right*. You already know the guy, which gives you first dibs. But the next sexy rich man is all mine."

"Rich men are a pain in the ass," Bernie said, hoping her words would counter her thoughts and Lawanda wouldn't see the hot flush inching across her cheeks. "You can have all of them."

"Well, then," Lawanda said. "I'd be a fool to turn that down, wouldn't I? But don't you forget that I did offer to share."

"And don't you forget to check out the other thirty-five cameras," Bernie said.

"Hey! You think I can't multitask? Multitasking is my middle name." She gave Bernie a smile and a wink, then turned her attention back to the monitors.

Bernie slipped out the door and started down the hall, feeling as if she were walking in a daze. She decided she'd leave through the door that was as far away from the atrium as possible, then circle around to the parking lot at the back of the building. She'd get in her car and go home, where she'd spend the rest of the evening as she always did, with the TV remote and something bland for dinner, and then endure an irritatingly chatty telephone call from her mother before she finally went to bed and got up to do it all over again. The thought of it actually made her sick to her stomach.

No. I can't do it. I can't.

She doubled back, ducked into the ladies' room, and sat down on the sofa, letting her backpack slide to the floor. She dropped her head to her hands, feeling breathless. Hopeless.

Manless.

She couldn't do it. She couldn't go home alone to the painful silence of her apartment, where all night long she'd picture Jeremy with Madeline and wish to God he was with her instead.

What's wrong with you? Shake it off. Did you really think he wasn't spending the past few months with every other woman in the Dallas metroplex?

This was stupid. *Stupid.* She knew what kind of man Jeremy was. That he'd decided he might like to experience a little fatherhood didn't mean he had any feelings for *her.* So why was she acting like a lovestruck fool?

Enough was enough. She was just feeling sorry for

herself. She didn't want Jeremy. She was just feeling overwhelmed and underappreciated and fat and ugly and *pregnant* while he was out there living it up. But that was his life, not hers. And it never would be.

Jeremy had assumed that Madeline would be working the room like the fundraising professional she was, so it might be a while before he could steer her into his limo for a night on the town, followed by a trip to his bedroom. But even as she greeted one guest after another and chatted it up with the philanthropic crowd, she used every opportunity she could to touch his arm, move in closer, and laugh softly at anything remotely funny he happened to say.

They'd be out of there sooner than he expected.

"So you're an art history major," Jeremy said. "This pre-Columbian exhibit must be very exciting for you."

Madeline looked left and right, then spoke quietly. "Can you keep a secret?"

"Of course."

"I hate pre-Columbian. I'm more of a modern art girl."

"But because of your position, you have to make nice about the exhibit?"

"Exactly." She leaned in so close he could feel her breath on his ear as she spoke. "The sculpture garden is more to my liking. Have you seen it?"

"A time or two," he said.

"There are a few new pieces. Would you like to take a look?"

"I'd love to."

"Follow me. I know a shortcut."

They dropped their glasses on a passing waiter's tray,

and Madeline led him on a circuitous route through the atrium, around an exhibit of semiprecious gems, and finally through a door that led to the sculpture garden. Max followed at a deferential distance, taking up his position at the window beside the door and turning statuelike once again.

The sun had dropped below the horizon, bathing the garden in a dusky glow. The landscaping was beautiful. The sculptures weren't, but Jeremy pretended to admire the latest addition—a few gigantic iron pieces twisted around each other. It looked like the wreckage of a 747.

"It's from Carillo's Warrior series," Madeline said. "What do you think?"

"What I think," Jeremy said, "is that it takes a trained eye to appreciate something of this quality."

"You're a very diplomatic man," Madeline said with a smile. "I suppose beauty *is* in the eye of the beholder."

They strolled over to another sculpture that Madeline described in glowing terms. Jeremy thought it looked like a giant garbage can with a weather vane on top.

"How do your patrons feel about these new pieces?" he asked.

"They've generated some excitement," she said. "Unfortunately, in this economic climate..."

"Everybody's a little strapped for cash."

Madeline sighed. "Yes. You have no idea how tiring it can be spending all day every day smiling and making nice with potential donors."

"Donors like me?"

Madeline moved closer, the evening breeze tossing her blond hair over her shoulder. "If you'd like to write a great big check, I certainly wouldn't turn it down. But trust me when I tell you—my interest in you has nothing to do with a donation to the museum."

Her subtle flirting had vanished, replaced by a blatant stare that let him know exactly what she was thinking.

"If you'll let me know when you're tired of smiling," he said, "maybe we could slip out of here. Hop in my car. I could show you a little bit of Dallas. The city lights—"

"I'm tired of smiling."

As she looked at him expectantly, clearly offering everything he thought he wanted and more, he actually felt disappointed. Was there any woman left on earth who was *hard* to get?

Truth be told, though, he wasn't sure he wanted to get this one.

No, you idiot. Of course you want her. She'll get you back in the swing of things where you belong. Do it now.

He pulled his phone from his pocket, intending to call Carlos to bring the car around. Then he heard a door open across the garden. He turned automatically and saw a woman emerge from the building.

Bernie?

For a few seconds, he just stopped and stared at her. It was the wrong time. He knew for a fact she worked the day shift.

But there she was.

"Stay here for just a minute," he said to Madeline, and started walking in Bernie's direction.

"What? Where are you going?"

"Just stay put," he said over his shoulder. "I'll be back in a minute."

He strode down the flagstone path behind Bernie. He called out to her. She turned around, looking surprised.

She was dressed as she always was. T-shirt. Jeans. No makeup. Straight, dark hair tucked behind her ears. He'd always thought of her as the kind of woman who faded into the wall the moment a woman like Madeline entered the room. Why, then, was he having a hard time even remembering what Madeline looked like?

"Hey, Bernie," he said, stopping in front of her. "What are you doing here? I thought you worked the day shift."

"Uh . . . I usually do, but I had to stay late tonight."

And suddenly he realized he didn't have a thing to say. So why had he even walked over here? For reasons he couldn't imagine, his heart was suddenly beating like mad.

"So . . ." he said finally, "how's the job?"

"Good. It's good." She glanced at the tux he wore. "Looks like you're here for the event tonight."

"Yeah." He smiled to himself. Okay. Here it came. *For God's sake, will you tie that tie? When are you ever going to grow up and dress like an adult?*

"So how do you like the Pre-Columbian exhibit?" she asked.

Jeremy frowned. What kind of question was that? She couldn't possibly be interested in his opinion of the exhibit. Why was she making stupid small talk as if they barely knew each other?

"To tell you the truth, it sucks." He glanced over his shoulder at Madeline, then lowered his voice. "Honest to God—only a moron would think that crap is art. And it's not just the new exhibit. Look around this garden." He pointed to one of the sculptures. "That one looks like somebody slashed a gigantic piece of aluminum foil with a machete."

She shrugged offhandedly. "I guess beauty is in the eye of the beholder."

Jeremy winced. Wasn't that what Madeline had said? What kind of response was that from Bernie, who once told him the painting in his foyer looked like two pigeons fighting over a ketchup-covered French fry?

"And speaking of beauty," Bernie went on, "it looks as if you met the new development director."

"Uh . . . yeah. Phil Brandenburg's wife is on the museum board. She introduced us. She thinks we'd make a perfect couple."

"She's right."

Jeremy blinked. "She is?"

"Of course. What more could you possibly want in a woman?"

Jeremy was growing more confused by the moment. "Aren't you going to tell me it's time I stopped dating blond bimbos?"

"No bimbo there," Bernie said. "I hear she has a master's degree from Vassar. Frankly, it's about time you dated a woman who's your intellectual equal."

"Intellectual equal?" he said. "When's the last time I chose a woman based on her intellect?"

"Never. But clearly you're branching out." She smiled sweetly. "Good for you."

Jeremy felt as if he'd landed on another planet. *Stop not being Bernie. I hate it.*

Then he had a thought. Maybe she was uncomfortable seeing him with Madeline like this, and it impaired her sarcasm. He wouldn't have thought that was possible, but what other explanation could there be?

"I know this must feel strange to you," he said.

Bernie's brows drew together. "Strange?"

"Seeing me with another woman."

"Why would that be strange? I've been seeing you with other women for years."

"You know what I mean. Me dating other women when you're . . . you know."

"Pregnant?"

"Yes."

"With your babies?"

"Yes."

"So you think it upsets me to see you with another woman?"

"Does it?"

Bernie laughed. "Of course not. No more than it would bother you to see me with another man."

Jeremy raised his eyebrows. "Another man?"

She smiled. "The fact that we're having children together doesn't mean we have to step on each other's personal lives, does it?"

"Uh . . . no. Of course not."

"Which means it's time for you to get back to Madeline." She paused. "And I'll get back to Dave."

Jeremy snapped to attention. "Dave? Who's Dave?"

She shrugged nonchalantly. "Just someone I'm spending the evening with."

"I didn't know you were seeing someone."

"Actually, I've been seeing Dave quite a lot lately." She looked at her watch. "And look at that. I'm late, and he's waiting for me." She nodded across the garden. "And Madeline is waiting for you."

Jeremy glanced over his shoulder to see Madeline pretending to look at one of the godawful sculptures even though she was clearly watching him and Bernie.

"Uh . . . yeah," Jeremy said. "I guess I'd better go, too."

With a tiny wave of her fingertips, Bernie started back down the flagstone path to the gate. As she walked away, he noticed—maybe for the first time ever—what a truly nice ass she had, filling out her jeans in a way that would get the attention of just about any man alive.

Jeremy frowned. It had obviously gotten *Dave's* attention, anyway. He'd never even met the man, and already he didn't like him.

He watched as Bernie went through the gate and out to the parking lot. He watched as she flicked open her car door with her remote. He watched as she got inside. He watched as she started the car. He watched as she—

"Jeremy?"

He spun around to find Madeline behind him.

"Do you know her?" Madeline said.

"Uh...yeah."

"From where?" Madeline said, as if she wasn't quite believing him.

"She used to be my bodyguard." Which was the only relationship to Bernie he cared to mention to Madeline.

"You're kidding."

"Nope."

"Hmm," Madeline said as she watched Bernie drive away, "now that you mention it, she does seem a little rough around the edges."

"Rough around the edges?"

"You know. As if a day at Elizabeth Arden would benefit her greatly."

For some reason, that irritated the hell out of Jeremy. He had a better idea. Maybe a day at boot camp would benefit *Madeline* greatly.

She sidled up next to him with a seductive smile. "Are you ready to go?"

A few months ago, he wouldn't have hesitated a single second. But now, as he looked at her, all he could think about was Bernie.

"Something's come up," he said suddenly.

Madeline drew back. "Excuse me?"

"I'm afraid I'm going to have to take a rain check for tonight."

Madeline looked positively astonished. She was clearly a woman who wasn't used to fighting for a man's attention. Jeremy sensed her weighing her options, trying to decide if risking a little humiliation was worth it.

"Of course," she said coolly.

Evidently it wasn't.

"Maybe we can get together another time," Jeremy said.

Madeline's eyes swept over him slowly, and she raised her nose a notch. "If I'm free in the next week or two, maybe I'll give you a call."

"That'd be great. Thanks, Madeline. It was very nice to meet you."

Evidently that was an even quicker dismissal than she'd expected. Astonishment flashed across her face, but she erased it as soon as it appeared. With a dismissive look, she simply turned around and walked away. Jeremy knew he was going to catch hell from Alexis for this, but he'd cross that bridge when he came to it.

A few minutes later, he and Max were in the limo, and Carlos was driving them back to his house. For once, Jeremy didn't mind that Max was mute. His thoughts were so consumed with Bernie's apparent plans for the evening that he wouldn't have been able to carry on a conversation with anyone. He sat back in the seat, his arms crossed, irritation eating away at him.

Dave? Who the hell was Dave?

That question loomed larger in his mind with every moment that passed. Also looming was the image of another man touching Bernie at that very moment. Logically, there was nothing wrong with that. He had no hold on her. This was a new century. That a couple had a baby together didn't mean they had say-so over each other's lives.

So why was it driving him straight up the wall?

He tried to get a grip. Tried to tell himself that he had no business getting in the middle of Bernie's relationships. Then again, didn't he have a right to know who she was dating? What if she hooked up with some guy who would be a bad influence on his children?

Once they were born, anyway.

And they grew up enough to be influenced.

But the day would come when it would be critically important that she associate with the right men. The more he thought about that, the more he decided that he was well within his rights to ensure that the mother of his children wasn't roped in by a guy who might not be good for her or the babies. He definitely needed to find out more about him.

"Max?" he said.

"Yes, sir?"

"Does Bernie know anybody named Dave?"

Max paused, presumably thinking about it. Jeremy hoped he hadn't suddenly forgotten how to speak altogether.

"Not to my knowledge, sir."

There it was. Proof positive that whoever this guy was, he wasn't somebody who'd been in Bernie's life for very long. Which meant that she'd probably just met him, which meant she was in that danger zone where a guy could be Mr. Perfect or Mr. Serial Killer or a hundred questionable things in between, and there was no way to know which one. Under normal circumstances, Bernie could take out any guy who might be a problem, but she was pregnant. Sometimes she didn't feel well. And the more the babies grew, the more off-balance she was going to be. As he'd told her once, pregnant women made excellent targets.

This could be a very serious situation in the making.

A few minutes later, they pulled up to his house. Carlos and Max left, and Jeremy went inside, grabbing his phone from his pocket and dialing Bernie's number. For a moment he thought she wasn't going to pick up, but after six rings, he finally heard her voice.

"Bridges? What do you want?"

She sounded a little snippy, which meant he'd definitely interrupted something. Evidently she and *Dave* were already in the middle of . . . well, whatever they'd planned to be in the middle of.

Don't think about that. Just make sure it comes to a halt. "We have some business to discuss."

"Business?" Bernie said disbelievingly. "What kind of business?"

"The kind we need to talk about right now. Can you come to my house?"

"Now? *Tonight?*"

"Yes."

"Aren't you with Madeline?"

"No."

"She's not there?"

"No."

"I thought she went home with you."

"I told you something came up," Jeremy snapped. "And I need to talk to you."

"No way. I'm right in the middle of something."

No. She wasn't in the middle of some*thing*. She was in the middle of some*one*. "I know. You have a date. But—"

"Why don't you just tell me what this is all about?"

"I can't discuss it over the phone."

"I told you I'm *busy*."

Jeremy didn't like the way that sounded. "But you have to come over right now," he said. "This concerns . . ." What the hell did it concern? "Creekwood Apartments."

"Creekwood?" When the pitch of her voice went up a couple of octaves, he knew he had her attention. "Is something wrong?"

"Will you just come over here so we can talk about it?"

"Bridges?" she said, skepticism creeping into her voice. "What's going on?"

"I'll tell you everything when you get here."

"Can't this wait until tomorrow?"

"I'm sorry to break up your date, Bernie. But I wouldn't ask you to do this if it weren't important."

He heard her let out a heavy sigh. "Okay. I'll be there in about fifteen minutes."

Jeremy felt a flood of relief. *Take that, Dave.*

Then he heard something in the background. A man's voice? Yes. That was exactly what it was. Well, it didn't matter now. Bernie was coming to his house, which meant that for this evening, anyway, the owner of that voice was out of luck.

As Bernie hung up, at first Jeremy felt victorious. Then a little underhanded.

Then a little clueless.

He needed some reason for dragging her over here. Something to talk to her about. Then he could work in questions about this guy she was seeing who had come out of nowhere who was only going to make her miserable.

He only wished he knew what that something was going to be.

Chapter
19

B ernie held out her phone, staring at it with confusion. Jeremy wasn't with Madeline after all? That made no sense. Anytime a tall, incredibly gorgeous blond popped up on his radar, he always went in for the kill. And given the way Madeline had been hanging all over him at that event, the two of them getting horizontal together should have been a foregone conclusion.

"Hey, lady!"

Bernie spun around, suddenly realizing that as she'd been talking to Jeremy, the man at the drive-thru window had been trying to get her attention.

"That'll be seven eighty-five," he said.

Bernie tossed her phone aside and dug through her purse to come up with a ten. She handed it to the man. He gave her change, then passed her the sack through the window.

"Thanks for coming to Dave's," he said with a smile. "Have a nice evening."

Bernie put the sack in the seat beside her and drove

away from the window, feeling dumber than she ever had in her life. The green neon "Dave's Hamburgers" sign reflected off the hood of her car, taunting her with just how ridiculous she'd sounded when she'd talked to Jeremy at the museum. A date with Dave? Had she actually told him that? Just the thought of it made her want to hide her head in shame.

She didn't know why she'd done it. She only knew that the moment she saw Jeremy with Madeline, she quit being rational. She imagined going home alone, right after stopping to pick up her favorite comfort food for the evening. Ever since her morning sickness had subsided, she'd had the appetite of a nutritionally challenged lumberjack, which meant that while Jeremy was making love to Madeline, Bernie would be making love to a double burger with cheese, an order of tater tots, and a chocolate shake.

Good Lord. How pitiful was that?

But now, it appeared, he wasn't with Madeline after all.

She swung back onto Park Boulevard and headed for Jeremy's house, feeling pretty good about that. Then again, if he wasn't with Madeline tonight, there was always tomorrow night. And if not Madeline, there was always some other woman. Jeremy would spend the rest of his life in the arms of one beautiful blond after another, and what would Bernie have?

Endless lonely evenings with nothing but fast food to keep her warm.

Ten minutes later, she was knocking on Jeremy's door. He answered quickly and motioned for her to come into his living room, talking as they walked.

"I'm sorry to interrupt your evening with... what was his name again?"

"Dave," Bernie said, and swore she felt her nose grow.

"What did you say his last name was?"

"I didn't say."

"What is it?"

"What is it? It's, uh...Berger. Dave Berger."

And just like that, her nose grew another inch and her pants caught fire. She was definitely going to hell for lying.

"Where did you meet him?" Jeremy asked, motioning her to the sofa.

She sat down, wishing he'd shut the hell up about it. "At a restaurant."

"How long have you known him?"

"Not long."

"What does he do for a living?"

"Will you knock off the dumb questions and tell me why you called me here?"

"Oh. Yes, of course." He pulled a stack of papers from his briefcase and sat down beside her. "I have six candidates for the manager's job at Creekwood. I need your input on which ones to interview."

For a moment, Bernie was absolutely certain she'd heard him wrong. "What did you say?"

"There are some good resumes here, but I want to be very careful about whom I hire."

"Hold on," Bernie said, holding up her palm. "Let me get this straight. You interrupted my date and called me over here at eight o'clock at night to see what I think of a bunch of *job candidates*?"

"You said I needed to find exactly the right person, so I thought I'd get your opinion."

He handed her the papers. She flipped through them.

As impossible as it was to believe, he really had handed her a stack of resumes.

"Is this some kind of a joke?" she said.

"Joke?"

"There's nothing here we can't talk about tomorrow."

"But you of all people should know how important that job is. Charmin terrorized those tenants for years. I need to find somebody who can undo all the damage she did and move forward from there."

"Yes, you do," Bernie said, trying to keep from shouting. *"Tomorrow."*

"If you'll take a look at the one on top, you'll see—"

Bernie stood up suddenly. "I'm going home."

"Hey! I thought you cared about the people at Creekwood."

"Oh, come on! It doesn't change anything for the residents if I read these tonight or in the morning. It is, however, starting to make me think you've completely lost your marbles."

She tossed the resumes onto the coffee table and headed for the door.

"Bernie! Wait!" He jumped up off the sofa and came after her. "You're here now, aren't you? Why can't we just get the job done tonight?"

"Because I have a *date*, that's why!"

She yanked open the front door and trotted down the steps with Jeremy in close pursuit.

"Bernie, wait."

She reached her car and grabbed her driver's door handle, but before she could open it, he put his hand against it the door.

"Will you *wait*?"

She spun around to face him. "You're doing it again. You're just so damned sure that whatever you want to do is way more important than what anybody else wants to do, and the moment you snap your fingers, they're supposed to jump. Well, I'm getting pretty damned tired of it."

"Hey, I was willing to give up my date. Why can't you do the same?"

"You dumped Madeline so you could stay home and read a bunch of resumes? What's *wrong* with you?"

"Nothing's wrong with me. It's just business."

"Business. Right." She shook her head with disgust and yanked open her car door. She slid into the driver's seat, but he grabbed the door before she could close it.

"Bernie, wait."

"Let go of the door."

"You're not leaving. Not yet."

"I don't believe this," Bernie said. "I had a date with a great guy, and you screwed it up for me? How rotten is that?"

"I didn't mean to screw it up!"

"Yeah? Well, what did you think would happen if you insisted I drop everything and rush over here?"

"Okay," he said with irritation, "so I meant to screw it up. But only because I was worried about you."

"Worried?"

"You've never talked about this guy before. How am I supposed to know if he's on the up and up?"

"Okay," Bernie said, looking up at him, "before I completely blow my stack, I'll give you about ten seconds to explain why you think you're entitled to know anything about the men I date."

"Because those are my babies you're carrying."

"*Your* babies? My God. Could you *get* any more prehistoric?" She yanked her keys out of her purse. "I'm leaving now. And as soon as I'm out of here, I'm calling Dave to apologize for leaving him high and dry. With luck, he'll forgive me. But if he doesn't, it's *your* fault!"

"Bernie?"

She stopped short. "What?"

Jeremy tilted his head. "What's that?"

"What's what?"

He looked past her, pointing to the passenger seat of her car. *"That."*

Bernie whipped around. And the moment she was reminded of what was sitting there, she knew she was screwed: the fast food sack with "Dave's Hamburgers" emblazoned on its side in huge, cherry-red letters.

She looked back at Jeremy, hoping he wasn't putting two and two together, but judging from the look on his face, math was clearly his strong suit.

He reached into the car and plucked her keys from her hand.

"Hey!" she said. "What are you doing?"

Jeremy circled around the car and yanked open the passenger door. She grabbed the sack, but as he slid into the seat, he managed to snatch it away from her.

"Well, look at this," he said, his voice laced with sarcasm. "You're dating a hamburger."

Bernie's cheeks heated up with embarrassment. She opened her mouth, praying words of explanation would miraculously materialize. They didn't.

"Do you two see each other often?" Jeremy asked.

Bernie had never felt so humiliated in her life. She had a fleeting thought that maybe Jeremy would believe she was dating the *owner* of Dave's Hamburgers, but she'd already put so many lies out there tonight that she wasn't sure she could sell one more.

"I can't believe this," he said, dropping the sack on the floorboard. "You laid a guilt trip on me for making you miss your date with a man who doesn't even exist?"

"But you didn't know he didn't exist!"

"That's not the point. You're the one who started all this by lying to me in the first place!"

"And you would have never known I lied if you hadn't tried to get in the middle of things!"

"Your fictitious boyfriend was obviously for my benefit," Jeremy said, "so what were you trying to do? Make me jealous?"

"If I was trying to make you jealous, then why did I tell you I thought Madeline was perfect for you? Wouldn't I want you *not* to leave with her?"

"Reverse psychology," he said, tapping his temple. "You know I always do exactly the opposite of what you tell me to."

She snorted. "Well, *that's* certainly the truth."

"I still don't have an answer. Why did you make up a boyfriend?"

Bernie hated the knot that formed in her throat when she tried to come up with a response. But even more, she hated that the only thing left to tell him was the truth.

"Fine," she said. "I'll tell you why. Because you were going home with a gorgeous woman, and I was going home with a sack of fast food." She paused, her voice dropping into the humiliation zone. "I didn't want you know just how pathetic I am."

"Pathetic? You're not pathetic."

"Knock it off, will you? I'm only a few years from forty and pregnant with twins. What man is going to want to buy into that?"

"Is your self-image really that crappy?"

"I'm just being realistic. Even before I got pregnant, men weren't exactly standing in line, waiting to ask me out."

"Maybe that's because you intimidate the hell out of them. It's hard for the average man to get up close and personal with a woman when he knows she can dismember him with her bare hands."

"I don't intimidate you."

He smiled. "That's because I'm above average."

"And so humble, too."

"Frankly, Bernie, you're pretty above average yourself. And I'll admit it. When I thought you were with another man, I got just a little bit jealous."

Bernie was astonished. Jeremy Bridges, a man who could have any woman on the planet, was telling her he was jealous of her seeing another man? She basked in the thought of that for a whole five seconds. Then the truth of the matter struck her right between the eyes, making her feel even more pitiful than before.

"You're such a liar," she said, turning away. "You're just saying that because you feel sorry for me."

"Feel *sorry* for you?" He actually laughed a little. "Uh...no. I'm afraid I'm not the pitying kind."

"You dragging me over here has nothing to do with jealousy. It has to do with your stupid controlling nature. You're every bit as possessive of me as you are of these babies. And, for that matter, everything else within range of your voice. You need to work on that, Bridges. It's a real character flaw."

"One vice at a time," he said. "Let's deal with my jealousy issues first." He came forward, resting his forearm on the console between them. "Come closer."

She looked at him skeptically. "Why?"

"I want to make sure you hear every word I'm going to say so you don't jump to any more dumb conclusions."

The intensity of his gaze drew her in, enticing her to lean toward him.

"Closer," he said.

When she didn't move, he took hold of her arm and pulled her forward until their lips were only inches apart. Suddenly in his space, she felt every bit of the magnetism he held for the women of the world and realized she wasn't immune to it. She'd never be immune to it. No matter how maddening his arrogance could be, no matter now much she protested to the contrary, she'd be drawn to this man until her dying breath.

"Listen up, Bernie," he said softly. "Are you listening?"

He was so close now that she could feel his breath as he spoke. In the darkness of the car, each second seemed to drag on endlessly. The August heat, even after dark, permeated the car, adding to the feeling that everything was moving in slow motion. Everything except her heart, of course, which was fluttering like a pair of hummingbird wings.

"I'm listening," she said.

"I told you the truth. I was jealous. Don't ask me why, because I'm still not completely sure myself. All I know is that by time I left that museum, I'd already decided that if any man was going to touch you tonight..." His voice dropped to a near whisper. "It was going to be me."

Very slowly, very deliberately, he leaned in, closing

the gap between them, until his lips fell against hers. His hand was warm on her shoulder, and she leaned into him, letting the heat of his kiss wash over her. He was strong and solid and confident and most of all, he wanted her, and, God, how she wanted him, so much that her breath deserted her. All she'd been able to think about all night was Jeremy, and the thought of him being with Madeline was just about the most painful thing imaginable. But now, unbelievable as it was, he was here with her. With *her*.

Her hand found its way around his neck, and she threaded it through his hair to pull him closer, her whole body tightening with desire, every cell aching for him. His hand seared a path along her arm, then moved to her thigh, his fingers grasping, releasing, at the same time his lips moved across her cheek and down her throat. She tilted her head back, asking for more, and he kissed her again and again, then dragged his lips back up until she felt his breath hot against her ear.

"Do you want me, Bernie? Do you?"

"God, yes," she said breathlessly. "You know I do. I made up a boyfriend just to get your attention. Hell, *yes*, I want you."

"My house. *Now*." He jerked himself away and opened the passenger door, giving Dave an accidental kick that sent a few tater tots flying. Or given the way he felt about Dave, maybe it hadn't been so accidental. Jeremy circled around the car and yanked open her door. By the time he offered his hand, she was halfway out, and he helped her the rest of the way.

He started to shut the door, only to stop short, breathing hard, as he stared down at the driver's seat.

"What?" she said.

"I don't know," he said, pointing. "What's that?"

She leaned in and looked at the spot where she'd been sitting only a few seconds before. "Oh, my God."

Jeremy swallowed hard. "Is that . . . ?"

She looked closer, still unsure, but then she realized it could be only one thing. She could barely choke out the word. "Blood."

"The hospital," he said. *"Now."*

Chapter

20

Twenty minutes later, Bernie was in the emergency room, flat on her back on an ultrasound table. Jeremy sat in a chair beside the table, his elbows on his knees, his hands clasped in front of him. He looked genuinely worried, which made Bernie worry even more. In spite of all the hard times she knew were coming her way because of the babies, she knew now just how desperate she was *not* to lose them.

The doctor squirted the goopy stuff on her abdomen and ran the transducer across it. "Any bleeding before today?" she asked.

"No," Bernie said. "None."

The doctor moved the transducer one way, then another, watching the screen the whole time. Bernie tried to make sense of the images, but for all she knew, the black-and-white blobs could have been the topography of the moon.

"Are the babies okay?" Bernie asked, terrified of the answer she might receive.

"Take it easy," the doctor said. "They're fine. You're in no immediate danger of losing the pregnancy."

"Thank God," Bernie murmured. She turned to Jeremy in time to see his eyes drift closed and his shoulders sag with relief.

"But there is something going on we need to watch. See that dark spot?" she said, pointing to the screen. "That's a subchorionic hematoma."

"What's that?"

"A gathering of blood between the membranes of the placenta and the uterus. In other words, a blood clot."

"Is that dangerous?"

"It's not a big one, so probably not. Most of the time a clot that size will bleed out or be absorbed. But until that happens, it'd be a good idea for you to go on bed rest."

Bernie came to attention. "What?"

"If you'll just stay in bed for a couple of weeks, it's possible that—"

"Wait a minute. No. I can't stay in bed. I have to work."

The doctor shook her head. "Not a good idea. A clot increases your chance for miscarriage. Activity only aggravates it. You need to be on bed rest. You can get up to go to the bathroom, maybe have dinner at the table if you want to. No heavy lifting, though, and no sex. Have your doctor recheck you in a few weeks. If the clot is gone, the danger is over, and you should be able to go back to work."

"And if it isn't?"

"More bed rest. More monitoring. Depending on the severity of any future bleeding, possible hospitalization until delivery."

Bernie felt a flood of anxiety, her thoughts spinning a hundred miles an hour. If she didn't work, she didn't get paid. If she was gone long enough, her health insurance would be in jeopardy.

"But I have only a few days of sick leave left. I can't possibly stay home from work all that time. And my job is very sedentary. I do nothing but sit all day. Surely that would be okay."

"For the health and safety of you and your baby, my recommendation is bed rest. But in the end, it's up to you."

After the doctor left the room, Jeremy looked at Bernie with worried eyes. "Are you okay?"

Bernie closed her eyes. "Not really."

"The babies are going to be all right."

"As long as I don't work. That's going to be a problem."

"Maybe not the problem you think. You get dressed. I'll go to the desk and make sure they have your insurance straight and the bill is settled. Then we can get out of here."

As Jeremy left the room, Bernie took off the gown and put on her shirt. The nurse had given her a plastic bag for her jeans and a pair of scrub pants so she'd have something to leave the hospital in. She stuffed the jeans in the bag and put on the pants. They had little hearts all over them. Bernie had never felt so ridiculous in her life.

A few minutes later, she walked out to the waiting room, barely slowing down as she passed Jeremy. "Let's go."

He rose and followed her. "We need to talk about this."

"There's nothing to talk about."

"How are you going to work out this bed rest thing?" he said, walking alongside her.

"I'll figure something out. It's only for a few weeks."

They went through the sliding glass doors into the parking lot. It was dark now, with only the weak halos of a few streetlights gleaming through the moonless night. "What if it's for more than a few weeks?"

"I'll figure that out, too."

Jeremy clicked to unlock the doors to the car and they got in.

"So what's your plan?" he asked her.

"Start the car."

"As soon as you tell me what's going to happen if you can't work for a few months."

She didn't want to go into this. She didn't want to tell him that she needed every spare dime she had now, along with every one she'd earn in the future, for her mother's care when she got to the point that she couldn't take care of herself. The idea of her mother going into some dark, depressing nursing home filled with heartless employees because she didn't have insurance and couldn't afford anything better was more than Bernie could stand.

Only now it wasn't just her mother she had to worry about. It was the babies, too. Being a mother herself meant she'd never work as a bodyguard again and make that kind of money, and whatever money she did make would undoubtedly come from some boring eight-to-five job she hated. It was an uphill battle that seemed harder to fight with every day that passed.

"It'll put me in a bind," she admitted. "I have some sick leave coming, but only a few days. I need the money."

"Screw the money."

"Spoken like a man with plenty to spare."

"That's right. I have plenty to spare. Which is why,

number one, your rent checks are no good with me, so
don't even waste the paper it takes to write one. But right
now, that's irrelevant, because, number two, you need to
stay with me."

Bernie froze. "What?"

"Just until you're back on your feet again. It's a rational
solution. It'll cut your expenses, and you need somebody
helping you. Mrs. Spencer will be there to get your meals
and anything else you need."

Bernie was flabbergasted. "No way. I'm not staying
with you."

"Why not?"

"Because it's not necessary. I just need groceries. My
mother can bring them to me."

"You heard the doctor. It could be two weeks or two
months. Do you really want to be stuck inside your apartment all that time? In bed, no less?"

She opened her mouth to respond, but when a lie was
all she could manage, she shut it again.

"I'll take that as a no," Jeremy said.

"I can stay with my mother."

"Is that what you really want to do?"

Once again, she didn't respond.

"Another no," Jeremy said. "You're staying with me."

She looked at him with irritation. "Have you ever
thought about asking instead of demanding?"

He looked confused. "Asking?"

"Is it really so hard to be nice?"

"Nice?"

Good Lord. Was she speaking Farsi? "You know. Offer
something nicely. Instead of saying, 'You're staying with
me and that's that,' why don't you try this: 'Bernie, I'd be

delighted to have you stay with me until you're back on your feet again.'"

"Sorry. I'm not very good at nice."

"Oh, give me a break. You pour on the charm so thick sometimes it damn near smothers people."

"So that's what you want me to be? Charming?"

"Let's put it this way. Right now, I'd rather you be insincerely nice than sincerely demanding."

"How about I just give you a good, logical reason? In the weeks you're staying with me, I can move your apartment to the top of the list for renovations. New paint, new appliances, new window coverings. You shouldn't be around those fumes when you're pregnant, anyway. You want the place nice for the babies, don't you?"

She thought about that for a moment. "Okay. So that's logical. But there's still something you haven't considered when it comes to the two of us occupying the same house."

"What?"

"You know our history. We fight about everything. Sooner or later we'll kill each other."

A sly smile stole across his lips. "There are a lot of things I'd like to do to you, Bernie. Killing you isn't one of them."

She felt a tremor of awareness that shuddered right down to her fingertips. The memory of him kissing her in the car came back so vividly that for a moment all she could think about was him touching her again. How would she ever be able to deal with those feelings if she was living in the same house with him?

"You heard my doctor," she said. "Sex is out of the question right now. Not that we'd be having it even if it weren't."

"Oh, yeah? An hour ago, you wanted it as much as I did."

"Okay. So let's say it eventually happens. What comes after that? You wait for me to chase you for an encore so you can avoid my calls and pretend I don't exist?"

"What?"

"It's your pattern with every woman you've ever been with, and I'm not interested in being one of them."

"I think you're protesting too much."

"And I think you have an ego the size of the Grand Canyon and can't comprehend a woman telling you no."

"You didn't tell me no tonight."

"You're right," she said with a sigh. "And if I'd gone through with it, it would have been a big mistake."

"Why?"

She leaned back in the seat, suddenly feeling even older than she was and so tired she could have slept for a week.

"Do I even have to explain it? The last time we had sex, things got a little complicated. I don't want any more complications. I'm only a few years from forty. I'm pregnant with twins. I have responsibilities you can't even fathom. You have the time and the money for fun and games. I don't."

"Okay, then. Forget sex."

Bernie's eyebrows flew up. "Did you just say 'forget sex'?"

"Yes. It was hard to form the words, but I managed. Do I get points for that?"

"Only if you stick to it. If I stay with you, you have to promise me that what happened between us in the car tonight will never happen again."

Jeremy didn't like the way that sounded. Too final, as

if she didn't mean just for now, while she was on bed rest. She meant forever. And he was shocked at how miserable that made him feel.

But it didn't have to be final, did it?

The problem was that she didn't trust him. She assumed as soon as she moved in with him, he'd move in on her. Not that they could actually have sex. The doctor had ruled that out. But she thought that was all he was after. The truth was that he knew Bernie, and it wasn't in her nature to take it easy. If she was under his roof, he'd know for sure she was following doctor's orders. But he had to be smart about it. After the thing with Madeline, Bernie thought she had a monopoly on reverse psychology.

Not true.

"I have a guest suite," he told her. "Living room, bedroom, bathroom, balcony. Very comfortable. It's in a separate wing of the house. Practically in another zip code. Mrs. Spencer can bring your meals to you. You'll be well taken care of. And the best part?" He paused. "You'll never even have to see me."

She looked a little undecided about that, and for a moment he thought she was going to object right off the bat and tell him she didn't want to spend weeks in that guest suite all by herself.

"Thank you," she said. "That sounds perfect."

Jeremy felt a little quiver of disappointment, only to tell himself it would be short-lived. He'd just have to let solitary confinement take its toll. Within a few days, she'd be clawing at the door, begging for a little company, and he'd be happy to oblige.

Chapter
21

Bernie had been a little uptight at the prospect of telling her ultraconservative mother she'd decided to live with a man without the benefit of marriage. She needn't have worried. As it turned out, when the man she was moving in with was the father of her babies, it wasn't a sin. It was a blessing.

Blessings. She'd had an awful lot of those lately. Maybe more than she deserved. *Way* more. She tilted her eyes heavenward. *Thanks a lot, God.*

As she lay in bed, squinting against the morning light pouring through the blinds, her mother swept through her closet and bathroom, collecting clothes and toiletries for her to take to Jeremy's house. It made Bernie dizzy just to watch her.

She'd called Gabe first thing that morning to tell him she'd be out for at least two weeks, maybe more. He told her not to worry, that she had sick pay coming, and of course her job would be waiting. All wonderful things, assuming her incarceration lasted only two weeks. If it lasted longer, she didn't want to think about the consequences of not drawing a paycheck.

"There! I think that about does it." Her mother came back into the room pulling a large suitcase on wheels and parked it near her bed. "That should be everything you need. When did you say someone is picking you up?"

"Noon."

Eleanor sat down on the end of the bed where Bernie lay. "Bernadette? Now that the two of you have cleared up that little misunderstanding about his involvement with the babies, does this mean..."

"What?"

"You know...that the two of you..."

"No! Absolutely not. *No.*"

"But you're going to be living with him, aren't you?"

"Mom, I explained this. He's just helping out. There's nothing between us."

Her mother tilted her head with a knowing smile.

"I mean it," Bernie said. "Don't think for one moment that anything is going to come of this."

"I know you say that now, but—"

"No *buts.* I'll be on one side of that big house of his, and he'll be on the other."

"Speaking of his house," she said, leaning in, her eyes bright. "What's it like?"

"It's a big, overblown monstrosity that's a ridiculous place for a single man to live."

"Well, there'll be two of you now, so maybe it won't be so lonely for him."

"I told you I won't even be seeing him."

"But you never know what might happen in the future."

"To tell you the truth, Mom, I thought you'd be upset about me living with a man I'm not married to. You don't really like that sort of thing."

"Well, of course it's not the ideal situation," Eleanor admitted. Then she looked down at her daughter's ever-expanding waistline and whispered, "But I think that horse has already left the barn, if you know what I mean."

Once again, Bernie was amazed. If it meant Eleanor could have yet one more thing she wanted desperately—a son-in-law—her power to rationalize was staggering. *No problem, sweetie. Once you've cavorted in sin, why not live in sin?*

Then Eleanor's face grew serious. "Bernadette? Will you promise me something?"

"Sure, Mom. What?"

"Promise me you'll at least try?"

"Try what?"

"Try to show . . . you know. That other side of you?"

"Other side?"

Her mother sighed. "Where men are concerned, you tend to be . . . well. You know."

Okay. Now Bernie understood what her mother was saying. *Try to be girly enough that the father of your babies will fall madly in love with you so then you'll get married and have a perfect family and we'll all live happily ever after.*

Her mother had been singing that same song since Bernie was seventeen and didn't have a date for the prom. *Here, try on these earrings. Isn't this eye shadow pretty? Maybe you should wear something besides black. There's that nice boy in your algebra class. If you'd just smile once in a while . . .*

Most of the time, Bernie could just blow off her mother's not-so-subtle hints. But it was harder to take these days than usual, especially since she was going to be staying with Jeremy. She couldn't stop thinking about how she measured up to the women he dated. It felt stupid and shallow and desperate, but she just couldn't help it. Yeah, he said he was jealous last night, but that was just his nature. He wholeheartedly believed that there wasn't a solitary thing on planet earth he couldn't have if only he decided he wanted it. And Bernie had discovered he wanted something the most when he thought he couldn't have it.

She started to tell her mother for the hundredth time that all the prodding in the world was never going to turn this frog into a princess, and it didn't matter anyway because *she wasn't even going to see Jeremy,* only to be interrupted by a knock at her door.

"That must be Carlos," Bernie said.

"Do you want me to come along? Help you get settled?"

"No!" Bernie said, then took a breath. "I mean, no, you don't have to bother. Jeremy's housekeeper is there to help."

"My. A housekeeper. He's very wealthy, isn't he? It's always nice when a man has plenty of money to provide for his family."

Bernie was practically clawing the bedsheets in frustration. "Family? No, Mom. That's not the way it's going to be."

A sly smile crossed her mother's lips. "I've been praying, you know."

And knowing her mother, she would take all this as a sign that God was listening.

Bernie rose and went to the living room to let Carlos in. As her mother was leaving, she told Bernie to stay off her feet, which made sense, and to have a wonderful time at Jeremy's house, which didn't. What did she think this was? A vacation at a luxury hotel?

As Carlos grabbed her suitcase and lugged it down the stairs, Bernie stopped by Ruby's apartment and told her she'd be gone for a while. Then she went down to the parking lot, where a few of her neighbors were hanging around, furtively eyeing the limousine. She just hoped nobody had stolen the hubcaps while Carlos was upstairs.

Carlos opened the back door for her. She ignored him and got into the front seat on the passenger side. Carlos gave up and came around to get behind the wheel.

"You're not supposed to sit up here," he said. "Bridges told me to bring the limo so you'd be comfortable in the back."

"I'd rather sit in the front."

"But he told me—"

"I know what he told you. I'm sitting in the front."

Carlos sighed. "Okay. But I'm telling him you sat in the back."

"Will you stop being such an ass kisser? His bark is way worse than his bite."

"Hey, he's the one who pays me, so when he barks, I listen."

Carlos started the car and headed out of her apartment complex, turning the heads of every resident who happened to be hanging around outside. Seeing a limo here was like seeing a diamond in a pile of cow chips.

Carlos made a right onto Fourteenth Street. "So," he said, "you really are pregnant?"

"Yep."

"And Bridges is the father?"

"Yep."

"*Damn*. That's..." He paused, then shook his head. "Oh, hell. I don't even know what that is."

"Surprising? Astonishing? Completely beyond belief?"

"You know I like you, Bernie. But it's still pretty weird."

"Weird? You mean that a man who could have any woman on earth knocked up a woman like me?"

Carlos shrugged. "Well, yeah." He flicked his gaze to Bernie. "No offense."

"Oh, don't worry, Carlos," she said. "I can't imagine any woman who would take offense at that."

"You know what I mean."

She did. And he wasn't going to be the last person with a reaction like that. Unlike Carlos, most people had filter in their brains that prohibited them from actually *saying* how weird it was, but it didn't stop them from thinking it. She had a feeling the strange looks and disbelieving stares were only just beginning.

Fifteen minutes later, they arrived at Jeremy's house, and Mrs. Spencer escorted Bernie to the guest suite. Bernie was prepared to yawn a little and pretend it wasn't much better than a room at Motel 6, but when Mrs. Spencer opened the door, it was all she could do to keep her jaw from hitting the floor.

Her gaze went from the overstuffed sofa to the leather recliner to the mahogany floors to the flagstone fireplace with a television above it. The bedroom was equally stunning, with a king-sized four-poster bed, luxurious linens, and a massive cherry wood armoire that spanned almost the entire width of one wall. The walk-in closet was nearly as big as Bernie's bedroom in her apartment. And the bathroom. Marble sinks, a shower with all kinds of strange shower heads for the water to squirt out of, and a Jacuzzi tub big enough to swim in.

"Why don't you lie down and relax while I unpack your things?" Mrs. Spencer said.

It made Bernie a little uncomfortable to have somebody else going through her belongings, but she was supposed to be resting, so she decided not to argue. She sat down on the bed and settled back against one of the pillows. The bed seemed to close in around her, cradling her in a peaceful warmth that sucked every bit of the tension out of her muscles, leaving her feeling as limp as Raggedy Ann. Okay. This was nice. *Really* nice. Way better than her own bed, the one she'd gotten at an end-of-the-year clearance sale at Furniture Depot. The salesman with the scary hairpiece had promised her high quality at a low price. What Bernie had gotten instead was a lesson in basic economic theory: You get what you pay for.

Mrs. Spencer puttered around in the bedroom and bathroom, sticking stuff in the closet and armoire, humming softly as she worked. She was dressed as she always was, in a starched white shirt, a calf-length skirt, and leather flats. Bernie had always thought she'd been born a century too late. She should have been serving tea to the monarchy in Victorian England rather than beer to a womanizing bachelor in a Dallas suburb.

"How long have you worked for Jeremy?" Bernie asked.

"Eight years."

"That's a long time."

"It's an excellent job."

"Excellent?" Bernie laughed a little. "With a boss as difficult as Jeremy Bridges?"

The woman blinked. "Difficult? Oh, no, ma'am. Mr. Bridges isn't difficult at all."

"He's not?"

"Actually, he's quite easy to work for. Not at all fussy about his meals, and in spite of his casual dress, he's quite fastidious about his person and his surroundings. And he's most generous with compensation and time off."

"They say he's pretty ruthless in his business dealings," Bernie said.

Mrs. Spencer looked a little confounded. "Mr. Bridges? Ruthless?" She shrugged. "I'm afraid I wouldn't know about that. All I know is what wine he drinks and how he likes his eggs."

She slipped into the closet to hang up a pair of Bernie's jeans. When she popped out again, she said, "I'm so delighted you're going to be staying with us. Maybe now Mr. Bridges won't be quite so lonely."

There was that word again. First her mother, and now Mrs. Spencer. "I'm sure he told you we won't be seeing each other."

"Yes. I believe he mentioned that. But you may be here quite some time."

Which wasn't going to change a thing.

"With all the women he brings home," Bernie said, "when does he have time to get lonely?"

"A man can feel lonely in a room full of people, Miss Hogan." She smiled. "And having two little ones in the house is going to do him a world of good, too."

"Mrs. Spencer... I think you've misunderstood. I won't

be here after the babies are born. I'm staying just until my doctor takes me off bed rest."

"No, ma'am. I understand completely." She shut the closet door. "There. All done. Your clothes are in the closet, along with your silk nightgowns and robe. And I put your toiletries and cosmetics in the lavatory, along with—"

"Hold on. Did you say silk nightgowns and robe?"

"Yes, ma'am."

"And cosmetics?"

"Yes, ma'am."

Bernie tilted her head, confused. "But I didn't bring those things with me."

"Oh, yes, ma'am. They were in your suitcase."

"But... but they couldn't have been. I don't even own—"

Oh, no.

Bernie slumped back against the pillow as the truth struck her. Her mother. How in the *hell* had she pulled it off?

Then she remembered the tote bag she'd been carrying over her shoulder when she came into Bernie's apartment that morning. Evidently it had been full of contraband, and she'd managed to smuggle it into the suitcase.

"May I see the robe?" Bernie said.

"Of course."

Mrs. Spencer brought the robe out of the closet on a padded hanger, and Bernie nearly groaned out loud. It was long, full, flowing, emerald green, and silky shiny, the kind of thing Bernie wouldn't wear even if there were nothing else on earth and she had to go naked. She could hear her mother's voice in her head as she imagined what she'd say. *Just because you're pregnant doesn't mean you can't be pretty.*

Pretty? She hadn't been pretty even without being pregnant, so what were the chances that pregnancy would suddenly make that happen?

"It's lovely," Mrs. Spencer said. "And the matching gowns are lovely, too."

"Yeah. Lovely. I don't suppose you came across a couple of pairs of pajama pants and some T-shirts? Maybe a terrycloth robe?"

"Yes, ma'am. Those were there, too."

Well, thank God. At least she'd have something comfortable to lounge around in. She didn't bother asking what cosmetics were sitting in the bathroom. It would only make her want to scream.

"Mr. Bridges tells me that you're to stay in bed as much as possible," Mrs. Spencer said. "Which means you're to notify me if there's anything you need. There's an intercom in all three rooms. Just push the button and speak, and I'll respond."

"Thank you."

"Mr. Bridges also said you'll be taking your meals in your suite."

"Yes. That's right."

"But if things should change and you wish to dine together, I'll be happy to set the table for both of you."

"I don't think that's going to happen," Bernie said, "but thank you."

Mrs. Spencer nodded and left the room.

Silk gowns. Good God. If Jeremy ever saw her wearing something like that, he'd laugh his head off. Fortunately, there was no chance of that. For the next couple of weeks, at least, she'd be on one side of this house, and he'd be on the other. That was a good thing. There could never be anything between them that was stable and permanent and long-lasting, so the last thing she needed was to get caught up in his charm and follow him down a road that led nowhere.

Chapter
22

It had been six days since Bernie had moved in, and Jeremy was on the verge of going nuts. He'd offered her total isolation, which he assumed would have her flinging the door open in a few days and at least coming down for dinner. But she'd stuck to their arrangement like glue. She hadn't poked her head out of that suite a single time, at least when he was home. As one day blended into the next, he wished he'd never offered her that deal in the first place. He'd discovered that there was nothing quite as excruciating as knowing she was in his house but not even being able to speak to her.

"Don't bother fixing dinner for me tonight," he told Mrs. Spencer when he got home from work. "I have a dinner meeting."

"Yes, sir." She pointed to a tray on the kitchen counter. "Miss Hogan's dinner is right there. I was just getting ready to take it to her." She paused. "Perhaps you'd like to instead?"

No. He wasn't going to her. She was going to have to

come to him. "Uh...no. Just carry on the way you have been."

Mrs. Spencer wiped her hands on a dishtowel. "Actually, I think she's getting a bit lonely in there all by herself."

"You told me her mother has dropped by a few times."

"Yes."

"She's perfectly free to have any guests she wants to."

"Of course," Mrs. Spencer said. "But perhaps it's your face she'd rather see."

Jeremy's heart stuttered. "That's unlikely. She's staying here because it's the practical thing to do, not because we intend to keep each other company."

"She asked about you."

Jeremy froze. "Oh?"

"Yes. She was interested in knowing if you were out of town."

"Why would she ask that?"

"Perhaps because she expects a visit from you, and she's searching for a reason why it hasn't been forthcoming."

A visit from him? That was the last thing Bernie would want. "I doubt that. She expects nothing from me."

"Sometimes the most welcome events are the ones we *don't* expect."

"Not in this case."

"Perhaps I could give her a message?"

"Mrs. Spencer," Jeremy snapped. "This isn't high school. I don't need you to pass a note for me."

She turned away. "Of course, Mr. Bridges."

Jeremy blew out a breath, hating that he'd snapped at her. "I'm sorry. I didn't mean to bite your head off."

"That's quite all right. I clearly overstepped my bounds."

"You didn't overstep your bounds. I overreacted."

Mrs. Spencer nodded. She picked up Bernie's tray and walked out of the breakfast room, leaving Jeremy feeling more alone than ever.

Two hours later, Jeremy left Gallagher's Steakhouse, his stomach full of steak and lobster and his head full of statistics he probably wouldn't remember in the morning. Hell, he didn't remember them *now.* He'd just spent the past hour and a half discussing demographics and pricing strategy with his senior vice president in charge of European sales and marketing, and he couldn't have been more distracted from that conversation if a marching band had come through the room.

Phil fell in step beside him as they left the restaurant. Thank God he'd come along to absorb some of the information, or the meeting might have been a total bust.

"European sales look good," Phil said. "We're a little down in Germany, but with that shift in distribution, I think we can pull it back up."

"Yeah. I'm sure we can."

"What did you think about the numbers from Italy? They were way better than what I expected."

"Uh-huh."

Phil walked along silently for a moment more, then turned to him again. "How did you feel about that pink elephant wearing the tutu who took our dinner order?"

"It was—" Jeremy stopped short. *"What?"*

"You haven't heard a word I've said since we left the restaurant."

"Wrong," Jeremy said, walking again. "I heard the elephant thing."

"You weren't exactly on your game tonight. What's up?"

"Nothing. I was just a little distracted."

"Well, I hope you're up for the strategy meeting tomorrow with the acquisitions team. I'll have organizational charts and employee lists for you then."

"Thanks."

"Meant to ask you," Phil said. "Are you planning to go to that donor appreciation event at Texas Southwestern? Every year at that thing Alexis spends the whole evening yammering with her sorority sisters. I just want to know if I'm going to have a drinking buddy."

"It's not for several weeks yet. Check with me later, will you?"

"Fine. But don't you even consider not going."

"Actually, I'm kind of afraid to go. Has Alexis forgiven me yet for what happened at the museum?"

"Hey, man. You know she loves you. She won't stay mad."

"Good."

"Particularly since it was Bernie who diverted you from Madeline."

"What? How did she know—" Jeremy stopped short. "Oh, yeah. Madeline knows who Bernie is because they both work at the museum."

"And Madeline told Alexis. So are you and Bernie seeing each other after all?"

"No. It's not like that."

"Then what is it like?"

Jeremy stopped short, facing Phil. "You're the nosiest son of a bitch I've ever known."

"That's not an answer."

Jeremy sighed. "Okay. Bernie *is* living with me, but—"

"*Living* with you?"

"Will you *listen*? There was a small problem with her pregnancy, and she had to go on bed rest for a few weeks. It only made sense for her to stay at my house where Mrs. Spencer could take care of her. We're not even seeing each other. She's in a suite on the other side of the house."

"You're not even speaking to her? Isn't that kind of weird?"

Yes, it *was* weird. And Jeremy was still kicking himself for his brilliant plan that turned out not to be so brilliant after all. "It doesn't matter, because there's nothing going on between us, just as I've been saying."

Jeremy started toward his car again.

"Okay," Phil said with a shrug. "If you say so."

"I say so." Max opened the door for Jeremy, and he slid into the backseat. "See you at the meeting in the morning."

"I'll be there," Phil said.

As Phil walked away, Jeremy tried to remember if his friend had always been this intrusive, or if Alexis was rubbing off on him. Jeremy wasn't used to his friends' getting in the middle of his personal business. But frankly, that was because up to now he'd had very little personal business for anyone to get in the middle of.

He had received the invitation for the donor appreciation event at Texas Southwestern, but he hadn't been all that interested in going. His primary goal in attending events like that one—picking up women—just didn't interest him anymore. And he knew why.

Ever since Bernie had shown up in his office that day

and announced she was pregnant, his interest in other women had all but vanished. He just couldn't stop thinking about her. During dinner at the restaurant, all he did was imagine *her* having dinner. In her room. By herself. Not even thinking about him.

She had asked Mrs. Spencer if he was out of town. Did she want to know because she wanted to see him? Or did she want to know because if he was out of town, she could relax, knowing she *wouldn't* see him?

Jeremy closed his eyes with frustration. He'd told Mrs. Spencer to stop with the high school behavior, and here he was speculating about every thought Bernie was having, like some stupid kid with a crush trying to figure out how to get a girl's attention.

A few minutes later, Max drove into his motor court. With a mumbled, "Good night, sir," he got into his own car and left. Jeremy headed for his kitchen door. But before he could stick his key in the lock, the door opened, and his heart practically leaped out of his chest

Bernie?

She was dressed in jeans and a T-shirt, but her hair was mussed, as if she hadn't even bothered to run a brush through it, and she looked more than a little distressed.

"Bernie?" he said. "What are you doing?"

"I have to run an errand."

"Run an errand? You're not even supposed to be out of bed."

"I'll only be a little while."

"No. You're not going anywhere."

"I have to."

She started to walk through the doorway, but Jeremy stepped in front of her.

"Damn it," Bernie said, "will you let me go?"

"Not until you tell me where you're going."

"I have to go *now*!"

"Absolutely not. You're not going—" All at once, he realized there were tears in her eyes. "Bernie? What is it? What's wrong?"

"Please. Will you just let me go?"

"Whoa, now. Wait a minute. Is it something with the babies?"

"No. The babies are fine."

"Then what? Tell me."

"It's—" She exhaled, closing her eyes. "It's my mother."

"What happened?"

"She called me. She's at the grocery store. The one she goes to all the time. She told me..."

"What?"

Bernie closed her eyes. "That she doesn't remember how to get home."

Jeremy blinked with confusion. "I don't understand."

"I tried to get somebody else to help. But my friend Teresa doesn't answer. My aunt is out of town. My grandmother's driver's license expired two weeks ago and she hasn't gotten another one. I wouldn't trust my cousin Billy to do anything. And I knew Max was with you."

"Wait a minute. Hold on. What do you mean she doesn't know how to get home?"

"She's been forgetting," Bernie said. "Even more lately. But it's never been anything like this. And in a few months...a year...oh, God. I don't know what I'm going to do."

For several more seconds, Jeremy just stared at her,

trying to understand. And when he finally did, the realization nearly knocked him senseless.

"Alzheimer's?"

Bernie took a deep, shuddering breath and nodded.

He closed his eyes for a moment, absorbing that, then opened them again. "Is she in immediate danger? Maybe we should call the police."

"No! If the police came, it would scare her to death. She's in her car, so I told her just to stay put, that I'd be there in a minute. She was worried about me getting out of bed, but what was I supposed to do?"

"Where is the grocery store?"

"At Park and Greystone."

"Call your mother back. Tell her who I am and that I'm coming to pick her up."

"No. She doesn't know you. She's going to be embarrassed. I'm the one who needs to go."

"No. You shouldn't be out of bed."

"And you shouldn't be leaving this house without a bodyguard."

"Here's a little secret, Bernie. Every once in a while I slip out by myself no matter what my board of directors says."

"Maybe I should just call Max now that he's free. I'm sure he'll—"

"No."

Jeremy spoke sharply. Too sharply. But the instant he imagined Max doing this instead of him, for some reason his irritation level shot through the roof.

"I can take care of this," he told Bernie, speaking more quietly. "Just tell me what kind of car she drives."

"A 2006 Camry. Silver."

He grabbed his phone from his pocket. "Her address?"

Bernie told him, and he punched it into his phone.

"What's her first name?"

"Eleanor."

Jeremy nodded and slid his phone back into his pocket. He took Bernie gently by the shoulders. "Then get back in bed, okay? You take care of the babies. I'll take care of your mother."

She ducked her head and nodded, and when she lifted it again, a single word formed silently on her lips. *Thanks*.

Jeremy waited until Bernie was back in the house and he heard her lock the door. Then he got into his car, and ten minutes later he pulled into the parking lot of the grocery store, looking up and down the aisles for a silver Camry. It was nearly dark, and the halogen lights of the parking lot cast a garish glow. As he turned down the last aisle, he felt a twinge of foreboding. What if Eleanor had tried to drive home after all? If she had, he couldn't imagine where she might—

There.

When he finally spotted the Camry, he pulled into a space two cars away and got out. He saw Eleanor in the driver's seat. He knocked softly. When she turned around and smiled weakly, he opened her car door and knelt beside her.

"Hi, Eleanor," he said.

"Are you Mr. Bridges?" she said, her voice a little shaky.

"Jeremy. Bernie mentioned you need a ride home. Is that right?"

"Yes. I'm afraid so." She laughed nervously. "This is so embarrassing. I can't imagine why I'm having such a problem tonight. I guess that happens sometimes when you get old, doesn't it?

"It happens sometimes even when you're young," Jeremy said.

"I shouldn't have panicked and called Bernadette. In fact, I think I know how to get home now, but she told me to stay put until you got here."

"I'm glad you did," Jeremy said. "It's late. Why don't you hop into my car? I'll have you home in a jiffy."

"But my car—"

"I'll send somebody for it tomorrow. It'll be back in your driveway by the time you wake up in the morning."

He took her hand and helped her out of the car, shutting and locking the door behind her. He escorted her to his car. He checked his phone for directions and headed toward Eleanor's house. She sat in the seat beside him, looking very much like the grandmother she was getting ready to be. She wore a flowered shirt over polyester pants and tiny pearl earrings. She'd pulled a tissue out of her pants pocket and spent most of the way home twisting it into a knot.

A few minutes later, he pulled up to a tidy brick house with a thick St. Augustine lawn and beds full of holly bushes, all of it resting beneath the canopy of a huge oak tree. As Jeremy escorted her to the front porch, the rhythmic chirp of crickets sounded through the dusky evening.

"I shouldn't have called Bernadette tonight," Eleanor said as they stepped up onto the porch. "She needs to be resting. But I just…." She shrugged weakly. "I just didn't know what else to do."

"You did the right thing. And then Bernie did the right thing by asking me to come." He smiled. "All's well that ends well."

Eleanor nodded, her face looking strained and tired beneath the weak glow of the porch light. "Thank you for helping me, Jeremy."

"No problem."

Jeremy turned to leave, but she touched his arm. "Before you go, may I talk to you for just a moment?"

"Yes?"

She took a deep, shaky breath. "By now it should be obvious to you why I had such trouble remembering tonight."

"Yes," he said gently. "Bernie told me."

"Bernadette swears there's nothing between you two. That there never will be, which means that your interest in her situation may just begin and end with the babies. And that's wonderful. The babies will need a good father. But where Bernadette is concerned..."

"What?"

"She's always been so independent. She'll tell you she doesn't need help, and she usually doesn't, but caring for two babies is something even she's going to find difficult. Taking care of me only adds to her burden, but she'll do it, because that's the kind of daughter she is." She pulled another tissue from the pocket of her pants and twisted it between her fingers. "I was just hoping that maybe... while she's taking care of me..."

"Yes?"

"You'll do what you can to take care of her."

Looking into Eleanor's eyes, he could see how desperately she wanted to protect her child, even as the tables had turned and any power she had to do that was slowly slipping away from her.

"Of course," Jeremy said.

"I know it's a lot to ask of you, but she is the mother of your children, and—"

"Eleanor. Please believe me. You never have to worry about that."

She nodded, dabbing the corners of her eyes with the tissue. "Are you a churchgoing man, Jeremy?"

"No, ma'am. I'm afraid not."

"Doesn't matter. I've known plenty of good men who've never set foot inside a church. And I can tell— you're a good man."

For a moment, he found himself feeling sorry for her, because the truth was that he wasn't a good man. He was a wealthy man. A successful man. But good? Not in the way she thought. If she knew the way he conducted his business sometimes, she'd be shocked. If she knew his history with women, she'd swear he was going to hell. If she knew the carnal thoughts he'd been having lately about her daughter, she'd probably slap him right across the face.

Good?

No. He was here now simply because it was the logical thing to do. Bernie needed to stay in bed, so he went. And there was nothing else to it.

"Eleanor?"

"Yes, Jeremy?"

"Is this house where Bernie was raised?"

Eleanor smiled. "Yes. Her father and I bought it right before she was born." She paused with a gentle sigh. "He's gone now. But I still have such lovely memories."

For an awkward moment, Jeremy had to turn away. He couldn't look into her eyes and see the pain she must be feeling. It was one thing for her husband to be taken from her. But to know that the memories of him would eventually disappear as well? How in the world did she stand it?

And how in the world was Bernie going to bear watching it happen?

Jeremy said good night, and Eleanor went inside. He started to walk toward his car, only to stop and stand on the porch for a moment to watch what was going on around him. Two doors down, a couple of kids were chasing each other around the yard, a shaggy brown mutt nipping at their heels. Across the street, an old lady was watering her petunias. A young couple passed by pushing a stroller. Fireflies hovered lazily in the dusk, blinking on and off.

All at once, Jeremy felt an unaccustomed tightness in his throat. Did Bernie have any idea how lucky she'd been?

As a child, all he'd known were nasty landlords, cracked concrete, and walls full of graffiti, along with the dismal hopelessness of old people and the angry defiance of young ones. Even now, even when he had everything in life he could ever have hoped for, he still wondered sometimes if people could look into his eyes and see a shadow of what he used to be.

Just then he heard the sound of a car engine running rough, punctuated by an annoying clatter. He turned to see a tired old Chevy Malibu pulling to the curb in front of Eleanor's house. Its missing passenger window was covered with cardboard and duct tape, its muffler nearly dragging the ground. The man who got out was in his early thirties, scruffy, poorly dressed, and in dire need of a haircut. He zeroed in on Jeremy's Mercedes in the driveway.

"Hey, man," he said, as he walked across the lawn toward Jeremy. "Is that your car?"

Jeremy stepped off the porch, then stopped and held his ground. "Yes," he said warily. "It's mine."

"Wow," the man said with a grin. "Nice. Who are you?"

Jeremy didn't like the looks of this guy. Why was he loitering around Eleanor's house? "I'm Jeremy Bridges," he said. "And you are ...?"

Recognition lit the guy's face. "Jeremy Bridges! You're Bernie's baby daddy!"

"Uh ... yeah."

"I'm Billy. Bernie's cousin. So what are you doing at Aunt Eleanor's house?"

Jeremy still didn't like this guy. Not one little bit. "She had a little problem when she was out, so I gave her a ride home."

"Oh," Billy said. "I'm staying with her for a little while. Just while I'm between jobs. You know."

When Billy didn't bother asking what Eleanor's problem was, Jeremy knew right away that he didn't give a rat's ass about her. And Jeremy sensed that his being "between jobs" was a fairly permanent state for him.

"You're one of those computer inventor dudes, right?" Billy said. "Like that Gates guy? No wonder you can afford a great car like that." He shook his head with awe. "Man, oh, *man*, I bet you've been with some really hot women. If I had a car like that, I'd be boinking hot babes every day of the week."

That statement told Jeremy that Billy likely had an ongoing problem with women, and it had nothing to do with the car he drove.

"I read the blog at *Dallas After Dark* sometimes," Billy went on. "They talk about shit goin' on around Dallas at all the hot clubs and stuff. I swear I saw a picture of you at one of those once with a supermodel. Can't remember her name. Something from one of those really cold places where everything's spelled funny. Tall blond chick in a long black dress. Was that you?"

Jeremy had dated more than one Scandinavian supermodel, and he'd gone to clubs, but other than that, he didn't have a clue what Billy was talking about. "Yeah," he said. "That was me."

"Whoa! I knew it!" He shook his head, a big grin on his face. "Man, you're living the *life*."

What an idiot.

Now Jeremy remembered. Hadn't Bernie mentioned her cousin Billy? Said she wouldn't trust him to help with anything?

Smart woman.

"I'm going to be living the life myself one of these days," Billy said. "As soon as the right opportunity comes along. But you know, my problem right now is cash flow. Hard to get anything going with no walking-around money." A calculating expression came over his face. "So you've got the big bucks, right?"

"Yep."

"I don't suppose . . . you know. That you could you help me out a little?"

"Help you out?"

"A loan."

"Nope."

"Oh, come on, man! You got all kinds of money, and you're practically family. Surely you can loan me a few bucks just to tide me over."

Jeremy was astonished. Did this guy have any shame at all?

"I don't lend money," Jeremy said. "But I do give advice."

"Yeah?"

"If you want money, earn it. Good night, Billy."

With that, Jeremy turned and walked to his car, leaving Billy standing in the driveway practically snarling with frustration. Jeremy couldn't imagine under what circumstances Eleanor would even think about putting a roof over that little deadbeat's head, but he intended to find out.

Chapter
23

Fifteen minutes later, Jeremy came through his kitchen door and shut it behind him. Looking through the kitchen to the den beyond, he saw a light on. Bernie was lying on the sofa. The TV was on but muted.

He hung his keys by the back door and went into the den. Bernie stirred a little, then opened her eyes, blinking against the light.

"I must have fallen asleep," she said, sitting up. "How is my mother?"

Jeremy sat down beside her on the sofa. "She's fine."

"She sounded so upset when she called."

"Don't worry. She's okay now."

Bernie let out a breath of relief. "I hope you don't mind that I stayed in the living room to wait for you."

"Of course not. Are you okay?"

"Yeah. Just a little tired."

Her eyes were heavy with sleep and worry. A strand of hair lay across her cheek, and he had to resist the urge to lean in and brush it away.

"About your mother," he said. "How advanced is her disease?"

Bernie rubbed her eyes, then sighed. "Up to now, it's just been small things. But if more stuff happens like this tonight..."

"She shouldn't be driving."

"I know that now. But if she doesn't drive, I'm going to have to help her even more than I do now." She put her hand to her forehead. "What am I going to do if I'm stuck in bed for several more weeks?"

"That's not a problem."

"Of course it's a problem. She can't get groceries, go to church—"

"I'll put a car and driver at her disposal."

Bernie froze. "You can't do that."

"Yeah? Why not?"

"Because it's not your problem. It's mine."

"Starting tomorrow, if your mother wants to go somewhere, all she has to do is pick up a phone. I'll call her and explain everything."

"But—"

"It's just temporary. Once you're off bed rest, you can handle things again, right?"

"Of course."

"Until then, she'll have a way to get around. Problem solved."

Bernie looked at him a long time, blinking with disbelief. "You'd really do that for me?"

It made him uncomfortable for her to act as if he'd done something wonderful. When he could throw a minuscule portion of his massive fortune at a problem and it ceased to be a problem, he couldn't exactly claim it was a gesture from the heart.

"If this happens again and you get out of bed to run all over town, it's not good for the babies." He picked up the remote, clicked the TV off, and changed the subject. "Tell me about Billy."

Bernie's smile faded. "So you met him?"

"I did. He tried to borrow money from me."

"Oh, God." Bernie closed her eyes. "I'm so sorry."

"He says he's living with your mother because he's a little down on his luck right now. Is that a normal state for him?"

"That's a long, ugly story."

"I've got time."

Bernie sighed wearily, as if it wore her out just to think about it.

"Billy's mother died when he was only eight years old," she began. "My mother has been making excuses for him ever since. She thinks if she can just lend him another hundred dollars, or let him stay with her for a week, which always turns into a month, then he'll get back on his feet again. The truth is that he's twenty-nine years old and he still can't hold a job. He borrows money from her and never pays it back, because my mother won't tell him no, and I'm not there twenty-four hours a day to keep it from happening. I think the total now is $640."

"Why haven't you kicked his ass by now? You're just the woman who can do it."

"Oh, God, I wish I could. I've threatened him more times than you can imagine. But my mother always asks me to take it easy on him. He grew up without a mother, you see, so he just needs some understanding."

"I grew up without a mother, too, so I don't have a lot of sympathy for that. Kick his ass, Bernie. Things will be better in the end."

"Truthfully, it wouldn't matter even if I did. In the end, Billy knows I won't kill him, and if murder is off the table, there's only so much I can do. He pretty much gives me the middle finger and keeps on being a problem. Unfortunately, he has one thing in his favor that nobody can ever take away."

"What's that?"

Bernie shrugged helplessly. "He's family. And in my mother's eyes, that trumps everything."

If there was one kind of person on this earth that irritated Jeremy, it was a deadbeat like Billy. If only he could go back in time and drop the guy into his own life as a kid, he'd find out what hell *really* felt like. And family or not, if a man crossed him the way Billy had crossed Bernie, he'd make damned sure it never happened again.

"When did your father die?" Jeremy asked.

"About eight years ago. After he was gone, I had to leave the military to come home and take care of my mother."

"Why? That should have been long before her diagnosis."

"I came home for my father's funeral. I stayed two weeks, made sure my mother was okay. Three months later, I came home on leave, and I couldn't believe what I found. Billy and his skanky girlfriend of the month had moved in with my mother. The spare bedroom was trashed. My mother had missed paying several of her bills since my father died. She'd never been terribly good at taking care of herself—my father handled everything—but I assumed she'd at least write all the checks she needed to. If I'd been gone another month, they would have started foreclosure proceedings on her house. I was stupid not to realize how impractical she really was, and how devastated she was by my father's death. It just paralyzed her. And now with her illness..."

"Did your father have life insurance?"

"Some. My mother gave it to a 'financial planner' at her church to invest for her. He lost most of it before I even knew what was happening."

Jeremy couldn't believe this. It was pretty clear that Eleanor trusted just about anybody she met, and it got her into trouble every time.

"So you moved back to Dallas," he said.

"As soon as I could. In the meantime, I had all her bills rerouted to me so I could make sure they got paid. I'm still doing it."

"Then you went to work for Gabe Delgado."

"Yeah. And I've been there ever since. I still worried when I had to travel for a week or two at a time, but I got home often enough to keep things from falling apart." She sighed. "Guess traveling isn't something I'm going to have to worry about anymore."

He'd had no idea. The entire time she'd been working for him, she'd been dealing with all this?

"What kind of health insurance does your mother have?"

Bernie closed her eyes. "She doesn't have insurance. She let it lapse after my father died."

"Nobody else would cover her?"

"She was fifty-seven years old with high blood pressure. Then she was diagnosed with Alzheimer's. No insurance company in America would cover her now. I have to make sure I have options when the time comes."

Jeremy couldn't believe just how much Bernie was having to deal with. And now she was pregnant? He had always known she was a tough woman, but he'd had no idea just how tough.

Then all at once he understood something he'd never understood before, and the realization hit him like a brick to the side of his head.

"Is that why you're living at Creekwood?" he asked. "To save money for your mother's care?"

She shrugged weakly. "Doesn't help much, but I've reached a point where every penny has to count."

Jeremy's stomach twisted with the realization of just how much of an ass he'd been. Telling her again and again to stop being cheap and go live somewhere decent, never knowing that circumstances were driving her to sacrifice her own well-being to help somebody else.

"You've taken on a lot where your mother is concerned," Jeremy said.

"You'd have done the same thing. If someone in your family—"

"I don't have any family."

"Come on. Everybody has family."

"A few distant relatives, maybe."

"What about your mother and father?"

"I never knew my mother. And my father is dead."

"Oh, God. I'm so sorry. When did he die?"

"Several years ago. But I hadn't seen him since I was eighteen."

"Really? Why?"

"Because the moment I graduated from high school, I was out of there." He paused. "And I never looked back."

"Why didn't you want to see him?"

"Now, Bernie. Are you sure you want to hear my sad story?"

"You listened to mine."

He shrugged offhandedly. "Let's see. My mother ran off when I was three years old. My father was a shiftless, alcoholic bum who couldn't hold a job. We lived in a hell-hole of an apartment in the worst part of Houston."

"Oh, my God. That's awful."

He raised an eyebrow. "Now, I told you it was a sad story, didn't I?"

"Wait a minute. I read somewhere that you graduated from Stonebriar Academy. That's not exactly in the low-rent district."

"I did. When I was in the eighth grade, I had a teacher who thought I had a shot at getting a scholarship to Stonebriar. With his help, I did. Trouble was, I had to get there every day, and it was eighteen miles from where I lived."

"Your father couldn't take you?"

"My father refused to take me. In fact, he did everything he could to discourage me from going there."

"Why?"

"Because he was a bitter, jealous old man."

"So what did you do?"

"I rode a city bus thirty-six miles round-trip every day and walked the other two miles."

Bernie was astonished. She'd always known he came from a bad background, but she'd never realized how much he'd had to do to climb out of it.

"That took a lot of guts," Bernie said.

"I wanted a decent education. That was the only way to get it. But looking back, all the crap I went through turned out to be a real motivator. It got me where I am today. Everything turned out just fine."

His nonchalance astonished her. It was as if his past had been nothing more than a speed bump on a side street, and he'd simply hopped over it to get to the freeway. He was an amazing man in more ways than she'd ever realized, and she was glad he'd risen above that background to have some of the best things life had to offer.

"Did what you went through with your father growing up have anything to do with you wanting to be part of these babies' lives?" she asked.

He sat there for a long time, his arms crossed, staring down. Then he lifted one shoulder in a half-shrug. "To tell you the truth, Bernie, I don't know if I can be a decent parent or not. God knows I had a lousy example. But I don't want these kids growing up thinking they have a father who doesn't give a damn. Because I do. You know that, don't you?"

There had been a time when she would have sworn his capacity for caring was practically nonexistent, that he could never be the kind of man she or her babies could depend on. But tonight she'd seen a different side of him, giving her a feeling of warmth and comfort she'd never anticipated.

"Yeah," she said quietly. "I do."

"You look tired," he said. "Why don't you let me take you up to your room?"

Jeremy stood up and held out his hand. Bernie looked up at him, feeling elated and worried all at the same time. Elated because he'd gone so far to help her tonight, but worried that because of everything he was doing for her, one day soon she was going be so deeply in debt to him that getting out would be impossible.

She slid her hand into his. He helped her to her feet. She felt a little bleary-eyed and clumsy from falling asleep on the sofa, but then she felt Jeremy's palm warm against the small of her back, guiding her to the stairs. She felt so tired that each step she climbed was a little harder than the last. When they reached the second-floor landing, Jeremy slid his hand up her back and wrapped his arm around her shoulders, pulling her next to him as they walked. A little voice inside her head told her that just letting him touch her was a mistake, but it felt so good that she just didn't want to tell him not to.

They came to her room. She reached for the doorknob, but he gently pulled her around to face him.

"Bernie? Why didn't you ask for my help tonight?"

"Because it's not your problem."

"It's not Max's or Teresa's problem either, but you saw nothing wrong with asking them."

"You were at a meeting."

"I don't care if I have an audience with the pope," he said. "The next time you have a problem, you come to me. Will you do that?"

She shrugged weakly. "I guess it depends on the problem."

Jeremy smiled briefly, shaking his head. "Do you have any idea how hard it is to get through to you sometimes?"

"We're both a little stubborn like that, aren't we?"

He slid his hand behind her neck, leaned in, and kissed her gently on the forehead. She closed her eyes, savoring the warmth of his lips and the gentle strength of his hand against her neck.

"I promised hands off," he said. "Was that out of line?"

"No," she said, tipping her gaze up briefly before lowering it again. "It was nice."

"Bernie?"

"Yes?" she said, meeting his eyes again.

"Tomorrow evening... will you have dinner with me downstairs?"

"Yeah," she said. "I'd like that."

"Good. I'll let Mrs. Spencer know."

She nodded, then turned around and slipped through the doorway, closing the door behind her. She stopped and stood there for a moment, feeling breathless and lightheaded. She closed her eyes and put her fingertips against her forehead where he'd kissed her, feeling as if she was going to melt right into the floor. Then she lowered her fingertips to touch them to her own lips.

He's not who you thought he was. He's more.

He's so much more.

At five o'clock the next afternoon, Jeremy left his office at Sybersense and climbed into his car.

"Home, sir?" Max said.

"We're taking a little detour first," Jeremy said.

"Where to?"

Jeremy gave him Eleanor's address, which Max punched into the car's GPS.

"Bernie's mother lives on that street," Max said.

"That's where we're going," Jeremy said. "Bernie's cousin Billy is staying with Eleanor. I need to have a talk with him. Know the guy?"

"Only by reputation. I'm not impressed."

"Bernie's had some problems keeping him in line. Would you like to help me put a stop to them?"

Jeremy could tell he had Max's attention. "If it helps Bernie, yeah."

"Good. Once we get there, I'm going to bring him out of the house. As soon as I start talking to him, you'll know what to do."

A few minutes later, Max pulled into Eleanor's driveway and Jeremy went to the door. He rang the bell. Eleanor answered, giving him a big smile. "Jeremy. How nice to see you."

"Nice to see you, too, Eleanor. I need to talk to Billy. Is he around?"

"You two have met?"

"He got home as I was leaving last night. I spoke with him outside."

Eleanor stepped around the corner and looked into the living room. "Billy? There's somebody here to see you."

Jeremy heard some shuffling around. Billy appeared in the entry, looking confused when he came face to face with Jeremy.

"Got a minute, Billy?" Jeremy asked.

"Uh...yeah. Sure."

He gave Jeremy a wary smile, probably hoping Jeremy had reconsidered giving him that loan after all, or maybe had dropped by to take him for a spin in his Mercedes so they could pick up chicks. After all, weren't they almost like family?

Little did Billy know that hell wasn't even close to freezing over.

They left the house, and Jeremy knew the instant Billy saw Max. He jolted to a halt, his eyes widening.

"Billy, this is Max. He works for me."

He smiled nervously. "Uh, hey there, big guy."

Max never moved. He just stood there, his arms folded across his expansive chest, staring down at Billy through those mirrored sunglasses. With no eyes visible, Max looked remarkably like Robocop, only bigger and badder.

Billy turned to Jeremy, considerably less elated than before. "So. Jeremy. What's up, man?"

"We need to talk about you living with Eleanor."

"Uh ... what's there to talk about?"

"Sometime in the next two days, you're going to move out."

Billy licked his lips, then let out a nervous laugh. "Oh, man," he said. "You've been talking to Bernie, haven't you? *Sheesh.* Takes nothing to get her panties in a knot, know what I mean? Aunt Eleanor's got no problem with me living here."

"This has nothing to do with Bernie. This has nothing to do with Eleanor. This is between you and me, Billy." Jeremy inched closer, skewering him with a no-nonsense stare. "If I come back here in two days and you're within a hundred feet of this house, I'm sending Max here to find you. And when he gets finished with you, there's not going to be enough of your face left for a plastic surgeon to make you look human again. Did you hear that, Billy?"

Billy flicked a horrified gaze to Max, who deepened his frown, lifted his chin, and cracked his knuckles, like every hit man in every B movie ever made.

"But ... but I don't have anywhere to go!"

"That's not my concern," Jeremy said. "I don't care if it's ten degrees below zero and you have to sleep in the street; you're not living with Eleanor ever again. If I find out you are, I'm turning Max loose. Now, are we clear on that?"

"Uh...sure, man. Sure. I hear you."

"You also have a habit of borrowing money from Eleanor and not paying her back. That's going to stop, too. Do you know why it's going to stop?"

"W-why?"

"Because I hate deadbeats. And do you know who hates deadbeats even worse than I do?"

Max cracked his knuckles again, and Billy's eyeballs got so big and round they just about burst out of his head.

"If you so much as *mention* money to Eleanor again," Jeremy went on, "Max is going to be mentioning a few things to you. Got that, Billy?"

Billy swallowed hard. "I hear you, man. No more money from Aunt Eleanor. Yeah, I hear you just fine."

"And you're going to pay her back every dime you've borrowed. I believe that's $640."

"Now, wait a minute, guys," Billy said, laughing nervously. "I'm sure it's not nearly that much. It can't be. It's—"

Max took a step forward. Billy threw up his palms. "Okay, man! Just chill, okay?" He wiped his hand over his mouth. "Okay. Six hundred and forty dollars. Yeah. Now that I think about it, you're right. That's what I owe her."

"I don't want Eleanor knowing we had this little discussion," Jeremy said. "I'd just like her to think you suddenly became the responsible nephew she's always hoped you could be. Do you have any problem with that?"

"Problem? Hell, no, man. 'Course not. I won't say a word."

"One last thing," Jeremy said, dropping his voice to a malevolent drawl. "From now on, if I find out that you've said or done anything to Bernie that causes her one single second of worry, disgust, or dismay, *I'm* coming after you. Max has muscle, Billy. I have money. And you can't even imagine what kind of retribution money will buy."

For a moment, Billy looked as if he was having a hard time breathing.

"That's it, Billy. It's been nice talking to you."

Billy backed away one step. Then two.

"Get packing," Max snapped.

Billy turned and hightailed it back into the house, stumbling a little on a sidewalk crack. He flew back through the door, shutting it behind him with a solid *thunk*.

Max watched him go, shaking his head. "He doesn't even have to sponge off Bernie's mother. I'd be happy to mess him up just for being an asshole. Not sure why Bernie hasn't done that already."

"She feels as if her hands are tied with that guy," Jeremy said. "He's family. And her mother's involved. That messes with her judgment."

"Wish I'd known the extent of it," Max said. "I'd have taken the little bastard out years ago."

"You didn't know because Bernie has a bad habit of trying to deal with everything by herself. I'm doing my best to help her get over that."

"And what she can't deal with, you will?"

"Every chance I get." Jeremy nodded toward the car. "Let's go."

Max slid into the driver's seat, then glanced into the rearview mirror at Jeremy in the backseat. "Sir?"

"Yes?"

"If you need my help eliminating any more of Bernie's problems, just say the word."

"Thanks. I'll keep that in mind."

"Where to, sir?"

"Home."

"Yes, sir."

Jeremy sighed. "Max? I thought I told you to lose all that yes, sir, no sir crap."

Max slowly reached up and removed his sunglasses. He sat up a little straighter and met Jeremy's eyes in the rearview mirror.

"I'm just showing respect, sir."

Max continued to look in the mirror, without blinking, until Jeremy acknowledged his words with a nod. Max slipped his sunglasses back on, backed out of the driveway, and headed for Jeremy's house.

Respect.

It was as if all the negative feelings that had stood between them like a brick wall had suddenly been blasted away, leaving Jeremy with a feeling of satisfaction he'd never experienced before.

Bernie's trust and Max's respect. Two things he never wanted to be without again.

Chapter

24

At six o'clock that evening, Bernie came downstairs to find Jeremy already in the kitchen. He pulled out a chair for her at the table, which was already set for dinner for two. Bernie was used to dinner being something she nuked in the microwave and dumped onto a Corelle plate, so the pretty placemats and napkins and colorful stoneware felt positively decadent. And she loved that there was a fireplace right there in the breakfast nook. Even in August it made the room feel cozy and comfy. She could only imagine what it would feel like in December with a fire blazing.

"I'll have everything heated up in a minute," Jeremy said. "Wait until you taste Mrs. Spencer's lasagne. There's nothing on earth like it."

"Can't wait," Bernie said, and meant it. When she was gone, Mrs. Spencer's cooking was going to be one of the things she'd miss the most. "So how was your day?"

"About average," he said, as he peeked into the oven. "A little fortune building, a little backstabbing, a little corporate plundering. The usual. How about you?"

"Charmin may be on to something with those soap operas," Bernie said, picking up her napkin and spreading it on her lap. "It's like watching real life with the boring parts taken out. Assuming, of course, that your real life is filled with extraordinarily attractive people who can't act their way out of paper sacks."

"I take it you're a little bored," he said.

"You have no idea. Bed rest sucks."

"You'll be up and around soon enough."

God, she hoped so. She had to admit, though, that today had been her best day here so far. Just knowing she was going to have dinner with Jeremy made her feel as if she'd finally been released from solitary confinement. She might still be in prison, but her privileges had definitely been expanded.

Finally Jeremy pulled the steaming hot pan from the oven and brought it to the table, along with a basket of garlic bread. He dished up a piece of lasagne for Bernie and set it in front of her. It was a big, beautiful blob of thick, spicy sauce oozing through layers of cheese and noodles.

"Try it," Jeremy said.

She picked up her fork and took a bite, closing her eyes as she chewed. "Oh, my *God*, this is good. But everything Mrs. Spencer makes is wonderful. You're very lucky."

"I hire only the best." He held out the bread basket. "Try the garlic bread."

Bernie took a piece, bit into it, and went to heaven all over again.

Jeremy dished up a big piece of lasagna for himself. "I went to see your cousin Billy today."

Bernie froze, her fork halfway to her mouth. "Really? Why?"

"Just needed to settle a little problem."

"Problem? What problem?"

"The problem of him being a worthless deadbeat and sponging off your mother. But don't worry. It's all taken care of."

"Taken care of? What do you mean?"

"I mean that Billy will never bother your mother again."

Bernie felt a strange little glimmer of apprehension. "What did you do?"

"You don't need to worry about it."

Bernie slid her hand to her chest, that glimmer of apprehension growing brighter. "Bridges. Tell me."

"I told you it's taken care of."

"I don't like the sound of that."

"The sound of what?"

"The sound of you telling me it's taken care of and not to worry about it. That sounds a little...sinister."

"Sinister? Hmm. I wouldn't call what I did sinister, exactly. But trust me when I tell you that the problem has ceased to exist."

"Ceased to *exist*?"

"Absolutely."

"Oh, my God," Bernie gasped, dropping her fork with a clatter. *"Tell me what you did to Billy!"*

Jeremy turned, looking startled. "Will you lighten *up*? All I did was tell him to stay away from your mother, and that Max would rearrange his face if he didn't."

"But—but no rearranging actually took place? Or... worse?"

Jeremy drew back. "Of course not."

Bernie let out a long breath and dropped her head to her hands. "Thank God."

"Thank God? What do you mean?"

She glanced quickly at him, then looked away again. "Uh...nothing."

Jeremy looked confused for a moment more. Then his eyebrows flew up. "Oh, my God."

"What?"

"You thought I killed him."

"No! No, of course not!"

Jeremy smiled. "Yes, you did."

"I did not!"

"Then why were you so worried?"

"I wasn't worried. I just..."

"Just what?"

"Oh, all right," she muttered. "The thought crossed my mind. But just for a second or two!"

His smile grew bigger. "You've got to be kidding."

"No! It's...it's like when you hear a noise at night and you're absolutely sure there's a serial killer in the house. You know, of course, that there really *isn't,* but just for a second it's there in your mind, and..." She slumped with resignation. "Oh, hell."

Jeremy laughed. "You're still in the hole, Bernie. Stop digging."

"Hey! You did say the problem was 'taken care of.'"

"For God's sake, Bernie. This isn't a mobster movie."

"Yeah? Well, it sounded an awful lot like one there for a minute."

Jeremy kept smiling, as if this really were a laughing matter. "You actually thought I might have *killed* the man?"

"Not you personally. I thought maybe you'd..." She shrugged. "You know. Put a contract out on him, or something."

The longer she talked, the dumber she sounded, and Jeremy laughed again. "You know, if I wanted somebody dead, that's exactly how I'd go about it. Unfortunately, I wouldn't want to risk the death sentence that comes along with murder for hire."

"So you just threatened him? Even though Billy is just the kind of guy who's asking for *way* more than that?"

"Yes, we just threatened him. You know. 'We made him an offer he couldn't refuse.'"

"Oh, shut up," Bernie muttered.

"And once he makes good and moves out, I'll run him through the next phase."

"The next phase?"

"I'll give him a job. Nothing much. Just groundskeeping at the Sybersense facility. If he can mow a lawn, I'll put him on the payroll."

Bernie sat back, shocked. "You'd do that, knowing what he's like?"

"He only gets one shot," Jeremy said. "He screws up, he's out. But I think it'll make your mother happy to see him employed." He nodded toward Bernie's plate. "Now, eat your lasagne, or I'm going to."

Bernie picked up her fork again. But before she could take another bite, something struck her that made tears come to her eyes. *He did this for you.*

"What's wrong?" Jeremy said.

"Allergies," Bernie said. "Been fighting them a lot lately."

He just smiled and took another bite of lasagne.

Over the next week, spending her evenings with Jeremy was both heaven and hell for Bernie. She enjoyed every moment, even as she knew those moments were numbered.

As soon as Jeremy got home every evening, Mrs. Spencer would slip out the back door, leaving them alone in the house. They'd eat whatever she fixed for them—chicken and dumplings, meat loaf and green beans, linguine with clam sauce—heaping helpings of the kind of comfort food that warmed Bernie right down to her toes. Then came the brownies and chocolate cake and bread pudding, which she always swore she wasn't going to touch, only to take one orgasmic bite and then dive face-first into a whole serving. Or two. If she kept this up, she was going to gain fifty pounds and look like an elephant, but she told herself that she had plenty of time to go back to eating like a responsible pregnant woman when she was by herself again.

And then after dinner, they'd go to Jeremy's den to watch TV. At first Bernie had thought a seventy-inch LCD TV was a ridiculous waste of glass and plastic and expensive electronic components. But fifteen minutes into *Monday Night Football,* she found out what all the fuss was about when it came to gargantuan, prestige-brand televisions. She could practically hear the hits and smell the sweat. The only way to get a better experience would be to sit dead center on the fifty-yard line. On an off-sports night, they discovered they both liked the History Channel and crime shows but hated talk shows. But the truth was that Bernie could have watched the Weather Channel with Jeremy and been happy to do it.

And through it all, Jeremy would insist Bernie relax on the sofa because she was supposed to be on bed rest. The sofa was huge and soft and felt like heaven to lie on.

But what was really heaven was watching Jeremy sit at the other end of the sofa, his shoes kicked off and his feet on the coffee table, holding a bottle of beer. She'd always thought he seemed pretty laid back, but she hadn't realized until now just how much of an act it was when he was in front of other people. He always spoke and dressed as if he was totally relaxed, but in the past few days she'd watched him move into another realm. It was as if the worry lines in his forehead disappeared and the laugh lines around his eyes intensified, and he moved with a lazy kind of grace that said he felt comfortable and content and stress-free.

Which was exactly how she felt.

All too quickly, though, the days passed. On Tuesday evening, Bernie tried to concentrate on the episode of *CSI* they were watching, but her mind wasn't on the show. Instead she was thinking about the ultrasound scheduled for tomorrow to reevaluate her condition. She would know if bed rest was still necessary, which meant she'd know if staying with Jeremy was still necessary. Part of her was eager to get home, to see her newly renovated apartment, to start building her nest for the babies. He'd convinced her to move to a two-bedroom apartment, and she was looking forward to putting together an actual nursery.

But she was also going to miss Jeremy more than she'd ever thought possible.

"Tomorrow's my ultrasound," she said.

Jeremy picked up the remote and paused the show. "Yeah. I'll send Carlos for you, then meet you there."

She nodded. "I think it's going to show everything's okay."

"I think it is, too."

"By this time tomorrow, I could have the go-ahead to get back on my feet and back to work. That means I'll be going home, too."

"Yeah. I guess it does."

"My apartment is ready, isn't it?"

"It will be. They're installing the appliances today." He shrugged offhandedly. "But if you'd like to stay a little longer, that'd be okay."

Bernie couldn't tell if he was just being nice, or if he really did want her to stay. A few weeks ago, he had told her he wasn't good at being nice, but since then she'd discovered just how wrong that was. But either way, it didn't matter. In the end, they lived separate lives, and it was time for them to get on with living them.

"Are you kidding?" Bernie said with a smile. "You've done too much for me already. I'm spoiled forever by that bed in the guest suite, and I think I gained ten pounds from Mrs. Spencer's cooking."

Jeremy smiled. "Why do you think I spend most of my lunch hours at the gym?"

And then he nonchalantly picked up the remote and started the show again.

So there it was. If her ultrasound was okay, she was moving out. She told herself that was a good thing. What if she stayed longer, but didn't read the signs when she'd worn out her welcome? He'd have to ask her to leave, and that would be excruciating. And though he'd been kind enough not to bring women to his house when she was on bed rest, a man with Jeremy's sexual appetite couldn't abstain forever. Sooner or later she'd look up to see him coming through the door with a beautiful blond on his arm. Did she really want to witness that firsthand?

No. She didn't. As much as she enjoyed being there, staying indefinitely was a recipe for disaster. If her doctor took her off bed rest tomorrow, she was going home.

At ten o'clock the next morning, the ultrasound revealed the good news they'd both hoped for. The blood clot had been absorbed, so Bernie's doctor took her off bed rest and released her to go back to work.

Jeremy had never seen such a perfect case of "good news, bad news" in his life. He didn't realize until the doctor said the words just how much he was going to miss Bernie. But he also knew he couldn't coerce her to stay, because there wasn't a single concrete reason for her to continue to live with him. What was he supposed to say to her? That he didn't want her to get on with her life because he hated eating dinner alone?

Now *that* would be pitiful.

"Now that I'm mobile again," Bernie said as they left the building, "I have errands to run before I go back to work tomorrow."

"You heard the doctor," Jeremy said. "You're free to get up and around, but don't wear yourself out."

"I won't."

"And remember what else she said. If you have any more bleeding, you need to go straight back to see her."

"I will."

"I think you should start out slow. Not just jump right back in as if this never happened."

"I think so, too."

"In fact, just for today, at least, why don't you let Carlos take you on your errands? You can pack and go back to your apartment later this afternoon."

"Thank you," she said as they reached the limo. "That sounds nice. I think I'll let him do that."

Jeremy blinked. "Did you just agree with me about all of that? Right off the bat?"

"Why, yes, I did."

"Did the pod people come and take the real Bernie away when I wasn't looking?"

"Hey, just because I gave in on that stuff, don't think you're going to win them all. I have enough arguments left in me for a lifetime."

Bernie slipped into the limousine, tossing him a smile as he closed the door behind her. Carlos started the car, and Jeremy stood on the sidewalk watching as they drove away.

A lifetime?

In business, Jeremy was a long-range thinker. He could project his company's growth for the next ten years. He had his corporate strategy planned for the next decade. But where his personal life was concerned, he'd never considered what he would be doing next month or next year, much less over a lifetime. In fact, he felt as if he hadn't had a life at all until Bernie showed up at his office that day and turned his world upside down.

But now it was time for him to get on with things, just as she was. He'd been so distracted these past few weeks that he'd let things slide at work, and he needed to get back on track. Nose to the grindstone. Pedal to the metal. Now, finally, he'd be able to put Bernie out of his mind and concentrate on the hundred things he needed to do that required his undivided attention.

But wait a minute. She was packing to go home this afternoon. Even though she was off bed rest, should she be lugging a suitcase all over creation? He hadn't thought about that. And she didn't have her car at his place, which meant she'd need a ride back to her apartment. He hadn't thought about that, either. Yeah, Carlos could take her, but if Jeremy rode along, he could see her face when she saw her newly renovated apartment for the first time.

He thought about his schedule at work. It was tight, but he could certainly head home a little early to help get her squared away. After all, he was the boss, wasn't he?

Then he'd put his nose to the grindstone.

Chapter

25

Bernie asked Carlos to drive her to a nearby drugstore so she could pick up a few things, but she'd underestimated how dumb she'd feel taking a limousine to Walgreens. As soon as they drove into the parking lot, people's heads turned, and a few even stopped to watch her get out of the car. All she could do was ignore their curious stares and walk inside as if she traveled in luxury every day of the week.

She headed toward the aisles to grab shampoo and razor blades. On the way there, she passed a display of perfume. There wasn't anything much more girly than perfume, and any other time she might have walked right by it. But this time, for some reason, she slowed down, then stopped, letting her gaze travel from one bottle to another.

Some of them were shiny and sparkly. Some were curvy and pink with flowers all over them. They all had names that were either in French, and therefore unpronounceable, or something like Beautiful or Lovely or Radiance.

Dumb, she thought. *Not my thing.*

But for some reason, she glanced over her shoulder to see if anybody else was around, and when she saw she was alone, she tentatively picked up one of the tester bottles. She sniffed the squirter thingy and just about gagged. It was if she'd fallen face-first into a Rose Bowl Parade float.

She tried a few more. Same story.

Then she saw one that said something about sandalwood and jasmine, the scents of the Orient. She sniffed it. Okay, this one had promise. Low-key. Mysterious. Nonflowery.

She checked the area again for witnesses. When she didn't see any, she held out her wrist. Pushed the plunger.

Nothing came out.

She tried again, harder this time.

Still nothing.

She pushed it one more time, harder still, and the bottle suddenly spewed approximately half a gallon of perfume onto her wrist. Horrified, she set the bottle down and held her wrist out, shaking it, but all that did was make a few droplets fall from her arm to the floor, and her wrist was still wet with perfume. She rubbed her wrists together, hoping if she spread it around a little, it would dissipate faster, then brought her wrists to her nose.

Oh, God. She smelled like a Hong Kong whorehouse.

Without thinking, she wiped her wrists on her jeans, only to realize that it wouldn't obliterate the scent. It would just move it to another part of her body.

Abandoning the perfume display, she hurried to grab the shampoo and razor blades she'd needed in the first place and went to the checkout counter. The crinkling of the clerk's nose told the tale. Bernie still smelled as if she'd taken a dive into a vat of perfume.

She hurried out of the store and got back into the limousine. It took only about five seconds for Carlos to look into the rearview mirror, his nose crinkling with even more disgust than the clerk had shown.

"What the hell is that *smell*?" he said, with his usual display of tact.

"Never mind," Bernie snapped.

"Is that perfume?"

"It was an *accident*."

"*Whew*. If that was an accident, I think I'd be suing Walgreens."

"Just drive, will you?"

"Where to?"

Bernie gave him the address of her mother's house. As he punched it into the GPS, she sat back with her fingertips to her temples, trying to ward off the headache she was getting from smelling herself.

Note to self: *No girly stuff ever again as long as you live.*

Carlos pulled out of the parking lot. After a minute, Bernie spied a McDonald's and told him to stop, only to realize that if a limo looked dumb at a Walgreen's, it looked positively ridiculous at a McDonald's. She ran the gauntlet of curious stares and headed inside to the ladies' room, where she washed her wrists, which helped with the overall stench. Some of the perfume still clung to her jeans, but at least she'd no longer make birds fall dead out of the trees just by walking past.

A few minutes later, they arrived at her mother's house. Bernie knocked on the door, and her mother swept it open with a worried frown.

"Bernadette? Why are you here? Aren't you supposed to be in bed?"

"Good news," she said. "I went for an ultrasound today, and everything's back to normal. I'm off bed rest. Full speed ahead."

"Oh, I'm so glad!" Eleanor said. "I just knew everything was going to be okay." Then as Bernie walked past her into the house, her eyes grew wide with surprise. "Bernadette? Are you wearing...perfume?"

Give up. Right off the bat. Don't even try to explain. "Yeah, Mom. I'm wearing perfume."

"Well, it's a lovely scent," she said with a beaming smile, though how her mother could smell the Eau de Cheap Hooker over her Glade "Always Spring" air freshener, Bernie didn't know. "Now, see? Doesn't just a little dab behind your ears make you feel pretty?"

Behind her ears? How about smeared up and down her thighs? At least now that she'd washed it off her wrists, the scent had faded to a preasphyxiation level.

A few minutes later, she was sitting at her mother's kitchen table eating a chocolate chip muffin and drinking a cup of oolong tea. She'd chosen an Asian variety of tea because, of course, she'd didn't want what was going *in* her to clash with what was already *on* her.

"I don't see Billy around," Bernie said offhandedly.

"He moved out," Eleanor said.

"Oh, really?" Bernie said, feigning surprise. "What made him do that?"

"He found another place to live. And even better, he has a job. Your Jeremy hired him."

"*My* Jeremy?"

"He gave him a job at his office complex doing landscaping work. Isn't that nice?"

"Yeah. It is."

"And he was so generous to give me access to a car and driver. It helps me out so much, and he seemed genuinely happy to do it."

"Yeah, that was nice of him, too. But now that I'm on my feet again, I can take you wherever you need to go."

"Oh, no. Jeremy told me he intends for me to use the car and driver at least throughout your pregnancy. That way if you're not feeling well, or there's some other reason you have to stay off your feet, you won't have to worry about me." Eleanor smiled. "He's such a lovely man, Bernadette. You're so lucky to have him."

A queasy little feeling of apprehension slid through Bernie's stomach, because the truth was that she didn't have him. Wanted him, yes. She'd be a fool to keep denying it. But Jeremy Bridges had never been a one-woman man, and she knew he had no intention of ever becoming one. And now her mother had fallen under the charming spell he was so adept at weaving, leading her to believe that her daughter was Cinderella and her Prince had come.

"Mom, I don't think you understand," Bernie said. "There's still nothing between us. Not like you think. He's just not the kind of man who wants an ordinary family life. Do you know what I mean?"

"I think you're the one who doesn't understand," Eleanor said with a knowing smile. "That man cares for you more than you realize."

Maybe. But caring and loving were two entirely different things.

"So now that you're off bed rest, will you be going back to your apartment?" her mother asked.

"Yes. Of course. This afternoon, after I run all my errands."

Eleanor frowned. "Oh. I hoped you'd be staying with Jeremy."

"Come on, Mom. You know he was just helping me out until I was back on my feet."

"I know that's what you said. But I had hoped maybe—"

"He's going to be there for the babies," Bernie said.

"I know he is. But he'd also make a wonderful husband."

Bernie sighed with resignation. "You're not going to let go of this, are you?"

Eleanor gave her a small, knowing smile. "God hasn't stopped hearing from me about it yet."

Bernie decided there was no point in fighting it any longer. If her mother wanted to continue to petition God, so be it. She only hoped her mother wouldn't be too disappointed when God finally answered her, and the answer was no.

"Does Jeremy like your perfume?" Eleanor asked.

"He hasn't smelled it." *And he's never going to.*

Her mother smiled sweetly. "Always remember that no man can ever resist a woman wearing a pretty perfume."

Bernie sighed inwardly. She'd always been the kind of woman who was pretty darned easy for a man to resist, and a dab or two of perfume was never going to change that.

She ran a few more errands. It was nearly four o'clock before Carlos dropped her back at Jeremy's house. She headed into the kitchen and trotted up the stairs to the guest suite. Once inside it, she stopped for a moment to admire the place one last time. She'd told Jeremy the truth. She'd be forever spoiled after sleeping in this beautiful king-sized four-poster bed. And her thirty-two-inch TV was going to look positively pitiful after staring at the gigantic one over the fireplace for the past couple of weeks. And the Jacuzzi tub. There was nothing on earth to relax a person like one of those. And the balcony overlooking the property...

She sighed. It was all just too, too beautiful. But this was Jeremy's life, not hers. It was time she got back to her own reality: a nine-hundred-square-foot apartment with a postage-stamp-sized kitchen and a tiny bathtub whose only talent was holding water.

She flipped on the ridiculously expensive sound system and stuck in a CD, reveling one last time in music as it really should be heard. She hummed along with the melody as she pulled her suitcase out of the closet and opened it. She packed her jeans and shirts and pajama pants.

Then she saw the emerald green gowns and robe her mother had insisted on packing for her.

Oh, just leave them there. It's not as if you'll ever be wearing them.

She left the closet and started to shut the door, only to turn around to look at the gowns again. After a moment, she walked over and stared at them, then reached out to touch one. She ran her hand along the silky fabric. It felt absolutely decadent. She didn't know where her mother had gotten them, but they hadn't been cheap. Bernie might be a little out of place in this house, but these gowns certainly weren't.

On impulse, she pulled one off the rod, went back to the bedroom, and stood in front of the full-length mirror. She held up the gown in front of her and imagined for a moment she was wearing it. The fabric draped beautifully, and it would feel positively sinful against her bare skin.

She turned left and right. *Hmm.* Maybe it would be nice to wear a gown like this after all. Even if she looked funny in it, at least she could close her eyes and *feel* wonderful.

"Don't just hold it up. Try it on."

Startled, Bernie spun around, horrified to find Jeremy standing behind her. She yanked the gown away from herself at the same time she felt a hot flush rise on her cheeks.

"What are you doing here?" she said.

"I came up to see if you need some help with your suitcases. Didn't know I'd be interrupting a fashion show."

"You could have knocked."

"I did. I guess you didn't hear me over the music." He tilted his head. "The color's perfect for you. Let's see what it looks like on."

"Get real. I'm not putting it on."

"Where did you get it?"

"My mother. She has different taste in nightclothes than I do."

"Sorry. I'm going to have to side with your mother. Though your blue terrycloth robe is lovely, too."

"Will you shut *up*?"

Bernie tried to brush past him, but he grabbed her by the arm.

"Wait," he said. "What's this I smell?"

"Smell?"

He raised an eyebrow. "Perfume?"

Oh, *God.* Not that, too. "I don't wear perfume."

"No, it's definitely perfume."

She sighed. "It was a tester at the drugstore. I was just...you know. Goofing around."

He dipped his head to smell her neck, then pulled back, looking confused. "So where are you wearing it?"

"Never mind." She turned to walk away, but he caught her arm again and pulled her back around. He sniffed the air a few more times. Then he looked down.

She rolled her eyes. "Some got on my jeans, okay?"

"On your jeans?" he said. "How did that happen?"

"If you must know, the squirter thingy malfunctioned."

"A perfume malfunction. Never heard of one of those."

"Well, now you have."

"Might want to wear some perfume for real."

"No, thanks."

"Why not?"

"Because I don't do the girly thing."

He smiled. "Silk gown...perfume...sure you do."

"Wrong," she said, sticking the gown back into the closet. "Those things just aren't me."

"Were they ever you? What were you like in high school? Did you date?"

This conversation was really beginning to irritate her. "Let's put it this way. Boys didn't exactly hang out around my locker, waiting to ask me out."

"Why not?"

She went to the dresser. "They were too busy chasing the ones who spent all their time reading *Glamour* and *Cosmo* and painting their toenails."

"But you weren't interested in those things?"

"Nope. But God, how my mother tried to get me to be. Turn around. I'm packing my underwear."

"Oh, for heaven's sake," Jeremy said. "It's not as if I haven't seen women's underwear before."

Yes, but had he seen utilitarian white cotton underwear? She doubted that very much. "Turn *around.*"

With a roll of his eyes, he slowly turned around and kept his back to her until she had transferred her undies from the drawer to the suitcase.

"Do you know she bought me a pink angora sweater for my thirteenth birthday?"

"Yeah?" Jeremy said, facing her again. "What did you do with it?"

"Wore it to a family dinner. Then I stuffed it into the back of my closet and prayed she'd forget about it."

"Maybe it was just the wrong color. Do they make those in camouflage?"

Bernie sighed. "I am *so* not the daughter she wanted."

"You're wrong about that. The other night she talked about how much you help her. She loves you a lot."

"Yeah, I know. But she never really understood me. I guess that's why I miss my father so much."

"You said he died several years ago, but you never really told me about him."

She smiled softly. "He was so wonderful. He used to take me fishing. To ballgames. To the shooting range. My mother *really* hated that." She paused for a moment as the bittersweet memories overcame her. "It felt good to be with him. Natural. Like I was born to put on waders and go fly fishing, or get my hands greasy helping him change the spark plugs in his car. Every time my mother got frustrated by that, he'd just laugh and tell her to stop with the girly stuff and let me be *me.*"

"I take it that was hard for her to do."

"My mother wanted me to be a cheerleader. My father wanted me to be point guard on the varsity basketball team."

"So were you?"

"What?"

"Point guard on the varsity basketball team."

She smiled. "Yeah. I was. I only wish my father had been there to see it."

Jeremy nodded as if he understood completely. Given what he'd told her, it was pretty clear his own father hadn't been present at many school events.

"To give my mother credit," Bernie said, "she never missed a game. But she was far more concerned with making sure I wore ribbons in our school colors tied around my ponytail. All she ever wanted was for me to get married and have a family. Unfortunately, it looks as if that husband she'd like me to have isn't going to wander along anytime soon. And even if he does, trust me. He'll keep on walking."

Jeremy took a step toward Bernie, his chin in his hand. "You know, you're more attractive than you think you are."

She slumped with dismay. "Now why would you say something dumb like that?"

"Because it's true. You have great eyes. Irises so dark they practically melt into your pupils. Eyelashes the average woman would kill for. Perfect skin. Pretty hair, even if you don't do anything with it. And if you'll pardon my saying so, a really nice ass."

She glared at him. "I've strangled men for less than that."

"Nah. You need a compliment or two. Believe in yourself a little, Bernie. You're not the man repellent you seem to think you are."

"You're just trying to make a pudgy pregnant woman feel good." She closed the suitcase and zipped it.

"I meant what I said. Stop selling yourself short."

"Old habits die hard."

"That's one you need to get rid of."

Suddenly she realized just how serious he was, and she felt a warm shiver of awareness. "Thanks for everything," she said softly. "Including the ego boost."

That wasn't how Jeremy intended it at all. He wasn't trying to boost her ego. He was merely telling the truth. Lately he'd found it hard to believe he'd never noticed just how pretty she really was. All these years, her tough-girl attitude had masked all the good things in her heart that showed so clearly on her face right now.

Suddenly Jeremy heard a car engine outside. Bernie walked over and looked out the window to the motor court below.

"Gotta go," she said. "That's my ride."

"Your ride?"

"My friend Teresa is picking me up."

Jeremy felt a surge of disappointment. "She is?"

"Yeah. She has some things to give me for the baby. And she wants to see my new apartment."

Yeah, but Jeremy wanted to be the one who was there when Bernie saw her new apartment. *Damn.* What was he supposed to say now? *Go away, Teresa, I have this handled?*

Jeremy took the suitcase. Bernie flipped off the music, and they went downstairs. Bernie opened the back door and a woman came into the kitchen—a tall, pretty, perky woman Jeremy truly wished would go away.

"I *cannot* believe this place," Teresa said to Bernie, her

eyes as wide as searchlights. "I simply can't believe it." She hiked a thumb over her shoulder. "That lake out there has swans in it. *Swans.* And this house. My God. It looks like a freakin' castle. What is it? Like, eight thousand square feet?"

"Ten," Jeremy said.

Teresa whipped around, seeing Jeremy for the first time. A smile came over her face. "And the view keeps getting better and better." She strode over to Jeremy. "Hi. I'm Teresa Ramsey."

Jeremy shook her hand. "Jeremy Bridges."

"So you're the king of the castle."

"Yes. I guess I am."

"Well, it's *very* nice to meet you." She turned to Bernie. "Oh! Guess what? My cousin said she definitely doesn't want the crib anymore, so she's giving it to you."

"That's great!"

"Bill's going to get it right now and bring it to your apartment. It's been in pieces in storage, so he'll have to put it together."

"Uh-oh," Bernie said. "Bill? Put something together?"

Teresa turned to Jeremy. "She's referring to the time my husband tried to assemble a desk. When he got finished, he had a handful of hardware left over, and the file drawer fell off." She turned back to Bernie. "Don't worry. Lucky and Gabe are coming, too. They'll make sure he gets it right."

Jeremy knew who Gabe was. But who the hell was Lucky?

"Max, too?" Bernie said.

"He'll be by later to join everybody for poker."

Poker?

"And don't worry. I know you don't have any groceries yet, so I picked up a couple of six-packs and stuff for nachos."

"Thanks. You're an angel."

"We'd better get going, or Bill is going to beat us to your apartment." She turned to Jeremy. "It was nice to meet you."

"You, too."

He grabbed Bernie's suitcase, took it out to Teresa's car, and stuck it in the trunk. Then he opened the front passenger door and Bernie got in.

"Thanks for everything," she said.

"Any time."

He closed the door behind her. Teresa started the car, and in moments, they'd disappeared down the road.

And that was that.

Jeremy went back inside. For the longest time, he just stood in the kitchen, listening to the silence. In the time he'd known Bernie, she'd never spoken of family and friends, so he had taken her to be as much of a loner as he was. Now he knew just how wrong he'd been. The familiar way she and Teresa talked about the men told him just how close they all were, and it made Jeremy feel like the odd man out.

All at once he envisioned coming home in the evenings the way he used to, eating dinner alone in the breakfast room, doing a little work from the office, watching a little TV, then going to bed. Then he thought about women he used to date, the ones he'd never felt any connection with, and he couldn't believe that had ever been enough. And this house. He'd been so proud of it when he'd built it, but now when he looked at it, he didn't see the soaring ceilings, the beautiful furnishings, the expensive art. Instead he saw the space between all those things—the empty space that he'd never even thought about before, but that now seemed to surround him like a shroud.

If only Bernie hadn't left. But why shouldn't she? It wasn't as if she needed him anymore.

He went to his den and sat down, flipping on the television to fill the silence. Then he looked beneath the coffee table and realized she'd left her slippers. He felt a shot of excitement, only to have it fizzle. Returning them to her might be good for a five-minute visit. Then what?

Then Jeremy happened to look at the bookshelves on the opposite side of the room and saw the stack of resumes the agency had sent over, the ones he'd tried to get Bernie to go through with him the night she ended up in the emergency room. He hadn't looked at them since. The guy from his facilities department was doing a great job filling in as manager, but he really did need to hire somebody permanently.

Then all at once he had an idea.

He sat straight up in his chair, turning it over in his mind. It was the kind of plan he loved the most—a win-win for all concerned. And this time tomorrow, he'd have exactly what he wanted, and so would Bernie.

She just didn't know it yet.

The next day, Bernie sat in front of the museum's security monitors, her eyes crossing, checking her watch every five minutes. Unfortunately, around here, five minutes felt like fifty. She watched people milling around the central atrium. Having a bite of lunch at the café. Walking up and down in front of the exhibits. Wandering through the gift shop. On and on and on. She was thoroughly convinced that they could hire a marginally intelligent chimpanzee to do this job, except he'd probably get bored and quit.

The door behind her suddenly opened. Surprised by the noise, she spun around and was shocked to see Jeremy come into the room with Max following close behind.

Jeremy pulled up a chair backward, slung a leg over it, and rested his forearms on the back. Max took up a position along the wall.

"What are you guys doing here?" she asked.

"I need to talk to you," Jeremy said.

"How did you find your way back here?"

"Max figured it out."

"If the head of security finds you here, he'll kick you out."

"I have a proposition for you."

"Oh, boy. This can't be good."

"Hear me out. You hate your job, so—"

"I didn't say I hated my job."

"Your mouth hasn't said it, but your face always has."

"So now you're a body language expert?"

"She hates it," Max said.

Bernie turned and glared at him. "I can speak for myself, Max."

"Evasively," Max said.

"Anyway," Jeremy said, "yesterday I was looking over those resumes for the manager's job at Creekwood, and suddenly I realized who the perfect candidate was."

"Who?"

"You."

"Me?" Bernie just stared at him, more than a little stunned. "You want me to manage Creekwood Apartments?"

"That's right."

"But—but I don't know anything about managing an apartment complex."

"Neither did Charmin."

"I know, but—"

"Do you honestly think it's something you couldn't do?"

"She can do it," Max said.

Bernie glared at him again. "You know, for somebody who doesn't talk much, you're having a hard time shutting up."

Max smiled. Just a little.

"Of course I can do it," Bernie told Jeremy. "I just don't know if I'm the *best* person to do it."

"As far as I'm concerned, you are," Jeremy said. "And it's a win-win situation. You get a job where you can move around, solve problems, get things done. And I protect my investment by hiring somebody competent to run it. Would learning something new be too stressful for you?"

"Stressful? I'm used to stress. That's why this job is killing me. If I don't have stress, I *get* stressed."

"Even with the babies?"

"Even with the babies."

"Would it be too much activity?"

"No. At this place, I get too little activity. That's not good."

"We'd have to work together quite a bit to make sure things stayed on track. Any problem with that?"

"Hell, yes. You drive me crazy."

Jeremy smiled. "So will you do it?"

"Benefits?"

"Whatever you need."

Then he mentioned a salary figure that positively ensured his investment was going to show a huge loss. She'd have to talk to him about that, because she still didn't like the idea of getting something for nothing. And she still wasn't completely sure she was competent to do the job. But if it meant getting out of this place...

"Bernie," Jeremy said, "am I going to have to spend ten more minutes convincing you it's the right thing to do? Because if I am—"

"She'll do it," Max said.

Bernie slumped with frustration. "Will you let me speak for *myself*?" She turned back to Jeremy. "Okay. I'm in. But the second you start in with the micromanaging control freak crap, I'm out of there. If you pay me to run the show, *I'm* running it."

"Deal. You can start as soon as you can shake free from this job."

It would feel strange to quit working for Gabe after all this time, but realistically, as a pregnant woman and eventually a mother, was she really all that employable where he was concerned?

Maybe it was time to move into something totally different.

"Fine," she said. "But I still don't get why you're here. Couldn't you have just given me a call tonight?"

"I had to catch you at a vulnerable moment," Jeremy said.

"What?"

"At the height of boredom. If you were sitting here wishing you were anywhere else, you were much more likely to accept my offer." He rose from the chair and pushed it back up against the desk. "Come on, Max. Let's go."

"Who are you guys going to rough up now?" Bernie asked.

"Hmm," Jeremy mused. "I have a board of directors that doesn't always see things my way. I'm thinking of bringing Max in. Just to stand there. You know."

Max flexed his biceps, his mouth turning down in a bad-ass frown.

Bernie rolled her eyes. "You're both nuts. *Out.*"

Jeremy gave her a wink as they left the room, and she couldn't help smiling back. After all, it was a perfect opportunity he was offering her. She'd be exercising the brain she swore had atrophied from lack of use. She'd be talking to people and solving their problems. She'd be overseeing the renovation. And as much as she'd told Jeremy to stay out of her way, of course she'd be discussing things with him, implementing his plans, reporting her progress. Together they'd be turning Creekwood into a decent place for the residents to live. As time went on, they might even be able to figure out a way to make it a profitable business.

She couldn't wait.

Chapter

26

Bernie knew it had been the right decision to take the manager's job at Creekwood Apartments, but she didn't have any idea just how much she would love it. Within the first six weeks she was there, she subscribed to *Units* magazine. She joined the Apartment Association of Greater Dallas and attended webinars on tenant relations and the Fair Housing Act. She created a satisfaction survey that she sent to each tenant to get feedback for future services. She managed the work crews, fielded tenant complaints, and handled rent collections. Not that there weren't problems. A lot of them. But she never brought Jeremy a problem without also proposing a solution, and he had yet to disagree with her. Given Jeremy's incredible success as a businessman, that gave her ego a really nice boost.

When she thought about Charmin occupying the same job, she almost laughed out loud. Charmin had spent all day every day trying to find ways to avoid work, while Bernie couldn't wait for the next task. She knew there would come a day very soon when she'd have to slow down, and when that time came, Jeremy was going to send somebody over to help, eventually filling in for her until the babies were born. But for now, she was getting the job done and loving every minute of it.

One afternoon Jeremy was in her office at Creekwood, thumbing through the payables for some of the carpentry work.

"That guy charges an awful lot," Bernie said, pointing to one of the bills. "It's starting to really add up. I can get bids from another company if you want me to."

"What's the quality of his work?"

"Top-notch."

"Better to pay a lot to get it done right the first time then to pay again to have it fixed."

"Good point."

Jeremy glanced to Bernie's inbox. "What's this?" he said, picking up the booklet that was lying on the top.

"Something I picked up about childbirth classes."

He sat down on the edge of her desk to look at it. "Is that where they teach you all that breathing stuff?"

"Yeah. It's supposed to help with the pain."

"I thought painkillers were supposed to help with the pain."

"Not if you're having natural childbirth."

"Is that what you want? Natural childbirth?"

"My doctor says with twins, it's a pipe dream. Actually, I'd prefer they knock me out and wake me up when the kids turn eighteen, but I don't think that's an option."

"When do the classes start?"

"In a few weeks. I'm supposed to take them in my second trimester instead of my third, because a lot of twin pregnancies don't make it all the way to term."

"Says here you need a coach."

"Yeah. I thought I'd ask Teresa. She has two kids, so she knows what it's like. With her there to help me—"

"Hold on. What about me?"

"What about you?"

"Shouldn't I be your coach?"

"Uh…"

"Bernie. I am the babies' father."

"You want to be in the delivery room?"

"Why not?"

"Do you remember that PBS documentary we started watching that night about childbirth? When that baby popped out, I thought you were going to faint. You couldn't turn the channel fast enough."

"That was because it was somebody else's baby. It was ugly. That was why I nearly fainted."

"All newborn babies are ugly. It's the law."

Jeremy drew back. "My children will *not* be ugly."

"Yeah, but will their father be facedown on the floor?"

"Nope. Coaches are always in control." He smiled. "I like that. *Coach.* If I'm going to be in there when the babies are born, I might as well be in charge."

"Uh-huh. I'm thinking they call it 'coach' because it's a sports reference, which is an excellent way to convince men to show up."

"Did you sign up for the classes yet?" Jeremy asked.

"Not yet. We can go on either Tuesdays or Thursdays. Two hours a night for six weeks. Which day do you want?"

"I don't care. Just sign us up and I'll work around it."

"You sure you want to do this?"

"Yep." He tossed the brochure back in her inbox. "I've

got to get back to the office. Just let me know when it's a done deal and you have the schedule."

As Jeremy left the office, Bernie felt a little shell-shocked. He was actually going to be in the room with her when the babies were born? She had never imagined he'd want to do that, and she wasn't prepared for the feelings that overwhelmed her at the thought of it.

She picked up the brochure. On the front was a photo of a man and woman. The woman was in a labor bed, and the man was holding her hand and smiling at her. All at once she felt the same way she had that first day in her doctor's waiting room, when she'd seen that couple sitting together, smiling at each other as they felt their baby move. She'd felt a shot of envy so strong it was almost incapacitating, and she was feeling the same way now.

Sometimes at night, in that zone between waking and sleeping, Bernie imagined reaching over to feel a man beside her, a man who was good and kind and dependable who would love her forever. She imagined him turning over and pulling her against him; holding her close, and for those few moments, she could let down her guard, melt into comfort and safety, relax in the warmth of his arms, and all her problems would go away. In the last several years, that dream had become so hazy that she rarely even thought about it anymore, but there was something about the prospect of single motherhood that brought it right back into sharp focus.

She'd never actually visualized the man before. He was more of a thought, a concept, an ideal. But that night, when she lay down to sleep and that hazy dream returned, this time it was Jeremy's arms that were holding her, his warmth she was sinking into.

And she went to sleep feeling as if she didn't have a care in the world.

Two weeks later, on a Tuesday evening, Bernie and Jeremy walked down a hospital corridor to room 202 and peered through the glassed-in upper half of the door. Four other couples were already there, sitting in a circle on the floor. Bernie couldn't help thinking they looked like four beached whales with four clueless people sitting beside them who had no idea how to get them back in the water. And as soon as she and Jeremy joined them on the beach, they'd look just as lost, clueless, and stuck.

"Are we late?" Bernie said. "I hate being late."

"Yes, we're late. So we'd better get in there."

Jeremy opened the door for Bernie, then followed her into the room. Another woman was there in addition to the four couples, but since she was single and nonpregnant, Bernie guessed she was the instructor. She sat on the floor with the others, her legs crossed in a funny yoga position that only freakishly thin women could accomplish. She tilted her head, blinked her giant blue eyes, and gave Bernie a beatific smile.

"Hello. You must be Bernadette."

Bernie felt an instant sense of *ick* that she just couldn't quell. She knew women like this one. They were named Lilith or Harmony or Sapphire and spent a lot of time visualizing world peace.

"Uh...yeah," Bernie said. "Bernie, actually."

"Bernie," the woman said, that smile still stuck to her face. "I'm Crystal."

Of course you are.

"And this is your birth coach?" Crystal said, turning her attention to Jeremy.

"Yes. This is Jeremy."

"Hello, Jeremy. Please join us."

Just then, Jeremy's phone rang. As he reached for it, Crystal's saintly smile turned into an admonishing frown.

"Turn it off," Bernie whispered to him, and he looked back at her as if she'd asked him to sever his own arm.

"Off," Bernie said.

Jeremy twisted his mouth with irritation, but he turned off his phone and stuck it into his pocket.

"I'm sorry, Jeremy," Crystal said. "But we're learning how to make birthing a child a calm, tranquil experience. A ringing phone instantly destroys that tranquility."

Bernie had never thought of childbirth as being a particularly tranquil activity. But if Crystal could show her how to refrain from gnawing through Jeremy's jugular vein during labor because he was the one who'd put her there, she was all for it.

Bernie found an open spot on the floor. Jeremy helped her sit, which was becoming more difficult to do with every week that passed. If she was this unwieldy at eighteen weeks, what would she be like in another month or two?

She didn't even want to think about it.

Crystal suggested they go around the circle so everybody could introduce themselves. Fortunately, only two of the couples were of the traditional variety—husband and wife. One couple was a woman and her female partner, and the other was a woman with her boyfriend, so Bernie didn't feel even more out of place than she had walking through the door. But she did have the sense of the others sizing them up. As always, they had to be thinking the obvious: She's with *him*? What's the deal with that?

"Now," Crystal said. "Can anybody tell me the most valuable thing you can take into the birthing room with you?"

"Well, I'm pretty sure it's not an iPhone," Jeremy said under his breath, and Bernie raised an eyebrow. *No smart remarks. This is serious business.*

"The answer is a positive state of mind," Crystal said. "In light of that, we're going to learn some positive affirmations. Ladies, will you repeat after me?" She took a deep breath and let it out slowly, then spoke as if she were channeling Confucius.

"I believe in my capability to give birth."

Jeremy turned to look at Bernie, one eyebrow lifted. *Is this woman for real?* She shot him the evil eye. *If I have to say this stupid stuff, the least you can do is listen.*

Bernie repeated the words, even though she was pretty sure this baby was coming out no matter what she believed.

"I trust my body to birth my child," Crystal said.

Bernie said the words, but really. Ditto her previous thoughts. Bodily trust wasn't going to change a thing.

"I inhale peace," Crystal said as she sucked in a noseful of air.

"Inhale peace?" Jeremy whispered.

Bernie repeated the mantra, then sucked in some air of her own, smelling not one iota of peace.

Crystal tilted her gaze toward the ceiling, her eyes drifting closed. "My pelvis is like a flower opening to the sun."

"Pelvic flowers?" Jeremy murmured. "Good God Almighty. Now I've heard everything."

"Will you knock it off?" Bernie whispered back.

"Bernie?" Crystal said. "Jeremy? Is there a problem?"

"Yeah," Jeremy said. "I was just wondering exactly how one inhales peace. And that pelvis thing—"

"Never mind," Bernie said, digging her fingernails into his thigh. "I'll explain it to him later."

For the briefest of moments, Crystal's mystically enhanced demeanor gave way to a cranky schoolmarm expression. It was probably her way of warning Jeremy that even though she inhaled peace, she didn't mind exhaling a little kick-ass. Then she transported herself to the Land of Bliss once again.

"What's very effective during the more difficult phases of childbirth," she said, "is to distract yourself with positive mental images. Imagine yourself walking along a tropical beach with ocean waves lapping at your toes. Picture yourself in a beautiful country garden, picking a bouquet of roses…"

Uh-huh. And the whole time Bernie would be picking those roses, her entire lower body would feel as if somebody was smacking it with a sledgehammer.

"After the break, we'll work on visualizations such as these in conjunction with our breathing exercises," Crystal said. "So now we'll talk about the various kinds of breathing for each stage of labor…"

As she rambled on, Bernie thought, *Who knew there were other ways to breathe besides just in and out?*

An excruciating hour and a half later they were leaving the class, armed with a couple of book recommendations and breathing homework. Max swung the car around to pick them up.

"You don't seem to be clicking with our instructor," Bernie said as they got into the car.

"What's with her, anyway?" Jeremy said. "Shouldn't she be in a cult somewhere drinking Kool-Aid, waiting for the mothership to return?"

"Hey, you said you wanted to come to these classes."

"Yeah, but I thought they'd actually be practical. All that woo-woo stuff's about to kill me. And I figured if I got bored, I could text somebody, or maybe check stock prices. But Attila the New Age Hun made me put my phone away."

"You have the attention span of a gnat. Will you at least try to pay attention next time? If I don't learn to breathe right, I have it on good authority that I'll be in excruciating pain and scream my head off."

"You know, women had babies long before anybody ever heard of childbirth classes," Jeremy said. "They used to give birth on cave floors in subzero weather with a T-Rex growling outside, and not one of them sprouted pelvic flowers or inhaled peace. So why do we need all that affirmation crap?"

"We? Who the hell is 'we'?"

"Hey, I'll be right there to feel your pain. Or at least watch it."

Max glanced into the rearview mirror. "What the *hell* are you two talking about?"

Jeremy shook his head sadly. "Believe me, Max. You don't want to know."

A few minutes later, Max pulled up outside Bernie's apartment. Jeremy got out to walk her up the stairs.

"Okay," Bernie said, as she unlocked her door and Jeremy escorted her inside. "Now you have an idea what the process is like. Are you still sure you want to be in the room when things go down?"

"No problem," Jeremy said. "I'm not the one whose pelvic flower is going to be opening."

"She makes it sound so easy, doesn't she?"

"Yep. Gardening, giving birth...it's all the same."

Listening to Jeremy's easy banter about her upcoming screamfest made Bernie feel as if she wasn't in this alone, and a sense of contentment surrounded her like a warm blanket.

"Well," he said. "I'd better go. I have a flight to catch early tomorrow morn—"

All at once, Bernie felt a strange flip-flop in her stomach. She gasped a little, steadying herself by putting a hand against the door frame. She thought for a moment something must be wrong, only to realize it was just the babies moving.

Just the babies moving. That was like saying a tsunami was just a big ocean wave.

Jeremy took her by the shoulders. "Bernie? What's wrong?"

"Don't worry," she said. "Nothing's wrong. It's just the babies moving."

"Moving what? A piano?"

"Sure seems like it. Here. Feel this."

She grabbed Jeremy's hand and placed it on her belly, and a moment later, it happened again—a big, undulating shift beneath her skin that actually made his hand move. Her doctor had told her that she'd feel quite a bit of movement, since she was having twins, but she sure hadn't expected this.

"Whoa," she whispered, laughing a little. "Are you *believing* that?"

Bernie expected him to make some smart comment about the movie *Alien*, suggesting that maybe the babies were actually creatures from outer space, or maybe tell her if she thought the kids were acting up now, wait until they were thirteen and started screaming and slamming doors.

He didn't.

Instead, he continued to stare down at his hand where it rested against her, seemingly transfixed. He took a small step forward, easing so close Bernie swore she could feel the warmth of his body mingling with hers. Then he put his other hand on her. Spread his fingers. Waited for movement. When it finally came again, a tiny smile curled the corner of his mouth.

"My God," he said breathlessly.

The next few seconds seemed to stretch into hours. Barely able to breathe, Bernie lifted her hands and placed them on top of his. The moment she touched him, he slowly turned his gaze up to meet hers. When their eyes locked, she flexed her fingers in a gentle caress. They stared at each other like that until the moment was so charged with emotion that she thought she'd die from the intensity of it. Was he looking at her like this because of the babies?

Or because of her?

He turned his hands over to grasp hers, giving them a gentle squeeze, his eyes fixed on hers with unrelenting intensity. She felt as if he was reading every thought she had, and those thoughts were growing hotter by the moment. She'd never felt desire like this in her life. Never ached for a man's touch so badly she couldn't breathe. It was as if every hot, sexy thought she'd ever had about him was coming to life.

He pulled one of her hands against his chest, where she felt his heart beating wildly. He smoothed his other hand along her upper arm to the curve of her shoulder, then tucked it beneath her hair at the back of her neck. When he brought his lips to within inches of hers, she could almost feel him quivering with self-restraint.

"I want you so much," he whispered. "Please don't tell me no."

"Not a chance," Bernie said.

"Thank God," he said, and lowered his mouth to hers.

Chapter
27

Jeremy felt so good and Bernie needed him so much that she almost cried out with relief. He kissed her like a man who'd been deprived for a decade—rough, eager kisses so incredibly satisfying that she thought her whole body was going to liquefy and ooze right onto the floor. The almost incapacitating desire she'd felt for him for so long clashed with the sensations flooding through her—his taste, his touch, his scent—and she wanted to drown in every erotic moment. What kind of a fool had she been to tell him she didn't want this?

After a while, he took her by the hand, and somehow they made it to her bedroom. He opened the door and pulled her inside, turning and nudging the door closed with his heel. Then he was kissing her again, and any remaining doubt she had about being with him vanished, and the place inside her that had been desperate for this kind of intimacy was suddenly filled to overflowing.

Suddenly he pulled away, breathing hard. "Hold on. Wait a minute."

She froze. "Wait? Why are we waiting?"

"Because we have to take this slow. Slow and easy."

"Why?"

"Because you're pregnant," he said, still catching his breath. "But don't worry. I know how to do this. I've been reading up."

"Reading up on what?"

"Sex during pregnancy. Now, don't get mad about that. I wasn't presuming anything. I just like to be prepared."

"Uh...okay."

"You're in your second trimester. Did you know that's the best time for sex? Women are generally sick during the first trimester and tired during the third. The second is the sweet spot. So our timing's good."

"Then we'd better get started, huh? In case the timing turns bad?"

"And I'll be extra careful, because I know there are some things that may be uncomfortable for you when we're doing it."

The only thing making her uncomfortable right now was the fact that they *weren't* doing it.

"So we need to think about positions," he said. "Those are important when you're pregnant. I learned about three of them, but they're kinda hard to describe. Wait—one of the websites had photos. Let me get my phone."

No. This couldn't be happening. Surely he wasn't reaching for his phone. Surely he wasn't—

Good Lord. He was.

He pulled his phone from his pocket. He gave the screen a poke, then swept his thumb across it a few times.

"Bridges. Put down the phone."

"It'll only take a sec. I have it bookmarked."

"Are you actually going to show me pictures of people having sex?"

"They're wearing clothes," Jeremy said. "The photos are just for demonstration purposes."

She grabbed the phone from his hand and tossed it to the top of her dresser. "I want to have sex. You want to do research. What's wrong with this picture?"

"I just want to do it right."

"There is no wrong way to do it."

"Oh, yeah? You should read the websites. Women change a lot when they're pregnant. What turned them on before turns them off now. Some parts are really sensitive. Lots of conflicting messages. For the record, guys don't like conflicting messages. It makes it hard for them to…you know. Do the job."

She couldn't help laughing. "Do the *job*?"

"And now you're laughing," he said, turning away. "That's just *great*."

Bernie stood there for several seconds, totally confused by this decidedly non-Jeremy behavior. Then the most amazing realization struck her.

"Are you nervous about this?" she asked.

He whipped back around. "Nervous? *Me?*" He laughed a little. "Do you know who you're talking to?"

"Yeah. A man who's made love to umpteen women, and not one of them has ever been pregnant."

"Well, yeah, that's true, but…" As his words faded out, he turned away, his mouth tight-lipped with irritation. Then his eyes drifted closed and he let out a sigh of resignation.

"Okay. You're right. I told you I knew what to do, but the truth is that I don't have a clue. This is uncharted territory for me. I've wanted you so badly I could taste it, and suddenly here we are, and now...now all I can think about is messing it up."

"Messing it up?"

He let out a long breath. "I'm just afraid of doing something that makes you uncomfortable, or hurts you, or makes you want to stop."

She couldn't believe it. Jeremy Bridges, a man who'd left hundreds of satisfied women in his wake, was actually uptight about making love to her? Something about that made her want to start kissing him and never stop.

She inched closer and placed her hands against his chest, then leaned in and touched her lips to his. "That's not going to happen. And just for the record, I'm nervous, too."

"You are? Why?"

"Because you're a man who's made love to umpteen women, and not one of them has ever been pregnant."

"True, but—"

"I'm not like the picture-perfect women you're used to being with."

He kissed her neck. "And I thank God every day for that."

"I just don't want you to be disappointed in what you see. So I'm thinking maybe you should turn out the lights."

"Bernie—"

"I'm thirty-six years old, I'm pregnant, gravity and I are not on speaking terms, and I could fill the Great Lakes with the water I'm retaining."

"I don't care," he whispered in her ear. "I want to see you."

"Do you also want to see my white cotton underwear?" She rolled her eyes. "*God.* Why do I have to be so damned practical?"

He smiled. Then he laughed softly, shaking his head. "You're really something, you know that?"

"Now *you're* laughing," she muttered. "Wonderful."

"If you had any idea of how hot I am for you, you'd know just how fast that underwear is going to end up on the floor."

True to his word, he had her shirt off in an instant, and with a flick of his fingers, he unhooked her bra and tossed it to the floor. He circled her breasts with his hands, squeezing them gently. She draped her arms loosely behind his neck, tilting her head backward as he kissed his way down her neck to her shoulder.

"You were so wrong," he whispered. "You are so beautiful."

They were words she'd never heard from a man before, and she refused to believe them. But then he was taking off the rest of her clothes, and his, and by the way he looked at her in the dim lamplight with such an adoring, appreciative gaze, she started to believe he really meant it. Any remaining mistrust she might still have been clinging to seemed to fade away, and the place in her heart that had felt so empty for years was suddenly filled with warmth. He tunneled one hand into the hair at the back of her head, tilting her head so their mouths fit together perfectly and he could kiss her deeper and harder with the kind of passion she'd lain awake nights dreaming about.

She pressed a kiss to the side of his neck, then whispered breathlessly in his ear. "I want you so much. *Please* make love to me."

He eased her over to the bed, where he pulled back the covers and helped her lie down. She started to tell him that he didn't have to be so careful, that she wouldn't break, only to realize how special it made her feel that he thought she might.

He stretched out beside her on one elbow. Closing his hand around one of her breasts, he traced his thumb back and forth over her nipple. Her breasts were so tender that at first it hurt, but after a moment the pain was gone and there was only pleasure. And when he dipped his head to touch his tongue to it, sweeping it in slow circles, the satisfaction was so intense she thought she'd die from the feeling.

"I want you," she said breathlessly. "Please. I've wanted you so much, for such a long time now. *Please*."

He kissed the curve of her shoulder, then grazed his lips against her ear. "Say my name," he whispered.

"What?"

"You never say my name. Say it."

"Bridges."

"You know what I mean."

She swallowed hard. "Jeremy."

The last syllable fell nearly silent on the single breath she took to say it. She loved the rhythm of it, the three syllables, the way it sounded as it passed through her lips.

"That's better," he said softly. "So much better."

She laid her hand against his cheek, staring into those beautiful eyes, then stroked her fingertips though his hair and pulled him down for one kiss, then another, and then they all seemed to blend together in a single sea of sensation. Just as she thought she might cheerfully drown in it, he rolled away for a moment and she realized he was getting a condom.

"I don't know if you need that," she said. "I can't exactly get pregnant again."

"I'm just protecting you. I've been with a lot of women."

"Yeah, I know."

The moment the words were out of her mouth, she wished she could take them back. But all he did was stroke her arm and look down at her with an expression of total sincerity.

"It's been months since I've been with another woman, Bernie. Since that day you showed up in my office and told me you were pregnant, you're the one I've wanted."

She couldn't believe it. All this time? No other women?

But his gaze had remained strong and steady as he said the words, as if to assure her he was telling the truth. He gave her a gentle kiss, then eased her over to lie on her side with her back to him. He rested on one elbow behind her, his forearm beneath her pillow, his other hand splayed beneath her breasts.

"If you lie like this," he said softly, "it should be comfortable for you. But if it's not, there are other ways. We'll find the right one, okay?"

She felt him hard against her and knew just how much he wanted her, but still he spent endless minutes kissing her neck, her shoulder, caressing her breasts at the same time, and her body seemed to melt under his mouth and his hands. Then he slid his hand down to delve gently between her legs. He had to feel how slick and hot she was and how she was dying to feel him inside her.

His lips touched her neck, his hot breath fanning her ear. "Are you ready for me, sweetheart?"

A shiver of anticipation slid right down her spine, followed by a rush of pure desire. Until all this happened, her only image of him was of a demanding, controlling, self-centered man who used women for his own pleasure.

Nothing could have been further from the truth.

"Yes," she said. "God, *yes*."

He bent her upper leg slightly at the knee, giving him access, and then he slipped inside her. He inhaled a sharp, raspy breath, and she could feel his shudder of self-restraint. She was so hot and wet that there was no resistance, but he filled her completely, and it felt so good when he began to rock inside her. But while his strokes were deep and thorough, they were also so maddeningly slow that she thought she'd go out of her mind.

"More. Jeremy, please. More. *Faster*."

"No, sweetheart. I have to take it easy. We'll get there, I promise you."

She hadn't expected this. She'd assumed he'd want it quick and hot and satisfying, and that was what she thought she wanted, too. Their first encounter had been about anger and power and control and was so hot the sofa practically caught fire, but this was the opposite. It was soft. Sweet. Tender. With every touch, every word, he was telling her just how much he cared about her and how good he wanted this to be.

He slipped his hand between her legs again, caressing her there as he rocked inside her, whispering soft words of encouragement. He read every small shift of her body, every whimper of satisfaction, stroking one way, rubbing another, until every molecule in her body was dying for release.

And then she felt it. Something deep inside, like a tiny

piece of kindling catching fire. Barely burning. Then burning brighter. A soft moan of pleasure rose in her throat.

"That's right," he whispered. "I want to hear you. Let
me know what feels good."

"Everything feels good. *Everything.*"

She tightened her muscles around him, the incredible pressure and friction pushing her higher and higher
until she was teetering on the edge and going insane with
anticipation.

"Oh, Jeremy, oh, *God* . . ."

When the first shockwave hit, she gasped at the sheer
power of it. Then came one shuddering spasm after
another—hard, pulsing, endless waves of agonizing pleasure. As she clamped down on him, he began to move
faster, harder, his restraint crumbling, and she heard his
breath catch. He grasped her thigh, and with his next
stroke, he dropped his forehead against her shoulder,
every muscle going rigid, a heavy groan ripping from his
throat. His hips convulsed as he moved deeper inside her,
wringing out every bit of pleasure he possibly could.

Finally he slumped against her, boneless with satisfaction, his skin warm against hers, his breath hot against
her neck. They lay there like that for a long time, slowly
edging their way back to reality. Then Jeremy fell to his
back and gathered her in his arms, pulling her against him
as they settled into satisfied exhaustion. Their breathing
became softer, more measured, and the heat of their love-
making dimmed to a warm glow.

"I have to fly to Atlanta early tomorrow morning," he
said.

She felt a rush of disappointment. "How long will you
be gone?"

"Three days. I don't want to go. In fact, I think I'm going to cancel my flight and lock us up together in this room forever."

"I like the sound of that," she said. "Oh. Problem. Sooner or later we'll have to eat."

"We'll let Mrs. Spencer in to bring us food. But that's it."

"What about Sybersense? How will they manage without their CEO?"

"How long do you think it'll take them to figure out I'm gone?"

"About five minutes."

He sighed dramatically. "Okay. So it's not a practical plan."

"But I do like the way you think." She nestled closer to Jeremy, and he tightened his arms around her. Then she had a thought of her own.

"Oh, my God," she said suddenly. "Max. He's still downstairs."

Jeremy grabbed his phone and called him, telling him to go home tonight and come back at six in the morning. Bernie could only imagine what was going through Max's mind, but she didn't want to think about that right now. All she wanted to think about was falling asleep in Jeremy's arms.

He flipped off the lamp and came back to bed. As he settled back against his pillow, Bernie eased over to rest her head against his shoulder. She took a deep breath, and when she let it out, she felt so relaxed that just lifting a finger would be a chore.

"I made you mad when I bought this apartment complex," Jeremy said. "But are you mad now?"

She laughed a little. "God, no. I love my apartment.

The whole complex is looking beautiful. It was a good thing you did, Jeremy. I know the tenants appreciate it."

"I know I acted like a real ass about wanting you to move. But it just reminded me so much of the place I lived when I was a kid. Nothing was as bad as that, but it sure stirred up the memories."

She couldn't even imagine what it must have been like. "How bad was it?"

For a moment, she thought he wasn't going to answer. Then he went on, his voice slipping into a quiet, haunting tone.

"Just about the only paint left on the buildings was graffiti. Boards were rotted. Weeds grew through every crack in the sidewalks. There were drug deals. Gang violence. Sometimes I slept on the floor because of the gunshots I heard, because I never knew if one of the bullets was going to come through my window."

"That's terrible," Bernie whispered.

"My father was worse. Most of the time all he did was drink too much and pass out, but every once in a while he'd turn mean. I had to watch my back from the time I was six years old."

"He was abusive to you?"

"In just about every way there was."

"I'm so sorry," she murmured.

"I used to wish he'd come to school events. All I wanted to do was look up and see his face. Then once he did show up for a parent-teacher conference. He was dead drunk and made a pass at my teacher. I wanted to crawl into a hole and die."

Bernie felt a shiver of empathy, even though she couldn't possibly hope to know what that had felt like.

"He used to taunt me all the time about the fact that I was going to a fancy school, as if getting a decent education was a bad thing. He just felt so crappy about himself that he had to tear into me."

"At least you had the opportunity to go to a nice school."

"No. Not nice. It was a good school, but it sure as hell wasn't a nice one. I rode the bus to school. The other kids got there in their Lexuses and Mercedes. The guys treated me like shit. The girls acted like I had some kind of disease just because I didn't have a rich daddy paying my tuition. For four years, they never let me forget I was the poor scholarship kid."

"That's terrible. How did you ever survive that?"

"I survived it," he said, his voice low and harsh, "because I was driven to be such a success and make so damned much money that I could call my own shots and never be at anyone's mercy again. I pushed through. Graduated. Went to college. Got my degree."

"And built an amazing business."

"I knew I wasn't going to be able to make it big working for somebody else. But when I asked for loans, bankers told me to go to hell. Venture capitalists wanted to own every profitable idea I ever had. It seemed like the whole damned world was against me. But I finally made it. I've finally gotten my life to the point where nobody can touch me."

She'd been so wrong before. The things from his past she thought he'd gotten over still haunted him to this day. She knew now why he struggled for control of just about any situation he was in. When a child was raised at the mercy of a terrible environment, he learned very quickly to protect himself from the pain and confusion and chaos any way he could.

"Sometimes when I was a kid," Jeremy said, his voice agonizingly quiet, "I used to fantasize that a man would come to the door one day and tell me he was my real father. He'd take me away to live with him, and he'd be there all the time, doing all the father stuff with me. That's who I want to be. That father. The one a kid dreams of having."

She couldn't believe it. She couldn't believe this was the man she had wanted out of her children's lives forever. She turned her face up and kissed his neck, then settled her cheek against his chest again.

"I just couldn't bear the thought of my kids being raised anywhere that reminded me of my father or the place I came from," Jeremy said. "I want their home to be perfect."

"It is now. It's beautiful."

She put her hand against the side of his neck, gently stroking her thumb along his jaw. A tiny bit of moonlight skirted through the blinds, and by the faint light, she saw his eyes slowly drift closed. After a moment, his steady breathing told her he'd fallen asleep.

Bernie lay awake for a long time, trying to get a grip on the way she felt, trying to tell herself that this meant nothing even when it felt like everything. She just hadn't expected it to be like this. She hadn't expected that he would be so warm and kind and sweet, making her feel more cherished than any woman on earth. Being with him tonight had knocked one more brick out of that wall she'd been so desperate to maintain between them, and if she kept this up, sooner or later it would be gone altogether. And when that happened, either something wonderful would be waiting for her on the other side, or she'd be facing the biggest heartbreak of her life.

Either way, there was no going back now.

When Bernie woke the next morning, she rolled over and reached out for Jeremy, only to find the bed empty beside her. It was a few seconds before she remembered that he'd taken an early flight to Atlanta that morning. He'd gotten up and left without her even waking up.

Three days. God, she was going to miss him. Last night had been beyond amazing, and she couldn't wait for him to come home again.

She got up and took a shower, grabbed a bagel for breakfast, and headed to her office at Creekwood. A tenant was already outside the door, waiting for her to arrive so he could report that his refrigerator was on the fritz. Bernie couldn't wait until all the units had new appliances. When that happened, tenant repair requests would plummet. Not that she minded taking care of things that needed to be done. Charmin had virtually ignored these people for the past several years, and she was thrilled to be in a position to help them.

After she'd noted the tenant's complaint and he'd left her office, the door opened and Max walked in. He was carrying a manila envelope.

"Max? What are you doing here? I thought you guys were on a flight to Atlanta this morning."

"Bridges had something come up at the office, so we're flying out this afternoon." He handed her the manila envelope.

"What's this?"

"Haven't got a clue."

She opened it and pulled out an ivory envelope. It was addressed to Jeremy, but he'd written her name across it. She opened it to find an invitation from Texas Southwestern University to attend a formal event to honor their major contributors. Apparently Jeremy was one of those. But what just about made her heart stop was the three words he'd written across it: *Come with me?*

It took Bernie a few minutes to realize that he was actually inviting her to this event. As his date. And the very thought of it terrified her.

Well, there was no question what she had to do. She had to tell him no. Even though she'd been to several of these events with him, it had been in an entirely different capacity. She didn't have anything to wear. She didn't know how to act around the rich folks. And she would likely embarrass him in some way by the time the evening was out, making him wish he'd never asked her in the first place. Texas Southwestern was her alma mater—hers, and that of about a gazillion other people in the state of Texas—but she wasn't sure if that made things better or worse.

Then she realized there was a small arrow in the lower right corner of the invitation with the word "over" to the left of it. She flipped the card over. It was blank, except for Jeremy's handwriting again.

Don't make me beg.

And when she saw what he'd drawn beside those words, all she could do was stare at it with total disbelief.

A happy face?

She couldn't believe it. Jeremy Bridges, of all the people on this planet, had drawn a *happy face*?

Talk about playing dirty.

She'd never been a sucker for sappiness, but Jeremy's

doing something as silly as that to persuade her made her feel all warm and fuzzy inside. How was she supposed to say no now?

She grabbed a pen and wrote a single word on the face of the invitation. *Yes.* And she drew her own happy face beside it. She returned the invitation to the manila envelope and handed it back to Max.

"Can you take this back to him for me?" she said with a smile.

Max took the envelope, then looked back at Bernie. "I hope you're being careful."

"What do you mean?"

"You're sleeping with him."

She paused. "You figured that out, huh?"

"Yeah. I'm smart like that."

For a long time, neither one of them said anything, but she could tell what he was thinking.

"I'm afraid he's going to hurt you one of these days," Max said finally.

Bernie hadn't expected such a direct hit. "You thought it was a good idea that I go to work for him."

"That was for your own mental health. If you didn't get out of that job at the museum, you were going to go nuts and take hostages." He paused. "It isn't business I'm talking about. You can't expect a guy like him to change overnight, Bernie. If he ever changes at all."

Bernie swallowed hard. "I don't expect anything from him."

"I hope not."

"He's not what I thought he was."

"He's not what I thought he was, either. But he still has the capacity to cause you a world of hurt."

"You don't have to worry about me, Max. I don't believe in fairy tales."

Max stared at her a long time, his eyes like a pair of lie detectors, and it was all she could do not to blink. Finally he nodded. "Just be careful, will you?"

She nodded, and Max slipped out the door.

Bernie sat down in the chair at her desk, Max's words still haunting her. And that was because she'd thought them herself more than once in the past few weeks. But she'd told him the truth. She didn't believe in fairy tales, and she was perfectly well aware of Jeremy's shortcomings. But even if they ended up having no future together, she wanted as much of the present as she could possibly get.

Okay. If she was going to that event, she had three days to transform herself from a dumpy, fashion-challenged pregnant woman to a...well, she didn't exactly know what, but definitely something more attractive than the woman she was now.

And when she got there, she was going to smile. She was going to have a good time. She was going to do her best to forget who she was and be a woman who looked as if she belonged with a man like Jeremy. She didn't have a clue how she was going to accomplish that, but if he wanted her to come with him, she was going to stop whining and make it happen.

Later, when she got to work, she grabbed her phone and called Teresa to tell her she needed some help—clothes, makeup, whatever. Unfortunately, Bill answered and told him that Teresa had taken the kids and driven to Wichita Falls for a week to visit her mother. As Bernie hung up, she realized she had only one other friend she could impose on to get the extensive help she needed. The thought of it was just a little bit scary, but what other choice did she have?

She picked up her phone again, called Lawanda, and told her she needed her help.

"With what?" Lawanda asked.

"I have to go to a formal event. I don't have anything to wear. I was hoping maybe you could help me find something."

She could practically feel Lawanda grinning right through the phone. "Shopping? You want me to go shopping? As you well know, I am the *queen* of shopping."

"Now, listen to me," Bernie said. "It has to be something understated. I'd feel silly in anything else. I know you like to dress a little…extravagantly."

"That is because I dress to match my naturally flamboyant personality," she explained. "The clothes have to fit the woman. But no, you will not be wearing army green no matter how much you beg."

"And there's the small problem with me being pregnant and fat and—"

"You're forgetting that I am a plus-sized woman. Does that stop me from having an outstanding sense of style? No, it does *not*."

"Can I just go with something black?"

"You got any clothes that *aren't* black?"

"Uh…I'm sure I do." She paused. "Somewhere."

"If he sees you in black all the time, you gotta wear something else. Shake him up a little."

"And I need a little help with makeup, too. *Understated*."

"Ah," Lawanda said with a sly smile. "So you want the

full Lawanda treatment. You're a very smart woman. I like that about you."

Bernie thought about Lawanda's false eyelashes and started praying.

"Don't worry, girl," Lawanda said. "By the time I get through with you, you're gonna be a knockout."

Chapter
28

The days later, Jeremy and Max were returning home to Dallas on a flight from Atlanta. Their flight had been delayed an hour, which frustrated Jeremy to no end. It meant he'd barely have time to get home and change into his tux before he and Bernie had to leave for the university.

When he sent her the invitation, he'd been prepared to have to talk her into coming with him, only to be pleasantly surprised when she accepted his invitation immediately.

Things are good, he thought. *Very, very good.*

When they reached cruising altitude, he closed his eyes, rested his head on the seat behind him, and thought back to making love to Bernie the other night. He'd been obsessed with having her again, but he'd had no idea it would be like that. It had been slow and soft and dreamy, every moment singular and intense, but it was her tiny whispers and cries and shudders of pleasure that told him how much she wanted him. He still remembered the expression on her face when she looked up at him and whispered his name, and he couldn't wait to hear it pass her lips a thousand more times.

If he'd been obsessed before, he was a fanatic now. The moment they got home from the event tonight, he was sweeping her upstairs and straight into his bed again.

"May I get you a pillow, sir?"

Jeremy opened his eyes, irritated that his thoughts had been interrupted. Ever since he'd boarded the flight, the first-class flight attendant had been fawning over him, a stunningly beautiful blond with the most spectacular breasts money could buy. She'd gone through the entire safety recitation with her attention focused mostly on Jeremy, a subtle smile of invitation on her lips.

"No, thank you," Jeremy said, and started to close his eyes again, only to have the flirting begin in earnest. First she asked the standard flight attendant questions, but with a sexy edge. Then she eased into more personal stuff designed to scope out where he lived, his marital status, and the approximate size of his bank account. By the time they were making their final approach into Dallas, Jeremy was surprised she hadn't taken him by the hand and led him into the bathroom for a trip to the Mile High Club.

She rested her forearm on the top of the seat in front of Jeremy and leaned in. "I'm Jennifer," she said, in a low, sultry voice. "If you'd like to get together, give me a call."

She slipped him a piece of paper, then walked away to prepare for landing.

Jeremy couldn't count the number of times this had happened to him. And most of the time, if the women were beautiful enough, he'd taken them up on their offers.

He remembered back to the time when Bernie was his bodyguard. She'd watch him collect those little pieces of paper from flight attendants, rolling her eyes the whole time, usually adding a snarky comment or two. He smiled to himself. That was what he liked about her. He never had to wonder what she was thinking, because she'd always been quick to tell him.

Without even unfolding this piece of paper, he crumpled it in his fist, then stuck it into the magazine pouch on the back of the seat in front of him.

"Better hang on to that," Max murmured. "She was a hot one."

"Nope. She doesn't do a thing for me."

"Beg to differ. She'd do all kinds of things for you."

"You're baiting me, Max."

"Yes, sir, I am."

"You appear to be gauging my interest in a completely different woman."

"Tell me if I'm out of line."

Oddly enough, Jeremy didn't feel that way at all. There had been a time when Max's comments had irritated him to no end, but now it actually made him feel good that Bernie had people in her life she could count on.

"You care a lot about her, don't you?" Jeremy asked.

"We go way back."

"I care a lot about her, too, Max. You have nothing to worry about."

Max nodded, then returned to his usual comatose state, and Jeremy closed his eyes for a last-minute daydream to entertain him until he could see Bernie again. She'd told him she was going to meet him at his house and they'd go from there.

He couldn't wait.

He got home an hour and a half later. He took a quick shower, put on his tux, and went back downstairs. When he stepped into the kitchen, he found Bernie sitting at the breakfast room table. She held a compact and was staring at herself in the mirror. She glanced up when he came into the room. Looking a little flustered, she closed the compact and tossed it into her evening bag. She stood up, fidgeting and frowning. He knew she was waiting for him to say something, but for a moment, he was speechless. She was still Bernie, but a different version of Bernie that was all soft around the edges, and he loved it.

Her hair was swept up in one of those messy-but-sexy styles anchored with a couple of rhinestone clips that he never would have imagined her wearing. She had makeup on. Very little, actually, but just enough to bring out her features, particularly those long, dark eyelashes. Her dress was made of royal blue satin that skimmed over her breasts and hips and her baby bump, then fell to her ankles in soft folds. Low neckline, but not plunging. He'd never noticed just how pretty her collarbones were, particularly with the diamond drop she wore falling perfectly between them.

"Wow," he said.

She winced. "Is that a good wow, or a bad wow?"

"Let's put it this way," he said, walking toward her. "You look so incredible in that dress that all I want to do is take it off you."

But she still looked worried. "Are you sure it's all right?"

"Oh, I'm very sure."

"Is the hair too weird? My friend Lawanda helped me with it. I told her it was weird, but she said it was perfect."

"Lawanda is a very wise woman."

Jeremy leaned in to kiss her, but she put a palm against his chest. "No. You can't do that. You'll smear my lipstick, and I won't be able to fix it."

"How about if I kiss you here instead?" he said, dipping his head and touching his lips to her neck.

"That's fine. Even I know not to put lipstick on my neck."

"Smart girl."

"Are you sure I look okay?"

"Why don't we go get a second opinion?"

They left the house and walked toward the limousine. Max was leaning against the back door. As they approached, Jeremy knew the exact moment he spotted Bernie. He pushed away from the car and reached up slowly to pull his sunglasses off, a look of utter amazement on his face.

"Holy shit," he said. "Bernie?"

"Max," Jeremy said. "Mustn't ogle the boss's date."

"Or the boss's date will deck you," Bernie snapped.

"Don't mind her," Jeremy said. "She doesn't know how beautiful she looks."

"Did she bother to look in a mirror?"

Jeremy tapped his temple. "Mental block."

"Will you two shut up?" Bernie said. "We're going to be late."

Max opened the door for them, and they got into the car. Max sat in the front passenger seat next to Carlos, leaving Jeremy and Bernie in the backseat alone. As they wound their way down the driveway to the front gate, Jeremy leaned in and spoke softly to Bernie.

"I sense you're a little uptight," he said. "There's no reason for that."

She took a deep, cleansing breath. "I'm just not used to being around this kind of people. Are you sure I look all right? I think you and Max are just trying to make me feel good."

"Bernie, when Max turned around and saw you, his tongue was hanging so far out of his mouth I thought he was going to step on it. You look incredible. And I want very much for you to enjoy yourself tonight."

She nodded, but he could tell she was still uneasy. Then she glanced at his neck, her brows drawing together with confusion.

"Wait a minute," she said. "You tied your tie?"

"Haven't you been telling me to for years?"

"Well...yeah."

But she kept staring at it. Finally she reached up and tugged on it until it hung loose around his neck.

"Hey!" he said. "It took me ten minutes to get it right. I was proud of myself."

She picked up both ends of the tie, pulled him toward her, and kissed him.

"If you wear it tied, how are people supposed to recognize you?"

Finally she smiled at him, and for a long, unguarded moment he just sat there basking in it, wondering why she'd always been so stingy with smiles when they lit up her face like Christmas. It had been so long since he'd actually looked forward to an event like this, but tonight...

Tonight was going to be magic.

Twenty minutes later, Carlos swung the limo onto the grounds of Texas Southwestern University, then pulled up in front of the building where the event was being held. He leaped out and opened the door for Bernie, giving her the kind of deferential treatment he'd never shown her before. Carlos was a little too afraid of the boss to focus too much on Bernie's physical attributes, but Jeremy could tell that he was seeing her in an entirely new light. He only hoped Bernie was enjoying it.

They walked into the ballroom where the event was being held, and Bernie's eyes grew wide with wonder.

"My God," she said. "Isn't it beautiful?"

Actually, it wasn't much different from any other event he'd ever attended. Gauzy fabric was draped all over the room, with tiny white lights wound up in it. A string quartet was playing something soft and classical. Ice sculptures abounded. Ridiculously opulent buffets stretched from one wall to another. But judging from the look on Bernie's face, she felt as if she'd just walked through the gates of heaven.

"You've been to these things with me before," he said.

"I was on the outside looking in," she said, her voice hushed. "This is different."

Over the next hour, a dozen people came up to speak to Jeremy, and when he introduced Bernie, he saw more than one set of eyes travel downward. After tonight, speculation was going to run rampant about his being there with a pregnant woman, and he couldn't have cared less.

"Everybody's wondering about us," Bernie said, as they eased away from the people they'd been talking to.

"Why? Because you're pregnant?"

"Uh, yeah."

"Do you care?"

"I thought you might."

"Think again. Let's dance."

She looked at him dumbly. "Do I strike you as the kind of person who knows how to dance?"

He took her by the hand. "Come on. It's easy."

"Jeremy—"

He ducked his head and whispered in her ear. "It's the only way I can get my hands on you at a public event without being thrown out of the place."

"I changed my mind," she said. "Let's dance."

Once they were on the dance floor, he pulled her around to face him. He saw her glance quickly at other women, and she put her hand on his shoulder the same way they were doing with their partners. He took her other hand in his and moved to the music, and after a minute, he felt her relax.

"See?" he said. "Not so hard, is it?"

"No. Not as long as I'm following you."

As they moved around the floor, he rubbed his hand gently up and down her back, already wondering just how quickly he could get her out of this dress once they got home. He thought it was quite possible he was going to find something under it other than white cotton undies, and he couldn't wait to see what she'd picked out. And if it made her feel pretty, he'd buy her a whole trunkload of it.

When the song was over, there was a polite smattering of applause, and Bernie's expression became pained.

"I have to sit down for a minute," she said. "These shoes are killing me."

"So why are you wearing them?"

"Because Lawanda says pain is a significant component of beauty."

"So kick them off."

"Nope. If I walk around in my bare feet, I'll look like your family friend from Arkansas."

"Let's grab a table."

Jeremy pulled out a chair for Bernie, and she sat down with a heavy sigh.

"Okay. That's better. But I'm pretty sure I have blisters on top of blisters."

"I'm going to get a drink," Jeremy said. "Would you like me to bring you something?"

"No. I'm fine."

"Back in a flash."

He wound through the crowd to the bar in the corner of the room, where he asked the bartender for a Scotch and water.

"Thank God you showed up."

Jeremy turned around to see Phil standing behind him.

"Second martini," Phil said, holding it up, then pointing to Alexis and the group of women she was with. "Did you know that five women talking aren't five times as loud as one woman talking? It's more like five *squared*."

"Keep drinking," Jeremy said. "Pretty soon you'll pass out and you won't hear them at all."

"I'm working on it."

Jeremy picked up his Scotch and water from the bar, then turned back to Phil.

"So you're here with Bernie tonight," Phil said.

"That's right."

"Alexis is thrilled. She wants to meet her."

"And I'd like her to meet Alexis."

"So there's still nothing going on between you two?"

Jeremy took a sip of his drink. "I wouldn't say nothing."

Phil got a big grin on his face. "So you're finally seeing the light."

Maybe he was.

Never in his life had Jeremy been so entranced with a woman that he had a hard time taking his eyes off her, but he hadn't let Bernie out of his sight for more than a few seconds all evening.

"Doesn't she look great tonight?" Jeremy said.

"Actually, yeah. She does. I barely recognized her. And to think she's been under your nose all this time."

That was a little hard for Jeremy to believe, too. But this was a different woman from the tense, unsmiling one he'd known for so many years. It was as if she'd vanished, and in her place was one who was so happy and relaxed she almost glowed with it.

"Sorry, Phil," Jeremy said. "I need to get back."

Phil sighed. "So I'm going to be all alone tonight listening to the chipmunks chatter?"

"I'm afraid so."

Phil looked at Bernie with a smile. "Don't blame you a bit, buddy."

Jeremy wound his way back through the crowd toward their table. He was halfway there when he saw a man approach Bernie. He tapped her on the shoulder. She spun around. They talked for a bit, and then a big smile came over Bernie's face. She stood up, and before Jeremy knew it, they were hugging each other.

Jeremy stopped short, feeling an instantaneous shot of jealousy. The guy was maybe in his late thirties. Tall. Not bad looking. And Bernie seemed extraordinarily happy to

see him. It was one thing for Max and Carlos to appreciate how great Bernie looked. He had control over their
behavior. But this guy... who the hell was he?

Jeremy continued through the crowd and came up
beside Bernie.

"Jeremy!" Bernie said. "Where have you been? You
have to meet Kyle."

No, I don't.

The guy gave Jeremy a big smile and stuck out his
hand. "Kyle Davenport."

Jeremy shook his hand. *Nice to meet you. Now go away.*

"Kyle was a classmate of mine at TSU," Bernie said.
"He and I lived in the same dorm."

Kyle turned away from Jeremy as if he wasn't even
there, focusing on Bernie again, giving her an appreciative smile. "It's so good to see you again. I barely recognized you. You look great."

"Thanks," she said, beaming. "So do you."

"Oh!" Kyle said. "Do you remember the day in micro-
biology class when Dr. Perez caught her hair on fire?"

Bernie laughed. "How could I forget?"

And then they were laughing in stereo, and for some
reason, that irritated the hell out of Jeremy.

"Gee," he said. "Sounds hilarious."

Bernie turned to him. "Dr. Perez leaned over to look
into a microscope. She didn't know the Bunsen burner was
so close, and when she stood up, her hair was on fire."

Kyle chuckled. "She couldn't figure out why Bernie
was smacking her on the head with a spiral notebook."

*Yeah. That's hilarious, all right. I bet you've got a mil-
lion of them. Feel free to take them somewhere else.*

But no. They kept talking. He had to hear reminiscences

about everything from stuck quarters in a dorm washing machine to a mixer their freshman year where a guy got so drunk he shoved his own mattress out a third-story window.

Jeremy heard somebody call his name. He turned to see the president of the university standing behind him, talking to a couple of other donors.

"Can you join us for a moment?" he said.

Jeremy held up his finger, then turned to Bernie. "The president wants to speak to me."

"Go ahead," she said. "I'm fine."

No. That wasn't the response he was looking for. He was looking for something more along the lines of "Bye bye, Kyle" as she followed him over to meet the president.

"Don't worry," Kyle said with that irritatingly cheerful smile. "I'll take good care of her. We have plenty of catching up to do."

A sharp spark of jealousy tightened every muscle in Jeremy's body, but he wasn't about to let it show. He just nodded as if it was fine with him and joined the president's group. For the next ten minutes, he was forced to listen to endless chatter about the university's plans to build a new facility to house the school of business. What Jeremy really wanted to do was grab Bernie, take her home, and drag her straight to bed, and by the time the night was over, he'd make absolutely sure she couldn't even remember that guy's name.

Then, out of the corner of his eye, he saw Kyle reach into his wallet and pull out a couple of business cards. He handed them to Bernie. She stuck one in her evening bag. Then she flipped the other one over, wrote something on it, and handed it back to Kyle.

Okay. That was it. Enough was enough.

Just as he was extricating himself from the conversation with the president, Kyle gave Bernie another hug and walked away. Jeremy came up beside Bernie, and she looped her hand around his arm.

"That Kyle is sure a friendly guy, isn't he?" Jeremy said.

"Yeah. He is."

"Did you date in college?"

"No. We were just friends."

"I didn't see a ring."

"He was divorced a few years ago."

Big red flag.

"He gave you his card," Jeremy said.

"Yeah. We're going for coffee on Thursday to catch up a little more."

Jeremy nearly choked. Coffee? *Coffee?* Didn't she know that was a male code word for *I want to get naked with you?*

Maybe she did know.

In that moment, Jeremy realized the awful truth. He had no hold on Bernie. None at all. He might be the father of her babies, but her life was her own, and she'd always made it very clear that she intended to live it any way she wanted to.

The question was, where did he fit in?

He imagined what might happen after she met that guy for coffee. They might start to date. Get engaged. Get married. Pretty soon Jeremy would be nothing more than that weekend guy, the one who picked up the kids on Friday, endured the glare of her husband, tried too hard with the kids and spoiled the hell out of them, then returned them on Sunday. He'd be the odd man out. Biological father, but not really essential in the day-to-day lives of his children, and virtually nonexistent in Bernie's eyes. And for the rest of his life, he'd be forced to imagine another man making love to her, and that was absolutely intolerable.

With other women, it had always been about the conquest. Once he had sex with them, the need he felt for them disappeared. But making love to Bernie had only sharpened his desire. That confused him. Unnerved him. Made him feel as if his emotions weren't his own anymore. Bernie was holding them now, and every smile she directed at another man felt like a knife straight to his heart, as if the time they spent together and the closeness they'd shared meant nothing to her.

By the time they left the university half an hour later, Jeremy's nerves were in a knot. Once they were in the limo, Bernie kicked off her shoes with a satisfied sigh. He looked at her feet and was shocked.

"Red nail polish?" he said.

"Lawanda did it. She put the light frost on my fingernails, but she said I needed red on my toenails even if it didn't show. She said I'd feel like a wild woman just knowing it was there."

"Do you?"

"What?"

"Feel like a wild woman?"

She laughed. "Yeah. I kinda do." She slid down in the seat and turned a little, crossing her arms and resting her cheek against the leather seat, her laughter fading to a soft smile. "Thank you so much for inviting me tonight. I had such a wonderful time."

Every word she spoke only irritated him more. The Bernie he knew was supposed to gag at red nail polish and feel insecure at a formal event. This Bernie looked beautiful and chatted with other men and felt like a wild woman.

Bernie's smile faded. "What's the matter?"

"Nothing's the matter."

"You're frowning."

"I've had a long day."

"How was your flight from Atlanta?"

"Fine."

"Did your meetings go okay?"

"I told you everything's fine," Jeremy said, even though things were about as far from fine as he could imagine. "I'm just ready to get home. Get out of this tux. Like I said, it's been a long day."

Ten minutes later, the limo pulled up to Jeremy's house. Carlos and Max left. Jeremy and Bernie went into the kitchen. She put her purse down onto the breakfast room table, and he pulled her into his arms for a kiss.

"Thanks for a wonderful evening," she said.

"It's not over yet," Jeremy said. "Stay with me tonight."

Bernie smiled. "Okay. But I have to be out of here at the crack of dawn tomorrow morning."

Jeremy frowned. "Why?"

"The guys are coming over to help me paint the nursery."

Jeremy came to attention. "That room was just painted."

"I know. But not in baby colors."

"Your friends don't need to do that. Just pick out a

paint color and send one of the crews in. They'll take care of it."

"Come on, Jeremy. It's no fun if professionals do it. And they cost a lot of money. All the guys cost is a couple of boxes of doughnuts."

As Jeremy imagined the whole group of them at Bernie's apartment, the strangest feeling welled up inside him. She was going to be living it up with her friends, painting a nursery for *his* children, and where would he be?

At home by himself.

"Go ahead," he said with an offhand shrug. "Do whatever you want to." What else could he say?

Bernie's probing stare came back again. "Okay. You've been acting weird ever since we left the university. What's up?"

All the way home, the what-ifs had piled up inside Jeremy's mind, and now he was on the verge of exploding with them. Bernie thought her choices were nonexistent where men were concerned, but she was dead wrong. There were hundreds of other men in this world she could have, and once she figured that out, Jeremy had no doubt she'd want to make up for lost time and try a few of them out. Pretty soon one of them would stick—maybe even Kyle after that cup of coffee—and he'd be out in the cold. And she had friends—old friends, close friends, friends who put together baby cribs and painted nurseries. And she had a mother who loved her. In light of all that, he could see only one way for him to fit into her life that would ensure he didn't get sidelined and eventually shoved out of the way altogether. And that was to offer her something no woman in her right mind could possibly turn down.

He took off his coat and draped it over the back of a chair, then turned to face Bernie. "I have a proposition for you."

She smiled and moved closer, draping her arms around his neck. "I'm listening."

"I think," he said, "that we should get married."

Chapter
29

Bernie had never felt so flabbergasted in her life. She dropped her arms and backed away from Jeremy. "*What* did you say?"

"I think we should get married," Jeremy said.

After she got over the first few seconds of total astonishment, part of her wanted to throw her arms around his neck again and tell him that yes, of course she'd marry him. After all, hadn't she thought about it dozens of times since they'd made love three nights ago? Fantasized that he'd suddenly fall in love with her, they'd get married, and live happily ever after?

But even as she entertained those thoughts, she knew fantasies were dangerous things, and they sure as hell couldn't be wished into reality. Things had been good between them, but a marriage proposal right now just didn't fit the whole picture.

"I'm not sure I heard you right," Bernie said. "Are you asking me to *marry* you?"

"I've been thinking about it, and I've decided it's the logical thing to do."

"Logical?"

"You say you don't think you'll ever get married. It's not in the cards for me, either. We have two babies to raise. Doing it in one household will make it easier."

"Let me see if I have this straight," she said. "You want to marry me because it makes things easier for you?"

"For both of us."

"That's crazy."

"Is it really?" he said, pulling his tie from around his neck and tossing it on the table. "We get along well, don't we?"

"Yeah, but—"

"You liked living here, right?"

"Of course I did. But—"

"You'll have everything you'll ever want or need, and so will our children." He took a few steps toward her. "Think about it, Bernie. Think of the advantages of being married to a man like me."

She didn't doubt that. But this didn't feel like a marriage proposal. It felt like he was negotiating a merger, and that made her very uneasy. As unsentimental as she was, she assumed if a proposal ever came, it would be accompanied by a ring and at least a small mention of how he felt about her. But that wasn't what he was offering.

Not even close.

"I can only imagine the prenup you'd want me to sign," she said. "Is there enough paper on the planet to put that one together?"

"That's a necessity. Otherwise you could divorce me in a month and take half of everything I have. What kind of idiot would run headlong into a marriage under those circumstances?"

"What kind of idiot would run headlong into marriage under *any* circumstances?"

"If it's the right thing to do, time changes nothing."

"No. I told you. This is crazy."

"I explained why it makes sense."

"Great. Why don't you draw up a business plan for that little venture and give me a call?"

"We're both practical people. So why are you surprised that I'm being practical?"

"I don't get it. If all you want is for me and the babies to stay here, we don't have to get married to make that happen."

"Yeah? You say you can't ever see yourself getting married, but what if you do? Where does that leave me? As that guy who gets his kids on the weekends? I have no intention of letting another man have more control over my children than I do."

All at once, light dawned, and Bernie understood what was really at the heart of this. "Okay. Now I get it. It's a matter of control. You need to get over that, Jeremy."

"I have nothing to get over."

"Please. I've never seen any man so determined to get what he wants no matter what the cost. You want to run my life. You want to run the babies' lives. But it can't always be about what *you* want."

"You'll be getting plenty of what you want, too."

"Like what?"

"Like a beautiful place to live. Everything you and your children could ever want. You can work only if you want to. What woman wouldn't want those things?"

"And where do I sleep?" she asked.

For the first time, he seemed a little flustered. "Wherever you want to."

"How about in another man's bed?"

He frowned. "Another man's bed? When you're married to me?"

"But it's not a real marriage you're offering me, is it?"

"What I'm offering you is the best of everything. Can't you see that? For you, for our children—"

"I'm not interested."

"Good God, Bernie!" he said, flinging his palms out. "I offer you the whole universe, and you won't marry me? What the hell is *wrong* with you?"

"I deserve more than that."

"More than the goddamned *universe*?"

"It's always about money to you, isn't it?" she said. "You think if you throw enough of it at somebody, they're yours to command. I know you don't believe this, but there really are some things money won't buy."

"Will you stop being so damned self-righteous? You're acting as if money isn't important to you. That's bullshit. You need my money, and you need it badly."

"And you're praying I'll take it, because you have nothing else to give."

Jeremy slowly lifted his chin, his eyes narrowing. In the years Bernie had known him, she'd never seen him truly angry. Irritated, maybe. Frustrated, yes. But she'd never seen the fury on his face that she was looking at right now.

"Try crawling out of the cesspool I was raised in and see how *that* changes the way you look at things," he said hotly. "I worked my ass off for the life I have, and I'm not going to apologize for living it."

"Yes. You have an incredible life. Exactly the kind of life a helpless, desperately unhappy kid dreams of."

His brows drew together. "What are you talking about?"

"When you speak, people listen. Nobody tells you no. You have every toy you've ever wanted. You built a castle filled with pretty stuff on a piece of property that looks like Disney World. You drive dream cars, fly fast jets, and keep company with beautiful blond princesses who answer your every whim. And you keep doing more and building more because it's all you know to do, waiting for the day when it finally becomes enough and happiness arrives."

He glared at her. "You don't know what the hell you're talking about."

She took a step closer to him, her throat tight with emotion. She tilted her head to catch his gaze, but he averted his eyes. "You've never loved anyone, have you? Not even when you were a child." Tears welled up in her eyes, and her voice fell to a plaintive whisper. "Nobody was there to show you how."

"I don't need this," he said, a warning tone creeping into his voice.

"So now you've gotten to a place where you put money and casual sex where real relationships should be, and you can't understand why you're still miserable."

"Bernie—"

"And the women. God, Jeremy. That only makes things worse. You can't keep people at arm's length all these years and not have it take a toll on you."

"I told you to stop."

"You're going to have the babies now. You have a shot

at something good and real and lasting with them. You can be the father with them your father wasn't with you. But I'm afraid of what's going to happen. I'm afraid if you don't let your guard down and focus on what's important and learn to *love* them—"

"Will you just leave me the hell *alone*?"

His shout echoed through the kitchen. Bernie recoiled, shocked at his sudden outburst. But the agonizing silence that followed was worse. In spite of his anger, her heart was bleeding for him. She knew deep down he was a good, compassionate man, but until he saw himself that way, he was always going to be trapped in a terrible cycle of reaching for happiness in all the wrong ways. And the last thing she needed to do was get trapped in it with him.

"I know that because of where you come from, marriage doesn't mean anything to you," she said. "But it means everything to me. Given my situation, my chance of getting struck by lightning is probably greater than my chance of finding another man who wants to marry me. But I'll tell you this. If it ever happens, it'll be for real. He'll be a good, kind, dependable man who will love me forever. That's when I'll get married, Jeremy. And not until."

She grabbed her purse from the breakfast room table and headed for the back door, only to stop and turn back.

"You want to hear something funny?" she said through her tears.

He turned slowly to face her.

"That man I've been looking for? The one who will love me forever?"

"What about him?"

Bernie paused, emotion choking her words. "I thought maybe that man was you."

She searched his face, looking for even the tiniest chink in the wall he'd built around himself, but all she saw was stoic denial.

"Well," he said, his voice tinged with sarcasm, "I guess that means you don't know me as well as you think you do."

Bernie blinked, and tears cascaded down her cheeks. "Yeah. I guess it does. Good-bye, Jeremy."

"The babies—"

"I'll be in touch."

She opened the door and left the house, hurrying to her car, and she managed to drive almost to the front gate before the tears came, so hard and so fast that they practically blinded her to drive. She pulled a tissue out of her console and dabbed her eyes, then kept on going, needing to get as far away from there as possible.

Max had been right. Jeremy had the capacity to cause her a world of hurt, and that was exactly what he'd done.

Jeremy went to the window and watched as Bernie's car disappeared down the driveway, and soon all he saw were her taillights glimmering in the darkness, growing dimmer and dimmer until they finally disappeared altogether. He stood at the window for a long time, feeling so alone he could barely breathe. An empty, gnawing sensation ground through his stomach, the silence of the house hanging over him, until all he could hear was the incessant ticking of the heirloom clock in his breakfast room and the blood pulsing through his ears with every beat of his heart.

He couldn't understand it. He just couldn't. Any other woman would consider herself the luckiest person on the planet at his proposal, but Bernie acted as if he'd done something wrong by offering her the moon and a few distant galaxies to boot.

He strode over to the counter to his iPod docking station and turned on some music. Then he went to his den, where he flipped on the television and jacked up the sound. Anything to drown out the godawful silence. Then he sat on the sofa and dropped his head to his hands, the music and the voices of the news anchors pulsing through his skull.

His desperation turned to anger, gradually building to a fever pitch. He rose and went to the bar. Grabbed a shot glass. Poured himself a drink and tossed it down. Before the burn in his throat had even begun to diminish, he'd already poured himself another one, only to slam down the bottle, pick up the glass, and throw it across the room. It crashed into his cherry-wood bookcase and shattered in a starburst of glass fragments and alcohol.

He gripped the edge of the bar and ducked his head, his breaths hard and raspy.

She'd walked out on him. He'd offered her everything he had, and still she'd walked out. What the hell was he supposed to do now?

He'd worked like crazy to be where he was now. To have the kind of life most men only dream about. But she acted as if that wasn't enough. And that had made him want to grab her and hold her and explain to her that he only wanted what was best for all of them. To keep her right here in his house until she accepted everything he wanted to give her.

Instead, he'd driven her away.

Jeremy felt a shiver of desperation that went soul deep. Good God. What had he done?

He sat on the sofa again, dropping his head back and closing his eyes, his heart still hammering in his chest. His thoughts drifted back to Bernie talking about her father. Not once had she mentioned any material things he'd given her. Her relationship with him was all about love and acceptance and time spent together. Jeremy had offered her none of those things. That she'd refused to take his money should have told him something. It should have been a big red traffic light demanding he stop and think about what he was doing. But no. He'd been so stuck in the past, so firm in his conviction that his life was wonderful, that he'd refused to see just how pitiful it really was.

He'd built this house because he could. It had become the outward representation of every age-old resentment he felt inside, every desire he'd ever had to stick it to anyone who looked down on him, who told him he couldn't make it. Not a solitary soul could pass by this house without knowing what a success he'd become.

But what good was it when he had nobody to share it with?

He sat up again, bowing his head, feeling sick to his stomach. He'd given her what he thought was every reason on earth for her to stay, and she'd rejected every one of them. And he knew why. It was because she wasn't like other women, who cared only about his money, his power, his prestige, who would agree to any condition on earth just to become Mrs. Jeremy Bridges.

And that was why he loved her.

When that realization struck him, he felt as if he'd been hit by a thunderbolt. It had hovered at the edge of his consciousness for weeks now, maybe longer, but he'd refused to let it rise to the surface. It had been there in the lazy evenings they'd spent on his sofa together, in the meals they'd shared in his kitchen, in the quiet warmth of her bed as they'd made love. How could it be? How could he have spent all that time with her and never realized until this moment how he truly felt?

Bernie had tried to tell him what she wanted in a man, and it wasn't power, money, or prestige.

He'll be a good, kind, dependable man who will love me forever…

After what he'd done tonight, he felt like none of those things. But he would be willing to try every day of the rest of his life to live up to them. Somehow he had to tell her he loved her, knowing if he didn't have her in his life, his life wouldn't be worth living.

Please, God, tell me I haven't lost her forever.

Suddenly he heard sirens. He thought for a moment they were outside, only to realize they were coming from the television. He glanced up at the screen and saw flames. Emergency vehicles. A reporter standing out in front with a microphone, shouting to be heard over the commotion.

Then an address flashed across the bottom of the screen, and his heart slammed against his chest. No. It couldn't be.

He looked closer.

It was.

He leaped off the sofa, ran to the kitchen, grabbed his keys, and hurried out the door.

A few minutes later, Bernie pulled up in front of her apartment and got out of her car, her feet so pinched by her shoes that she'd probably have to amputate both feet. When she thought about how wonderful she'd felt only a few hours ago and how horrible she felt now, she thought she was going to cry all over again. She'd known all along that things could end badly, but she'd never expected anything like this. She'd never expected that he would ask her to marry him, and it would end up being the worst thing he could possibly have done. He'd offered her everything under the sun except the one thing she couldn't do without, and it broke her heart to finally know that was one thing he wasn't capable of giving her.

She went into her apartment. She still wasn't used to being in such a pretty place, and every moment she spent there from now on, she knew she'd be reminded of Jeremy. After what had happened tonight, everything she felt for him should have vanished in an instant, but right now the pain of leaving him was still so raw and so sharp she ached with it.

The worst part was that she couldn't just cut all ties and move on. He was the father of her babies. A man who would be in her life forever. She only hoped that one day they could reach the place where it wouldn't kill her to see him and think about how things might have been.

Just as she'd kicked off the shoes from hell and collapsed on her sofa, her phone rang. She rose again and grabbed it from her evening bag. She looked at the caller ID and groaned out loud.

Her mother. The last person Bernie wanted to talk to right now. Her mind instantly leaped to the conversation she was going to have to have with her about Jeremy, the one where she told her mother that the man she thought could do no wrong had done something so wrong that her daughter could never be with him again.

Yeah, that conversation was coming. Just not tonight.

She'd talk to her about Jeremy tomorrow, after she got her emotions back under control and her heart had at least begun to mend.

She hit the TALK button. "Hi, Mom. What's up?"

"Bernadette?" she said in a shaky voice. "Are—are you there?"

Bernie felt a rush of panic. "Mom? What's wrong?"

"Fire," she said. "My house. There's a fire."

Bernie jerked to attention. "Fire? Mom, are you out of the house?"

"Yes. I'm out. The firemen are here, but it's still burning. My house is burning. Please, Bernadette. Come now. *Please!*"

Chapter
30

Bernie threw on a pair of jeans and a T-shirt and jumped into her car, and by the time she reached her mother's house, the firefighters had extinguished the blaze, but smoke was still pouring out through the open front door and a few broken windows. A fire truck, an ambulance, and several police cars were parked in front of the house, along with a couple of vans from local news stations, and Bernie had to leave her car down the street and walk the rest of the way. As she made her way along the sidewalk toward her mother's house, the acrid smell of smoke filled her lungs.

She worried when she didn't see her mother right away. Then she spotted her in the next yard over, huddled with three of her neighbors. Her mother saw her coming and walked over to meet her, tears streaming down her face.

Bernie hugged her. "Mom! Are you okay?"

"Oh, Bernadette. I'm sorry. I'm so sorry!"

Bernie held her by the shoulders. "Sorry? Why are you sorry?"

"It was my fault," she said. "The fire was my fault!"

"What do you mean?"

"I put something on the stove, but then I guess I forgot about it," she said, her words tumbling over each other. "Then I smelled smoke. I came back into the kitchen and it was on fire. I didn't know how to put it out, so I just grabbed my purse and ran outside."

"You did the right thing. The most important thing is that you got out without getting hurt."

"But what am I going to do now? My house! What am I going to do?"

"Calm down, Mom. That's what insurance is for. Everything can be repaired."

"Our family photo albums were on the bookshelf in the living room. What if they burned up in the fire?"

"We won't know what was damaged for a day or two. Then we'll deal with it, okay?"

"I have no place to live," Eleanor said.

"You'll stay with me. Just until we can get the damage repaired."

But even as she was reassuring her mother, Bernie felt the most horrible sense of foreboding. She'd thought her mother would surely be safe in her own home for a while longer, but if she couldn't even turn on the stove without causing a fire, how could she ever live alone again? And if she couldn't live alone, what the hell was Bernie supposed to do?

Damn it! It wasn't supposed to happen this soon!

The crushing responsibility she felt overwhelmed her. If she had to work, she was going to have to find somebody to care for her mother during the day. How was she ever going to pay for that?

Okay. The insurance money would fix the house. And if she sold it, she'd have that equity. But with the cost of a marginally decent facility or even home health care, that money would be gone in no time.

One of the firefighters approached them, sweat pouring down his temples. Bernie asked him about the damage.

"It really isn't that bad," the firefighter said. "We got here quickly, and it was pretty much contained to the front of the house. Most of the damage is from smoke and water." He turned to Eleanor. "You're sure not going to want to stay there, though. Do you have a place you can go tonight?"

"Yes. This is my daughter. I can stay with her."

"There's nothing you can do here tonight," he told her. "Feel free to go to your daughter's house and get some sleep."

As the firefighter walked away, Eleanor turned to Bernie. "Bernadette? Where is Jeremy?"

Just hearing his name made Bernie feel sick inside. She'd had a terrible feeling her mother was going to ask that question, and she didn't have a good answer. But just as she started to make something up, her mother glanced off into the distance, a look of relief passing over her face.

"Oh, thank God," Eleanor said. "There he is!"

Bernie whipped around, shocked to see Jeremy striding across the lawn toward them. He still wore his tuxedo pants and shirt, and even at this distance, he looked so handsome her breath caught in her throat. She put her hand against her chest to try to calm her heart, which was suddenly beating like mad.

"I need to talk to him," Bernie said to her mother. "Can you stay here with your neighbors for just a moment?"

Eleanor nodded, and Bernie turned toward Jeremy. She didn't know why he was here. How he knew to come. What he would say when she talked to him. She walked hesitantly toward him at first, in contrast to his strong, purposeful strides, and the closer she came to him, the more her chest tightened. His face was in shadow, and it wasn't until she drew closer still that she saw it clearly. Gone was the cynical expression that had been on his face when she'd walked out his door, and in its place was a look of overwhelming concern that went straight to her heart.

The swirling soot and ash seemed to drive away the memory of the hurtful words they'd spoken to each other, and when they were still several strides away from each other, he held out his arms. She didn't walk the rest of the way.

She ran.

When she finally fell against him, he wrapped his arms around her, holding her close, and all she could think was, *He's here. He's here. Thank God.*

"I saw it on the news," Jeremy said. "I came as soon as I could. Is your mother all right?"

"She's a little shaken up, but she's fine."

"What happened?"

"God, Jeremy...it's awful..."

He eased her away and held her by the shoulders. "Tell me."

Bernie felt as if she were sinking in quicksand, and every word she spoke about it only weighed her down more. "She was the one who started the fire."

"What?"

"She left something on the stove and forgot about it. When she came back into the kitchen, it was on fire. She forgot. She forgot about what was on the stove. She could have been killed. If she'd gone to sleep before she saw it, then—"

Bernie's voice suddenly choked up, and she put her hand against her mouth, squeezing her eyes closed and gritting her teeth against the tears she felt building behind her eyes.

"Take it easy, sweetheart. It's okay."

"No, it's not! It's my fault! I should have known she was getting too forgetful. But with everything going on, I just wasn't paying close enough attention. I can't stay with her because I have to work, but I can't afford to pay somebody else to stay with her. At least, not for long. And then the babies are coming, and—"

"Bernie. Listen to me. I'm going to take care of everything, okay? Everything. I'm going to make sure you never have to worry about anything again as long as you live. Do you understand?"

"You're all I need right now," she said. "Just you."

He pulled her into his arms again, surrounding her with the kind of warmth and security she needed above all else. "I'm here for you, sweetheart," he whispered against her cheek. "I'll always be here for you."

Jeremy insisted on taking Bernie and her mother back to his house for the night, which he said would be more comfortable for both of them. Bernie didn't argue. His house had come to mean comfort and relaxation and contentment to her, and that was exactly what she needed tonight. Mrs. Spencer met them at the door and told them she had the guest suite ready with fresh linens, cups of tea, and nightclothes for Bernie and Eleanor. Bernie sent her mother upstairs with Mrs. Spencer and told her she'd follow in a moment.

As the ladies disappeared up the stairs, Jeremy took Bernie by the hand and led her into the den, where he sat down on the sofa and pulled her into his arms. She lay her head against his chest, soothed by the rhythmic beating of his heart.

"How are the kids?" he asked, putting his hand against her belly. "As tired as you are?"

"They're pretty quiet. I think they're sleeping."

A long silence stretched between them.

"I'm sorry," he said softly. "So sorry."

"I know."

"No. I need to say it. You were right about everything. I've been chasing things that were never going to make me happy. But not anymore. I've found out what really makes me happy, and it's not making the next buck." He paused, his voice rough with emotion. "It's you, Bernie."

Bernie felt a shiver of awareness when he said those words, astonished that after everything that had happened, she was with him now and he was telling her that. She turned slowly and sat up, wanting to see his eyes, needing to see if they echoed the sincerity of his words.

They were glistening with tears.

"I'm so sorry about tonight," he went on. "The things I said to you. You have so much going for you. You don't know it, but you do. I was just so afraid of losing you that I did something stupid and drove you away. That's never going to happen again. Do you believe me?"

The earnest tone of his voice sent shivers between her shoulder. "Yes."

"You told me you were looking for a man who was

good and kind and dependable who would love you forever. I want to be that man." He took her face in his hands, strumming his thumbs along her cheeks, looking at her as if she were the most precious thing on earth. "I love you, Bernie. Do you love me?"

The answer seemed so clear that she was surprised he even had to ask. Yes, she loved him. Not because of his looks, even though she practically fainted every time she set eyes on him. Not because of his intelligence. The world was full of intelligent men who didn't make her heart go crazy every time she heard their voices. And certainly not because of his money, because he could be dead, flat broke, and she would still love him.

It was so much more than those things.

It was his rescuing her mother that night at the grocery store. Straightening out her cousin Billy for the first time in his adult life so she could quit worrying about him. Researching sex positions on the Internet so he could please her when he made love to her.

It was his showing up tonight and telling her he'd be there forever.

"Yes," she said. "God, *yes*, I love you."

"I want you to marry me."

She sat up straight with surprise. He wanted to *marry* her?

"Don't worry," he said. "It's nothing like earlier. I'm talking about the real thing."

She was so stunned she couldn't speak.

"Love, honor, cherish, till death do us part. All of it."

And still she stared at him.

"And no prenup. Prenups are for people who plan on getting a divorce. I have so much, Bernie. But I've never had anyone to share it with. From now on, what's mine is yours."

Bernie swallowed hard, trying to say something, but her voice had deserted her completely.

"Miss Hogan?"

Bernie looked over to see Mrs. Spencer at the doorway.

"Your mother is asking for you," she said.

"I'll be there in a moment."

"I know it's a lot to think about, so don't say a word now," Jeremy said. "We'll talk tomorrow. Come on. I'll walk you upstairs."

He helped her off the sofa and guided her up the stairs. When they reached the door of the guest suite, he slid his hand beneath her hair at the back of her neck, leaned in, and kissed her softly on the forehead. She closed her eyes, savoring the warmth of his lips and the gentle strength of his hand against her neck.

"Good night," he whispered.

As Jeremy disappeared down the hall, Bernie closed her eyes and put her fingertips to her forehead where he'd kissed her, so in love with him she thought she'd faint with the feeling. Then she lowered her fingertips and touched them to her own lips.

He's even more than what you thought he was. So much more.

When her heart rate finally returned to normal, she opened the door and went into the living room of the guest suite, then into the bedroom, where she found her mother lying in bed in her pajamas, sipping tea.

"Mrs. Spencer is a lovely woman, isn't she?" Eleanor said.

Bernie smiled. "Yes, she is."

"She has four grandchildren, you know."

"Yes. I know."

"She's very excited about the twins. She says Jeremy is, too."

"Yeah. He is."

"You look so tired, dear. You need some sleep."

"I know. I'm going to change clothes."

Bernie went into the closet and grabbed one of the emerald-green gowns. She went into the bathroom, got undressed, and put it on. When she came back to the bedroom, her mother placed her palm against her chest and sighed with delight.

"Oh, Bernadette! That gown is just beautiful on you."

"Thanks, Mom."

"I'm so glad you've enjoyed wearing them. That you're pregnant doesn't mean you can't be pretty, now does it?"

Bernie couldn't help smiling at that. She walked over and sat down on the bed beside her mother. "It's been kind of a rough night, hasn't it?"

"Yes. But Jeremy has been just wonderful. He loves you very much, doesn't he?"

"Yeah, Mom. He does." She paused. "He even wants to marry me."

Eleanor's mouth dropped open. "*Marry* you?"

"Yeah. He asked me tonight. What do you think? Should I say yes?"

Bernie could almost see her mother quivering with restraint. "Well, I don't know. You've always had your own mind, Bernadette. I wouldn't presume to get in the middle of such a big decision."

"Okay."

"But maybe you should ask yourself a few questions," she added quickly.

"Like what?"

"Well, do you love him, too?"

Bernie smiled softly. "Yes. I do."

"Do you believe he'll make a good husband?"

"The best."

"A good father?"

"Absolutely."

"Well. Those are all very good things, aren't they? Things I'm sure you'll want to take into account when you—"

"I'm going to marry him, Mom."

In that moment, Eleanor's restraint went right out the window. She threw her arms around Bernie and hugged her, rocking back and forth, joy and excitement pouring out of her like sunshine.

"I knew it would happen," Eleanor said. "I knew it! I knew eventually you'd all become a family."

Bernie couldn't say she'd been equally sure about that, but she was thrilled it was happening just the same.

"Will you live here?" Eleanor asked.

"Yeah. Probably."

"Oh, my," Eleanor said on a breath of delight. "It's like a fairy tale, isn't it?"

It was. Bernie would have sworn she didn't believe in those, but she'd had to change more than a few of her paradigms in the past couple of months. And every change had been for the better.

Her mother chattered for the next few minutes about dresses and flowers and music and all those other things that made a wedding a wedding. Bernie listened dutifully, only to let a yawn slip past her lips.

"Oh, my," Eleanor said. "Here I am talking when you should be sleeping. You look so tired. Come to bed." She smoothed her hand over the soft linens. "Heaven knows this one is big enough for a family of four."

"I'm going to stay with Jeremy tonight."

Her mother froze for a moment, the slightest bit of concern crossing her face. Then she lifted her shoulder in a tiny shrug. "Well, considering the circumstances, I suppose it would be silly to wait to share a bed until after the wedding, wouldn't it?"

"Yeah, I guess it would."

"And don't worry about me, Bernadette. I have no intention of going downstairs to do any cooking anytime soon."

"I don't want you to worry about what happened tonight, Mom. Jeremy's going to take care of everything."

Her mother nodded. "I know."

Bernie couldn't have imagined how wonderful it would feel to say those words, and to know that the man behind them would do anything to love and protect them.

"You go on now," Eleanor said, with a flick of her fingers. "I need to have a word with God." She paused. "Actually, two words."

"And what might those be?"

Eleanor's eyes shone with tears. "Thank you."

Bernie smiled. "Good night, Mom."

"Good night, Bernadette."

Bernie left the guest suite and made the long walk to Jeremy's room. When she reached the door, she took a deep breath and knocked.

After a moment, Jeremy opened it. He still had his tux pants on, but he'd taken off his shirt. He looked so sexy it was all she could do not to leap right into the room and rip the rest of his clothes off. He looked her up and down, a sly smile playing across his lips.

"I was right," he said. "That gown is just your color."

"It is, isn't it?"

"My proposal," he said. "Can I take this as a yes?"

"Yes," she said. "You can take this as a yes."

He took her by the wrist, pulled her into his room, and shut the door behind them. Before the night was over, with his whispered words, his gentle hands, and his adoring eyes, he told her he loved her a hundred times more. And when she woke the next morning, cradled in his arms, she knew she was home to stay.

Chapter
31

"If you so much as touch me again, I swear to God I'll eviscerate you!"

Jeremy ignored Bernie and took her hand anyway, wincing when she dug her fingernails into him instead of the bedsheet. But it was all in a day's work for a labor coach. What Jeremy couldn't figure out was why they called him a "coach" when absolutely nobody listened to anything he had to say.

"You always did have a way with words," he said, smiling down at Bernie.

"I'm not kidding, Jeremy. This is your fault. You started this whole thing. If sex so much as crosses your mind again—oh, *God*!"

"Remember your visualizations," he said. "Picture yourself in a beautiful country garden, picking a bouquet of roses..."

"Oh, shut *up*! That birth class instructor was a New Age goofball. How many flowers would she be picking if *her* uterus was tied in a freakin' knot?"

He helped her breathe through another contraction, and then the pain subsided. Barely. At this point, one was kind of blending right into the next one.

"Oh, God, Jeremy," she said, gasping a little, looking worried. "I don't think I can do this. It hurts so much. Are you sure everything's all right?"

"Hang on, sweetheart," he said, brushing her hair away from her temple, then kissing her there. "Everything's going exactly as it's supposed to. Our babies will be here soon."

"I know. We're having babies. Two of them."

"That's right."

"That's a hundred percent more babies than most people have."

"Yes, it is."

"One for each of us. Like Twinkies."

He smiled. "But we can share."

Then her brows drew together. "But they can't come out yet. I'm not ready to be a mother."

"Sure you are. You're going to be the best mother ever."

"No," she said, breathing hard. "When they come out, I'm stuffing them back in."

He smiled. "Sure you want to do that?"

"Yes. But don't worry. It won't be forever. Just until I know I can do this. I'll let them out in a couple of years. Or maybe a decade or two."

He squeezed her hand. "But I'll be there to help you, sweetheart. We can do it together."

She took a deep breath and let it out, actually smiling a little. "Oh, yeah. Together. That'll work."

Jeremy couldn't have imagined being this much in love with anyone.

A month ago, on a cool, crisp Saturday afternoon, they'd gotten married in the sanctuary of Sunnyside Baptist Church. Teresa was Bernie's maid of honor, and Jeremy asked Phil to be his best man. Eleanor didn't stop crying all day. Jeremy hired the best photographer in the metroplex and made sure she had all the photos she needed to show her family, her friends, the ladies at the church, the postman, the clerk at the drugstore, and the poor woman who was just out walking her dog and minding her own business.

After her first night's visit in the guest suite, Eleanor never left. At first she wasn't sure about taking Jeremy up on his invitation, telling him the suite was entirely too luxurious for somebody as ordinary as she was. But it wasn't long before she felt right at home on the pillowtop mattress, raved about how helpful the Jacuzzi was for her arthritis, and had tea every morning on the balcony. In her spare time, she chatted endlessly with Mrs. Spencer, planning exactly how they intended to spoil the twins when they made their grand entrance into the world. And when the time came that Eleanor needed more help, Jeremy insisted that she would never have to leave the comfort of her new home to get it.

Bernie continued to oversee the renovations at Creekwood, and they were well on their way to being wrapped up when she went into labor three weeks before her due date. The tenants were thrilled to have such a nice place to live. They thought the owner of their complex was just about the greatest guy on earth, and Jeremy couldn't have imagined how wonderful it would feel to be that guy.

Life was good. And it was getting ready to be even better.

Another contraction came. Then another. Bernie swore she couldn't do it, but Jeremy held her hand and got her to breathe with him. Half an hour later, their babies came into the world—a boy and a girl—and just like that, Jeremy had the family he never could have imagined.

And he couldn't have loved them more.

An hour later, Bernie lay resting in her hospital bed, exhausted and ecstatic all at the same time. Jeremy sat beside her, holding her hand with a look on his face that said there was nowhere he'd rather be. Eleanor stood by the isolettes, admiring her new grandchildren.

"They're so beautiful," she said, rubbing her thumb gently over one of the babies' hands. "I can't believe I'm actually a grandmother."

And Bernie couldn't believe the chain of events that had led to this moment. The night in Jeremy's safe room. A pregnancy that never should have happened. Jeremy's insistence that he was staying in her life no matter what. Two highly dissimilar people falling in love, only to find out they weren't so different after all.

Her mother was right. It was a blessing.

"What about names?" Eleanor asked. "Have you made the final decision?"

"Our son is Jeremy, Junior," Jeremy said.

Bernie rolled her eyes. "That discussion was closed weeks ago. He loves the idea of having a mini-me." She sighed. "Two of them in the same house. Can you imagine?"

Eleanor trailed her fingertip over the other baby's face. "You have a little girl here, too," she said. "What have you decided to name her?"

Bernie looked at Jeremy. "Unfortunately, that's still up for discussion."

"No, it isn't," he said.

She closed her eyes. "Jeremy—"

"I'm naming this baby."

Bernie looked at her mother. "He's been coming up with some weird names, but don't worry. He thinks he has the final word, but I still have veto power. If it's something awful—"

"Her name is Eleanor."

Bernie froze. Slowly she turned back around to look at Jeremy. Then suddenly he looked all blurry, because tears were filling her eyes.

"You're naming her after me?" Eleanor said.

"If that's all right with you," Jeremy said. "Maybe we'll call her Ellie for short."

"That's what they called me when I was a little girl," Eleanor said, and then she was crying all over again.

Bernie pulled Jeremy to her, putting her arms around him, hugging him tightly. "I love you," she whispered in his ear. "I love you so much."

And he hugged her back, stroking her hair and whispering that he loved her, too. When she finally let him go, he scooped up little Ellie. He stared down at his daughter, then lowered his lips and kissed her gently on the forehead, and Bernie thought she'd die from loving him so much. Eleanor sat down in a nearby chair. Jeremy brought the baby to her, and she held her as if she were the most precious thing on earth. Then he picked up Jeremy, Jr., smiling down at him like the proud father he was, one who Bernie knew would be there for his children every day of their lives.

Then he brought the baby to Bernie. As she cradled him in her arms, he blinked a few times. His eyes got heavy. Then he stuck his fist in his mouth and fell asleep.

"Well, he's certainly not like his father," Bernie said. "He's not demanding anything."

"Give him time. He'll be a chip off the old block soon enough."

Jeremy sat down beside them, leaning in and resting his hand on the baby's blanket. "My family," he said softly, then turned to kiss Bernie on the cheek.

She couldn't believe there had ever been a time when her only goal had been to keep him out of her life, because she couldn't imagine living life without him now. In the end, he was all she'd ever wanted—a good, kind, dependable man who would love her forever.

One newly minted matchmaker
meets his match.

Please turn this page
for a preview of
Jane Graves's
next irresistible novel

Heartstrings and
Diamond Rings

Available in August 2011.

Chapter

1

*R*elationships, Alison Carter thought, *are all about modest expectations*. As she watched Randy inhale the last of his honey-glazed pork chops and drain his wine glass, then swivel his head to watch their waitress's ass as she passed by, Alison added, *And that soulmate thing is a crock*.

The more she repeated those mantras to herself, the better she felt. After all, there was nothing really wrong with Randy. They'd met at a party where he'd gotten too drunk to drive and she'd taken him home, and then they'd started to date. A sales rep with a big paper company, he had a townhome in Plano, not large, but bordering a somewhat prestigious area only a block from a golf course. He wore suits you couldn't tell from designer originals, and shoes that looked like real leather. He did drive an actual Mercedes, a few years old with a great big payment, but a Mercedes nonetheless.

"You look great tonight," Randy said, now that the waitress with the perfect ass had disappeared into the kitchen.

"Thank you," Alison said. "So do you."

She wasn't lying. He wore a pair of slacks, a sharply starched dress shirt, and a sport coat, looking as nice as she'd ever seen him, which really wasn't bad at all. In the candlelit ambience of the restaurant, he actually looked handsome.

As for her looking great, she wasn't so sure. Yesterday she'd spent ten minutes in front of an evil three-way mirror at Saks as Heather convinced her that the dress she wore really didn't make her butt look big. Since junior high, Heather had always been one of those rare friends who never told her she looked good in something when she really didn't. Sometimes the truth was hard to swallow, but in the end it meant there was at least one person on earth she could trust. And if Randy truly loved her for her, did the size of her butt really matter, anyway?

They'd been seeing each other for nearly eight months now, and it had been a decent eight months. No, she didn't have hot flashes of pure sexual hunger whenever he kissed her. She didn't sit around at work all day doodling his name on a sticky note pad. She didn't always leap up to answer the phone when she knew it was probably him. But after she'd turned thirty a few months ago, she'd decided there were tradeoffs she was willing to accept. She could wait for burning sexual attraction to strike her out of nowhere, or she could knock off the lottery mentality and go for the sure thing if it meant she might actually get to have the home, husband, and family she'd always wanted. It might not be great, but if they worked at it, it could certainly be good.

One day last week on her lunch hour, she'd seen Randy in a jewelry store at the mall. Then there was the conversation she'd overheard him having with somebody named Reverend McCormick. And then she'd spotted a Hawaii travel brochure on his desk at home. She brushed all those things aside, telling herself they didn't mean ring-wedding-honeymoon, only to have Randy tell her he had something very important to talk to her about and make dinner reservations at Five-Sixty, the hottest new restaurant in the Dallas metroplex. Oddly, the only emotion she seemed to be able to summon was relief. But that was okay. Relief beat the hell out of desperation.

The waiter poured them more wine, then took their plates. Alison cuddled up next to Randy and stared out the window. Five-Sixty sat at the top of Reunion Tower, fifty stories in the sky, offering sweeping views of the Dallas metroplex. Dusk was becoming night, and with every second that passed, the city lights grew brighter and more mesmerizing. In that moment, Alison truly believed there wasn't a more romantic place on earth. Then Randy turned and kissed her, and she was surprised to feel a little of that first-date flutter she thought was long gone.

"Alison," he said finally, fixing his gaze on hers, "I think we've grown very close over the past few months."

Her heart bumped against her chest. This was it. After all these years, after all the wrong men, after all the blind dates, after all her waiting and wishing and hoping, she was finally making the leap toward matrimony.

Thank God.

"Yes," she said. "We have."

He brushed a strand of hair away from her cheek and stared soulfully into her eyes. "And I wouldn't even be asking you this if I didn't think our relationship was very, very strong."

Alison nodded. "Of course."

"Like a rock."

"Yes," she agreed.

"You're so beautiful. Have I told you that lately?"

She gave him a smile that said, *Yes, but don't hesitate to tell me again.*

"And you're open-minded." He pondered that a moment. "Very open-minded, I'd say."

Actually, she'd never thought of herself as particularly open-minded. But it was okay if he thought so, because that was a good thing...right?

He shifted a little, suddenly looking uncomfortable, and Alison smiled to herself. It was so cutely traditional for him to have a hard time with this. In fact, she was sure she saw him blush.

"I think Bonnie is open-minded, too," Randy said.

Alison blinked. "Bonnie?"

"Yeah. And you seem to get along well with her."

Alison worked with Bonnie, but Randy didn't really know her all that well. Like all men, he was far more acquainted with Bonnie's breasts than her face. God bless Bonnie—she could sprout two heads and the men of the world would never know it. But why was Randy bringing her up now?

"Uh...yeah," Alison said. "I guess we get along okay."

"I assume you think she's, you know...attractive."

Yes. Bonnie was attractive. In a wide-eyed, short-skirted, body-flaunting way. "I...suppose so." *What is he talking about?*

"Anyway, I was wondering..." He inched closer and stared directly into her eyes, and her heart practically stopped. She stared up at him adoringly.

"Yes?"

"You. Me. Bonnie. What do you think?"

Alison just stared at him. "What do I think about what?"

He laughed a little. "You know. The three of us. Together." He leaned in and kissed along her neck. "Seeing you with another woman would be such a turn-on."

For the next several seconds, it was as if Alison's entire circulatory system contracted, stopping the blood flow to her brain. Surely he must have said, *Will you marry me?* but somehow it had come out sounding like, *Wanna have perverted sex?*

"What did you say?"

"A threesome. You, me, and Bonnie."

Don't just repeat it, damn it! Change it!

"When we were at that party at John's house last month," Randy said, "Bonnie seemed to be as open-minded as you are." Then his voice slipped from soothingly sexual to blatantly carnal. "I think she'd go for it, don't you?"

Alison yanked herself away from him. "Are you completely out of your mind?"

He stared at her dumbly. "What's the matter?"

"What's the matter? *What's the matter?*" Alison sputtered aimlessly for a moment, words escaping her. Then she leaned in and spoke in an angry whisper. "That's what you wanted to talk to me about?"

He shrugged. "Well...yeah."

"You brought me here to ask me that?"

He looked befuddled. "Well, it is kind of a big step, so I—"

"What were you doing in that jewelry store three days ago at lunch?"

"Jewelry store? How'd you know I was at a jewelry store?"

"Just answer me. What were you doing?"

"Getting a battery for my watch. Why?"

Alison felt a wave of nausea. "You had a Hawaii vacation brochure on your desk at home."

"I did?"

"Yes. You did. Where did it come from?"

He shrugged. "I don't know. It was probably junk mail."

The nausea continued to roll in, like surf crashing over a rocky beach. "Okay, then. You haven't been to church since you were twelve. So who the hell is Reverend McCormick?"

"Who?"

"Randy," she snapped, "I overheard you talking to somebody named Reverend McCormick last week."

Randy blinked. "Oh. I donated some of my old clothes to a church charity. Tax deduction. How did you—"

"Never mind."

Alison dropped her head to her hands, feeling more dumb and deluded than she ever had in her life. How had this happened? What could she have seen in those bland brown eyes of Randy's that made the concept "together forever" seem like an actual possibility, particularly since he was still staring at her with a look that said, *Now don't be too hasty—have you ever actually considered the advantages of lesbian sex?*

"Randy, listen to me carefully. Are you listening?"

He nodded, a hopeful look on his face. Hopeful. What did he think she was going to do? Suggest a plan to catch Bonnie off-guard in the shower?

"My answer is no," she told him, her voice quivering

with anger. "Now, that's not just any old no. It's no, not in a million years, not if we're the only three people left on Earth and I'm the odd woman out and it's the only chance I have to participate in sex again for the rest of eternity. It's that kind of no. Are you getting my drift?"

His face fell into a disappointed frown, as if he were a spoiled six-year-old who couldn't understand why a spotted pony with a silver-trimmed saddle or a month-long tour of Disney World was out of the question.

"Maybe you just need a chance to think about it," he said.

Think about it? Was he *serious*?

"Randy," she said with a growl in her voice, "you're going to get up from this table right now. You're going to leave. And if you so much as glance back over your shoulder, I'm shoving you through the window. It's fifty stories to the ground, and I don't give a damn. Do you hear me?"

Randy drew back with a startled expression. "But why? Just because I had one little idea to spice up our sex life that you didn't like?"

Alison's mouth dropped open. "One little idea? *One little—*"

"So forget I mentioned it," he said with an offhand shrug. "No big deal. We can still have regular sex. Just you and me—"

She grabbed him by his lapels and dragged him forward. "Get. The hell. *Out.*"

"Come on, Alison," he said, a nervous laugh in his voice. "You really don't want me to—"

She leaned away and whacked him on the arm with her doubled-up fist. "I said *out*!"

When she reared back to smack him again, he threw up

his arms to ward off the blow. He scooted out of the booth so quickly he banged the edge of the table with his hip, knocking over his glass of Pinot Noir. The wine spread like a gigantic Rorschach blob on the white linen tablecloth. He stared down at it dumbly.

"Out!" Alison shouted.

He took two shaky steps backward, his shocked expression shifting to a vindictive glare. "Yeah, well, you know what?"

"What?"

"That dress makes your butt look *huge*!"

A pure, unadulterated, I-hate-you kind of anger welled up inside Alison that she'd never felt before. As he spun around and stalked off, she closed her hands into fists and banged them on the table. The last wine glass standing shimmied a little, but she managed to grab it before it fell over. In three seconds she'd drained its contents and smacked the glass back down on the table, feeling the wine burn all the way down her throat. It hit her nauseated stomach like cold rainwater on hot lava, and she swore she could actually feel the sizzle.

She closed her eyes to try to gain back a modicum of control, and when she opened them again, she realized the restaurant had fallen silent, the waiters had frozen in place, and everybody was looking at her as if she were a rabid dog foaming at the mouth. She sat up straight and put her hands in her lap, trying to look calm, sane, and sensible. Judging from the fact that everyone was still staring, she wasn't succeeding.

The waiter walked tentatively back to the table, staying slightly more than arm's length away. "Uh...madam? Will there be anything else?"

Yes. A gun so she could chase Randy down and blow him away. A big, fat box of Kleenex so she could cry her eyes out. A trench coat so everybody in this restaurant wouldn't be looking at her ass as she walked out the door, wondering if Randy had been right.

"No. Nothing."

In the time it took for her to decide that the wine-red Rorschach blob on the tablecloth looked like a pissed-off woman castrating a depraved man, the waiter returned with the check.

The check. Well, crap. Not only had this been one of the worst nights of her life, now she had to pay through the nose for the privilege of participating in it.

She winced, paid the check, and left the restaurant. And sure enough, she felt the collective gazes of every patron in the place focused squarely on her backside. The moment she got home, she was burning this dress.

She went into the elevator and leaned against the wall, feeling a little woozy as she shot down fifty stories. But it wasn't until she stepped into the hotel lobby that it dawned on her that Randy had driven her there, and she had no way home.

No car, no fiancé, no hope, no nothing.

Alison trudged through the underground passage to Union Station, where she went to the surface again and sat down on a bench to wait for the northbound train. She grabbed her cell phone, called Heather, and asked her to pick her up at the Fifteenth Street station in Plano. Since Alison wasn't exactly radiating the excitement of a newly engaged woman, Heather started to worry, but Alison told her she'd fill her in when she got there.

Just last week, Heather and her husband, Tony, had

returned from celebrating their first anniversary in Las Vegas. Alison tried not to be pea-green with envy about that, but it was a hard-won battle.

You got the last good one, Heather. Hang on to him.

Anger had carried Alison this far, but now in the silence of the aftermath of her future going right down the tubes, she couldn't stop the tears from coming. God, she hated this. Sitting alone at a train station by an over-flowing trash can beneath garish lights wearing a dress she now despised, crying her eyes out. Could it get any worse than that?

When the train came several minutes later, she sniffed a little, dried her eyes with her fingertips, boarded a car, and plopped down on a seat. Evidently she looked really piti-ful, because even the insane homeless people shied away from her. She thunked her head against the window, her thoughts a jumbled mess. This couldn't have happened. It just couldn't have. How had all her marriage dreams morphed into a scenario only a pornographer could love?

Easy answer. Because she was a fool.

Randy had never given her any indication that he was Mr. Wonderful. She'd just chosen to hope that maybe he was. He was merely a clueless degenerate who'd taken a wrong turn and wandered into her life. She, on the other hand, should have pulled off those damned rose-colored glasses the moment she met him and smashed them into a million pieces.

As the train went underground and picked up speed, whizzing through the tunnel toward Cityplace, Alison thought about how other women were getting married and having families right and left. What was wrong with her?

Okay, so she hadn't exactly been a genius when it came

to picking the right men. First there had been Greg Chapman. A few months in, she'd woken up one night to find him licking her toes. That she might have been able to overlook, but when he wanted her to wear six-inch heels in the bedroom and carry a whip, she'd decided enough was enough. Then there were the two years she wasted on Richard Bodecker, who turned out to be gay. Alison might have realized it sooner, but since he owned a Harley dealership and spat a lot, she'd stayed in denial even longer than Richard himself.

And then there was Michael Pagliano, who scratched his balls in public. Just stood there in a movie line or whatever and scratched away, as if nobody was watching. But since Alison had been three months away from her twenty-ninth birthday and feeling a little desperate, she'd decided to overlook it. Then he took her to a five-star restaurant, which was good, and blew his nose on a cloth napkin, which wasn't. It was then Alison decided she couldn't close her eyes to his downside any longer.

Then came Randy.

So there they were. The men she'd been able to attract over the years. A clueless degenerate, a foot fetishist, a gay biker, and a ball-scratching nose-blower. She wasn't dumb enough to think all men were rotten, but she was beginning to believe she was a magnet for the ones who were.

Thirty minutes later, Heather met her at the Fifteenth Street station. She wore a pair of faded jeans and a white tank top. Her wild, curly brown hair was backlit by a halogen streetlamp, glowing like a halo around her head.

"Uh-oh," Heather said. "It's bad, isn't it?"

"If eight months of my life going down the tubes is bad," Alison said, "then yes. It's bad."

"Tell me what happened."

"Let's see. The *Reader's Digest* version. Randy's an asshole, and I'm an idiot."

Heather winced. "Get in the car. Then I want to hear everything."

Once they were inside the car and heading home, Alison told Heather the whole story, and Heather's eyes grew wide.

"He wanted a threesome? With Bonnie?" She paused. "Well, okay. If a guy's a big enough jerk to want a threesome, of course it would be with Bonnie."

Alison dropped her head against the headrest, feeling miserable. "I'm a dating disaster. I'm done with men."

"No, you're not."

"Yeah, I am. I'm going to become a nun."

"You're not Catholic."

She rolled her head around to look at Heather. "I could adapt. I'm not too fond of kneeling, but I do like wine. Tradeoffs, you know?"

"What about confession? That won't exactly be a walk in the park for you."

"Yeah, maybe the first one will be a little lengthy. But once I purge the past ten years or so, the next ones will be a breeze. I mean, come on. After I'm a nun, what could I possibly have to own up to?"

"Oh, right. Like the moment a cute priest walks by, you won't be lusting in your heart?"

Alison sighed. "That's my problem, isn't it?"

"What?"

"Doesn't matter if he's Mr. Right or not. I'll find a way to cram that square peg into that round hole or die trying. God, Heather. What's *wrong* with me?"

"Nothing's wrong with you. Randy's the one with the problem."

"But what if I end up with somebody even worse than Randy because I'm so desperate to get married that I'll settle for anyone?"

"You would have figured Randy out sooner or later, even if he hadn't... you know. Gone all pervert on you. Just be glad you're rid of him."

"And who am I supposed to put in his place?"

"Do you have to figure that out now?"

"Sometime before I'm eighty would be nice."

"You have fifty years before you're eighty."

And Alison knew what that fifty years was going to be like. A few years would pass. Then a few decades. And before she knew it, she'd be staring at some hairy-eared octogenarian over their morning oatmeal at the home and wondering how long it might take to get him to pop the question.

"It's not like you've exhausted every possibility out there," Heather said. "You just haven't met the right guy yet. Give it some more time."

"But I've already tried everything! Singles bars. Speed dating. Video dating. Match dot-com. E-Harmony. I've even considered setting fire to my own condo to try to meet a cute firefighter."

"Now there's an approach I wouldn't have thought of."

"Yeah, but it'd be just my luck that he'd be a firefighter who wore women's underwear or had a wife he wasn't telling me about." She sighed. "Do you understand how much I suck at picking out men?"

"Have you thought about letting somebody else pick one out for you?"

"No," Alison said with a wave of her hand. "No way. I've had enough bad blind dates to last me a lifetime."

"I'm not talking about letting your aunt Brenda fix you up. That was a disaster."

Alison cringed at the memory. She'd never met a man before who wanted a sex change operation so he could become a lesbian.

"I'm talking about a professional," Heather said.

"Huh?"

"A matchmaker."

"Matchmaker? You mean, like one person who decides who you're supposed to spend the rest of your life with?" Alison screwed up her face. "Sorry. That's just weird."

"No, really. I work with a woman who went to this matchmaker in downtown Plano, and she set her up with a really great guy. She was engaged four months later and married within the year."

Just the words "engaged" and "married" in the same sentence made Alison's heart go pitty-pat. But she knew the truth. Nothing was ever that simple.

"Pardon my skepticism, but what's this friend of yours like? Tall? Skinny? Blond? Ex-cheerleader? Trust fund?"

"Short, a little overweight, brown hair, ex–debate team, good job."

Now Alison was listening. Minus the debate team thing, Heather could be describing her.

Alison pulled out her phone. "What's this matchmaker's name?"

"Uh . . . I can't remember. Rosie . . . Roxanne . . . something like that."

Alison Googled "matchmaker" and "Plano."

"Oh, my God," she said. "Did you know there's a

matchmaking service dedicated to finding you somebody to cheat with?"

"You're kidding."

"I guess that one's for later. Before I can cheat on a man, first I have to find a man." She flipped to another site. "And here's one called Sugar Daddies. They match rich old men with hot young women."

"How young?"

"Judging from these photos, barely legal." Alison flipped her thumb across the screen. "I'm still not seeing... wait. Rochelle Scott? Matchmaking by Rochelle?"

"Yeah. I think that's it."

"Hmm. Says she's been in business for thirty-five years. Nobody stays in business that long if they're not successful, right?"

"Oh, she's successful, if you judge by what she charges."

"How much are we talking?"

"That's the downside. She charges fifteen hundred dollars for five introductions."

Alison winced. Three hundred dollars per man?

Then she thought about the thousand dollars she'd once paid to spend a week at a singles resort in Florida. Instead of coming back with a man, she'd returned with a horrible sunburn and so many mosquito bites she looked like flesh-colored bubble wrap. She wasn't one to throw money around indiscriminately, but if the woman could actually deliver, it might be worth it.

She looked back at her phone and clicked through the website. "Listen to this," she said, reading from the woman's bio. "Rochelle Scott has a degree in psychology. She's been matchmaking for thirty-five years. Out of more than three hundred marriages, there have been only sixteen divorces." She looked at Heather. "That blows the national average out of the water. I'm going over there Monday."

Heather's eyebrows shot up. "Now, wait a minute. I just threw that out there as something to think about. You need to let the sting of tonight wear off a little before you hop right back out there."

"Nope. I'm thirty and alone, and it's bad. I imagine forty and alone is even worse."

"Doing anything on the rebound is usually a mistake. Forget about it for tonight. Come up to my place. Tony's working late at the bar, so we can trash-talk men all we want to."

"Right. You have nothing to bitch about where Tony's concerned."

"Yeah? That's what you think. He still hasn't grasped the concept that dirty underwear goes in the hamper and that onion rings aren't health food. And don't get me started on his collection of *Sports Illustrated* swimsuit editions. You'd think they were the Dead Sea Scrolls the way he—"

"Heather," Alison said, "right about now, I'd kill for a messy guy eating onion rings while he's staring at hot women in bikinis. Particularly if he looked like Tony." Her eyes teared up again, and she hated it. "You know, when we were both single, it wasn't so bad. But now...now you have Tony, and..." She sniffed a little. "I'm happy for you, Heather. I really am. But I'm really starting to feel like the odd woman out." She let out a painful sigh. "It sucks to be me."

"Don't you say that," Heather told her. "Don't you *dare* say that. You already have a good life. You have a great job. A nice place to live. Good friends. Money in the bank. That's more than some people can say. And you're a good person who does nice things for other people. So it does *not* suck to be you."

Alison sighed again. "Is it really so wrong to want the last piece of the puzzle?"

"No. Of course not. I'm just saying that maybe you need to give the husband hunt a rest for a while."

"I would, except for that damned clock ticking inside my head."

Heather smiled. "He's out there, you know."

"Who?"

"Mr. Right. Your knight in shining armor. Your forever guy. You just have to be patient. One day, when you least expect it—"

"Don't try to cheer me up. I'd rather wallow in my misery."

"No problem there. I have a really nice bottle of vodka I've been saving for an occasion like this. And did I mention I also have a gallon of Blue Bell Cookies 'n' Cream?"

"Perfect. That's why I can't find a man, you know. My hips aren't big enough."

Heather pulled into the condo complex where they both lived. Alison ran to her place, got out of the big-butt dress, and put on sweatpants, a T-shirt, and a pair of flip-flops. By the time she was climbing the stairs to Heather's condo, she was feeling marginally better.

She decided she was going to eat enough ice cream to get brain freeze, then warm her head back up with half a dozen vodka shots. And through it all, she intended to obliterate everything Randy from her phone, her Facebook page, and her e-mail. If she got inebriated enough, when she got home, she'd head over to the forums at the Knot and spam them with *love sucks* messages, then grab a couple of issues of *Modern Bride* from her magazine rack and shred them.

Now, *that* was wallowing in misery.

Then Monday on her lunch hour, she'd head over to see Rochelle and pray the woman could work miracles.

THE DISH

Where authors give you the inside scoop!

From the desk of Vicky Dreiling

Dear Reader,

While writing my first novel HOW TO MARRY A DUKE, I decided my hero Tristan, the Duke of Shelbourne, needed a sidekick. That bad boy sidekick was Tristan's oldest friend Marc Darcett, the Earl of Hawkfield, and the hero of HOW TO SEDUCE A SCOUNDREL. Hawk is a rogue who loves nothing better than a lark. Truthfully, I had to rein Hawk in more than once in the first book as he tried repeatedly to upstage all the other characters.

Unlike his friend Tristan, Hawk is averse to giving up his bachelor status. He's managed to evade his female relatives' matchmaking schemes for years. According to the latest tittle-tattle, his mother and sisters went into a decline upon learning of his ill-fated one-hour engagement. Clearly, this is a man who values his freedom.

My first task was to find the perfect heroine to foil him. Who better than the one woman he absolutely must never touch? Yes, that would be his best friend's sister, Lady Julianne. After all, it's in a rake's code of conduct that friends' sisters are forbidden. Unbeknownst to Hawk, however, Julianne has been planning their nuptials for four long years. I wasn't quite sure how Julianne would manage this feat, given Hawk's fear of catching *wife-itis*.

After a great deal of pacing about, the perfect solution popped into my head. I would use he time-honored trick known as *The Call to Adventure*. When Tristan, who can not be in London for the season, proposes that Hawk act as Julianne's unofficial guardian, Hawk's bachelor days are numbered.

In addition to these plans, I wanted to add in a bit of fun with yet another Regency-era spoof of modern dating practices. I recalled an incident in which one of my younger male colleagues complained about that dratted advice book for single ladies, *The Rules*. I wasn't very sympathetic to his woes about women ruling guys. After all, reluctant bachelors have held the upper hand for centuries. Thus, I concocted *The Rules* in Regency England.

Naturally, the road to true love is fraught with heart-break, mayhem, and, well, a decanter of wine. Matters turn bleak for poor Julianne when Hawk makes his disin-terest clear after a rather steamy waltz. I knew Julianne needed help, and so I sent in a wise woman, albeit a rather eccentric one. Hawk's Aunt Hester, a plain-spoken woman, has some rather startling advice for Julianne. Left with only the shreds of her pride, Julianne decides to write a lady's guide to seducing scoundrels into the proverbial parson's mousetrap. My intrepid heroine finds herself in hot suds when all of London hunts for the anonymous author of that scandalous publication, *The Secrets of Seduction*. At all costs, Julianne must keep her identity a secret—especially from Hawk, who is determined to guard her from his fellow scoundrels. But can he guard his own heart from the one woman forbidden to him?

My heartfelt thanks to all the readers who wrote to let

me know they couldn't wait to read HOW TO SEDUCE A
SCOUNDREL. I hope you will enjoy the twists and turns
that finally lead to happily ever after for Hawk and Julianne.

Cheers!

Vicky Dreiling

www.vickydreiling.com

♥ ♥ ♥ ♥ ♥ ♥ ♥ ♥ ♥ ♥ ♥ ♥ ♥ ♥ ♥

From the desk of Jane Graves

Dear Reader,

Have you ever visited one website, seen an interesting
link to another website, and clicked it? Probably. But
have you ever done that about fifty times and ended up
in a place you never intended to? As a writer, I'm already
on a "what if" journey inside my own head, so web hopping is just one more flight of fancy that's *so* easy to get
caught up in.

For instance, while researching a scene for BLACK
TIES AND LULLABIES that takes place in a childbirth
class, I saw a link for "hypnosis during birth." Of course I
had to click that, right? Then I ended up on a site where
people post their birth stories. And then . . .

Don't ask me how, but a dozen clicks later, my web-hopping adventure led me to a site about celebrities and baby names. And it immediately had me wondering: *What were these people thinking?* Check out the names these famous people have given their children that virtually guarantee they'll be tormented for the rest of their lives:

Apple	Actress Gwyneth Paltrow
Diva Muffin	Musician Frank Zappa
Moxie Crimefighter	Entertainer Penn Jillette
Petal Blossom Rainbow	Chef Jamie Oliver
Zowie	Singer David Bowie
Pilot Inspektor	Actor Jason Lee
Sage Moonblood	Actor Sylvester Stallone
Fifi Trixibell	Sir Bob Geldof*
Reignbeau	Actor Ving Rhames
Jermajesty	Singer Jermaine Jackson

*Musician/Activist

No, a trip around the Internet does *not* get my books written, but sometimes it's worth the laugh. Of course, the hero and heroine of BLACK TIES AND LULLABIES would *never* give their child a name like one of these. . . .

I hope you enjoy BLACK TIES AND LULLABIES. And look for my next book, HEARTSTRINGS AND DIAMOND RINGS, coming October 2011.

Happy Reading!

Jane Graves

www.janegraves.com

♥ ♥ ♥ ♥ ♥ ♥ ♥ ♥ ♥ ♥ ♥ ♥ ♥ ♥ ♥

From the desk of Paula Quinn

Dear Reader,

Having married my first love, I was excited to write the third installment in my Children of the Mist series, TAMED BY A HIGHLANDER. You see, Mairi Mac-Gregor and Connor Grant were childhood sweethearts. How difficult could it be to relate to a woman who had surrendered her heart at around the same age I did? Of course, my real life hero didn't pack up his Claymore and plaid and ride off to good old England to save the king. (Although my husband does own a few swords he keeps around in the event that one of our daughters brings home an unfavorable boyfriend.) My hero didn't break my young heart, or the promises he made me beneath the shadow of a majestic Highland mountain. I don't hide daggers under my skirts. Heck, I don't even wear skirts.

But I am willing to fight for what I believe in. So is Mairi, and what she believes in is Scotland. A member of a secret Highland militia, Mairi has traded in her dreams of a husband and children for sweeping Scotland free of men who would seek to change her Highland customs and religion. She knows how to fight, but she isn't prepared for the battle awaiting her when she sets her feet in England and comes face to face with the man she once loved.

Ah, Connor Grant, captain in the King's Royal Army and son of the infamous rogue Graham Grant from A

HIGHLANDER NEVER SURRENDERS. He's nothing like his father. This guy has loved the same lass his whole life, but she's grown into a woman without him and now, instead of casting him smiles, she's throwing daggers at him!

Fun! I knew when these two were reunited sparks (and knives) would fly!

But Connor isn't one to back down from a fight. In fact, he longs to tame his wild Highland mare. But does he need to protect the last Stuart king from her?

Journey back in time where plots and intrigue once ruled the courtly halls of Whitehall Palace, and two souls who were born to love only each other find their way back into each other's arms.

If Mairi doesn't kill him first.

(Did I mention, I collect medieval daggers? Just in case . . .)

Happy Reading!

Paula Quinn

www.paulaquinn.com

♥ ♥ ♥ ♥ ♥ ♥ ♥ ♥ ♥ ♥ ♥ ♥ ♥ ♥ ♥

From the desk of Kendra Leigh Castle

Dear Reader,

It all started with the History Channel.

No, really. One evening last year, while I was watching TV in the basement and hiding from whatever flesh-eating-zombie-filled gore-fest my husband was happily watching upstairs, I ran across a fascinating documentary all about a woman I never knew existed: Arsinoë, Cleopatra's youngest sister. Being a sucker for a good story, I watched, fascinated, as the tale of Arsinoë's brief and often unhappy life unfolded. And after it was all over, once her threat to Cleopatra's power had been taken care of in a very final way by the famous queen herself, I asked myself what any good writer would: what if Arsinoë hadn't really died, and become a vampire instead?

Okay, so maybe most writers wouldn't ask themselves that. I write paranormal romance for a reason, after all. But that simple, and rather odd, question was the seed that my book DARK AWAKENING grew from. Now, Arsinoë isn't the heroine. In fact, she's more of a threat hanging over the head of my hero, Ty MacGillivray, whose kind has served her dynasty of highblood vampires for centuries, bound in virtual slavery. But her arrival in my imagination sparked an entire world, in which so-called "highblood" vampires, those bearing the tattoo-like mark of bloodlines descended directly from various darker gods and goddesses, form an immortal nobility that take great pleasure in lording it over the "lowbloods" of more muddied pedigree.

Lowbloods like Ty and his unusual bloodline of cat-shifting vampires, the Cait Sith.

Now, I won't give out all the details of what happens when Ty is sent by Arsinöe herself to find a human woman with the ability to root out the source of a curse that threatens to take her entire dynasty down. I will say that Lily Quinn is a lot more than Ty bargained for, carrying secrets that have the potential to change the entire world of night. And I'm happy to tell you that it really tugged at my heartstrings to write the story of a man who has been kicked around for so long that he is afraid to want what his heart so desperately needs. But beyond that, all you really need to know is that DARK AWAKENING has all of my favorite ingredients: a tortured bad boy with a heart of gold, a heroine strong enough to take him on, and cats.

What? I like cats. Especially when they turn into gorgeous immortals.

Ty and Lily's story is the first in my DARK DYNASTIES series, about the hotbed of intrigue and desire that is the realm of the twenty-first century vampire. If you're up for a ride into the darkness, not to mention brooding bad boys who aren't afraid to flash a little fang, then stick with me. I've got a silver-eyed hero you might like to meet. . . .

Enjoy!

Kendra Leigh Castle

www.kendraleighcastle.com

Find out more about Forever Romance!

Visit us at
www.hachettebookgroup.com/publishing_forever.aspx

Find us on Facebook
http://www.facebook.com/ForeverRomance

Follow us on Twitter
http://twitter.com/ForeverRomance

NEW AND UPCOMING TITLES

Each month we feature our new titles
and reader favorites.

CONTESTS AND GIVEAWAYS

We give away galleys, autographed copies,
and all kinds of exclusive items.

AUTHOR INFO

You'll find bios, articles, and links to personal websites
for all your favorite authors—and so much more.

GET SOCIAL

Connect with your favorite authors, editors, and
other Forever fans, and share what's important to you.

THE BUZZ

Sign up for our monthly romance newsletter,
and be the first to read all about it.

VISIT US ONLINE

@ WWW.HACHETTEBOOKGROUP.COM.

AT THE HACHETTE BOOK GROUP WEBSITE YOU'LL FIND:

CHAPTER EXCERPTS FROM SELECTED NEW RELEASES

•

ORIGINAL AUTHOR AND EDITOR ARTICLES

•

AUDIO EXCERPTS

•

BESTSELLER NEWS

•

ELECTRONIC NEWSLETTERS

•

AUTHOR TOUR INFORMATION

•

CONTESTS, QUIZZES, AND POLLS

•

FUN, QUIRKY RECOMMENDATION CENTER

•

PLUS MUCH MORE!

BOOKMARK HACHETTE BOOK GROUP
@ WWW.HACHETTEBOOKGROUP.COM.